UNFICTION

GENE DOUCETTE

For Luigi

'Gainst death and all-oblivious enmity
     Shall you pace forth; your praise shall still find room
     Even in the eyes of all posterity
     That wear this world out to the ending doom.

— WILLIAM SHAKESPEARE, SONNET 55

Dear audience, we are now coming to
     The point where we must hang him by the neck
     Because it is the Christian thing to do
     Proving that men must pay for what they take.

But as we want to keep our fingers clean
     And you are people we can't risk offending
     We thought we'd better do without this scene
     And substitute instead a different ending.

Since this is opera, not life, you'll see
     Justice give way before Humanity.
     So now, to throw our story right off course
     Enter the royal official on his horse.

— THREEPENNY OPERA, BERTOLT BRECHT

CONTENTS

PART ONE

Stories

Chapter One

KINGDOM

"I understand you are a sorcerer."

The speaker was a vast example of humanity, a truly gigantic man who easily could have been mistaken for a giant with dwarfism, if there were such a thing. He was heavily armored in thick leather, atop chain mail, underneath a fur cloak that appeared to have been manufactured from the remains of an entire bear.

He was from the northern climes, clearly. There was no reason to wear this much clothing on the southern side of the Ailing Mountains.

"Yes, indeed," Osraic said. "I am a sorcerer. Can I be of service?"

This was only a partial truth.

"I am Cant of the Warven tribe. I have need of magics."

Cant was standing in the middle of Osraic's tiny shop, which was at the edge of the only slightly larger town of Lantor, one of the northernmost settlements in the nation of Kalspar.

Lantor was one of a chain of mud towns, so named because the streets were a perpetual morass of thick mud. This was in part due to the snowmelt runoff from the mountains, and in part because the range had a tendency to attract and retain storm systems.

Much of the mud from the mud town appeared to have found a new home on Osraic's wood floor thanks to the heavy boots of the man from the Warven tribe.

"Of course," Osraic said. "Is it a remedy you're looking for? I have a number of potions on-hand for any variety of ailments." He gestured around the room, which was wall-to-wall with exotic items.

"No, nothing like that," he grumbled. "Do these offer protections?"

"Ah yes! These are fortune charms. They will improve the luck of the wearer threefold."

"Hah. And what if you are a man with only bad luck? Does it triple your misfortune?"

"That's not how they work, no. Ha-ha. So, no remedy or charm for you, then, Mr. Cant. A potion?"

"It's Cant. There is no 'mister' or 'sir', there is only Cant of the Warven tribe. And you seem young for a sorcerer. Have you no master?"

Osraic looked young because he was actually very young, which was the reason he had elected to set up his first shop in a distant little mud town rather in than in the city. Well, it was one of the reasons. Another was that he wasn't formally a sorcerer yet, but nobody this far from the center was going to check.

"Mine is the only name on the door, Cant of the Warven tribe. I've no need for a master."

Cant grunted and stared at the door. "I can't read. What does it say?"

Osraic sighed.

"Osraic Tal Nar Drang. Sorcerer. And again, that's me. I would proffer my city papers if you require further proof, but as you've said, you can't read so I don't see how this would help. But, see the nice symbol?"

Most of the town of Lantor couldn't read either, so the symbol on the door—an owl, more or less, rendered by a carver who didn't know what an owl looked like—was mandatory. Most of the shops on the main road followed a similar symbol-based method of self-identification. All except for the alehouse, which used to have a sign up until either a boisterous wind or a boisterous guest tore it down. It hadn't been replaced because if there's one thing everyone knows the location of, it's the nearest alehouse.

"You have too many names, you people," Cant muttered. He was holding up a gingerroot homunculus and looking puzzled about it. "And, that symbol on the door looks like a baby covered in feathers. I walked past here thrice before asking someone on the street. You should fire whoever did that for you. I thought sure this was a nursery for malformed infants."

"A valid complaint. I'll take it up with him when next we speak. But in the meantime, once more, what can I *do* for you?"

"I told you, I need a sorcerer. How many times shall I repeat this?"

"Yes, yes, but for what? Potions are right over there."

"I don't want any of these trinkets. I need to *hire* a sorcerer. I need for you, Osraic Tal Nar Drang, to accompany me, and for this I will give you gold. I assume you southerners still do business in gold and at least *that* much hasn't changed since the last time I came down the mountain."

Osraic was oddly pleased that Cant remembered his entire name.

"Accompany you where?"

"That is a complicated question."

"It's really not."

The door behind Cant opened. Osraic couldn't see who had come in, at first, because the northerner was blocking his view. He could hear her voice just fine, though.

"What's taking so long?" she asked.

He didn't recognize the voice, and when the voice's owner stepped around Cant, he didn't recognize anything else about her either.

"It's impossible to hire a sorcerer in this town, it seems," Cant said. "The only one they have appears to be too stubborn."

The woman was much more human-sized than Cant, about the same height as Osraic. She had brown hair, pulled back behind her head and partly hidden in a fur-lined hood that hung from her shoulders, attached to a heavy cloak. Her face was freckled, and she had maybe the most amazing green eyes he'd ever seen.

Those eyes looked him up and down. "You there, call your boss down so we can discuss terms."

"He says *he's* the sorcerer," Cant said.

Another ten minutes passed in which Osraic attempted to reiterate his bona fides to the young woman without sounding cross about it. He didn't want to sound cross because while going over his résumé he realized first, that her eyes were actually emerald green, which was simply extraordinary, and second, that she was most likely an elf. He'd never met an elf before, and was tempted to go wherever it was she wanted him to go just to get to know her better.

"I apologize," the girl said. Cant called her Atha, and Osraic was busy rolling her name around in his mind during her apology. "I've never met a sorcerer without a beard. I assumed it was mandatory for your profession."

"I've never met a *man* without a beard," Cant said. Osraic decided the large northerner was making a joke, as it was not difficult to find a clean-shaven man south of the Ailings. Cant either had a very dry wit or was a poor joke-teller.

"It seems the two of you have traveled a long way specifically to hire me for some reason," Osraic said. "So why don't we—"

"We needed a horse too," Cant said. "And dried food."

"Yes, and those things as well. But as you've said, the reason for this is complicated so maybe—"

"And rope."

"Yes fine! How about if I close the shop and we go down the road to the alehouse, sit down and have ourselves a few pints and maybe you can tell me what mad quest shook you off the side of the mountain and through my front door. Would that be all right?"

Cant shrugged. The elf smiled.

"That's a splendid idea," she said.

～

Borric's Saloon was easily the most important establishment in town. Nearly everyone who worked on the main street of Lantor spent at least part of their day there; was large, bright where it needed to be and dark where it didn't, surprisingly clean, and served food at least two measures above edible.

And of course there was the ale.

"This is the only reason to bother with this side of the Ailings!" Cant said, regarding the drink in his half-drained stein.

"There's no ale in the north?" Osraic asked.

"There is," Atha said, "but only in the baldest definition of the word. Alcoholic, and brownish."

"Stay clear of the ale in our travels, sorcerer," Cant barked. "If it doesn't make you ill, the next day you'll wish it had."

"Yes, our travels. Why don't you tell me more about that? Before I agree to anything?"

Osraic had no intention of agreeing to go anywhere further than Borric's with the two northerners, no matter how often Atha transfixed him with those eyes. But he was willing to seem interested for quite a long while.

Atha smiled. "I think first I would like to see some demonstration from you, master sorcerer."

"Call me Osraic."

And I am no master, he thought.

"Osraic, then," she said.

"A demonstration of what?"

"Use your magics. No large feat, just a minor proof."

Something Osraic learned early in pursuit of this career was that there was really very little true magic in the world. It existed, certainly, but not as widely as anyone unfamiliar with the profession believed. Most times, when called upon to prove himself he could get away with a simple sleight-of-hand. The art of "magic" tricks was nearly as important to a professional sorcerer as scholarship and the innate ability to manipulate true magical energy. Sleight-of-hand and real magic was often indistinguishable to citizens.

Osraic debated whether Cant and Atha would be swayed by a disappearing coin or one of a thousand card tricks he knew. Elves were reputed to have better eyes than humans, and might not be counted upon to fall for a proper misdirection, so it was a risk. And he wanted to hear their story.

"Do you have a quill?" he asked.

"I don't," Atha said. "I can read, but have no need to write. Cant does neither."

"How about an arrow?"

"Yes, those I have."

On the floor at her feet was a large sack, from which she extracted a single arrow. He took it, and examined the sack.

"You have a bow in there?" he asked.

"No, not there." She pulled a hairpin from the brown tangle on her head and held it up in the sunlight. It turned out to not be a hairpin at all. "This is my bow."

"Enchanted!"

"Yes, obviously. You've no idea what a pain it is to carry a longbow everywhere."

Osraic wanted a closer look at the bow. He knew of this enchantment but hadn't ever tried it; examining a stable one would be helpful. He wondered why they weren't bringing the sorcerer who'd done that for her to go on this trip of theirs, but decided against asking.

"Why didn't you have the quiver enchanted as well?" he asked instead.

"I tried once, but arrows the size of toothpicks have a tendency to go missing."

"That was a disaster," Cant said. "She was afraid to speak the words to resize the arrows for fear one had become lodged in an awkward place."

Atha laughed. "It would be an embarrassing way to die."

Osraic studied the arrow. "You make your own," he observed.

"There are no armories from which to buy such things in the mountains. But trees and birds we have plenty of."

"Falcon?" he asked, sniffing the fletching.

"Very good."

"Are you going to fondle it all day or will you be demonstrating your magic, sorcerer?" Cant asked.

"Right."

Osraic held the arrow, tip down, on the table. Beneath his breath he muttered the necessary phrase, and let go. The arrow remained upright, point-down, apparently balanced in place.

"This?" Cant said. "This is a vagabond trick."

Osraic twirled his finger above the arrow, and it began to spin in place.

"Is that better?" he asked the large man.

"Marginally better," Atha answered. Cant only grunted.

With a twitch of his fingers the arrow rose off the tabletop and turned until it was horizontal with the surface. With another twitch Osraic made it drift toward Cant's face until the point was inches from his eyeball.

"And now?" Osraic asked.

He sincerely hoped this would be an adequate demonstration, because it was just about the only trick he could perform reliably.

The ability to levitate small, light objects was one of the first things any sorcerer learned. It had a surprisingly wide range of applications, so wide it was possible for most to make a perfectly respectable living without advancing any further. Osraic expected to reach a much more advanced level of aptitude in time, but he hadn't yet.

Also, if called upon, Osraic couldn't have used the arrow as a weapon. The full degree of force he could apply to the arrow would at best have caused it to bump into Cant's face gently. He was confident so long as the eyeball was the target he would not be called upon to do this.

Cant and Atha shared a meaningful glance.

"This is sufficient proof, thank you," Atha said.

Osraic gestured and the arrow floated to the elf. He spoke the words, and the object was released. It fell into her waiting hand.

"Now why don't you explain what you need from me?" he asked.

"Very well," Atha said. "We seek the Cydonian Kingdom. I'm certain you've heard of it."

Osraic laughed. But for some reason, he was the only one laughing.

~

There was a legend. Nobody knew how old it was, or if it represented some sort of true history, and if it did, what that history might have looked like.

But the legend itself, everyone knew.

The Cydonian Kingdom—known by most as simply *the*

Kingdom—was supposed to have been the birthplace of all the races of the world: humans, elves, giants, trolls, goblins and so forth, from a single ancestral people. The inhabitants of the Kingdom—a race of beings called Cydonians—lived harmoniously up until the day they didn't any more, an event known as the Fall.

Every take on the legend came with a different version of what caused the Fall: a war; a plague; an accident; and so forth. The Fall of the Kingdom was an entire literary genre unto itself, and whether those stories were to be found among the histories or in the fictive mythologies depended on whose library one happened to be standing in.

Osraic didn't take the Kingdom seriously in any real sense, but he did have a favorite version of the Fall. It was the one his mother told him.

There was a mighty sorcerer named Orsak—sometimes Orak, or Ossic, or a half-dozen others including Osraic's own name— who came to rule the Kingdom. At that time, magic was much more common and much more important, which meant Orsak's power, as the ruler of a land of mighty sorcerers, was tremendous to a godlike extreme. This was a problem when Orsak went mad.

In some accounts, the madness was due to grief over the loss of a true love, which is how the poets and the bards told it. Other accounts told of a betrayal, and an act of violence meant to kill Orsak, which succeeded only in causing his derangement. This violence was a physical blow or a magical spell, depending.

A less popular account had the sorcerer falling into a great sleep and dreaming the spells that caused everything that came next. As a child, that was the one Osraic preferred, because it was the least horrible. As an adult, he leaned toward the violent attack / betrayal story as the most plausible, when he bothered to entertain the idea that it was true at all.

What came next was that Orsak spoke a new set of spells of a kind nobody had ever attempted before. These spells took the combined attributes of the Cydonians and divided them up. No longer were his subjects as tall as giants *and* as clever as goblins *and* as strong as trolls, and so forth.

It was the most implausible part of the story, so far as Osraic was concerned, because none of the races were *just* one or two things. Elves could be tall, and strong, and fast, and so could goblins. Trolls were strong brutes, but had a capacity for cleverness. Humans could perform magic, but were as capable as any of brutishness and stupidity, and all of the other traits that had been assigned to other species. The whole thing only managed to simplify the races into caricatures.

Really, the only way the story made sense was that it provided an explanation as to why humans were the one race that could manipulate magic.

As the story went, once the entire population of Cydonia had been de-mongrelized by his spell, Orsak scattered the races across the realm and sealed the gates of the Kingdom, which made it an origin story for the entire world. That was another reason not to take anything regarding the Kingdom seriously, because nothing in the world Osraic knew was this simple.

The mad sorcerer king then either died, continued to live alone in the vast and empty land he had personally depopulated, or left the Kingdom as well, only to walk the world in a series of incarnations. Again, it depended on whose version was being told.

Some adhered to the theory that the Kingdom was a true physical place to actively seek out, and that Orsak had left clues to its location in different parts of the world. One day—and this was the redemptive part that every version of the myth seemed to have—someone worthy would come along and either find the clues or otherwise piece together the location of the Kingdom, and enter.

Not that it mattered. It was only a myth.

～

ant ordered a new round of ale as Osraic tried to figure out what the two of them could possibly mean.

"The Kingdom is a fairy tale," he said. "Everyone who isn't a child knows that."

"I happen to know a fairy," Atha said. "She didn't think there was anything imaginary about it."

"You're actually making my point for me."

"It's very real, young sorcerer," Cant said. "And we need your help to find it."

"Why *my* help?"

"It's said to pass through the gates at least one of each race must be represented," Atha said.

"One of each *kind* is the exact wording of that passage," Osraic said. "It could mean race; it doesn't have to. And a lot of things are *said* when it comes to the Kingdom. It's said one must also defeat a dragon, and drink the tears of a raven. Or an owl. Or a hawk. I have personally met two scholars who've devoted their entire adult lives to a debate on the correct bird's tears, and I don't even know if birds weep. But you've skipped those debates on the necessary requirements and gone with *all races*. Also, why me when Cant here is a perfectly acceptable human representative? You've forgotten all the other races and doubled up on one you already have."

"Yes, but he isn't a sorcerer, and we need one of those."

"Why is that?"

"There's a spell," Cant said.

"What kind of spell?"

"We are not sorcerers, or we would tell you."

Osraic took a large gulp of the ale. It was really annoying to learn that after all of this mysteriousness, the story he'd been waiting to hear was just another foolish Kingdom quest.

There had always been, and always would be, people who had convinced themselves they'd cracked the secret behind the Kingdom's location. Some of them were ranting loners, but a few had the charisma to convince others or the finances to pay them. Every few years, it seemed, there was a formal expedition planned. All of them failed, sometimes spectacularly so. Osraic had an entire volume on the more famous Kingdom quests, and it made for highly entertaining reading.

"If it's a spell, where is it written?" he asked.

"On the stones of the world," Cant said.

Osraic rolled his eyes. He had only a modest tolerance for stupidity before what most people considered an off-putting level of sarcasm settled in, and Cant's answer had just about tipped the scale.

"Really. The stones of the world. Not in a book or anything useful. Do you mean for me to read a cliff face?"

"*And Orsak's words fell upon the stones of the world,*" Atha recited, "*and rent the earth in twain.*"

"I… don't think I've heard that version. Where's it from?"

"The Benja Codex."

"The Benja Codex doesn't exist."

"You say this a great deal, sorcerer," Cant said. "I'm not sure you realize how often. You're a very untrusting sort."

"It doesn't exist," Atha said, "and yet, I've seen it. You noted the distinction, I trust?"

The Benja Codex was nearly as legendary as the story of the Kingdom itself, which was why it was so unlikely for these two northerners to have stumbled across a copy. It was the ur-text from which all the other renditions of the tale sprang. The last historical mention of it was a thousand years old.

"I did," Osraic said. "In your version it wasn't Orsak that rent the earth in twain, it was his words."

"When they fell upon the stones," Cant said.

"And it's your interpretation that these words are a spell, and these stones are non-metaphorical."

Atha and Cant shared a meaningful look.

"It's not precisely *our* interpretation," the elf said. "But we will show you, and you can decide for yourself."

"Well, I'm very sorry," Osraic said, pausing for an unexpected yawn, "but I'm afraid you two are going to have to find yourselves another sorcerer."

"We've already decided on you, Osraic Tal Nar Drang," Cant said. "It's been settled."

"I would love to, but really I can't… Cant. I can't. I have the shop…" he yawned again.

Why am I so tired? he wondered.

"Are you feeling all right?" Atha asked.

"I'm fine. Seems this ale has gone right to my head."

"Yes," she said with a smile. She had a lovely smile. He wanted to tell her that before she ran off on her ridiculous quest, but surely a nap first would be a decent idea. "The ale is quite strong, isn't it?"

~

"Thank the gods he's awake."

Osraic didn't like horseback riding. It was essentially impossible to get around in the countryside without hopping onto a horse, but he'd set up a shop beneath his residence and could walk everywhere he wanted to be—Lantor wasn't at all large—so he simply didn't spend much time in the saddle. He didn't even own a horse.

This meant he tended to suffer more frequently and more intensely from saddle-sore than most people. On this occasion, he was *woken up* by it, which was a new experience entirely.

Cant's voice came from directly behind Osraic, but he was far too disoriented initially to figure out why that was, because it turned out he was still on top of the horse that was causing him so much pain.

He was also dizzy and out of balance, but that wasn't a significant problem as he appeared to be lashed to something steadier than him. That thing turned out to be Cant.

"Why am I tied to you?" he asked, but not quite loud enough to be heard.

His eyes began to focus, revealing a landscape he was unfamiliar with. They were in a mountain pass. The terrain was rocky and almost without vegetation of any kind.

He knew a type of cactus that grew out of harsh rocky outcroppings of the sort they were encountering. The plant's juice made for an excellent poultice when mixed with the proper secondary ingredients. He also knew the plant didn't grow south of the Ailing Mountains, and further that he had just seen one.

"Stop struggling, sorcerer," Cant said.

Atha rode up next to them, her green eyes looking him up and down. "He'll need water," she said. "We stop at the next clearing."

Osraic tried to speak, but she was right: he needed water, and food, and a few other things that didn't involve being tied to a horseman on the wrong side of the mountains.

They drugged me, he realized.

The path they were on opened up to a flat area mostly clear of snow and with a small pool of water for the animals. Atha brought her mount to a halt, along with a second, riderless, horse that was carrying the bulk supplies. She dismounted, and a few seconds later was helping Cant untie himself from Osraic.

"Easy," she said, although it was hard to say to whom she was speaking.

Osraic had never felt so weak before. Once off the horse he tried to stand but collapsed immediately into the elf's arms.

"I have you."

Atha was surprisingly strong, but then it was the first time he'd been supported by an elf so he had no idea what the standard was. Elves tended to be thin and lithe, and were usually described as graceful and elegant. Atha was far from elegant, but sorcerers were supposed to have beards so who was he to say?

She helped him to the edge of the water and sat him down on a rock that was blessedly not shaped like a horse's saddle, her hand on his shoulder to keep him still.

"Can you hold yourself a'right?" she asked, after a moment.

"Yes."

She left him there. Staring at the pool of ice-cold water Osraic decided he had never been more thirsty in his entire life, but he had his wits about him enough to understand that throwing his body into the pool in order to obtain some of that water was not a wise course of action. It might, however, wake him up.

What am I wearing, he wondered.

He was in a heavy fur cloak he'd never seen before. Then his hand went from the soft fur to his chin, where he discovered stubble. *Two days. It's been two days.*

Atha returned with a canteen, and knelt beside him.

"Drink," she said. "Slowly, not all at once."

He sipped the water, which was cool but not nearly as cold as what the horses were sampling. It was without question the greatest thing to ever pass his lips, and he began to chug it down manically, before her hand came down and pulled the canteen away.

"I said slowly. You'll just vomit it back up again if you aren't careful."

"You drugged me," he said.

"That we did, yes."

"And you gave me too much."

She looked over her shoulder at Cant, who was unloading some of the gear from the supply horse.

"It might have been a dose for a… larger man, yes," she said. "I'm afraid our friend Cant overestimated."

"Tell me what it was."

"The drug?"

"Of course, the drug."

"Cant?" she called "What did you give him?"

"The man called it Lot's…something."

"Lot's Fortitude?" Osraic asked.

"Yes, that's it!" he said. "Odd name for a potion, but we couldn't well go to the local sorcerer for it, could we?"

"It's a tranquilizer for cattle."

"I did buy it in the stable."

To Atha, Osraic said, "I need salt. Right now."

"That will only increase the thirst."

"And nullify the poison that idiot fed to me. Salt pork, salt beef, hard tack, whatever you have."

~

It was an hour before Osraic calmed down enough to decide he wasn't going to die. His first gulps of water had not stayed down, as Atha predicted, but the next sips did, as did the dried beef strips that followed. The entire time he ate, Cant eyeballed him angrily, because he was digging into provisions that were meant to last longer than this.

Atha started a fire, which seemed unnecessary until the sun started to set and the cold emanating from the land beneath their feet became more self-evident.

"I assume," Osraic said, "that if I start down the path in that direction I'll eventually end up at Lantor?"

"It's dark," Cant said. "It's not wise to travel the hills at night, sorcerer."

"In the morning, then."

"On foot?"

"You have an extra horse I assume is meant for me."

"It's a northerly horse. He only travels in one direction."

"You made that up."

"I may have."

Atha stood up from the edge of the fire pit. Her cheeks were red from the heat and her green eyes danced with the flame.

"You don't want to travel alone," she said, "with no sword and no clear idea of where you're going or how to get there. You'll never make it."

"Yes, because the people who kidnapped me are a reliable source of information."

"I'm sorry about that. We didn't have a choice."

"You could have tried hiring another sorcerer. There are at least three within a days' ride of Lantor."

She smiled. "It had to be you."

"Why is that?"

She didn't answer. Her attention had been redirected to a space somewhere over Osraic's shoulder. She'd gotten very still.

"What do you hear?" Cant asked quietly. His hand was already buried in his furs, looking for what Osraic assumed was the hilt of a weapon.

"Not sure," she muttered. "I think we share the clearing with something other than rock right now."

"Lion?"

"Possibly."

Osraic held his breath. He'd never seen an Ailing Mountains lion before. He'd seen captive ones, as a child, but rumor was the wild versions were twice as large. He was both excited to see if this was true and worried that it might be.

Atha studied the darkness for a few heartbeats and then shook her head.

"It's no lion," she decided. "This is something larger."

"*Larger?*" Osraic asked.

"Yes. And airborne."

"A dragon?"

"Not a dragon," Cant said, as Atha pulled out her quiver. "If it was a dragon there would be no question. Now keep quiet and still."

Osraic went back to holding his breath, and ruminating on the number of different things he knew about that were larger than a lion and smaller than a dragon, could fly, and were predatory. He couldn't think of any.

With her quiver slung over her back, Atha pulled the longbow out of her hair and whispered something. Osraic strained to hear the command, but couldn't quite pick it up. Whatever it was, the bow responded appropriately. And quickly. Osraic blinked, and the longbow was in her hands at full size.

She held it parallel with the surface, put one hand on the shaft of an arrow, crouched, and waited.

Her eyes were closed. This was, he realized, so she could regain the night vision she'd lost because of the fire.

When she fired, it happened so quickly Osraic was ready to ascribe it to another enchantment. The arrow was out and notched, the bow raised, and the arrow loosed, and it happened between heartbeats. Considering how rapidly his heart was beating, this was very fast.

The arrow flew nearly straight up and apparently hit its mark, making a sick sort of noise Osraic last heard in a butcher's shop. He still hadn't seen what was out there, and didn't until it fell to the ground a few yards from their campground.

"A greathawk," Osraic said, jumping to his feet.

"Yes," the elf agreed.

The beast was taller than Cant, with feet large enough to wrap around a man's head and talons sharp enough to remove that head. Atha's arrow was buried in its brown feathery underbelly, and had found the creature's heart.

Even half-crushed by its impact with the rocky earth and gored by the weapon that killed him, Osraic was worried that the thing might jump up and attack when the elf crouched down and pulled out her arrow

"I don't understand," Osraic said.

"When they attack is when they are most exposed," she said. "Provided one knows where to hit them."

"But greathawks don't hunt by night."

"No," she said. "They don't."

⁓

The attack by the greathawk was enough to shelve any discussion of Osraic venturing home on his own, at least until the following morning, when he was disappointed to see his companions had no interest in changing direction.

"You will never make it back," Cant said, as Osraic stared up the wrong path. "Cities are built on straight throughways and flat ground, but up here the path is dictated by the land. Lost men die in the hills, even in the spring."

"The horse knows the way."

"That horse was bought in Lantor on the same day we retrieved you, sorcerer. She is just as lost. Now are you going to help or continue to whine?"

Helping meant reorganizing the distribution of weight. The third horse had been tasked with most of their provisions while Osraic had been unconscious and tied to Cant. Now that he was awake and reluctantly prepared to ride unaided, they had to move things around.

This only took a few minutes, though, and then Osraic was in the saddle and faced with a decision.

Atha rode up next to him.

"We go north," she said. "There's nothing for you the other way except for death."

Appropriately enough, they stood only a few yards from the body of the greathawk.

"You won't escort me back, then?" he asked.

"No. You're welcome to stay here and sulk, but I wouldn't recommend it. This is a common area for travelers, but you'll find most of the people you meet up here are less friendly than we are."

"Maybe. Maybe I'll meet some people who don't try and drug me the minute we've been introduced."

"We apologized for that. But you didn't leave us with much of a choice."

"You left me with no choice whatsoever. That's what kidnapping is."

She laughed. "You need to relax, sorcerer. We'll take care of you."

"I didn't need taking care of in Lantor. Nothing was trying to kill me there."

"Are you so sure of that?" She patted the head of his mount. "By the way, her name is Jenna, and she's nearly as frightened as you are, so talk to her. We have a long day of travel and it would be better if neither of you were spooked the entire time."

Osraic's anger—at himself, at his companions-cum-kidnappers, at the horse that was brutally harming his posterior—subsided over the course of the day. The view afforded him as they descended the northern face of the Ailing Mountains was often breathtaking, and as much as he resented the circumstances that brought him there he was thankful for the experience.

They were nowhere near the top of the range, and had truly never been, as the pass they had used when he was still unconscious cut between two peaks rather than summiting one of them. This was just as well, as he'd read about the troubles men and animals had at that elevation, not just with heavy winds and deep snows, but also with things that should be taken for granted, like air thick enough for breathing.

Osraic was still higher and further north than he'd ever been before, seeing things he'd only ever read about or examined in etchings. The open sky was so vast and close that for the first time in his life he understood why some men wrote poetry. He'd seen cloud banks that were close enough to touch, and distant storms writing sigils in lightning.

Their descent was heading for a forest floor he couldn't see due to a perpetual ground fog. He'd have thought they were lowering themselves into a cloud if not for the pine forest poking through.

And he saw dragons.

At first he didn't even grasp what he was looking at. The problem with being so high up in such an open space was that he lost all understanding of distance and size. In the cities and mud towns he'd grown up in, how far he could see was limited by how many things were in the way—buildings, trees—and how bright and plentiful the evening torches were. He was unaccustomed to an unobstructed view that went for miles in all directions. So when he saw the dragons, they were so far away he initially mistook them for peculiar birds of the approximate size of actual birds, and not monstrous lizard beasts the size of houses. It wasn't until one of them expelled fire—playfully, it appeared—that he realized his mistake.

Osraic must have gasped audibly at the sight, because he caught Cant's attention. They were riding with Atha in the lead and Cant in the rear. Whether this was because they were concerned he might wander, or fall off his horse, he wasn't sure.

"Don't worry," the large man said. "We shouldn't expect to face a dragon until we've reached the gates of the Kingdom."

"Right. What if one of them decides to show up early?"

"Well that would just be bad luck. Perhaps we should have taken one of your charms."

He rode up beside Osraic.

"Here," he said, "have a look."

Cant pulled out a vial and handed it over.

"What's this?" Osraic asked, holding it up. It was blue glass with a clear liquid inside. He might have thought Cant palmed one of his potions from the shop, but the container was unfamiliar.

"Tears of a raven, of course."

Osraic handed back the vial.

"You're both mad," he said.

"So you say. When you see what we have seen, you might consider if madness is such a terrible recourse."

"How do you mean to defeat one, when the time comes?"

"Have you ever met a dragon, sorcerer?"

"I haven't, no."

"When the time comes, we'll probably just negotiate terms. They're mostly quite reasonable."

"I can never tell when you're joking."

Cant laughed. "That's because I never am."

~

They didn't stop riding until the sun fell past the western edge of the mountain range. By then everyone was starved. Osraic felt a bone-deep soreness and general exhaustion he wished he could have attributed to the aftereffects of the drug, but which likely had more to do with the riding.

Before the sunlight disappeared he took a look back at the hills they had spent the day climbing out of, and was pretty sure he could spot the point where they emerged from the clearing that morning. It didn't seem far at all. But, as with the dragons, distance and size expectations were confounded by the scale of the mountain range.

Atha helped Osraic off the horse, and then ignored him for several minutes while she spoke to his mount.

"She says you didn't talk to her," the elf said, after what sounded like an entirely one-sided conversation. "I told you to talk to her."

"You can talk to animals?"

He couldn't recall any lore on elves having the ability to communicate with animals. There was no lore on *anyone* having that innate ability, actually. There was a spell that could do it, but it was complicated, and Osraic was years away from even attempting such a thing. That was provided it even worked, which was doubtful. About three quarters of the volumes on spells were flim-flam.

"Anyone can talk to animals," she said. "You should try."

"I'll rephrase. Do they talk back to you?"

"In their own way, yes."

Cant clapped him on the shoulder. "I would not press this point, if I were you," he said. "We have to make camp. Let her tend to the animals. They *did* do all the work today."

Making camp didn't involve a fire this time. For most of the day, a sharp wind had been cutting through the heavy furs, leaving Osraic raw and uncomfortable, if not actually cold. The undermost layer of his clothing was damp with his own sweat, though, and whenever the wind touched it he shivered.

But there was no firewood to be found in this terrain, and what they'd been carrying had been used up the night before. They were somewhat less likely to attract the attention of another greathawk without a fire, but probably more likely to freeze to death before morning.

The three of them spent the next hour chewing dried meat and drinking water, which only made them feel colder. Nobody spoke, but this could have been as much from exhaustion and the amount of energy involved in chewing dried food as from any residual belligerence.

"Can I see your bow?" Osraic asked, both to break the silence and because he'd been wanting to examine it closely since Atha first showed it to him in the tavern.

I was warm that day, he lamented.

Atha shrugged, and removed it from her hair.

"*Alavas,*" she whispered, and as before it jumped to a normal size in her hands. This time Osraic was watching carefully, and still didn't see it happen. It was as if the bow had only two sizes, and jumped between them without pausing at any of the intermediate sizes first.

He took it from her.

"Is it specific to you?" he asked.

"Yes."

"*Alavas*," he said.

Nothing happened.

"As I said."

"I believed you. I was just curious. This is the most powerful enchantment I think I've ever touched. Who did it for you?"

She and Cant shared a quick glance.

"I'd rather not say at this time," she said, "if that's all right."

"Yes."

Maybe he should have gone on this damn quest, he thought, *instead of me.*

Osraic would have said this aloud, but his reading of the enchantment on the bow was much more interesting than any answer they could have provided.

Magic was a craft, just like anything else.

Most people thought of it in the same way they thought of blacksmiths. That is, a smithy could forge a sword, and nobody who later held that sword would be able to discern the technique used to make it, beyond a general understanding of fire and hammered metal. But the truth was, magic was more like carpentry. To an untrained eye it might appear that a chair, or a table, or a house was assembled in a process as mysterious as that of the sword-maker. An experienced carpenter, though, could examine the joints and ascertain how the object was assembled, and in what order.

So it was with an enchanted thing. If one knew how to read magic, it was possible to see the joints and hinges and figure out how the enchantment did what it did.

"Are you going to give that back, or fondle it all night?" Atha asked.

"Sorry," he said. He held it out for her to take back. When she touched it, he held on for an extra half-second, enough time to examine the part of the spell that made it particular to her. "It's an amazing piece of work."

"The bow, or the magics?"

"Both."

He nearly understood the spell, which was surprising enough on its own. He had plenty of experience reading other sorcerers' enchantments—this was an essential element of apprenticeship— but never anything so complex. He had imagined it as something that would take hours to grasp. But the only part he couldn't quite get had to do with the different materials that made up the bow. Mostly, he couldn't figure out how the drawstring had never broken.

Osraic decided he wanted to know more about the sorcerer who had performed such a complex enchantment, but it was too dark and too cold for any further conversation. Atha returned the bow to her hair and the three of them huddled together for mutual warmth, and slept.

"All right, let's stop here."

The loose collection of individuals that constituted the Tenth Avenue Writers' Underground was assembled in a haphazard fashion across the surprisingly spacious living room belonging to Wilson Knight. The room had several appropriate places to sit and lounge, including the floor, which was covered in a heavy pile carpet and was deemed by many to be quite comfortable in the event a short nap was needed.

The room was a part of a seventh floor condo, which was either owned by Wilson's parents or by Wilson himself, depending on who asked and what kind of mood Wilson happened to be in at the time.

It was Wilson who told Oliver to stop reading. Under most circumstances this interjection would be considered rude, except: everyone expected rudeness from Wilson as a matter of course; and Oliver was glad to be stopped. The truth was, what followed was another two pages of description of a forest that just didn't work, ending with the note MORE WORLD-BUILDING GOES HERE.

Oliver put down the pages and looked up expectantly, but for the moment, Wilson looked as surprised as everyone else in the room regarding his interruption.

"Do you have notes?" Oliver asked.

"I… yes. I mean, that seemed like a good place to stop. You don't have a lot more, do you?"

"Not a lot more, no."

"It's quite a bit already," Wilson said. "What you've done so far."

"It's a start."

"For the purposes of the assignment, it's more than enough. You didn't write an entire epic in a week, I'm just assuming."

"No, I didn't."

"Then let's talk about what you've got here."

If it seemed like Wilson was a little too professorial for someone who was, age-wise, a peer to the entire writer's group, that was because the Tenth Avenue Writers' Underground—which everyone called either TAWU or "the woo"—was his idea. More exactly, people involved in it got involved because Wilson Knight ran the thing.

There were two reasons for this. First, Wilson Knight had a MFA in creative writing from a university everyone had heard of.

Second, and possibly more importantly, Wilson Knight had been published.

Neither of those facts meant nearly as much to the people who had accomplished both of those things as they did to the people who had not. The publication involved a short story in a literary magazine that was so obscure, if Wilson (or anyone else) announced one day that the magazine itself was a work of fiction, nobody would be all that surprised. But the value of having been published far outweighed the exposure from it, the money he might have made in selling it—if any—or even the quality of the piece itself. (In truth, hardly anybody had *read* the story either, for the same reason nobody had really heard of the magazine it was featured in.) The value came from the accolades that followed.

Wilson Knight was a certified Important Generational Voice. There had been more articles published on the significance of Wilson Knight, author, than things published by Wilson Knight, author, by a factor of at least ten.

This didn't mean Wilson was not a good writer. By all accounts, he was very good indeed, it was only that the people who had first-hand experience with his prose were greatly outnumbered by the people who only knew of it by word-of-mouth. It was probably true that were Wilson to never write another word, he could still survive as an Important Generational Voice in literary circles for several years. Whether or not this theory was put to the test depended on when and if he actually finished his novel.

"Fantasy is a challenging first choice," Wilson said, somewhat grandly. "Bold, I mean."

"All right," Oliver said, not sure whether or not he agreed with this but willing to take whatever ride his ostensible mentor was thinking of taking him on. "Why do you say it's bold?"

"It's a well-worn path, isn't it? An entire genre built on mimicry of an early, original voice."

"You mean Tolkien."

"Of course I do. I don't mean any disparagement when I say this, by the way. It's generally a respected genre."

Oliver thought everything Wilson just said was disparagement, and he doubted anybody in the room took it as anything less than precisely that.

"I think that's an over-simplification," he said.

"Sure, sure. A little reductionism to make a nuanced point."

Wilson used more expensive words when challenged. If he ever got into a hot enough argument, he'd likely start speaking entirely in Latin.

"And what's your nuanced point?"

"That you shouldn't start a quest to find your own voice by imitating someone else's."

The writing assignments for the TAWU were given out weekly, and based on nothing more than whatever letter Wilson felt particularly close to that day. Since there were ten members, all in various states of skill and experience, there was no expectation that each week would result in a new bit of writing from all ten. In fact, the likelihood that any of the participants would have something corresponding to the letter handed out in the prior week was pretty low. Mostly, everyone brought in what they had to share when they were ready to share it, which made Wilson's whole letter-assignment concept kind of silly.

Also, single letters as writing prompts was a pretty limited system.

Still, it tended to work more often than not. For the most part, the weekly discussions about the act of creating fiction proved sufficient to inspire two or three new pieces a week, and the letter was a decent jumping-off point.

Oliver had been coming to TAWU for a year. For six months of that year he wasn't at all sure he even wanted to be a writer, but he very much enjoyed discussing other people's attempts at it. Sometime around month seven Oliver decided everyone else in the group—possibly excepting Wilson, although it was difficult to tell since he never showed anything—was a worse writer than he was. But, since Oliver had never written anything he had no way to prove this.

It was another five months, give or take a week, before he actually gave it a try. That was the week the letter K was assigned.

Well, no, that wasn't entirely true. Yes, the week in which he finally wrote something coincided with the letter K, but there had been other letters before K, letters that sat at the top of the blank word document on his computer screen, alone and abandoned, with no inspirational collection of additional letters used to form words and then sentences and paragraphs, adding up to things someone might call a story.

Then came K. Everything felt different with K, although Oliver couldn't begin to explain why. For starters, as soon as he got the letter—while still in Wilson's living room, even—he decided K stood for Kingdom. By the time he got home he had the first sentence: "I understand you are a sorcerer." And then he was writing, and he didn't stop until he was well past the TAWU minimum word-count and further, on his way to what he imagined was a full novel, written in under a week.

It didn't end up being a novel—not yet—but he was pretty proud of what he'd accomplished.

All of which made Wilson's reaction kind of disappointing.

"Hang on," Tandy said.

Oliver thought Tandy was a pretty good writer. She liked to write about serious things using dangerously large compound sentences and making what seemed like decent observations about the human condition. The biggest problem she had was that very few people seemed willing to concentrate long enough to figure out the gist of those observations, because despite being a *good* writer, Tandy wasn't an *interesting* writer.

"Don't we all learn how to write by imitating others?" she asked.

"Do you mean fan fiction?" Gerald asked.

Gerald was *not* a good writer, but he was an excellent rabble-rouser. Saying *fan-fiction* in front of Wilson was a lot like waving a red cape in front of a bull while also blasting the bull in the ear with an air horn.

"I don't mean fan-fic," Tandy said quickly. "I mean we learn to write by reading, and if we assume we like what we're reading, of course our first efforts are going to be imitative based on what we enjoyed, conscious or not."

"Yes, yes, but that isn't my point at all," Wilson said. "My point is, this particular sub-genre is derivative *when you're doing everything right*. That's the *goal*. Whether one is performing an homage to the source text or writing something deliberately contrary to it, all versions of the sword-and-sandal epic are a conversation with Tolkien. And there's nothing wrong with that! All I'm saying is that given this is Oliver's first attempt at something he can call his own, that the challenge of finding himself in his writing is going to be *that much harder* when he's attempting to occupy a space that's already taken. And it has to be taken, if he's doing it properly."

This assertion broke the group up into a number of mini-conversations and debates that Oliver could barely keep track of and wasn't sure whether or not he should even bother. The topic soon strayed from any direct critique of what he'd written into the concept of originality, the implicit challenge of writing something truly original, and the source of inspiration and creativity in the act of creation.

It was interesting, or rather it *had* been interesting, the first five or six times the debate came up. But after a year, he doubted he was going to hear anything different than the other times, so he elected not to participate actively.

He also wasn't sure he *should* participate actively.

Presenting his own writing was a weird experience. After all the time he'd spent in the group, listening to other people's stuff and actively engaging them on what they'd just read, he now felt as if he had a duty to be silent and wait for opinions to form. Or for a decision to be reached. Like he was listening to his parents argue about something he'd done, while he was still in the room: surely, the punishment would be agreed upon shortly.

Oliver was only half-listening, then, when he made eye contact with the other person in the apartment not directly engaged. Her name was Minerva. She was Wilson's live-in girl-friend-slash-something-something-fiancé. Everyone called her Minnie except for her boyfriend, and her parents, probably.

Wilson was the sort of person to favor full names in all circumstances. As Oliver had a rather long name—his last name was Naughton, but due to some complicated family dynamics he had two middle names—he was glad Wilson's preference didn't go beyond surnames, or they'd never get anything done.

Minnie was a petite, auburn-haired, adorable woman with turquoise eyes and about fifteen different versions of a smile. Each one was devastating. There were times when Oliver thought she had to be invented by someone, as he didn't think it was possible for the natural world to produce her without some kind of guided supervision.

There was, he reflected, a pretty decent chance he was in love with her. This wasn't necessarily extraordinary, as he couldn't imagine a world in which everyone didn't also feel this way. It fit in perfectly well with all the other known facts about the universe: the sun rises; the sky is blue; everyone is in love with Minerva.

She was standing at the edge of the kitchen, a bystander to the TAWU meeting, as always. Very, very occasionally, she would interject an observation, but it always felt like a protest vote sort of circumstance. She wasn't a writer, and more precisely, she had no interest in becoming one. (If one were to measure the identifi-cation of a person as "a writer" with the minimum standard of "writing things", one third of the regulars in the writers' underground weren't writers at all. Until recently, Oliver would have been one of them.) Sometimes, Minerva sat quietly at the far end of the room, and maybe once or twice brought in cookies. On certain occasions, she wasn't even in the apartment. Those were the bad weeks.

Minnie gave him a little head gesture, which he interpreted to mean, *come over here*, and so he did. This in no way interfered with the debate.

Once he got close enough, she took his elbow and pulled him into the kitchen.

"It's really good," she said.

"It's…"

He lost his train of thought. She did that to him.

"*The Kingdom*. It's really good. Wilson thinks so too."

"Are you sure? He's trying to talk me into writing something else instead."

"That just means he thinks you're worth rescuing."

"Rescuing? Like a puppy?"

"Yes, like a puppy."

"I still don't understand."

"Then you aren't paying attention, except I *know* you are. C'mon, Ollie, he props up the bad ones and tears down the good ones."

He *had* noticed this, but this observation led him in the direction of thinking unkind things about his ostensible mentor, so he dismissed it. Hearing it presented so baldly by someone he would have expected to be on Wilson's side was a little jarring.

"Why does he do that?" he asked.

"The good ones need to be challenged to get better. The bad ones need encouragement just to become good. I mean, that's what *I* think. He could just be out to destroy the good ones."

Oliver laughed, because he wanted to think she was kidding. She hadn't delivered one of her fifteen known smiles with the line, though, so he couldn't be sure.

"Listen, you should get back in there," Minnie said.

"Yeah, probably."

"Oh, and what are you doing later?"

"What?"

This was the longest private conversation he'd ever had with Minerva and his head was exploding. He thought he was out, and then she asked the most terrifying open-ended question she could have asked that didn't involve an explicit sex act.

"Tonight," she repeated. "A bunch of us are going to that new club. You're invited if you wanna come."

"Thanks, okay, sure. No, I mean. No, can't. I have to work."

"Aw, too bad. Next time?"

"Sure, next time."

~

The debate ended to the complete satisfaction of nobody as usual, and then came the final part of the meeting: the critique circle.

Oliver had already managed to detach himself from the current reality to some degree, in that he was no longer *in* the moment so much as he was sitting outside of it and watching dispassionately.

Practiced disengagement was more or less his default mode. In it, he managed to be involved but at the same time listening to a running meta-commentary in his head. It was like having his own narrator accompany him through life. About the only times he could remember being fully engaged was when he was talking to Minnie, and when he was writing.

The critique circle was pretty painless, because everyone there had certain predilections, which led to similar-sounding criticisms, which fit pretty much anything placed in front of them.

Take Ivor. He had a lot to say about the title. In the two or three minutes in which he had the floor at least half was taken up by this. On the occasions when the piece being critiqued had no title, he'd talk for twice as long, specifically to crowdsource a title for the author.

Jennifer took a similar approach, only she had a habit of finding one particular word—not the title, since that was taken—and talking at length about how striking the word choice was and why it worked.

Then there was Tandy and her Big Themes and Gerald's fascination with alliterative passages, and Danny's love of dialogue. And so on.

Oliver didn't know any of these people outside of this particular space. They didn't do anything socially together—or if they did, it was without him—and there was never any time to discuss their lives above and beyond fiction writing. Because of this, Oliver, in self-narrative mode, had been providing them with their own backstories.

Ivor, in his late thirties, was chubby and unshaven. He had a job during the week, which required him to shave daily, so when Saturday came around he treated himself by not doing it. Ivor was unreasonably preoccupied with how much things cost. He carried a real estate property values spreadsheet around in his head, and could tell you how much it cost to buy a condo in any part of the county. He was also single, not currently dating anyone, and liked to blame women—as a monolithic whole—for the fact that he was unable to find love.

Aside from the physical observations—the man was indeed chubby and unshaven—everything else was either deduced observationally by Oliver or invented whole cloth. Oliver no longer knew where the line was between reality and something he made up. Since he doubted the day would come when he got to know Ivor well enough to figure out where that line was, he didn't much care.

Tandy was probably a lesbian. She had a habit of staring overlong at Minerva when Minnie was in the room, which Oliver only noticed because he had the same habit. She was a copy editor for one of the five or six literary magazines that hadn't gone out of business yet thanks to the Internet. This either made her a stickler for textual precision and clarity—and a complete lunatic about semicolons—or those innate tendencies were what led her to copy editing. Tandy liked to wear sandals in all but the worst weather, along with lots of brown clothing, and carried pinecone-and-allspice potpourri in one of the pockets of her jacket.

These were the most thorough backstories Oliver had, because Tandy and Ivor had been there as long as he had. Others were just initial impressions written out into longer sentences. Gerald, for instance, spent too much time gaming online, but had a girlfriend who also spent too much time gaming online, so she was a good match. Nathan was in his early twenties and was attending community college part-time. Ollie didn't have a profession for him yet, but it was something that required clean fingernails.

Most of the rest of them were represented largely by mental index cards with two or three words on them, and a lot of the time those words weren't even going to make it to the final draft. Like Bibi, who'd only been to three meetings. Her card said "boobs", because so far that was all Oliver had noticed about her. Undoubtedly, the longer she participated, the more likely it was his eyes would drift northward—to focus on what she was saying —and east and west to review other physical characteristics which may come in handy when he got around to building out her imaginary life. Until then, "boobs" was it.

Interestingly, he had almost no backstory for the two people he was most likely to have real facts on: Wilson and Minnie. For Wilson, what he had was the hagiographic edition, which was surprisingly short on real details. As for Minnie, Oliver didn't want to ruin her by inventing a life outside of the condo that was anything less than amazing.

The bullet-point version of the critique circle, on the subject of the quality of *The Kingdom*, was:

- Dialogue: good
- Magic: okay
- Some wanted less limited and more explicit magic, which led to a new lengthy discussion on the merits of placing artificial limitations on what Wilson called "the ultimate *get out of trouble free* card"
- Some wanted no magic at all
- Characters: okay
- Ivor ended his dissection of the "kingdom" in the title to talk about how the main character's name began with the same letter as Oliver's name, which he seemed to think was important but couldn't explain why
- Several complained that it was confusing to name a character "Cant" and wanted to know why he did that, and he didn't know
- Dragons: bad
- This was just Wilson, who apparently hated dragons without cause
- Conclusion: do something else

In spite of all the back-and-forth regarding the merits of the fantasy genre (specifically the 'sword-and-sandal' variety) the group tended to follow Wilson's lead: *The Kingdom* was good, but put it down and go write something different.

Then, Wilson ended the TAWU meeting with a new letter—P—and the group was adjourned.

Oliver didn't stick around for any after-meeting conversation. He never did, which could have been why he had to invent everyone's backstories. A couple of times, he became convinced that the others *were* meeting outside of Wilson's condo, and Ollie simply wasn't invited, but he always either talked himself out of this or convinced himself he didn't care, depending on his mood.

Either way, he wasn't along for socializing. Plus, he was about to be late for work.

~

The condo was conversationally identified as belonging to Wilson, but nobody in TAWU was actually sure if this was true. What *was* true was that it was on the top floor of a walk-up brownstone in the center of Tenth Avenue, which meant the place was worth a substantial amount more than it seemed either occupant was capable of owning. The owner—be they Wilson or Minnie—was either independently wealthy due to some sort of unusual windfall, or they came from a wealthy family that earned money via a more traditional long-term means.

Oliver liked to think the money was on Minerva's side, but he wasn't sure why he preferred that. Maybe, in his own backstory, he was secretly harboring a wish to steal her away from Wilson, and had a complex fantasy of them running off using her father's credit card, making it all the way to a Caribbean island before daddy cut off the funds in a fit of pique, because he always liked Wilson's family and wanted to punish his little girl for going against him. Then Oliver and Minerva would be forced to go native, live off the meager earnings of their menial jobs, share a cot in the back of a bar, and maybe later solve a murder mystery.

Maybe.

The condo was part of one building in a row of buildings that were attached to one another, all the way down the street to the end of the block. The same thing existed on the opposite side of the street, with the middle occupied by a grassy median that was called a vertical park. It had statuaries and fountains and ran all the way down the length of Tenth.

Oliver worked in a coffee shop two blocks away, on Market

Street, a stretch of road that featured some of the most high-end shops in the country. Oliver couldn't afford to buy anything on Market, except possibly the coffee, and only because he got an employee discount.

It was in the shop, a year earlier, where he'd seen the sign posted advertising an opening in the Tenth Avenue Writers' Underground. He took it down almost as soon as it went up, because they had a strict policy about that sort of thing and also because he wanted to reduce the competition for this presumably coveted opening.

Wilson and Minnie didn't know he worked there, and he liked that just fine. They lived in a world where top-floor condos on Tenth Ave were affordable things, and where they could just up and head to "that new club"—whatever that was—without having to budget ahead of time for a night out.

Oliver took the five cement steps down from the door of the brownstone to the street, and suffered a moment of disorientation. The high walls of the buildings created a kind of forced perspective, in which he felt even smaller, somehow, as if standing beside a mountain range instead of a seven-story walk-up.

At the far end of the street, around a flagpole, a flock of birds circled, on their way to settling at the high edge of the cornice, where there was probably a nest of some kind. The mountain range effect conspired with what he had to admit was probably an overactive imagination, and for a half-second he thought he wasn't looking at nearby birds at all. He was looking at faraway dragons.

Write something new, he reminded himself.

He already had something in mind. It came to him as soon as Wilson handed out the assignment.

"P is for Phone," Oliver said aloud, to nobody. Nobody responded.

Chapter Two

PHONE

A fat drop of water clung to the white ceiling tile for an indescribably long period, before it surrendered to gravity and plummeted to the carpet. It made a gentle sound—*POIT*—as it added itself to the moisture already collected down there, on the floor of the Young Misses section, to the left of a rack of discount blouses and the right of more discount blouses.

It was a leak. It had been going on for hours.

Orrin stood there with the beam of the flashlight he only grudgingly employed, trained on the space above the damp carpeting, waiting for the next one to fall. Every drop of water caught the light on the way down, a tiny, brief flash. They could be tracer rounds—time to reload the gun—except they didn't announce that the ceiling was about to run out of water. If anything, the next step was going to be an increase, possibly damaging the racks of discount blouses on both sides.

It'd rained all day, and now at three in the morning with the rain *still* going, Orrin had to think that what he was looking at was the first indication of something very bad rather than the final act of a minor inconvenience. If the roof above the ceiling had a leak, there was no telling how much water was pooled up there and how long it had been happening. The gradual darkening of the ceiling tile was a good sign, though, that a bigger mess was pending.

That was provided the tile was really darkening. It was hard to tell with the flashlight.

During the day, the sales floor of Mad Maggie's Shop-O-Rama was a shadowless consumer mecca, a shining shopping plaza city on a hill, with industrial strength fluorescents to keep everyone awake and make the products look newer and cleaner and less flawed. But when the store closed, the main lights went away and the emergency lights kicked in. These were small spotlights mounted in odd places throughout the store, pointed at weird angles and creating a chthonic nightmare of shadows in every direction.

The shadows weren't so bad as long as one resisted the urge to eradicate them, such as by using a flashlight to get around.

Orrin kind of preferred the nighttime version of the place. All the light made him uncomfortable. Sure, it was probably because he was mostly only there after hours, which meant the cozy half-lit aisles he was accustomed to looked artificial and alien in full light. He was also a night person by nature and a loner by social standards. He was reasonably sure he was those things first, and therefore a good night watchman, but it was possible he became those things in order to be a *better* night watchman. It was hard to say.

He'd been doing the job for a little over two years, which officially made him—even counting the other shifts—the longest-running office-holder. The watchmen who came before him could have simply gotten better jobs, which was possible since it wasn't a well-paying position, although there were worse ones out there. But Orrin didn't think that was the case.

When Mad Maggie's hired him he was told the job had high turnover. That tended to mean his predecessors quit or were fired, at a frequency atypical in the eyes of the hiring manager. He was pretty sure the reason was that the others used their flashlights.

That was the thing he figured out his first month: the extra light just made the darkness worse. Shine a beam in semi-darkness and it ruins your night vision and makes the shadows seem deeper and much more foreboding. Sometimes, it creates the illusion things out there are moving when they aren't, and it's hard to climb out of that psychological rabbit-hole once you've started going down it.

So he taught himself to see in the native dimness of the off-hour lighting, figured out where all the weird shadows were—the ones that looked like something to run away from all got their own names—and things had been just fine since.

Then the ceiling in Young Misses started leaking, and that screwed up his whole schedule.

He'd been hearing the steady *poit-poit-poit* for a couple of hours before discovering the source. Now that he had, other than spending entirely too long watching the plump droplets flash across his light beam one-by-one he didn't know exactly what he was supposed to do.

He turned to the nearest mannequin, a twelve-year old in a poodle skirt and a floofy blouse.

"I guess I should get a bucket," he said.

She didn't register any kind of satisfaction or dissatisfaction with this idea, because she had no eyes or mouth.

*B*uckets were in the maintenance closet on the other side of the room.

This implied a nearness not borne out by facts. Mad Maggie's Shop-O-Rama was a repurposed warehouse, so getting to the *other side of the room* meant traversing a space that was once used to make battleship guns, among other things.

That was back in the Second World War, and probably for a little while after. Then, for some reason—probably not because battleships stopped needing guns, as that seemed unlikely—it became something else, and then something else again, and then something else after that. It housed an overstock of lawn statuaries in one of its iterations, Orrin was told. He didn't know when or for how long, or even why an overstock of such a thing would exist, but he did know that he was glad to be the night watchman for Mad Maggie's, and not for a warehouse full of statues, because the shadows in such a place would be so, so much worse. Mannequins were bad enough.

Getting to the maintenance closet meant exiting Young Misses by way of the central causeway, heading past Young Men's, and then diving into the Kitchen section at about the halfway point, after the endcap of blenders. This also took him through the weird motor oil smell he was apparently the only one to notice.

It was an odor Orrin picked up on in three different places in the store, and it was especially curious because while Mad Maggie sold home furnishings, clothing, kitchen goods, plumbing supplies, toys, costume jewelry, electronics, gardening tools, seasonal doo-dads, and dry groceries, she didn't sell motor oil. He'd checked. The only thing he found that came close was the cleaning stuff in the kitchen section, and when "seasonal" meant barbecue grills there was usually lighter fluid around. But neither of those smelled like motor oil.

He guessed that one of the things the warehouse was used for before the statuaries and after the battleship guns was auto storage and maintenance, but he'd never been able to confirm that. It didn't help that when he asked around—either the night crew handing the store off to him or the day crew taking it back— nobody copped to smelling it too.

The other option, then, was that it was all in his head. If he had some deep-seated motor oil trauma to revisit, this might make sense. He didn't, though.

At the end of the aisle, past the food processors and juicers, was a door leading off the sales floor and into a space used for the employee break room, locker rooms, manager's office, and the employee bathrooms, along with the janitor supply closet. Orrin didn't usually go there during his shift. There were no emergency lights in back, so in order to see he had to either turn on the bright fluorescents or use the flashlight. He didn't even go back there for the bathroom; he used the customer one instead, which was nicer anyway, and it had an emergency light. It still meant leaving the floor, and when he did that he always had to do a pass afterwards, through the whole store to make sure nothing happened while he was away. But the bathroom was the sort of thing he couldn't *not* visit, so he planned his trips near his scheduled rounds, and tried to keep his fluid intake down.

The visit in back blew up his night vision completely, because he couldn't figure out which key belonged to the closet, and there were a lot of keys on a big ring. The fourth time he dropped the ring, he gave up trying to juggle both the flashlight and the keys, and just turned on the overhead light.

~

*A*fter dumping the mop, Orrin had a bucket-on-wheels that didn't seem nearly large enough to handle the growing problem in Young Misses. He was starting to wonder if it wouldn't have been a better idea just to head over to Storage and grab one of the big plastic bins instead. Sure, it would have ruined a sellable product, but the water was well on its way to ruining the carpet already. It would probably end up being a net gain.

Back on the floor, blinking repeatedly and waiting for his pupils to adjust, he tried very hard not to jump to any conclusions about what he was seeing that just wasn't there.

That was the problem: there was exactly enough light to mess with your head. If it was total darkness, he could invent monsters in the dark if he wanted, but they were entirely subject to the limits of his imagination. In partial light, though, he was getting information from the world around him, and the animal part of his brain that held the fight-or-flight mechanism was going totally bananas as a consequence.

He could have sworn he saw something move, two aisles to his right. That would have put it at the start of the Sporting Goods section, and he knew for a fact that there were two particularly athletic mannequins in the middle of that extra-wide aisle, posed in mid-run so as to show off clothing to sweat in and sneakers to wear for it. Their peculiar stances—one man mannequin, one woman mannequin—combined with the lights to fool the eye into thinking a whole bunch of bad things that weren't true. He *knew* this. But his peripheral vision wasn't on board. So his heart raced and his breathing picked up, and no matter how often he looked over at Sporting Goods and talked himself out of seeing the movement that wasn't really movement, the bile kept rising in the back of his throat and the panic set in, until finally he just closed his eyes and counted to ten.

This was a terrifying exercise in its own right, but it worked. The way he figured, if the part of his mind that knew perfectly well he was alone in a locked building—with nothing but inanimate objects and the shadow nightmares of his own imagination —if that part wasn't driving, the smartest thing to do was also the dumbest: close his eyes and stand still. If the monster his instinct told him had to be out there didn't grab him during the ten-count, it probably wasn't there.

Probably.

It worked. It always worked, because of course it did. Because of course, he was alone. The running mannequins were just that. And to make absolutely 100% sure, he walked down to Sporting Goods, dragging the bucket-on-wheels with him, until he was in the aisle.

"Nothing but you guys, see, I told you," he said, to his own imagination.

The mannequins had no comment, which was great.

He pulled the bucket past them and returned to the main concourse, as his vision got back to normal. The place felt comfortable, then. His heart rate slowed, and except for the fact that he could still hear the ceiling dripping, all was well. He would set the bucket up under the leak, maybe move the clothes racks further away from it in case the whole ceiling tile came down, then go back to his rounds and have a nice ordinary night.

That was when he heard the phone ring.

"Who's there?" he shouted, without thinking much about it. Whoever was hiding in the store certainly didn't need him to be announcing where he was while at the same time tipping them off that he knew they were there.

He spun around in place, until he was staring at the butt of the male jogging mannequin in stylish space-age fabric shorts.

Everything was where it was supposed to be. Two rows down, across from the last section of Sporting Goods, in the Home Health aisle, on the endcap, was a humidifier on a shelf. It had a long neck and offered omnidirectional humidification, and it cast a shadow that looked like a lizard head.

It was still there, it wasn't moving, and the lizard didn't much care that someone in the room was getting a call.

The phone rang again. It was a cell phone chirp, the generic kind that people get when they first buy a phone, before they change it to a Smashing Pumpkins song or something.

He didn't know what to think about it ringing a second time. It was perhaps good news because that meant whoever owned the phone didn't turn it off or answer it, which could mean there was nobody with him at all: just an abandoned phone.

That's probably all it is, he thought. *Someone lost their phone in the store and now they're calling it to see where it ended up.*

He'd find it, answer it, he and the owner would have a nice

chat and he'd confess that the guy's phone scared the balls off of him, everyone would have a nice laugh about it, and he'd leave the phone with the morning folks and that would be that. It'd end up being one of those funny stories he told about his time as a night watchman. The Night the Roof Caved In and the Phone Rang.

Everybody laugh now.

There was a problem with this theory: Mad Maggie's Shop-O-Rama was probably the most infamous dead zone in town.

Everybody knew this about the place, to the extent that when families made plans to shop at Maggie's, they either stuck together or set up a meeting place, because they couldn't call one another in the store, and by this point everyone had evolved to where they had no way to cope with department store shopping without being tethered to one another electronically.

Orrin had heard lots of theories about it: the store was so massive they needed to put a phone relay *in* the store; the steel beams of the World War Two architecture interfered; the telecoms were punishing the store owners for some reason; there were aliens in the basement.

He didn't think any of the theories were true, although he had a fondness for the last one, mainly because there was no basement, so it was verifiably false. The way he thought of it, the town probably had a lot of dead zones, it was just that they weren't as notable because they happened in areas people drove through, or didn't spend any time in. It was not, probably, that big of a deal.

Except when a phone was ringing in a place where that was historically impossible.

It rang a third time.

"It's the storm," he decided.

Saying it aloud made it truer, for some reason. The sound of his own voice demystified the sales floor in general.

The satellite signal is getting redirected by the storm clouds, making it so a call can get through. That was what it was.

He could check it on his own phone, but since there was no cell reception and the screen on the smartphone did to his vision the same thing the flashlight did, only worse, he didn't have it. Still, that had to be it. And the lucky bastard who lost his phone in the store was going to be the beneficiary of this cosmically rare event.

Just as soon as Orrin found the phone.

He thought it was coming from the far corner. Sound carried really well at night, but the store didn't have much of an echo to it, so that was probably about right. If he was pinpointing it correctly, that meant the phone was ringing in the Electronics section, and *that* opened up a whole new set of possibilities.

Like, maybe a display was going haywire—again, because of the storm, perhaps—and one of the sample phones was going off on its own.

That was a pretty good explanation. Orrin liked it.

He reached the edge of the Electronics section in time for the seventh ring, which never came.

"Hello?" he called out. Either the owner of the phone would answer or maybe the phone would. Neither did.

He didn't go through electronics all that often, even though it was just about the least frightening section of the store: TV's that weren't on; phones under glass; video game consoles in lock and key underneath embedded display versions that could be played by passers-by, provided the display version wasn't broken that day; racks and racks of movies on DVD, just in case there were still people out there who had DVD players and didn't know how to stream films. None of what was there looked like a human, a lizard, or a hell-beast. No mannequins, and nothing but right angles. A Cubist nightmare, perhaps.

He stepped up to the phone counter. Mad Maggie's offered the latest versions of most phones and contracts with three different carriers, which was a level of ecumenism that nearly offset the fact that nobody could try out their new phone in the store.

There was a long counter of test phones. These were tethered to the surface with heavy steel cables. Buyers could pick them up and hold them to their ear, but that was about all. They also had a second wire leading to their charge outlet.

He picked one up and flipped it over to confirm what he already thought must be the case: the battery pack was missing. The phones powered up when the store's main power came on, and only then. It would have taken a miracle for one of these to ring.

"I mean, I guess I could be hearing things," he said, once again reassured by the sound of his own voice.

"Let's review our options: one of you powerless phones rang in the middle of a cell signal dead zone, someone left a phone somewhere else around here and *it* rang in the middle of a cell signal dead zone, or, I'm losing my mind. Thoughts?"

The committee of cell phones had no answer. Neither did the two-dimensional cutout of the pretty cell phone spokeswoman on the wall behind the counter. The mannequin in the Men's Formal section on the other side of the causeway also offered no opinion.

Except for the part where he was polling the thoughts of nonliving objects, Orrin took the lack of response to be a good sign. Then he wondered for a couple of minutes how he would know if he was starting to go crazy from being alone in this place all the time, and decided he probably wouldn't, until at least morning, and then decided not to let it bother him before then.

The tremendous crash on the other side of the room made him jump about five feet in the air. It also stopped his heart and turned him into a religious man, for a few seconds, until he real- ized what had happened: the ceiling in Young Misses just collapsed. The bucket he'd gone through all that trouble to fetch was still resting in the concourse at the edge of Sporting Goods, serving no particular purpose.

At least, he thought, *I'm not hearing a phone ring any more.*

~

"What a mess," Leopold said.

It was two hours after Orrin called the morning shift supervisor, using the "just for emergencies" number taped next to the landline in the office. As it was the first time Orrin had ever classified anything going on in Mad Maggie's as an emergency, the call got Leopold into work more or less as soon as he was awake enough to operate a car.

Considering Leo lived only three miles away, Orrin assumed the manager's preparations also involved a shower and a stiff cup of coffee, neither of which fully eliminated the alcohol smell.

"Yeah, I tried to get…" Orrin kicked the side of the janitor bucket, which was still useless, but it was being useless much closer to the broken ceiling now.

"Points for effort, hombre, but that would'a been a teacup under a waterfall, I mean looky that."

Leopold was a shortish guy who was maybe only a couple of years older than Orrin, but spoke as if he was a fifty year old trying to relate to high school kids in a 1980's movie, and he dressed as if he was hoping mustaches and bowler hats were going to be coming back in style soon. Orrin was a full foot taller, and rail-thin skinny. Bernie, the elderly register lady who was usually the second or third one in the door after Leo, called them Mutt and Jeff. Orrin didn't get the reference, but he thought Leo probably did.

They stood there and looked at the carnage for a few more seconds. Leopold was mindful of the hard-and-fast rule that sales floor lights do not come on more than an hour before open, and so he was using a flashlight to assess the damage, which just made it all look worse. Four tiles had come down, there was water and white foam tile debris all over the floor. The local prepubescent girls were going to have to go down the street to Belles & Bills if they wanted to pick up the latest in cheap chemises, for the immediate future.

The rain had subsided, though, so just about the only good thing that could be said about this situation was that there wasn't also a steady stream of water coming down to destroy more merchandise.

"You know what I am going to have to do?" Leo asked, not apparently expecting an answer from Orrin. "I am going to have to call corporate. I'm sure we have insurance for this sort of thing. Don't you think?"

"I'm sure."

Orrin wasn't sure, but this was a circumstance in which he wouldn't suffer any for being wrong.

"We'll have to get everyone in early to clean up, and cordon off the area, and… oh, and it's a safety hazard. Should we open? Should we even open the store? I don't know!"

"Call corporate."

"Yes, right, yes. We'll need signs. 'Beach Closed'. Hahaha. *Jaws* reference, right?"

"Right." Orrin didn't know that it was, but Leo always assumed he and Orrin understood each other in a way that they actually didn't. He sometimes wondered if Leo acted the same way with the other night watchmen, but decided he wasn't sufficiently invested in Leopold to find out.

In all fairness, interacting with humans wasn't something Orrin excelled at, whether they were decidedly odd ones or the ostensibly normal ones. This was presuming he himself could distinguish between the groups. Since he imagined he probably fit well in the *decidedly odd ones* category, he was not the ideal judge of who went where.

It was no coincidence, then, that he took a job requiring little interaction with people. Not that he didn't sometimes want to have someone to talk to, but the mannequins were okay in that regard, on most nights.

Leo concluded his flashlight review of the damaged region and headed down the concourse, and then to the back and the office. Orrin followed, because now that there was someone else in the room with him, it felt weird being left alone.

A half an hour later, Leo had a plan. It involved getting all on-staff janitor people in early, locating every "CAUTION: WET FLOOR" sign in the building (there were only two) and committing the sin of turning the lights on early. This was to get some photos of the damage, which would then be uploaded to corporate, which would forward it to insurance adjusters and approved repair contractors.

Having the lights up was, as always, surreal. Orrin and Leo walked around the store, looking for signs of other future cave-ins. Now that the roof above the ceiling had been proven suspect, every minor tile discoloration was a possible new disaster.

Orrin gave the Electronics section an especially close review, although he wasn't looking up. He considered asking if Leopold ever heard a phone ringing in the store, but decided it was a silly question to ask of someone who spent his days surrounded by people on the sales floor. Even if it was a dead zone, the ambient noise of human interaction would be more than enough to hide a ring tone.

"Hey," he said, deciding to ask a different question instead, "what was this place used for, before?"

"Ahh... statues or something."

"Yeah, before that."

"Guns."

"No, after that. Between."

"I dunno."

Leo paused to take a picture of a brown spot directly above the cardboard cutout of the cell phone spokeswoman. The spot was shaped like Wisconsin, and had probably been there forever.

"Why do you ask?" Leo asked. "You getting the jeebies?"

"The what?"

"You know. The willies. The spooks. Are you a couple of days from ending up huddled in the corner near the front, holding your breath until one of us opens the door? Are you heading for a Section 8?"

"No, of course not," Orrin said, while privately wondering if hearing a phone ring where there couldn't be one might actually be an indication that precisely this was happening. "I just wondered. I pick up a motor oil kind of smell sometimes."

"Huh." Leo shrugged. "Never heard that one. I do remember… maybe. Yeah, something about a fire."

"There was a fire here?"

"Or near here. It could be something I heard one time. Was it just motor oil, or burning motor oil?"

"Burning, I guess. I don't know if motor oil smells at all otherwise."

"A fire. Look it up, could be my imagination."

"Yeah. I'll do that."

~

*O*rrin didn't look it up. As always seemed to be the case, he forgot about it—and everything else he promised himself he'd do—as soon as he left Mad Maggie's.

He likened the threshold of the store to an airlock. Once he got on the other side of it he was too busy taking off his space suit and being checked for alien parasites and just generally rejoining the world to remember to look up local fires of the past fifty years. He was happy to be home, and to get some sleep.

Orrin got back to the store that night to find almost half of the Young Misses section was gone. The ceiling had been replaced by a green trash bag-quality layer of plastic, the floor was cordoned off with caution tape and orange cones, and the whole scene was surrounded by several space heaters and fans, which were not in use at the time of the store's closing, but reportedly had been going all day.

This added a bouquet of mildew to the ambiance of the store—undoubtedly discouraging a number of shoppers. The trash bag ceiling was worse. It billowed with the air currents Orrin was not aware existed. This made a crinkly sound—probably not audible when the store was open—which threatened to drive him insane. Or, more insane, he supposed.

Over the course of the evening, he gained a profound appreciation of the sinister quality of the sound of plastic sheeting in the wind. Since it relied on the vagaries of a chaotic force, there was no way to predict when the plastic would go from silent to so loud he was nearly convinced something was trying to escape from the other side of it.

This made him unaccountably edgy, and that wasn't a good headspace to be in when alone in the store. He was reminded of the first month he worked, when every stray sound was *de facto* proof of an armed incursion.

Sometime on the other side of Midnight, he finally began to calm down and stop *hearing* the noise the plastic was making. He could still hear it, but he was able to shove it in a corner, where all the other random sounds the store made also lived. Like the creaking that came from the front doors on certain nights, when the air in the antechamber cooled and the metal contracted. Or the periodic squeak from a plastic wheel here and there, as merchandise racks gradually succumbed to gravitational pull in slightly uneven sections of the floor. Here and there, an improperly stacked product might resettle, and this might cause a loud noise, but Orrin was used to that as well.

The smell of mildew bothered him for a while, too, but by his two A.M. rounds, he'd largely become immune to that, which was how he still managed to notice the motor oil smell had returned.

It was impossible to miss. In the past, it was nothing more than a faint odor that went away quickly. This time, it was profound, if that was a word that could be used to describe a smell. It came on so strong, Orrin nearly gagged at first. Then he held his arm up to his nose and looked around for a source.

He was standing in the Kitchen area. The smell was strongest near the frying pans, but didn't emanate from any one thing. It was concentrated there, but in a five-foot space in the middle of the aisle.

Nothing was coming in from the ceiling, and there was no discoloration on the floor. The merchandise was unsullied and uninteresting and not covered in burning oil. It was a ghost smell.

If it was closer to the wrecked floor, he might have been able to entertain the idea that the moisture kicked up an older smell underneath, but Kitchen and Young Misses weren't proximate.

It was, he decided, something he would just have to add to the quirks of the place. At least now he had an idea of a source location. He surrendered to the conclusion that he would not be solving this that evening, and finished the circuit of the store.

A half an hour later, the cell phone rang again.

Orrin was at the desk at the front, his default state when not walking around. He spent most of his desk time playing solitaire under the gentle illumination of the overhead emergency light. The sound was a shock, almost literally: his heart acted like he'd touched a live wire, as all the sublimated fear and dread from the prior evening came back aggressively.

"HELLO?" he shouted.

There were no clouds out. No storm to confuse the sky and bounce a cell phone signal around, so that explanation was plainly wrong.

The phone rang again.

Orrin jumped from behind the desk and started running toward Electronics, which was at the polar opposite end of the store. Between the heavy boots and loose belt holding a large collection of keys on chains and loops, and the fact that he was not terribly athletic by nature, Orrin no doubt looked like a jangly, uncoordinated mess on the verge of doing himself harm, but he wanted to get there fast because someone in this place was screwing with him.

That had to be it. An electronic device of some kind, a tape recorder of a cell phone set to go off at a certain time of night, just to mess with him. Maybe one of the other guards was playing a joke on him. Or Leo. Or some other random daytime person.

"WHO'S HERE?" he shouted after the third ring. His sprint was along the back concourse, which took him by Young Misses and the jogging mannequins, rather than past Kitchen goods and the oil smell. It was probably so he could see straight ahead into the Electronics all the way down the corridor, rather than turn and face it at the last second (as the other path would have him do) but he also didn't want to smell the oil again, because it bugged him.

He got to the edge of the section before the fourth ring, and stopped. He could hear his breathing—he was panting—and the blood pumping through his heart, and the flapping of the plastic sheeting. Nothing else.

RING.

He jumped backwards, then calmed down enough to zero in on the source a little better, but only a little. It was from the left, where the life-sized cardboard display of the cell phone sales lady stood. He took a few steps in that direction.

"Whoever this is, you're in a lot of trouble," he said, raised voice but not shouting.

Whoever it was didn't answer.

"Not kidding. It would be better if you came out." When this didn't do anything, he added, "I have a gun."

He *did* have a gun, but not on him. It was sitting in its holster on the desk at the front of the store, because it rested awkwardly when he sat down so he always took it off until his rounds. Even if he did have it on, he barely knew how to use it.

The fifth ring came, and it sounded like it was right behind him, and that was terrifying. He spun around, brandishing nothing because his hands were empty, ready to punch someone or defend himself or just die from some ninja attack. And there was nobody there.

"C'mon," he said, to himself this time. "What is it, in the ceiling?"

He did a circuit around the area, but there was no cell phone. Yes, there was a display of phones under glass, but they had no power—as he'd previously verified—and aside from the two-dimensional one the cardboard woman was holding up, that was all.

No, not all, he thought.

He was being an idiot. He'd walked past the thing a dozen times and didn't even fully recognize what he was walking past, but there was a box at the end of the counter, on the floor. It was about three feet tall, had a lid with a lock, and a rectangular slot. The sign above the box read, *RECYCLE OLD CELL PHONES HERE*.

He stood in front of the box, and waited. It didn't ring again.

Orrin was relieved by this, although he felt like he probably shouldn't have been. Someone dropped a phone in there and the phone was still active for some reason, and now a call was coming in on the phone. Sure, the battery should have died by this time, and Mad Maggie's was no less a dead zone now than it was the night before, but this was an answer anyway, and it was a pretty good one.

It also had a tendency to stop ringing whenever he got too close, and that was the part he thought he should perhaps be wondering about. Although it had only happened twice.

Coincidence, he decided.

That was probably it.

That wasn't it.

Over the course of the next two weeks, at some time after midnight—always—the phone would ring. It was never at exactly the same time, and never for exactly the same number of rings. If he went near the box, the ringing stopped. Otherwise, it kept going, for sometimes up to an hour.

Orrin really didn't know what to do. At first he tried asking day shift employees leading questions about the phones in the box, but this didn't help. The questions included: how often is the box emptied; did any of the phones ever happen to, oh, goodness, let's say *ring*; have other night guards commented on… odd noises…? The answers he got were that nobody knew when the box got emptied, of course the phones don't ring, and no, why do you ask?

Further investigation—done when he should be sleeping, not wandering around the store—led to the discovery that the box had been sitting in electronics for longer than any of the current employees of Mad Maggie's had been employed there, because none of them knew how to recycle the disposed-of phones, nor had they ever seen it done. They were also pretty sure nobody had a key for it, but it seemed more likely the key existed and whoever had it didn't know they had it. All Orrin was sure of was that *he* didn't have it, but he did have a dozen keys that had no apparent use on the key ring he was handed when he started working there.

At least once a night he tried convincing himself it was all in his head. That he found incipient psychosis preferable to a malfunctioning cell phone was sort of interesting, but that's all it was. It didn't make the ringing stop, whether it was real or not.

What he really wanted was to convince someone else to stay in the store with him during his shift, so they could hear it too. But to do that he would have to explain why, and he had a feeling as soon as he explained it he'd be looking for another job. If that person were another employee, management would find out their longest-tenured night watchman had finally made it round that final bend and needed to be rotated out. If they were not an employee—he didn't know anyone who would do this for him, so this was a pure hypothetical—Orrin would end up fired for allowing a civilian into the store after hours.

This wasn't the only thing making his job much more difficult of late, just the worst. Whoever was hired to fix the ceiling above Young Misses was apparently deeply inefficient, because the plastic tarp was still there. One night he decided it sounded like someone trying to breathe with a trash bag over his head, and as soon as he made that comparison that was all it ever sounded like.

After a week of repetitive cell phone abuse, he finally decided to get on a computer and research the warehouse more thoroughly. He was hoping for a felicitous discovery that would explain the impossible ringing, whatever that might be. (Aliens, maybe, buried under the cement floor. Not in the nonexistent basement; entombed in the foundation.) He didn't find it, but he did find out that the building did indeed store vehicles for a time —emergency vehicles, actually, including fire trucks. This was over twenty-five years ago, and it was only for nine months, while the station down the road was torn down and rebuilt due to something unspecified by the historical record. Apparently the firemen even bunked in the building.

That was all he had, though. He figured the motor oil smell he kept picking up was some sort of combination of dry rot in the floor coupled with an old spill from one of the engines that used to be stored there, and the 'burning' part he just tacked on himself. This would be slightly easier to believe if he knew what motor oil smelled like when it was burning. He didn't, and so he had no reason to think that was the exact nature of the odor, yet he remained convinced this was right.

By the eleventh night, he'd had all he could take. He was, as always, at the front of the store, listening to the staccato breathing of the suffocating giant in the middle of the store and sniffing a cinnamon stick he'd started carrying around in his breast pocket to try and scrub the stench of the oil from his nostrils—it wasn't working—when the phone rang again.

"ENOUGH!" he shouted, jumping to his feet. "WHAT DO YOU WANT, DAMN YOU?"

In something like a real sprint he tore down the main concourse, his nightstick in his hand, not really thinking about anything but making the goddamn phone stop goddamn ringing, goddammit.

"AAAAHHHH!" he shouted, through the worst of the oil smell and around the corner, and of course... of course... the phone stopped just as soon as he got near enough.

"CALL BACK!" he screamed.

He knew there were security cameras in several key locations in the store, and he knew those cameras still recorded activity at night, because the little red lights stayed on. He also knew where the recordings were stored, although he didn't have direct access to them. This meant his little trip down crazy lane was going to be captured, and someone was going to see it, and he 100% did not care any more.

"I'M RIGHT HERE! COME ON, WHAT DO YOU HAVE TO SAY?"

Motionless, holding his stick, hearing nothing but the rasp of the plastic tarp and his own breathing, he was undeniably completely alone. He was shouting at nothing and nobody.

Then the phone started ringing again.

He lunged forward awkwardly, a disturbed marionette, nearly taking out a display rack of outdated nineties films on his way to the phone counter.

Destroying something in the store was absolutely grounds for immediate termination, so his lack of hesitation in striking the lock on the phone box with his nightstick should have warranted, at minimum, a moment of contemplation, and it did not.

It was a good quality nightstick, made of some sort of carbon alloy, and while the lock was pretty decent too, the hinge holding the loop through which the padlock was threaded was more or less decorative, because it took only three blows to pop it.

Orrin lifted the lid and peered inside.

The ringing hadn't stopped, but there were a hundred phones to choose from. He grabbed one, flipped it open, verified that it was not the right one, and tossed it on the floor and tried again.

It rang again, and it sounded like maybe it was at the very bottom of the box.

"I'm coming!" he said, trying phones two at a time now, still not getting the right one.

The decision to tip the box onto the floor wasn't really a conscious one; it was just the next logical step, and then he was ankle deep in discarded electronics, spread out as far as Men's Fashion, and only then did he find the right phone.

It was an ancient thing, by current standards. It felt like a walkie-talkie. He thought maybe he saw someone using a phone like this in of one of the nineties movies on the rack he nearly toppled.

He held it up and looked for a button to open the line, reminding himself at the same time that this was impossible, this phone was older than half of the employees at Mad Maggie's, it couldn't have a charge, or a phone plan. It couldn't be ringing.

He found the button.

"Hello?"

There was static on the other end.

"Hello?" he repeated. "Who is this?"

"O..." someone said. A woman's voice. "Orrin."

"Who is this?" he asked. His mouth was bone dry and his heart rate was trying for a record.

"Orrin," she repeated.

"WHO IS THIS? HOW DO YOU KNOW MY NAME?"

"You have to help us."

He screamed, and threw the phone as far as he could. It impacted with the wall above a luggage display, something he didn't see but heard well enough.

Then it was quiet again.

Finally.

Until another phone started ringing.

It was a different ring, certainly. Another phone, one he'd never heard ring before. He fell to his knees and started checking phones, but he wasn't going nearly fast enough because then a second phone was going, and a third. And then all of them, all at once, a horrible cacophony of noise. He grabbed one and activated the line.

"WHAT DO YOU WANT?"

"You have to help us," the woman said.

∼

∼

"*H*ow does it end?"

The early afternoon flow of traffic through the boutique coffee shop was gentle but constant. It was warm outside, which got a lot of people moving along Market Street, and a decent number of those people wanted to celebrate the nice day with hot coffee in a portable cardboard cup. True, a number of them wanted iced coffee, but this was a statistically irrelevant percentage.

Oliver was just busy enough to interact briefly with new people when they appeared before him, and too busy to fully acknowledge their existences as individual beings with their own independent realities. They were known only by the names scribbled in marker on their cardboard cups, or if no name was required—if they didn't require the services of a barista—then by their choice of bean.

He was really confused, then, when Ms. Medium French Roast took the cup he was handing over to her and then asked how *it* ended.

"What?" he asked, as his mind tried to catch up to the new reality, which was that Minerva was standing in front of him.

"*Mad Maggie's Midnight Madness*. How does it end? Great title, by the way. Ivor will love it."

"Ah, oh. Thanks. I didn't…" *I didn't think you knew I worked here,* Oliver was going to say, but then he would be admitting he did work there. Somehow it felt like if he said that, she would suddenly realize it. Like before that moment she might have thought he was a customer who'd jumped over the counter to assist in the pouring and distributing of caffeinated beverages. And that—again, as a customer—it just so happened he was wearing the same color Polo shirt as everyone else behind the counter.

"I didn't write the ending yet," he said.

"I know," she said, flashing smile #12, which was the one where only one side of her mouth curled, in time with her eyes, which rolled upward, a display of exasperation that was only taken in jest, thanks to that smile. "I mean, how is it going to end?"

He was a little confused by the question.

"I don't know," he said. "I won't know until I write it."

She laughed.

"That's wild, Ollie. Well finish it, I wanna know."

Adding to his confusion was that it didn't really even occur to him that she would have read the story already, or necessarily at all. After the last meeting, Wilson sent an email blast to the *woo* mailing list suggesting a process change: pieces to be discussed would have to be submitted in advance of the meeting so everyone could read it ahead of time. It was pretty obvious that this imperative sprang from the fact that the prior week, Oliver brought in an overlong epic fantasy. Minerva wasn't a member of TAWU, though, so he had no reason to think she would have read a copy. Maybe she was more intrinsic to Wilson's process than he let on.

A significant logjam had developed behind her in line, due to this incredibly brief, non-business-related exchange. It seemed as if nobody was all that put off by the extra delay. Possibly, if one is willing to wait five to ten minutes for four ounces of espresso, one is already temperamentally prepared for an *ex tempore* exchange of this magnitude. Oliver still felt the pressure to keep things moving, even if it was internally applied.

"Listen, I have to—"

"Oh, yeah, thanks for the coffee." She raised the cup as a salute, and turned to walk off. He forced himself to turn away and address the next customer's needs, when she returned.

"Almost forgot!" Minerva said. "Pallas, tomorrow night, are you in?"

"The... what?"

"Pallas! Have you been?"

His brain couldn't make sense of the words.

"I don't know what that is."

"The club, the club I was telling you about. Tomorrow night?"

"Um... sure, I think. Maybe."

"Catch me later, we'll work it out."

"Later."

"At the meeting, man. See you then?"

"Yeah, yeah. Yeah."

"Cool. Oh, and the story is *great*. Wilson thinks so too."

He took the next customer's order, and card, feeling numb and distracted, and unable to keep himself from watching Minnie leave the shop. The place—it was called the Jittery Canary, and featured a drawing of an over-caffeinated bird on all the signage— was below street level, with a patio space that was open on good days. When she left, Oliver could watch her heading past the tables and up the brick staircase to the street.

Before she did so, she stopped to have a conversation with an extremely large man, which was a little interesting only because Ollie couldn't imagine anything she and this big hairy guy could have in common that would warrant a verbal exchange.

But, whatever. He ran the card in his hand to charge Mr. Italian Roast for his drink, checked the clock, and thought about how he was going to tell Minnie he couldn't go to this *palace* place.

~

*I*f Wilson liked the new story, he certainly took the long way around in saying so.

"Horror, Oliver? Honestly." This was his first note.

"I'm not really sure what to do with that," Ollie admitted.

Sometime between the prior week and this one, he'd arrived at the conclusion that he should be challenging his mentor's criticisms at least a little bit. He told himself it was because Wilson was allowed to be wrong about these things—that not everything he had to say came from on high.

"Well, I don't know. It's so… base. Crude. Cheap."

"Cheap?"

"Easy."

"It wasn't easy," Oliver said.

"No, that isn't what I mean. Writing is hard, we all understand that. You sat down and put together a bunch of words that when strung together made meaningful sentences that stacked up into paragraphs, and that's great. You can hand those paragraphs over to anybody and say, *here, read this,* and assuming they can read, they'll receive the information behind all those words you've assembled in more or less the way you wanted them to. What *I'm* saying is that the information you've chosen to convey with this gift is something other than an exploration into the human soul. You decided to communicate with their animal brain instead. You decided to try and scare them, with—I think—a ghost story. Is it a ghost story? We never get to find out."

"It isn't finished yet."

"Yes, but do you imagine a ghost will eventually turn up, should you choose to finish this?"

"Yeah, I guess. I figured I'd work it out as I wrote." Ollie had an idea of the ending, certainly, and it was unquestionably a ghost story, but it felt wrong to talk about that before it was done. "So are you saying being frightened isn't a part of the human condition?"

"No, no, I'm saying fear is a crude component. I'm saying writing has the power to enlighten and illuminate and address, and I want you to think about aspiring for that."

"What if I just aspire to scare the crap out of someone?"

This elicited a gentle laugh from the otherwise dead-silent members of TAWU, which also evidently woke them from their slumber.

"I have to tell you," Jennifer said, "It… wasn't *all* that scary."

"There was dread," Ivor said. "And it has a great title."

Minerva, from the edge of the kitchen, covered up a laugh.

"Dread's not bad," Tandy said. "I mean, it's *good* stuff, Ollie."

"Just not scary," Oliver said.

"Not… really."

"I haven't finished it yet. I was going to build up to a big scare."

"Well, I thought it was scary enough," Bibi said. "My phone rang while I was reading it, Ollie, and I jumped three feet."

"That's a good question, though," Wilson said. "Is *scary* something universal? That's a real challenge, right? The old gothic horror stories that used to frighten us seem pretty tame now. Weeping statues, and creaking walls in old castles just don't do anything for us now, but maybe a moving mannequin and a haunted department store is what's replaced all that. But you're never going to write something that is going to scare both Bibi and Jennifer."

"I think it's *possible*," Oliver said.

"I'm not saying what is or isn't possible, I'm addressing the challenges of the genre."

"But you could say that about anything," Tandy said. "It could be a romance someone doesn't find romantic, or a thriller people don't think are thrilling. The best you can expect is to get the right reaction from *most* readers."

"I think just about everyone can agree that Shakespeare is exactly as brilliant as we all say he is," Wilson said.

"Shakespeare," Ollie repeated.

"Or, Poe. Poe is as effective now as he was a hundred years ago. We might not find his stories as disturbing as we used to, but the impact is there."

"So you're saying, you expect me to be as good as Shakespeare and Poe?"

"No, Oliver, I expect you to expect that from yourself. And I don't think you're doing that. Do you mean to finish this story?"

"I haven't decided yet."

"Give it a try. I think it would be good for you to have something finished. I'm also curious to see if you can follow through on the ending."

"How do you mean?"

"Make it scary, Oliver. Something that gives Jennifer nightmares."

~

*O*liver didn't stick around. Wilson had no other notes to give, and unlike just about every other time he'd attended, TAWU had nothing else to give him, collectively. He imagined if Wilson had opened up the floor there would be more feedback to be heard, but once the group decided any formal evaluation had to wait until there was an ending, whatever else there was to be said was put aside.

It wasn't until he'd already left the apartment and reached the street that he remembered he was supposed to be telling Minerva about his unavailability regarding any plans to go someplace. This was perhaps just as well. If she knew where he worked she had to know he wasn't making a lot of money—unless she assumed he owned the shop or something—and therefore likely knew he couldn't go someplace fancy on his own dime.

Or not. Oliver had known a few wealthy people in his life, and they generally showed a lack of comprehension regarding what *poor* really meant. She could be one of those. She could also see him as a charity case or something. He was pretty sure that would be worse than being confused with someone who could afford to go clubbing.

Either way, he wasn't going, and he hoped she would stop asking him.

~

*T*here were certain parts of the city where the rent per month and the available square footage intersected at a point allowable for someone of limited means. Oliver lived in such a space, on the sixth floor of an apartment complex, alone. It met all of his needs, which was to say that he wanted to be alone most of the time and he wanted to live in the city all of the time, and so he surrendered certain basic comforts such as an actual kitchen.

It was precisely enough space for a single bed, a hot plate, a tiny refrigerator, a shower, and a toilet. The bathroom had a door for privacy, but he found that if he wanted the door to open and close he didn't have enough room for the refrigerator, so he took the door off the hinges and stored it in the basement. (Ironically, the basement storage for the unit was larger, per square foot, than the apartment itself.) In the unlikely event he ever brought a girl over, and that girl elected to spend the night, he would have to make some hard choices about that bathroom just because, generally speaking, *I can watch you pee from the bed* is not the sort of thing most women would find enticing. Probably.

It took about forty-five minutes to get home by subway from Wilson's: one train line into the center of town, and a second one out of that center and in a slightly different direction. Oliver was nearly convinced the two locations were, geographically, a lot closer than the subway made them feel, but had yet to examine a map of the city to determine how close, and whether walking was a better idea.

On the way, he saw a couple of posters he'd never noticed before, for a place he never heard of.

M PALLAS, they read. The vertical portion of the letters doubled as ionic columns holding up a roof, underneath which, men and women in bright colors were dancing. A disco ball dangled above them.

There was fine print, no doubt featuring locational details and what-not, but while this sort of place likely appealed to a certain sub-group of people, Oliver was definitively not a member of that sub-group. He also didn't require any directions, even if he was going, because it was an odd but well-known detail of the city that all the big nightclubs in town were located on the same strip of road. If M Pallas was as big a deal as it was being made out to be in the subway poster, it was surely located on that strip.

It was a while before he realized this was probably the place Minerva had been talking about.

The apartment building had an elevator everyone was afraid to use. It creaked and bucked like it was riding the back of something old and powerful that didn't want it on its back. It had a habit of stopping just below where it was supposed to, such that riders had to step up to get off. At least half of the building's inhabitants also appeared to think the elevator was haunted, although the entire building—which was well over a hundred years old already, and which could be felt to move in heavy winds—lent itself to the sense that it was inhabited by spirits.

Oliver took the stairs, which was an adventure all its own. The handrail on the third floor landing was almost completely detached, every eighth or ninth step sagged to an alarming extent, and the hallway lighting was only hypothetical in several places. But he hardly even noticed these things any more.

The light on the sixth floor had a habit of flickering. He mostly ignored this too, but it was a little harder to sometimes, because the light bled into his apartment from under the door. When he turned out all the other lights, sometimes the periodic blinking created a kind of strobe effect that was hard to sleep through.

The flickering was particularly bad on this occasion, doubly annoying because it was taking him forever to select the right key to get into his own door. It didn't help that he had a keyring that included all of the ways to lock and unlock things in the Jittery Canary.

As he stood there, fumbling with keys, he thought he saw someone at the far end of the hallway. It was a peripheral vision sort of thing, and it was probably just a shadow, but for a half-second he thought it was a young girl, just standing there, staring at him. With that thought came the kind of fear that manifested as acid reflux and some kind of vertiginous panic, until he looked at the space and found it empty. No little girl ghost here, just his imagination messing with him.

That's the feeling, he thought. *That's what Wilson wants me to create.*

The question was, how?

He got the key right, and let himself in, and ten minutes later he'd settled down on the bed with his laptop in hand with the last words of *Mad Maggie's Midnight Madness* staring at him.

He held his fingers over the keys, and waited for the words to come. They did, but they didn't belong to this story. They went elsewhere, for another letter and the newest assignment.

Wilson's latest letter prompt was A, and Oliver had been trying to suppress where his mind went with that, but he just couldn't do it.

A is for alien.

Chapter Three

ALIEN

Nobody knew about the aliens until the attack, and by then it was much too late. But that was the nature of surprise attacks: the very best ones tended to be surprising.

The colony was the seventh one established in the Theta Quadrant Time Well. It was the most remote of the colonies, eighteen standard years from the hub. This likely made it the last, both for the lack of other potentially habitable planets in the quadrant, and for the distance. As a rule—and it was an actual rule, if one interpreted Starseed Bible as a book of rules, which most people did—local spacetime travel shouldn't exceed a radial distance of more than twenty standards. This was because for as long as the human race had been seeding the universe, nobody had been able to figure out how to extend the average human life-span much more than a hundred standards.

That rule was more for the sake of the families of travelers than for travelers. A colonist leaving the hub for Hockspit—the unfortunate name of the seventh planet in the Theta Quadrant Time Well—would be devoting only eight standard years of their life to the trip. But it would be eighteen years for any of their friends or family on either side of the journey. And if it was a round-trip, forget it.

This was why most freight was moved between planets around the hub, when possible, and by drone if it had to come from the hub. It was also why, in the unlikely event something that had never happened before happened—such as aliens showing up and attacking for some reason—individual planetary colonies tended to be on their own. It wasn't that nobody cared to help, it was that nobody could get there in time to effect meaningful change on the proceedings.

For the same reason, the colonies were typically well-defended, sometimes comically so. About half of the planet's workers were paid by the Intergalactic Matrix, and while a significant portion of those workers performed some bureaucratic role, all were trained and equipped to perform as members of a standing army, should the need arise.

The need had never arisen before, so far as anyone on Hockspit knew. Then, on an otherwise decent afternoon, the suborbital perimeter disappeared.

~

"All right, men, lock and load!"

Sergeant Jusp loved telling his men—a group of humans consisting of both genders, but never mind that—to 'lock and load'. It meant, *get your pulse cannons ready*, and was essentially meaningless, an antiquated bit of parlance that made sense back when soldiers fired bullets instead of bursts of concentrated energy from neutron blasters.

Corporal Opie Telluride nonetheless took his weapon off his back and performed a quick visual check to ensure that if he pulled the trigger, the most likely thing to happen next would be that it would fire. Short of firing it into the air, all he could do was check the energy readings and make sure he knew how to click the safety off and on. He did this, and then he put it back over his shoulder. He accompanied this with an eye-roll that did not escape the notice of Corporal Epic Wyn.

"Careful," she said under her breath. "Too much character will get you kicked out of this man's army."

Opie smiled back, and then they resumed positions, eyes-forward at attention. In a smaller group, this exchange could have gotten them into some trouble, but they were in the middle of the largest collection of citizens any of them had ever been a part of; Jusp couldn't even see them from the stage.

Commanding the soldiers to check their weapons was the end of the speech anyway. Next came the literal marching orders, as each unit was given an assignment. Assignments were greeted with whoops and hollers from the various units, a time-honored assertion of collective bravado to offset the fact that Sergeant Jusp's briefing was basically the most terrifying thing any of them had ever heard.

Opie knew a lot of the info already, although this was the first time he'd heard it all at once, and the first time he was forced to think of it from a tactical perspective. It was also probably the first time he thought of himself as one of the people who would have to do something about all of it.

The sub-orbital perimeter went down five days earlier. Opie was one of seven in his family who did full-time soldiering, and included in that seven was a cousin named Dino who worked communications. Dino told him about it that night, two days before the news was made public.

The colony had three perimeters. The first was a series of satellites in low stationary orbit. They were only there to detect any inbound traffic to the planet—be they ships or meteors or whatever—and had no built-in defenses. The satellites were also useful for communication, but less so on Hockspit than on a lot of the other colonized planets, because for the most part, this colony could communicate based on line-of-sight.

The second perimeter was airborne: military whirlybirds and stream riders, mostly. These were armed, and they did regular overpass sorties from one end of the habitable zone to the other so regularly, hardly anyone really noticed them anymore, up until they stopped happening.

Opie and Epic, and everyone else in the room constituted the third perimeter… or they would, once they reached the front line.

The speed with which this all happened took everyone by surprise. According to Dino, the sub-orbital satellites went down all at once, which was basically impossible for a network that stretched completely around the planet. They assumed for the first few hours that it was a natural cosmic event—a solar flare or a particularly impressive gravity wave or a dark energy pulse, maybe; the possibilities were pretty far-reaching. But all of those things would have had a directionality to them, affecting satellites on one side of the planet first, and also likely impacting surface-level equipment.

After a little more work and a lot more math, someone in the tower figured out that Hockspit had been attacked. Something—at least two somethings but probably more—hit the network with a disruption blast from multiple angles at once. This strongly implied an intelligence.

"Derby province," Epic said.

"What?" Opie asked. He hadn't been paying attention.

"It's where we're going, granite-head. Too early for a nap."

They started moving as a unit, toward the landing bay to the carrier that would transport them to—apparently—Derby province.

"Not that bad," he said.

She clapped him on the shoulder, which was painful but also a show of affection in Epic's world. Opie was tall and gangly, while Epic was smaller and generally more compact, but she packed a lot of muscle in that small frame.

"I swear, Telluride. You're on the smallest chunk of land in the quadrant and you're still flunking geography. Derby's at the edge of the hab zone."

"South?"

"Western limit."

"Cold, then, not hot."

"Temperate. And sure, I guess there are worse places we could be."

Hockspit was only barely habitable. There was a landmass on the planet that was essentially an enormous steppe, and that was where everyone lived. The weather went from extreme hot to extreme cold and the storm systems were incredibly violent, but on average it was livable for humans. That was the only part of the planet where this was true. There was an ocean that was highly acidic on the west and the east, the south—the equatorial region of the planet—was mostly a lot of lava, and the north was mostly one big chunk of ice.

So there were indeed worse places to be.

They marched double-time until reaching the carrier, up the ramp and into the wide-mouth bay door. All around them, people were talking about what was ahead with a combination of bragging to cover up fear, and out-and-out fear. Because none of them knew what they were in for.

~

*A*t the surface, the planet's atmosphere was a little thicker than standard. This meant defining the 'surface' as the ground of the plateau on which they all lived, and that was about a mile up from the sea level. It got a lot thinner higher up. The most efficient vertical travel was a whirlybird, until the air got thinner and then a more plane-like design tended to work better. Consequently, the grunts on the carrier were treated to a strangely unpleasant experience.

First, they rose slowly for about forty minutes. Then, quite suddenly and very audibly, the rotors stopped and retracted and the wings deployed. While this was happening nothing was keeping the craft aloft, so they were in free fall. Then, the jets at the rear of the carrier engaged and everyone went from zero gravity to two standards, sideways, in half a second. This was the transition that broke arms and legs and the occasional neck, and invariably made at least a couple of people vomit.

The good news was that it was a smooth flight the rest of the way, as the carrier skipped across the heavier atmosphere beneath it like a round stone on a pond of non-acidic water.

"Well that sucked," Opie said.

"Always does, soldier," the guy next to him said.

He turned for a look at the man. He was a lot older than just about everyone else aboard, which made him more interesting than everyone else aboard except maybe for Epic, although Opie was probably biased in that regard.

"You a first gen?" Opie asked.

"Yessir. I'm guessing you're a third."

"Second, but I was born on the ride over."

"A Zee Gee baby full-time soldiering? We really are in trouble."

He said it lightly, with a smile, but it was the same sort of thing Opie had been hearing in one form or another his whole life. Epic got the same grief for the same reason, and she liked it even less.

There was a myth that children born in zero gravity were too soft and weak for heavy labor. It had to do with the idea that bones only developed properly in an environment with something close to standard gravity. This was sort of true, except colony locals had gravity simulation areas. He learned to walk in one of those spaces. Granted, he didn't get to experience the gravity of a planet until he was two, but the natural pull on Hockspit was slightly less than one standard. It just didn't feel that way because the atmosphere was a good deal thicker. He remembered finding the air hard to adjust to, but that was all. He also remembered seeing the sky for the first time, and that was a much nicer memory.

"I'll make sure I stick by you if something heavy needs lifting," Opie said.

The man laughed.

"Sure, sure."

He extended his hand and introduced himself as Koestler.

"Born here, I take it?" Opie asked.

"Builder stock, yes sir."

Colonies were started by cleaners and builders. Cleaners came first, and mostly worked from ships in low orbit, and just above the surface. Most thankless job in the quadrants, from what Opie had been told. Cleaners spend their lives in space, either above planets that weren't ready for people yet, or traveling to those planets. They scrubbed atmospheres, cleared land masses and tested for native life.

Builders arrived later, to stand on the planet's crust and build things. Typically, the biggest buildings and largest land claims would go first to the descendants of the cleaners, which was only fair. Every now and then a builder would be a second gen cleaner, but that was pretty rare.

"Ever heard of something like this?"

Koestler looked him in the eyes. "No. Nobody has, far as I know."

He was referring less to what happened to the sub-orbital network than to what happened after that, which was how the rest of the colony was really introduced to the problem now facing them.

A day after the satellites were deactivated by an apparent deliberate attack, the armed sorties that constituted the second perimeter were shot down.

This was especially terrifying for someone sitting in a troop transport flying the same basic pattern as many of those downed airships. They'd all been told that analysis led to the conclusion that the assault on the second line worked because the flights were running on a predictable schedule. This seemed fair provided the weapons that took out the flights were fired from space, because that required predictive targeting, and that only worked if the target followed a consistent pattern. Opie happened to know that was an assumption not fully supported by facts: they hadn't figured out yet how the second perimeter was actually taken out.

The troop transport was making this jump at a new time, along a path the regular ships never took. Everyone involved still saw this as a huge risk, but it was at least a calculated one.

"Well, this is what we trained for," Opie said, repeating an oft-stated truism that never sounded all that true.

"True. Makes you wonder though," the older man said.

"How do you mean?"

"Nobody ever questions training up an army to guard a frontier settlement. That's just good common sense. But how many generations of us did that without ever facing an enemy? Other than a rogue faction of humanity from time to time? Point is, looks like we got ourselves some aliens, and that's a first. Sure, we've come across xenospecies here and there, but nothing current, right?"

"Current?"

"At the same scale as us. Mostly, it's bacteria, and maybe some more advanced life forms, with hair and all that. And we've found ruins, alien societies who died off before we got there. But you think about it, the universe is big and it's been around much longer than we have, and it'll be here long after we're gone. The odds of us bumping up against aliens who can shoot us out of the sky with weapons that match our technological level, well that's a pretty small number."

He leaned in closer, pressed up against the safety belt that was holding him in place.

"At the same time… somebody in the government knew. You don't build a society on the backs of conscripted military for kicks. You do it because you know someone's out there."

～

They didn't land in Derby province, because they needed a runway to land and Derby province didn't have one. There was a maneuver the carrier could have performed, but converting from stream rider back into whirlybird was considerably more challenging than the reverse, because the speed had to be bled off first. It could be done—the craft would essentially commit to a downward spiral in the heavier lower atmosphere, with the wing flaps up to create drag, until it was slow enough to convert to the rotors. The challenge was that it had to be done with precise timing, because if the ship began to fall too fast, the rotors would snap off before engaging. It was scary, anyway, so Opie was glad they weren't doing that.

What they were doing instead was chute diving from the carrier's belly. If it meant something that he preferred free falling to the ground over landing on a helipad, he didn't stop to consider what that something was.

Also, he liked chute drops. In drills, it was the thing he enjoyed the most. If you're going to live on a planet with a thicker-than-standard atmosphere, parachuting is definitely a pleasant recreational diversion.

It was the middle of the day, which would have been a bad time to drop into a war zone. However, they had significant cloud cover—this part of Hockspit got lots of storms thanks to the natural high/low pressure of the cliff side—and it was only a war zone in a philosophical sense. Nobody was shooting anybody over here, either out of the air or otherwise.

More precisely, nobody was shooting anybody anywhere. After the second round of attacks took out the airborne defense network, there had been no further escalation. That the military higher-ups had elected to deploy troops to certain specific territories suggested they knew something they weren't sharing, but so far as Opie knew, that something didn't involve direct engagement with the aliens.

He took in the terrain on the way down. There weren't a lot of colonists this close to the edge of the habitable zone, so what he saw was mostly hillsides, grasslands, and a few buildings here and there. The military had a weapons cache and general supply fortress buried in one of the hills, but that wasn't visible from the air. He had the coordinates for it, though; it was the recon point.

He landed on the edge of a livestock paddock. The best farmland in Hockspit was north of this spot, in soil enriched by a pre-colonization volcanic eruption and fed by runoff siphoned from the melting icecaps of the northern pole. The soil was poisoned by the acid Western Ocean, and only certain plants grew naturally. They raised animals here; ones that could survive on an acidic scrub grass diet.

They called these animals cows. Hockspit's cows were genetically modified specifically for this planet to the degree that one couldn't breed this animal with a cow from another quadrant's bovine, and it was highly likely the taste of the animal's meat varied widely from colony to colony as well. Still, the gene stock was cow, so they were cows.

Opie took to the task of collecting his chute, as he watched Epic float gently to the ground in the field next to his. A couple of the cows on the other side of the fence took a minute to look up from their lunch and moo some additional commentary.

"Storm coming," she said, as he joined up with her. "Can you smell it?"

"Yeah." There was ozone in the air, and the clouds were wet.

"Hope everyone gets down before the lightning kicks. I hear it's bad around these parts. You ever drop during an electrical storm?"

"No, but it sounds like a bad idea. Come on, we're a few klicks away."

~

The skies opened before they reached the recon point.

Epic and Opie grew up in downtown Burkin, the one place on Hockspit that could rightly qualify as a city. It was almost perfectly centered in the middle of the habitable zone, which made it as far as it could possibly be from the lava in the south, the ice in the north, and the acid seas of the east and the west. Aside from the fresh water canals that crisscrossed the landscape, Burkin was fully landlocked. Any storm that made it there—quite a few did—had to pass over the entire landmass first, and since it was an uneven landmass with lots of hills and valleys, city dwellers rarely got the real Hockspit high storm experience.

City storms had weaker winds, and the cloud formations usually relied on internal momentum alone to carry through. In Derby, though, the wind and rain was unforgiving. It was fed with new energy from the sea churn and there wasn't a lot between the town and the cliffs to cut down the force.

The water was also slightly more acidic than Opie was used to. Nothing that would do them immediate harm, but also not the sort of thing it was good to get in one's eyes. And it made everything smell like vinegar.

That wasn't the worst part, though. The worst part was the lightning.

Most of the bolts reaching the ground were drawn to the lightning rods dotting the landscape. The local cattle farmers used power from the frequent strikes to charge their generators, and also to keep the lightning from doing too much damage else-where. The straight-path route to the recon point was full of these, and they knew better than to get too close to one.

Flat, open fields were also probably a bad idea, but on that they had little choice because that described a large portion of the terrain.

"Why do you think they sent us here?" Epic shouted over the rain, between the thunderclaps.

"Don't know."

They were double-timing it together down a path between two farms. Their packs had a spotlight attached to the shoulder piece, which they'd both lit up. It helped keep the road visible in between the lightning flashes, but it was difficult to tell by exactly how much, because it felt like they were running through a strobe.

"I mean, this was a targeted landing, right? They sent a whole squad out here. So what was their intel?"

"I'm not gonna know any more between the times you ask me that," he said. He was thinking about what Koestler intimated on the ride over, though, about the government maybe working with a lot more information than they were sharing. Distrust of government was a little unusual coming from someone in the military arm of that government, but only a little.

"Just want to know what I'm running toward, lughead," Epic said.

"My guess is, a warm cot, three squares a day, and a whole lot of nothing."

She laughed.

"You sound pretty optimistic for cannon fodder."

"They sent us to the coast," he said. "Might be the front line. Could also be the back. Maybe the aliens land in Swampscrub and work their way across."

"Thought you were in this man's army to shoot some xenos."

"No ma'am. Three squares and a cot is all I ask for. Plus, what else am I gonna do? Government's the only one hiring. And I get this cool blaster."

Up ahead, they could see members of their squad hustling

along in similar fashion, in packs of twos and threes. Every now and again a civilian would pop a head out of a window to take in the spectacle, but that was about all. Opie was used to the heavy congestion of the city; he couldn't imagine a life this isolated. He wondered if the people here even knew to expect soldiers. And if not, what did they think was happening?

"I'm just saying it would be nice to have a better idea of what to expect here," Epic said. "I know our people don't know a lot, but they know more than nothing, and right now I know less than that."

"Maybe there'll be a brief at the bunker."

"Yeah, maybe. Hey, hold up."

She came to a stop at a street junction, at one of the first places Opie would argue constituted an actual block, meaning it had buildings on both sides of the street and around the corner of the cross-street. Other than the surprising existence of manmade structures in close proximity, it didn't seem in any way interesting.

"What's wrong?" he asked.

"Thought I saw something."

The road was pressed dirt. Very little out on the edge of the colony appeared to be paved, or all that well defined. There was no curb here, for instance; the side of the road was untended tall grass.

The scene reminded Opie of the old Westerns from the Earth-Eden history archives. He tried to remember what those bundles of hay that used to blow across the road were called. Turboweeds or something like that.

Epic popped the spotlight off the vest and into her hand.

"What did you see?" Opie asked.

"If I knew I'd tell you. Something shiny."

"Not a lot of shiny things out here."

"Well yes, that's why it stood out. Lightning played off it. Probably my eyes just playing tricks."

She kept walking along, though, as if she had seen something and her eyes were not playing tricks at all.

"Come on, we should keep moving," he said. "Get out of this rain."

"You worried you might not be following orders fast enough, soldier?"

"Little bit, yeah. And I'm starting to smell like boiled greens."

"There it is, did you see?"

She waved the light back and forth over a section of roadside grass. Something did flash back.

"Yeah, I see it."

Holding the beam steady, Epic ran to the spot and dug around while Opie put his hand on the butt of his blaster. He couldn't explain why he did that; it just felt right.

"Someone lost their light," she said.

"One of ours?"

"Yeah, same gear."

"So it fell off a vest on the way down or while they were running. Shove it in your pouch and let's get moving."

"Yeah, maybe."

She stood, and raised her discovery up, so Opie could see the rest of the story, which was that while someone had indeed lost their spotlight, they'd also lost a portion of their vest.

"It was torn?" he asked.

"You tell me. These things, they don't tear, right? What's the tensile strength of this material?"

She tossed it to him.

He ran his light along the tear, which was jagged. The cloth looked shredded. Or bitten, maybe.

"I know this is crazy, but this looks like..."

"Shut up," she said, cutting him off.

She drew her blaster and then they stood there for a while and waited for something to happen. Nothing much did, other than the rain.

"What did you hear?" he asked, after a respectful silence.

"Don't know. A squeak or something."

"Chasing rats?"

"Not that kind of squeak."

"You sure? I bet they got rats out here, same as us."

"Positive."

The vermin problem in the city was well-known, and seemed to be a persistent problem with every colony. When humanity first traveled the stars, it was by using long-distance haulers and a cryo-frozen crew. But cryo never got much better than a 20% mortality rate, and nobody much wanted to be the one-in-five who never woke up again. Still, back in those days there was no chance of a stowaway rat. Then the hub system was discovered—something people found and learned how to use, but didn't invent—and suddenly the galaxy was available, without costing three lifetimes to get somewhere interesting. Only then did the rats figure out how to stow away and discover the same new worlds as people. More than once, Opie had heard someone joke that if they ever did encounter an advanced alien species, that species might have trouble figuring out who the dominant Earthlings were.

"Well what *did* it sound like?" he asked.

"Like metal rubbing up against metal."

"So you heard a machine somewhere, or a... I don't know, a pinwheel or something. Do they have windmills out here?"

"I said that's what it sounded like. Didn't say that was what it was."

"Epic, you're not making any sense."

"Bet the guy who owned that vest said the same thing."

"Maybe he did. How about we bring it back to the bunker and let someone smarter than us have a good look at it and..."

There was a *loud* shriek. It came from above, and to their left, a little up the road. Something was on top of a roof.

The sound was, on the one hand, pretty similar to the noise of two stripped gears rubbing together. On the other hand, it was undeniably a vocalization made by something with a mouth.

"Did you hear *that*?" Epic asked.

"Yeah, that I heard."

He shoved the torn piece of vest in his sack and armed himself.

"Came from there. See anything?"

She pointed in a direction that differed from where he thought he heard it. He checked where she was looking, then where he thought he heard it coming from, and both times there wasn't really much of anything to look at. Their eyes were still iffy from the regular lightning flashes.

He switched his goggles to infra and tried again. This was not a good idea on a night with lots of bright flashes, but made for a decent enough spot-check.

"There's nothing there," he said, flipping the goggles back to normal.

"Think they're invisible?"

"I think I want to go back to what I was saying before. Let's get to the recon point."

She nodded. "Yeah. Yeah, let's do. Double-quick."

They high-tailed it back to the junction, caught a right, and headed down the road as fast as they could safely do so. This wasn't all that fast, because of the rain and the dirt roads.

Opie wanted to ask Epic what she thought happened to the guy who was wearing the vest, and maybe if she thought it was weird how alone they were at this point. The townspeople hiding inside in the middle of a downpour he could understand, but an entire squadron had chuted to this point. They saw a few folks in front of them earlier, but now there was nobody, in either direction. If they'd been the last to jump it would have made a little sense, but they weren't.

They'd gone about a kilometer before they heard the sound again—in front of them.

Epic, who was leading, pulled up.

"What the hell is it and where the hell is it?" he asked, as she looked over her shoulder.

"Don't know, keep moving… DROP!" she shouted.

He did, just before she filled the space he'd been occupying with energy from the blaster. The hand cannon made a familiar THUP-WHOOSH sound: the first from the aperture at the end of the barrel opening and closing, and the second from the air as it surrendered to the rock of hard plasma sliding through.

Epic fired twice, and both sounded like they hit their mark. He tried to get up and have a look, but she'd already grabbed him by the elbow.

"We have to move!"

"But…"

"Now, soldier!"

So he did. It wasn't the order he'd just received (she technically outranked him) that did it, though; it was her expression. He'd never seen Epic look afraid before.

He just really wanted to know what she thought she saw that warranted two rounds, and if that thing still existed after having absorbed them. Not many things could. If this had, maybe that was why she looked so frightened.

They didn't get far. Another few houses, another block, another turn, and then there was a new howl. Again, it came from in front, but since the last shout presaged a rear assault— multiple enemies, working in concert, showing effective deception techniques—the first thing Opie did was check their six.

Nothing there.

Then, from the rooftop to their left, an actual alien dropped to the ground…

∾

∾

here was a restaurant not too far from Oliver's apartment that specialized in something called 'gastropub' dining. It was really just pub food with fresher ingredients and real chef, but since every fifth eating establishment in the city featured a variant of the same concept, it appeared to be working well for all concerned.

This particular restaurant—it was called Four Horse, which was meaningless—was a favorite of college students. There were ten universities in the metropolitan area, and five of them were within walking distance of Four Horse, so it was well attended almost all the time. The same could be said for the twenty or thirty other bars and eateries along the same strip of road.

Oliver, whose education included community college at a regional campus, had never been to Four Horse, right up until Wilson invited him there.

The invite came one day after he'd submitted *The Battle of Hockspit*, and the dinner landed two days before the next TAWU meeting. It was such a weird occurrence, Ollie could hardly say no, even if it felt like he was in some sort of trouble.

"Oliver! Hey!"

The entrance to Four Horse was below the service floor. One had to go up a short flight of stairs to reach the tables, which also meant some of the tables looked down on the entrance. Wilson was at one of them, shouting over the alt-rock station playing everyone through their meals.

Ollie waved awkwardly and stumbled around past the hostess desk and through the small perpetual crowd occupying most of the standing areas, until he got to the table. The place felt a lot like a regular bar, and since Ollie wasn't terribly fond of bars—he wasn't great with crowds unless there was a counter between them and him—it wasn't a welcoming experience. He did take note that all of the employees were wearing plaid, which he thought was helpful. If there was a fire, he'd know who to follow.

Wilson gestured him to a chair, and a second later a plaid waitress was there, and a few minutes after that Ollie had a hard cider chosen at random (they had five to pick from) and there was a plate of tater tots covered in cheese and bacon resting in the middle of the table.

"I thought we should talk," Wilson said. "Outside of the group."

"All right."

"Oliver, I think you're a good writer."

"Oh." This jibed with what Minnie insisted, but hearing it was still a surprise. "Thanks."

"And, I'm not going to share your latest piece with the group."

"Okay, now I'm not sure what's going on. Are you kicking me out?"

"No, no of course not."

Wilson had a dark beer with a thick head, which he took a sip of. Ollie just assumed it was intolerably bitter. It seemed like something a person drank because he wanted to acquire the taste for it, rather than something a person enjoyed.

"Look," Wilson said, "I think you can do better."

"I thought that was the point of workshopping."

"Oh, it is. But… okay, let's talk about the latest one. I think you did a lot of good things there. You threw in a little omniscient narration, which is a first for you."

"Did I?" Oliver wasn't a hundred percent sure what the difference was, but he was willing to believe Wilson did.

"Third person, but not from a character's perspective. You understand the difference?"

"I guess I do, sure."

"Transitioning from third omniscient to third close is tough, but you did fine with it. But that's not… What I'm trying to say, Oliver, is that technically you have all the tools. It's your choice of subject that I want to push you on."

"What does that mean? *Technically* I have the tools."

"Not a lot of people can sit down and string together words in an order that makes people want to keep reading. You're a pretty good storyteller, and that's something that I don't think can really be taught. When I was getting my MBA, trust me, I met a *lot* of writers who didn't have that. You also find different ways to tell stories, and that's all good."

"But you don't like the stories I'm trying to tell."

"I honestly think they're beneath you. I think you should be striving for more."

Oliver grabbed a tater tot and popped it into his mouth. The cheese had already cooled, and room temperature fried potatoes were never quite right, so the combined flavor made for an unpleasant experience. However, it turned out he was hungry, so he took a second and third, while trying to assess exactly what he was being told.

"All right," he said finally. "So I should be aiming higher. But what am I aiming for? I just want to write stories people like."

"Right, I get that. I want you to write stories people *need*."

Ollie smiled.

"Who's to say people don't need a good space opera?" he asked. "Or a horror story? Or an epic fantasy?"

"I think *need* is too strong a word. People *want* romance novels. They don't need them."

"I think *need* is too strong a word for any piece of fiction, Wilson."

"Of course it isn't. All right, it's a little pretentious, but a good work of fiction can be important, and important things can change the world."

"It isn't pretentious to think fiction can change the world. It's pretentious to think you're the one who can write it."

Wilson laughed.

"I like that. All right, let me reframe this for you. I don't expect you to write the great American novel. I do expect you to *try* to write it."

"But I don't want to write that kind of thing. These are the stories I want to tell."

"They're beneath you."

Oliver didn't think they were beneath him. He didn't think there was any story that fit that description as long as it was a story he wanted to tell. He did think they were beneath Wilson, and he wondered if someone had this same talk with him once, when he was getting his Masters. And, once he was through wondering all that, he wondered once more what Wilson was actually working on. Was Wilson writing his own great American novel? If so, why was he pressuring Oliver to do the same? Surely, there can be only so many great American novels, and Wilson was supposed to be the important generational voice at this table.

"All right," Oliver said. "So what do you recommend?"

"I'd like to give you more specific assignments. See if we can force you out of your comfort zone and flex those muscles some. I was on the other side of a lot of these same exercises, and since you can't... sorry, I'm assuming you can't jump into an MBA program yourself, but maybe I can bring some of it to you."

For a second, the fact that Wilson annoyed the heck out of Oliver fell away and he was touched. Flattered, even. He didn't think his writing was nearly as good as Wilson did, apparently. Maybe that was reason enough to go along with him and see where it led.

He suspected it would end badly, because writing something someone else thought he should write, instead of what he wanted to write just seemed like a bad idea all around. It was a lot like the dark beer Wilson was drinking, actually. Sure, with effort Oliver could probably learn to appreciate it, but he would never get rid of the bitter aftertaste, and he might end up quitting beer altogether.

"Sure, what the hell. I'll try it."

"Great!"

Wilson held up his dark beer, and they toasted.

"Oh, and before I forget, Minerva wanted to know what the alien looks like."

Oliver almost choked on his cider at the mention of her name. "She wants to know..." he repeated.

"Yeah, you stopped before describing the alien. In the story. She wants to know what it's supposed to look like."

"I don't know," Oliver said. "That was the problem."

"That's why you stopped?"

"Yes. I mean, I want to create something new. All the alien species in these stories are variants of pretty normal creatures we can all relate to. Lizards, or, you know."

"Bugs," Wilson said. "Giant bugs. They're always giant bugs."

"But that's why these stories are more than you make them out to be, I think. These are archetypes."

"Sure, sure, I get all that. Put a bug under a microscope and it's terrifying. But you'd be the thousandth writer to get to that same place if it ended up being a giant bug."

"That's why I stopped. I wanted something like that, but different. It's the same reason I couldn't keep going with the horror story. By the ending, it's the same ghost story tropes all over again. I wanted something new, but couldn't think of it."

Wilson grinned.

"This is why we're talking at all, Oliver. This is your instinct. You don't want to do the same old thing."

"There's value in those same old things."

"Yes, yes. But you're resisting it yourself. That's why you haven't finished anything."

"I could."

"You don't know what the aliens are going to look like, and you don't know who the ghost is or what she wants, and I'm nearly certain you've no idea what this Kingdom is all about. All you do know is you want these things to be new and different and something nobody ever thought of writing before, and you're stopping because you can't find that thing. Your need to write something great and original is preventing you from being one of those people who just churns out another genre story."

"I don't think there's anything wrong with…"

"Yes, I know, I'm not being dismissive of genre as a whole. I *am* being dismissive of tropes, and expected beats and outcomes. But Oliver, if you want to blaze a new trail, it's that much harder if you start down the same path as everyone else."

Oliver didn't know what to say to this, so he stuffed a tater tot in his mouth and didn't say anything. They were legitimately cold now. He wondered if they were going to order actual dinner before they ran out of things to talk about.

"Look," Wilson said. "As long as you're writing it, it's going to be something original. Don't get all swell headed, because I could say that to anybody. Every one of us is an individual creating something unique that only we could create, and blah blah blah. You get what I'm saying. So if you finish these stories you probably will find a way to make them different, if that's what you want. But you'll still be using someone else's paintbrush. I'd like to see what happens if you start from scratch."

"All right. So what's my first assignment?"

"Excellent. Your first… oh wait, Pallas."

What?"

"That was the other thing I promised not to forget. Minerva is *insisting* you join us."

"I know; she's made that really clear a couple of times."

"Well now she's looped me into this, so if you don't attend we're both going to be in trouble. I'll give you plenty of advance notice, all right? We're going on the last Saturday of the month. Be at our apartment by 4 PM and we'll take it from there. And no, you do not have a choice. Blow her off at your peril, because her next step is going to be to find out where you live and drag you out the door."

"That sounds terrible. Why is she so insistent?"

"I think she wants to adopt you. Don't ask me why, and don't say no."

"All right, fine."

"Excellent. Now let's get some real food, these potato things are dreadful."

~

Dinner devolved into small talk about nothing in particular, and also a little about Wilson's super-secret writing project. A very little. What Oliver learned was that Wilson was writing something "stupidly ambitious" and "never-before-attempted" and that he expected to fail miserably. He'd only written one chapter so far, but it felt like more because he'd written it seventeen times.

Oliver wanted to talk more about Minerva, but worried that expressing too much interest might be construed (correctly) as inappropriately obsessive.

When the meal was done—he paid without asking, and it wasn't as awkward as Oliver thought it was going to be—Wilson handed out the new writing assignment.

"Write something personal," Wilson said.

"That's all?"

"Sure."

"Personal, but fictional?"

"Yes, stick to fiction. Maybe first person, if you feel up to it. You haven't done that yet."

"It's a little vague."

Wilson sighed, as if to say *something personal* was an incredibly precise instruction as far as he was concerned.

"All right. Stick to a small story. One person meets another person in a place. Describe the people and the place, have them interact, and then get out. No aliens, or ghosts, or dragons. Just two people having a conversation in a place."

"That really sounds boring."

"Maybe it will be. See what happens."

"All right. Oh, can you give me a letter?"

"A letter? That's really a gimmick for the… yes, all right. Um, E. The letter E."

Then they shook on it, and Oliver pushed his way out.

The crowd at Four Horse had only gotten worse over the course of the meal, with overflow from the bar filling up all the standing space inside, until it seemed as if people were actively looming over them as they ate, in anticipation of a table clearing out. Oliver had a burger made by someone overly fond of sriracha, which he somewhat regretted. Still, it was a free meal, and those were hard to complain about.

Once on the street, Oliver oriented himself and headed down the road. He wasn't too far from a subway station, but using the subway to get home from this spot just seemed lazy: it was only three stops, it was a decently warm night, and the walk was only a couple of miles. Also, he could save on train fare, and maybe work out a plot before he got home.

To end up going in the proper direction, he had to navigate the modest college pedestrian detritus littering the sidewalk for three blocks until he reached Common Ave and hung a right. It was exactly the kind of stretch of city that Oliver hated, because for the most part these kids—he called them kids even though they were only a couple of years younger than him—hardly ever looked where they were going even when they were sober. Here, most of them were not.

At one point, he had to step all the way to his left to avoid a phalanx of undergrads who thought it necessary to walk four abreast, and if that weren't bad enough, the one on the end did all his talking with his arms. Oliver nearly got struck in the face by an act of over-exuberant gesticulation, while the kid responsible for this near-collision didn't even notice.

Oliver's aggressive sidestepping, in turn, nearly resulted in a different collision with another person. The large man, just coming out of another bar, came to a stop just before he ran Oliver down.

"Careful," the man said, in a deep baritone.

"Sorry!" Oliver said, quickly getting out of the man's way and continuing along the sidewalk.

It wasn't until Oliver reached the next street that he realized the man he nearly ran into was the same one he saw lingering at the coffee shop before. He was the one who spoke to Minerva.

Also, he was following Oliver.

That couldn't have been right. It was a big, busy thoroughfare, with lots of people moving in both directions, so undoubtedly the guy was just heading the same way Oliver was, as were many other people.

Except none of those other people paced Oliver quite so exactly as the large man. Ollie kept looking over his shoulder to confirm that it was all in his mind, but instead, every time he checked he became more convinced that he was being stalked.

He got to a busy intersection just as the walk light ended and raced across. The cars rushed through as soon as he reached the curb. He turned back.

The large man was standing on the other curb, unable to go any further. That he was staring right at Oliver more or less cemented Ollie's concerns.

"Hey!" Oliver shouted, over the traffic. "Can I help you, man?"

"Can't," the man shouted.

"Then leave me alone!"

"Can't," he repeated.

"What?"

"I understand you're a sorcerer."

"What did you say?"

"You heard."

"Who told you to say that?"

It was a prank. It had to be. Maybe Wilson put him up to it. Or Minerva, who after all was seen talking to the guy. But it didn't seem like something either of them would really do.

"You did," the man said, smiling.

"You're crazy! Leave me alone!"

"Can't."

The light changed, and the man started across the street. Oliver decided this was a good time to start running.

He didn't stop until he reached his apartment.

Chapter Four

EATERY

liver didn't get any writing in that night, or the night after. He spent both evenings and an unreasonable portion of the day in between staring out windows and over his shoulder, looking for the large man.

He never saw him. He wasn't sure whether that was better or worse, because it raised the possibility the man was never there in the first place.

To walk himself back from that conclusion, Oliver pointed out —to his reflection, in the bathroom, which was when he found he was the most reasonable—that the man wasn't dressed in animal furs and carrying a massive broadsword like the character described in his story. He was dressed as one might expect of an individual who drove large trucks for a living: in heavy boots, coveralls, and a brown leather bomber jacket. Although he *did* have a thick, tangled beard, and he *was* unreasonably large as human beings went.

Maybe the most disturbing thing was how the man answered questions. *Can't,* he said. Was he saying he "cannot" or was he identifying himself? Did the man think his name was Cant?

Of course he didn't; that was ridiculous. The entire thing was, actually, so Oliver decided he'd just gotten it wrong. The encounter with 'Cant' was some combination of Oliver being more tired (or non-sober) than he realized, coupled with an actual run-in with a person, where things went a little differently than he remembered. That was all.

Maybe the guy was speaking another language or something, and Oliver just misheard some words. That was probably it.

The third day was the day of TAWU, and even though his Hockspit story wasn't getting presented, there were other stories to talk about and so Oliver attended. It ended up being the day Ivor presented an original piece for only the second time.

Oliver had read it on his phone on the train, on the way to the meeting. It wasn't a long story, and it was kind of a mess. Ivor had a penchant for unreasonably long paragraphs and liked to use dialogue to have characters deliver exposition in deeply awkward ways, by saying things nobody would ever say. When he got to the sentence, *Bob, as you know we need the reactor to power the lattice uninterruptedly or face catastrophic consequences of epic proportion that could trap someone inside for ever,* Oliver had to stop reading for a while and ask what he did to deserve this.

The story's idea was pretty good, if a little borrowed. The execution was terrible, though.

He decided the criticisms running through his head were starting to make him sound like Wilson, and he thought that was probably a bad thing, so when it came time, he didn't offer much of a thorough critique to Ivor. Wilson was also pretty gentle, and nobody had much else to say that particularly critical.

Oliver was beginning to wonder if groups like this could actually make a writer like Ivor any better. But he decided to put that thought aside and deal with it another time.

Minerva cornered him before the meeting ended.

"So you're on this time," she said, without preamble.

"Yes."

"You promise?"

They were in the kitchen again. The meeting had already broken up, but when Ollie tried to sneak out with the rest of the group, Minnie was ready to grab him by the elbow and hang on.

"I don't know what the big deal is," he said. "Clubs really aren't my thing."

"I promise you'll enjoy it. And this isn't like any other club."

"How's that?"

Ollie could barely tolerate a crowd like the one at Four Horse; he had no idea how he was going to survive an actual nightclub. In his lifetime, he'd been to three, and each of them was—by acclaim—the Best Thing Ever. As far as he could tell there was no difference between them though: loud house music with heavy bass; disorienting flashing lights; a small collection of attractive people evenly scattered in a crowd of people wearing poor-fitting clothing that didn't flatter them at all.

He didn't enjoy clubs, and never expected to. Although he was, by instinct, pretty introverted, so this wasn't a big surprise.

"It's hard to describe," she said. "It's a different theme, all the time."

"All right."

She laughed, and threw a cheese puff at his head. He would analyze this later to discern precisely how flirty it was, but in the moment the thought didn't come to him at all.

"Look, I know going out isn't your *thing*, but I can fix that."

"I guess that's something I can look forward to. Being fixed."

She threw another cheese puff.

∿

*I*t was such a positive encounter—retrospectively—that Oliver didn't even remember to check over his shoulder for the guy who might or might not be Cant. He did decide that the next time he had a conversation with Minnie, he'd ask her about the man, given Ollie had seen her interact with him. It was incredibly likely she wouldn't know what Oliver was talking about, but it was worth asking anyway, so long as he could figure out a way to ask without sounding nuts.

He spent the rest of his ride concentrating on Wilson's insistence that Ollie try *something personal*. It was a weird assignment. What did it mean to write something personal, yet fictitious? He got the sense that this wasn't about penning a *roman a clef* of any kind. This was more basic. *Something small.*

~

~

She sat in the booth of the eatery, this old woman he hardly knew. She was pale in every meaningful sense, with white skin that sagged and drooped over a skeletal system that didn't look fully up to the task of supporting the weight of her flesh. Her eyes, which he remembered as being a vibrant blue, had faded somehow, like a portion of cloth upholstery left under a sunlit window for too many years. Cloudy, but still alive, those eyes darted from object to object. No part of the diner was safe from her discerning gaze.

Her hair had thinned sufficiently such that each long, silky white strand claimed a large portion of her scalp. It reminded him of when he tore the hair off Karen's Barbie doll, leaving behind only the follicle pinholes, except Barbie's follicles spawned multiple strings of plastic platinum hair. The old woman's skull only managed one string per pinhole.

Even her blouse was pale: a simple frock that appeared too large and hung loosely from her shoulders. It was frayed along the seams, and there was historical evidence of a coffee stain at the midway point of the right breast, a spot that had no doubt been treated to an incredible amount of personal attention by the blouse's owner. Her fastidiousness had given way to practicality with time, and the fight between those two instincts could be seen in every millimeter of the stain.

The next battle in that war of the blouse would be fought over the loose thread on the left-hand sleeve. It was early evidence of the gradual unspooling of the entire thing, a vanguard of entropy rubbing against the Formica countertop as she ran her fingers along the handle of the spoon.

He wondered what would happen if he pulled on the string. Would the entire blouse come apart? Then his mind went to a more unsavory place and he wondered what would happen if he pulled on one of her few remaining hairs. Would she end up bald, like Karen's long-buried Barbie doll? Or would she simply unspool before his eyes? He imagined that hair was the one consistent piece of internal connective tissue keeping her together, woven in with her synapses and bones and cartilage, tracing the path of her capillaries and on down to her closed-until-further-notice womb and on to her overworked knees and the disasters that were her feet. Would she become a pile of disarticulated matter with one sharp tug? Nothing left of her but the memories of the fully assembled?

Is this how we all end?

He shook the thought loose like a dog out of the rain, and turned his attention to the cup of tea slowly cooling in his hands, as she tried to speak.

"Thank you," she said.

There was iron in her voice, still. It hadn't betrayed her like the rest of her body had done. He noticed her teeth were stained with the same coffee damage that had claimed part of her blouse, and wondered if she spent as much time trying to whiten them as with the blouse. For someone so defined by shades of ivory, it must have been maddening that the one part of her body meant to be white adamantly refused to commit to anything better than a brownish yellow.

"You're welcome," he said, which was a lie. *You're welcome* and *no problem* and *no worries* and all the other things one said in response, they were all just there to let the person giving thanks off the hook. He didn't want to be there and he didn't want her thanks, and it *was* a problem, he *had* worries and she was *not* welcome. He didn't want her let off the hook.

But this is what we do, isn't it? he thought. *We take care of the things we have to take care of because there isn't anyone else to do that.*

There *was*, for years, someone to do these things he was now going to have to be doing, because Karen wasn't there any more to do them. Karen was lying in a hole in a field on top of a hill surrounded by a heavily manicured lawn, beneath freshly upturned soil and a layer of grass seed. By the end of the summer, that seed would be sprouting new blades of grass to erase all evidence of the turned-up soil marking the hole in the field on the hill, and there would cease to be proof of Karen in the world. Karen's entire self gone, like the words on a chalkboard.

All except for the stone.

We've traded in my sister for a slab of limestone with her name on it.

It was not at all a fair trade, but death had a no-returns policy that was impossible to get around.

A slab of limestone couldn't do the things Karen could. Admittedly, he never spent a lot of time talking to Karen when she was more than a name carved out by a chisel, when she was still chalk on that blackboard. He wished he'd gotten around to doing more with her before her cosmic eraser was clapped. This is a sentiment everyone had, regarding the dead, and he recognized this abstractly, a vague awareness that what he was experiencing for the first time in this moment was a universal thing. He also appreciated that this particular kind of mourning was for conversations never had, and that made it deeply selfish. He was sad for the loss of his own hypothetical future enrichment. Not for Karen, but for how Karen's interaction with him might create a better version of himself.

This version also mourned the loss of what Karen *did*, for no matter how expensive and nattily carved that limestone slab might be, it couldn't do what he relied on Karen to do. It couldn't take care of mother.

Neither could he, and that was the problem. But as much as he couldn't, he had to, because there wasn't anyone else left to do it now.

"I kept your room," she said.

The waitress took this opportunity to intercede on behalf of their appetites, which they had been ignoring for the past several minutes while they drank their hot things.

She was attractive in the way waitresses could sometimes be attractive, meaning it was some byproduct of her interest in looking basically appealing to the general public, and the lowered standards that result in being the only twenty-something girl in a busy diner. She might look plain in another room, or a larger town, or a city in a different state. In the quiet diner, slinging java and eggs and unmeasured quantities of grease, she was pretty, or nearly so.

Her nametag insisted she was Cydonia, which was several orders of magnitude too exotic for this little upstate town, something he could say with great confidence having grown up in the town with the name Oscar. Somehow, this attracted abuse from boys named John and Steve, possibly an instinctive revulsion toward polysyllables they couldn't even explain.

Cydonia, then, was probably a transplant. Except there was no reason for a twenty-something to move to this place. There was no college nearby, or heavy industry. There was factory work two towns over, on the river, and a winery in the valley a half an hour's drive north. But no, this wasn't the place people moved to, it was where people got up and moved away from once they were old enough to hire a cab.

"Are you ready to order?" Cydonia asked. The question was addressed to the middle of the table, and to the notepad in her hands. The notepad was the only indicator of her station, other than the nametag. She could pocket the tiny spiral-bound pad and remove the nametag and she would be left with a loose short-sleeved shirt, her jeans, and well-worn sneakers. Hypothetically, at that point she'd be indistinguishable from the general public.

He didn't think that would be really possible for her, though. She had a wariness that was combined with a sort of hyperactive exhaustion that branded her as a service employee. That was without considering the aromatic bouquet of failing deodorant and aerosolized fryer grease that would mark her as *the waitress* in a wide range of circumstances.

He wondered if she could even go to other restaurants without people asking her for things, mistakenly assuming she worked there.

"Toast, please," mother said, without looking up. She had mastered the art of speaking around people with a casual dismissiveness that was easy to interpret as spite and, sometimes, outright antagonism, especially to strangers and her children. "Could you burn it? I like it burnt."

"Right. How burnt?"

His mother looked Cydonia in the eyes, as if nobody on the planet had ever, in her seventy-seven years of existence, asked this question. As if 'burnt' was a toaster setting with which everyone was familiar.

"Darker than brown and lighter than charcoal," Oscar said, as clarification, before the elderly widow Donovan found the most witheringly insulting way to answer the question as possible. Cydonia deserved better.

"Got it," she said. "And you? Want some more tea?"

His choice of tea appeared to be a source of amusement to the kitchen. It perhaps identified him as a person who didn't *live around here.* He suspected his clothing did much the same. It was also possible he was being overly sensitive, and seeing people from a provincial region with the foggy lens of a cosmopolitan. Perhaps they were possessed of some manner of down-to-Earthish homespun wisdom that he, in his urban liberal enclave, would only grudgingly learn to respect after a number of hard-won lessons about the value of hard labor and an honest day's work.

This was what the movies had told him to expect. But since he grew up in this town and fled at the earliest opportunity, he was not about to misapprehend isolationist xenophobia with good ol' American aw-shucks wisdom. He escaped this place for a reason.

"More hot water would be great," he said, trying on a smile. "Do you do egg white omelets?"

"Oh, Oscar, please," mother said.

She always found his peculiarities a symptom of his being *difficult*, but would then turn around and offer a lengthy dissertation on the importance of getting her toast exactly right. For her, being difficult was an exertion of common sense; in other people it was *little babies who wanted to have everything just so*.

"I'm sure we can do that," Cydonia said cheerily in a tone that indicated this was hardly the first request of its kind. "Two eggs?"

"That'd be super, thanks."

Cydonia flashed a little smile and took her small-town-attractive self to the other side of the room to place their high-maintenance order with the cook, who looked like he recently arrived in the twenty-first century directly from 1955.

Oscar very much wished that the conversation he was in the middle of was with Cydonia, instead of with mother. This was probably true when it came to everybody else in the diner as well, but that didn't mean he found Cydonia any less interesting.

"So you can stay there if you wish."

"Where?" he asked.

"In your room."

"Oh."

To his knowledge, the bedroom he called his own in the house in which he came of age, remained exactly as he left it when he stopped calling it his home. He was told—by Karen, some months prior, as a preamble to the unfortunate fact of her imminent demise—that mother held it aside from the rest of the house in the same way a woman who'd lost her child to an unfortunate sledding accident might: as a ghostly memorial. When Karen told him this he thought back to all the *things* that must still be there, collecting dust: odd collections of Matchbox cars and comic books, posters of bands now famous mostly for having once been famous, a shelf of those books everyone was assigned to read in high school, and so on.

He wondered how thorough she'd been, in her effort at verisimilitude. Did she pick up the laundry or leave it on the floor? He had a wooden box under his bed that contained a small water bong and a plastic bag that was about half weed and half oregano. Did she find this? Would she leave it there if she did? Would she even know what it was?

These were entertaining questions once. Now, he was about go to back to that room and he didn't want to, because now he recognized it for what it was: the phantom of his own childhood, back to reclaim his soul. It was as if he'd slain a dragon to escape this place—that was the approximate difficulty level, in his mind —and now, thanks to an awkward contractual detail, he was back, and not only did the dragon live, it didn't appear to have been inconvenienced in the slightest.

It wasn't a contractual detail. It only felt that way. Father had died from a fatal case of congenital bitterness ten years past, Karen only a week ago—from cancer, not bitterness, unless that was a kind of cancer—and now he was all that was left to care for mother, and the house she refused to part with.

He could already tell she expected him to take Karen's place. Like dropping everything and relocating to this highway rest stop of a town was something he could do. He couldn't, though. He had a job and a life and friends and an existence that would only ever see this place as the answer to a personal question, provided to unlock an online login, alongside the last four digits of his social security number.

She couldn't care for herself, and her daughter, his sister, was selfish enough to die first, and he wasn't going to be stepping up. He was going to be putting mother into a home, and paying for it by selling the house. That was what was going to happen.

He thought this probably made him a bad person. He could no longer tell. Maybe she knew this was going to be happening eventually, that the son you drive away—intentionally or not—is not the man you should be putting your future care into the hands of. She was going to be upset and he was going to be angry and they were going to have a terrible time of it, and that was before he got around to bringing up the subject of a nursing home.

He knew it was going to play out this way, just as he knew she was going to be asking too much of Cydonia on the subject of how to best burn her toast. *It must be edible,* she might say, *but not enjoyable. I'm working out a lifetime of Catholic guilt through my diet. It has to taste like sin. If you can't do that for me, I have some communion wafers you can sauté.*

Oscar and his mother were stuck in a Sophoclean tragedy. That they knew this wasn't going to change the outcome. All he could say for sure was that this very moment, in this diner, on the day they put Karen into her hole, was the wrong moment to discuss the future. Today was a day owned by the past.

~

~

"*The Eatery,*" Wilson said. "Okay."

"That's all you have to say?" Oliver asked.

"I have a lot more."

"I hated it," Minerva said.

It was only Wilson and Minerva, because this was not any

more a formal meeting of TAWU than the dinner in Four Horse had been.

Oliver felt like he'd been punched.

"You didn't like it?" he asked her.

"I liked the other stuff better. I mean I'm sorry, I know I don't get a vote since I'm not in the group, but I read all the stuff too."

"She does," Wilson said. "I keep telling her to get involved but—"

"But I'm not a writer."

Wilson took her hand, which was the first time Oliver ever saw a gesture of affection pass between them. He felt oddly uncomfortable, like he'd walked in on them in the bedroom.

"She says she's too busy being a character," he said with a laugh. "Kills me every time."

They were sitting outside, at one of the tables in the vertical park a few blocks from Wilson's condo, and around the corner from Oliver's work. It was a cold, wrought-iron setup, the kind of thing that makes sense on a patio or some other place where wind is the enemy. Heavy, with the table chained to the ground and the chairs chained to the table, it was designed to go nowhere, year-round. It made for a pretty uncomfortable place to sit for an extended period. This was likely just a byproduct of choosing iron furniture, but it was probably an outcome the city preferred, since nobody was likely to occupy one of the seats for all that long.

Wilson squeezed Minerva's hand for another second, let go and leaned forward.

"I thought it was excellent," he said. "I thought you made great progress. Even if the story doesn't show promise, I think you grew as a writer. You really focused your attention on the smaller details and teased out some interesting things."

"Thanks," Oliver said. "That means a lot to me."

This was something he thought he should say because he thought it was probably supposed to be true. Surprisingly, despite being the exact kind of accolades he had been hoping to get one day, it didn't feel true. He turned to Minnie.

"Tell me more about why you didn't like it."

"Oh, I'm not the expert here," she said.

"Go ahead," Wilson said.

"Well, okay. I don't think you should listen to him."

Wilson laughed, but didn't add anything else.

"No," she said, "I mean, it's… okay, *The Eatery* is pretty good, notwithstanding the title."

"What's wrong with the title?"

"I just don't know what an eatery is, I mean it's a diner. You call it a diner the whole time except for the first time."

The truth was, Oliver started writing the story without bothering with the letter-prompt. He completely forgot about it, until just before he handed it in. After combing the document for a good noun that would do for a title, he went back in and changed one of the diner references to 'eatery', slapped the title on, and sent it through. If he had more time he would have given the mother a name beginning with an E instead. Or the waitress.

"It doesn't tell me much about the story," Minnie added.

"All right, sure," Oliver said.

"And the writing's okay. But nothing *happened*. I'd rather see you go back and tell me what happens when Osraic gets to the kingdom, or Orrin figures out what's going on with the ghost, or Opie sees his alien."

Wilson laughed again. "I just realized you gave them all O-names," he said, which was not the first time it had been observed, but the first time he'd been the one remarking on it. "What's that about?"

"I don't know," Oliver said. "Just feels right."

"Someone's gonna accuse you of writing Mary Sues. Or, what are they for men? Gary Stu?"

"I don't know what that is," Oliver said.

"It's when the author puts idealized versions of themselves into their stories, basically."

"Oh."

Oliver did sort of think of all the main characters as a version of him. He thought he was supposed to be doing that.

"It's not really a thing," Wilson said. "I mean, it can be, but usually if you're getting accused of stuff like that it's because you're writing something that isn't very good anyway. I mean, basically every thriller with a super-competent protagonist is trafficking in the same idealization. Nobody throws that charge around until they're reading someone who can't pull it off."

Somehow, whenever Wilson named specific genres, it sparked an idea in Oliver. In this case, he was suddenly working on a spy thriller in his head.

"That someone is usually a woman," Minerva said. "Even if they're doing a fine job of pulling it off."

"Oh, hey, I don't think that's fair," Wilson said.

"Sure it is. You know it is. You guys write James Bond versions of yourselves and sketch the outline of the women characters and get movie deals out of it. Flip the genders and everyone starts throwing Mary Sue around."

Minnie clapped a hand over her mouth.

"Sorry!" she said. "I'm not supposed to know that much about writing."

"I don't understand," Oliver said.

"I mean I shouldn't say things like that. I'm not the expert."

"Why not? Who's stopping you?"

She laughed one of her cuter laughs.

"Never mind!" she said. "Go on, you guys talk about the thing some more, don't mind me."

What Oliver wondered was whether Minnie was drunk. It was a little early in the day for it.

"So Mary Sues are okay," Oliver said.

"Yeah, yeah they aren't really Mary Sues, I don't think. I mean if these guys are idealizations, you've got some issues. They're well-rounded characters, mostly. Probably. I'm not sure about the last one."

"Oscar."

"Right," Wilson said. "Another O. He's mostly present in the story as a reflection of the world he's judging. Nothing wrong with that at all, and the writing's really interesting. I'd love to see you explore that some more. Did you enjoy it?"

Oliver hated it. With the other pieces he felt like the only reason he stopped was that it was going to take two months to finish and he only had a week. With this, he could see it taking two years, he would hate the two years, and when he was done he would have an end product he would also hate.

"I guess," he said.

"Oh, come on," Minnie said.

"Minerva..." Wilson looked like he was jumping back into the middle of an argument they'd already had.

"Wilson, look at his face, he doesn't want to write more." She reached out and put her hand on Oliver's wrist. "Ollie, look, it's okay to admit you don't like writing the things Wilson thinks you should write."

"I don't know. I mean, if I'm good at it..."

"Yeah, but you didn't have any *fun*."

"Maybe you should try outlining," Wilson said.

"What would that do?" Minnie asked. It was starting to feel like Oliver was a child stuck between his parents disagreeing on how to punish him. His actual parents didn't ever do this, as far as he could recall, but it felt that way just the same.

Wilson ignored her question, and kept his attention on Oliver.

"It's the one thing we can consistently report about your efforts to date. You come up with things too large to finish. Even when I told you to just take something small, you focused in on a level of detail that made it impossible to write a whole story. I'm wondering if the problem is that you're just sitting down and typing, without any kind of plan."

"I've never tried an outline before."

"It'll be fun! You can work out the whole plot first, and then just fill in the gaps."

"But what do I write?" Oliver was worried he'd be forced to do something boring—an outline—in order to write something also boring, like the prestige pieces that got Wilson going.

"Whatever you want, I guess."

"Write a romance!" Minerva said.

"A romance?" Oliver thought he was probably blushing.

"With a female main character! You haven't done *that* yet, have you?"

"Um… okay."

"For me?"

Minerva gave him probably her best smile. It was really hard for Ollie to believe she didn't know what that smile did to him.

"Sure, all right."

Oliver didn't want to write a romance and he didn't want to work on an outline for a romance he didn't want to write. He would rather work on the spy story in his head.

It would start with a helicopter crash, he thought. That would be a less effective beginning for a romance. Or, he assumed that to be so.

Wilson, meanwhile, looked like he was developing a bad headache, and looked ready to go on a rant about the romance genre as a whole.

"Do you need a letter?" he asked, instead of ranting.

"Yeah."

"Okay. Let's go with U. The letter U."

"Sure. Romance, letter U."

"Start with an outline, see how far you get."

"Right."

"Oh, look at the time, Ollie," Minerva said. "You need to get back to work."

"Do I?"

He looked at his watch and saw that it was nearly two P.M. This was possibly bad, but he couldn't remember.

"When did I go on break?" he asked. He honestly didn't know.

"Like an hour ago," she said. "We don't want you to lose your job."

"Yeah. Yeah, no, we don't."

"Go on, then," Wilson said.

Oliver jumped to his feet and headed to the intersecting road that connected Tenth and Market. He noted that he was wearing his work shirt, the black slacks he usually had on accompanying the shirt, and the right footwear. There were coffee grounds under his nails and in a couple of spots on his shirt.

This must have been his lunch break, which was a problem because he didn't think he ate any food. Except he wasn't hungry. But that wasn't the real problem. The real problem was he didn't even remember being at work before this meeting.

Oliver hesitated at the corner and looked around. The traffic on the street was steady, but the foot traffic was light. Behind him, Minnie and Wilson had already gotten up from the table and disappeared in one direction or another, even though there hadn't really been time for them to reach a spot that was not in view from where Ollie stood.

The good news was that he didn't see the large man who thought he was Cant anywhere, because if he coupled that with the problem he was suddenly having with his memory, he'd be forced to conclude that there was definitely something wrong.

But no, of course that wasn't the case. Oliver'd just gotten so used to being at work he didn't even register it any longer. He must have sleepwalked through the whole morning. It only seemed like his day began on that uncomfortable wrought-iron chair chained to the middle of the vertical park.

Just to make sure—and he couldn't explain why this was a valid confirmation—he looked up at the corner of the building across the street. Birds still lived atop the cornices, and still circled around, and they still weren't dragons.

Everything is fine.

UNNAMED

O liver sat at his laptop and stared at the blinking cursor beneath his title page. The title was the only thing he'd been able to write up to this point, and that title was *Unnamed*.

It was an inauspicious beginning.

For weeks, this was how writing went for him: a blinking cursor on a white 'page' in a Word document with no actual words in either direction aside from the occasional title word that was a placeholder about fifty percent of the time. "Unnamed" was just such a placeholder, which meant his one accomplishment thus far in completing his latest assignment was not even an actual accomplishment. He'd typed a seven-letter word he expected to replace with another word in the near future. If he was looking for credit, he could argue that the new word would also have to begin with the letter U, so he had that going for him. But Wilson had supplied that letter, so he couldn't take credit for that either.

He didn't know what changed in the recent past to turn that blank page with the blinking cursor into a page full of words. (Still with a blinking cursor. The cursor was never satisfied.) All he knew was that one day he started writing, and everything just fell together, and the frustrating aspect of it all was that when he couldn't just sit down and start writing, he didn't know why that was. If you don't know how a machine is activated, you can't be expected to know how to get it going when it isn't running.

Oliver got up and took a look out the window. The apartment had a decent view of the city, really, and he only occasionally took in that view. It was the sort of perspective a tourist might appreciate, were this a hotel room. (It was too small to be a hotel room. It was perhaps large enough to be a sanitation closet in a proper hotel, but that was pushing it.) The city was dominated by seven or eight main thoroughfares, and four of those seven met at a central point, like an actual hub on a wheel. He thought that was probably where he got the idea of the outer space arrangement in his Hockspit story, but he tried not to overanalyze these things. It worked, and it made sense, and that was what mattered.

The roads headed off in diagonals, with boroughs popping up around various mini-centers that were called things like "such-and-such Square" or "this-and-that Circle", which was always curious because there was inevitably neither a square nor a circle involved.

The effect was a city map that looked like someone had smashed a spider against a wall with a shoe, and torn off a couple of the legs. It only really worked if one imagined spiders had big bulbous knees—to account for the squares and the circles along the legs—so it was a terrible analogy. It was the one most people went with anyway.

Ollie lived on one of the legs, on Common Ave., pretty close to the center of the city. When he looked to the left, he was looking inbound. In that direction the buildings all got taller, ultimately obscuring the view of downtown proper. Straight ahead was another row of apartments, but that side's buildings were shorter, and he could see over them as far as the ball field. Of that he could see only the outer wall and the lights. Thankfully, the lights faced away from the window.

He could see very far when he looked to the right. In that direction, the urban sprawl was really obvious. The intersection of Common and Harrod was fully visible—Harrod Ave. was where Four Horse was—and so was the road a long way past that. Common cut through two college campuses before vanishing into the hills that distinguished the suburbs.

Looking down on the street level Oliver was happy to note nothing unusual, like a large hairy figment of his imagination staring back up at him.

Wilson and Minnie lived in a section of the city on the other side of the downtown, so Oliver couldn't see Tenth from his window. If he had the city plans right, they were to his left, through downtown, and then left again at about a 120-degree angle. Tenth didn't head directly into downtown, though; getting to it was a series of right-left-right-lefts using connecting streets until getting to Trimount Ave., which went straight in.

Absolutely none of this was going to help Oliver write. The blinking cursor on the blank page remained both blinking and blank. But he'd learned that sometimes the best way to get his mind going was to distract it for a while.

He sat back down and put his fingers on the keyboard, and waited to see if they started putting out words.

They didn't.

"The problem is, you've never read a romance," he said.

There was no reason to say this aloud, but it broke up the monotony of the text in his internal narrative so he rolled with it.

"There are rules. You don't even know what the rules are."

At least with the other stories he had something to stand on, because he'd read things *like* them before. At the same time, he knew he broke a couple of rules here and there. The military sci-fi didn't have enough weapon porn in it, for instance. He didn't know exactly how to resolve that, since the characters were using guns he made up, leveraging technology that didn't exist and science that was probably completely wrong. Providing details on a made-up weapon just didn't make a huge amount of sense to him, yet his *characters* might care a lot, so Ollie should have given it to them. Even if it was all nonsense.

So there were expectations. There were tropes. He had been ignoring a lot of them. And he was okay with that. But maybe, for romance, he had better pay attention.

Story structure was another thing he had a habit of ignoring. In this, at least, he had Wilson's support. In one of the first TAWU meetings Oliver attended, Wilson talked at length about how stories have acts, and stages, and turning points, and so on, and all these things come at certain points in a story. Then, after listing all of this out he told them to throw it all away.

The story, he said, should have its own rhythm and pace, and if you learn how to tell a good story it will end up following a pattern all its own. That pattern might very well end up being the same as the one in the structure map he provided, but it didn't have to.

That the same person was now telling him to outline, was either funny or alarming. Funny, because Wilson seemed to be doing an end-around on his own advice, and alarming for the fact that Wilson might not know he's doing this. The possibility that his mentor was essentially making things up as he went—with the later things contradicting the earlier things—occurred to him, and not for the first time.

Oliver clicked over to a search engine and looked for romance story outlines, and then romance story tropes. The first search results made him think there was no room for creativity, and the second made his head explode. There were more tropes than he thought possible, and about the only one that looked mandatory was Happily Ever After, with a "Happy For Now" caveat that apparently existed to allow for sequels.

He had a nagging sense that he should maybe not try to write a genre he'd never read and wasn't really a fan of. He had nothing against romance as a genre form, but he also had no history of reading that form, and that was just a bad way to begin. Sure, he could grasp it conceptually: he had seen romantic comedies, and that was close. (Probably.) But unless he was going to write a screenplay—and this was something worth considering—it didn't make sense to try and do this.

Of course, he was also stalling. Writing an outline felt like homework, and he didn't enjoy writing nearly as much when it resembled homework. But Minerva asked him to write her one, so he had to try.

"Just write a crappy outline," he said to himself.

Act One

The protagonist: a nurse. Yes, a nurse is good, let's go with a nurse. A nurse who works at an old age home. Her name is… okay let's face it, I'm going to be basing her on Minerva whether I mean to or not (note: DO NOT LET HER READ THIS) so, no I can't call her Minerva, but okay, Athena, then. They're the same name, just Roman vs. Greek, so, cool.

Old age home? Why an old age home? Okay, stick with it for now. Athena has a boyfriend already, and she lives with him, but he's a jerk. (too close?) He's a jerk and he takes advantage of her and he's… in a band or something, and she's supporting them and she's also going to school. Yes, cool, okay.

She's incomplete somehow? Maybe she doesn't think she deserves better than jerk boyfriend. (childhood trauma?)
Love interest: he's, well okay, what the hell, his name is Otis.

Sounds like an old person name, but when you've got a theme, might as well stick to it, right? (right?) Otis. Yeah, I'm gonna be basing this on me, whatever, I'm writing a romance where the lead is Minerva and the love interest is me and all right, fine, I'm not really doing this stupid assignment anyway. (DO NOT LET HER READ THIS)

Otis is a paramedic, so they work together, except that doesn't make sense because I didn't put her in a hospital. Maybe I should move her to a hospital.

Okay, I'm gonna move her to a hospital.

Wait! Wait, wait no okay, so she's at like an *old* old person old age home. Like the kind of place that has paramedics there all the time, like two or three times a week. Maybe they have a special dock for the ambulance and he works for one of those private companies and they're there all the time just hanging out and waiting for someone old to have an event so they need to go to the hospital. That way I don't have to put Athena in the emergency room, because how else would she interact with a paramedic?

Yes, I like this idea. And this way the patients are always the same so I can build a character or two in the elderly ppls.

Yes.

Plot for act one: Do they already know each other?
I don't know. Am I supposed to put a meet-cute in? Is that only a movie thing?

Not just a movie thing, thank you Internet. But okay I think I want them to know each other already. They're supposed to be in conflict initially, though, so maybe they don't like each other? Maybe he flirts with her but she's got a boyfriend so, no, that's not okay, no they flirt with *each other*, yes, but they're like, this is all cool because she's got a boyfriend and everyone else is like, *this is totally not cool you guys* but they're sure it is.

So maybe open with her leaving for work, so hello here's crappy boyfriend being crappy, here's her getting in her car and going to work, describe work, and then there's a crisis! Medical something-something, someone's crashing oh no, call paramedics.

Athena goes with dying person to ambulance bay, and we meet Otis and they something-flirt-something, oops, Mrs. So-and-so's dying, gotta fly.

Too dark? Love story surrounded by death, characters only together because of repeated death and dying, reminders of mortality, enjoy life while you can (is this a trope?) yes I can work with this but is this okay for the genre?

Whatever, keep going. Never gonna write this anyway. Also, I'm doing outlines wrong, I'm nearly positive.

Conflict: I have no conflict, this is all setup. Where does the conflict come from?

A patient? I need another character. Conflict character: Nathan. Old guy, been in the home for a long time, has lots of health emergencies, so he gets to know both Athena and Otis. Maybe he's the guy who tells them they should really get together, seize the day blah blah. Lots of old-person wisdom.

This is not conflict, but maybe Nathan is just so awesome that every time he nearly dies it's a big deal, and then he *nearly* nearly dies, and asks Athena to go with him in the ambulance because he's sure he's going to really for real die this time, and then it's just Otis and Athena and Nathan.

Act Two

Nathan's faking! (note: figure out how to fool a paramedic into thinking you're dying; find out if paramedics can work alone, or if I need to account for a partner. If I ever decide to write this, I mean.)

Nathan's faking and he has a gun, somehow, and he's kidnapping them to take him somewhere. And it's not that he isn't actually a kind old guy with lots of wisdom and who wants these two crazy kids to end up together, it's that he's all of those things and he's also an old bank robber.

He saw some kind of something on the news and this something made him think, oh, no, I have to go find my stash, and he has money buried somewhere that he has to go find, and nobody knows he's secretly this old bank robber because he's using a fake name and the guy he actually is, is supposed to be dead. (How did he do this? How much do I care?)

So now they're hostages, even though Nathan is elderly and may have some sort of medical condition or something, and when he knows he needs sleep he, I guess, ties them up at first, until something. I need an inciting incident that gets them to agree to go along on his treasure hunt.

It's a road movie? Can I do a road movie that's also a romance? That can be a thing, I'm pretty sure.

Since people can't just disappear they end up being missing persons, and Nathan's face gets on the news and someone recognizes him, and now it's a manhunt for this famous crimi-nal, and all Nathan wants is to find the treasure trove before he dies…

…so he can give it to Otis and Athena? Sure, why not? He doesn't have any next-of-kin, not unless I want to make him Athena's long-lost father, but that's so tired, and besides, it's a huge coincidence, so no, unless some trope tells me I have to do that I'm not gonna do that.

Okay but our lovers, they're bickering a lot because maybe one of them is really into this and the other one isn't, something some-thing, so they're fighting, but it's the kind of fighting that makes you think they really care about each other. (I can't create charac-ters like this, this is so dumb.)

There has to be a puzzle. Either Nathan's memory isn't a hundred percent or he doesn't really know where the money is, he just has clues left behind by whoever actually hid it. Or, he knows but he doesn't want to go there directly, he want's Athena and Otis to figure it out.

A treasure map! Nathan drew it when his mind worked better (dementia? That's a thing) and they have to use it to find the treasure now, so they can do it even if Nathan isn't there or can't figure it out himself because of his old age thing.

Act Three

Otis and Nathan go off on their own, Athena leaves them, figures out the final clue where the treasure is, somehow recon-nects/saves them or something, they find the treasure, Nathan dies of whatever it is that's been killing him, they can't save him, there's something in the treasure that is important somehow. Not money, something else, important for a different reason. Like, a long lost something that, upon being revealed, results in the couple facing no charges? Somehow?

I need to figure out what that is. There's a story around that something, it's the part to build around.

~

~

Oliver's phone was ringing.

It was a little while before he even recognized this was happening, because he was concentrating on the outline, and because his phone basically never rang.

There were perhaps a dozen people who had the number, and five of them were from the coffee shop. Three of those five were essentially the only ones who might call, and only to discuss important matters like shift coverage.

His phone didn't seem to think this was a number that had ever called him before, though. Perplexed, he answered.

"Hello?"

Only static. If there was anyone talking on the other end, he couldn't hear them.

He hung up, and returned to the outline. They'd call back if it was important.

He was thinking maybe this would work better if he could start writing the characters out. In the past, plot came second, after the fleshing out of the main character. Plus, if Athena was the main character instead of Otis, he had some work to do.

There was a loud BANG at the door. If he wasn't sitting on his bed with his back against the wall this would have been when he fell out of his office chair.

"Hang on," he said.

The response was multiple blows to his door. Someone was hitting it with a fist.

"I said, hang on!"

The bed was a futon mattress on the floor. Climbing out required a little bit of rolling around to get his knees underneath before he could stand. He reached for the knob, and took note that the hallway light appeared to be going wonky again: he could see it flickering underneath his door.

He slid the chain on, and then opened the door two inches so he could look into the hallway. There was no peephole, so this was all he had.

"Hello, what is it?"

With that kind of insistent banging, at minimum there should have been an active fire in the hallway, but there wasn't. There also wasn't anyone there.

He closed the door, disengaged the chain, and opened it all the way, so as to get a proper look.

Nobody was there, in either direction, or at least not near the door. It was hard to tell for sure at the far end of the hall, because the overhead light had gone out again over there. It was intermittent in Ollie's part of the hallway, but there was a window at the end of the corridor and streetlights shone through that window, so if someone had been standing there in the dark he would have seen some evidence, and he didn't.

This was despite the irrefutable fact that someone had been banging on his door a few seconds ago.

Oliver thought about going to one of his neighbors and asking if they'd just been banging on his door, but that seemed like a waste of time. There were a few doors to choose from, and he really didn't know anybody all that well, so at best it would be an awkward conversation.

The phone began to ring again, which startled him a little more than it should have. The number on the phone was the same as before. He shut the door.

"Hello?"

More static.

"If you can hear me, I can't hear you. Call from a different phone, or from a different place."

There *was* someone there. The static wasn't constant; it had gaps, and he got the sense that in those gaps, someone was speaking.

"Look, I'm sorry, I can't hear you."

"Wilson?"

It was a woman's voice, and it sounded familiar, but the interference was making it tough to pin down.

"This isn't Wilson. Who is this?"

"You need to come back."

Come back?

"This is Oliver."

"Come back, Oliver."

He looked at his watch. It was nine-thirty, and the Jittery Canary closed a half an hour earlier.

"Into work?" he asked. "Who is this?"

More static. Some kind of low bass line rumble, like there was a boat in the background, or a horn on a train, or someone with a tuba.

"Hello?"

"You have to..."

"What? I have to go back, I heard you."

"You have to help us."

"What? What did you say? *Who is this?*"

The line went dead. Oliver threw it across the room like it was burning his hand. The light as his feet continued to flicker, and now it felt like his heartbeat was matching the frenetic strobing in the hall.

What the hell is going on?

He opened the door again and looked up and down the hall, unconsciously associating the weird phone call with the banging on the door. Someone was pranking him, so it didn't seem all that far-fetched. It was someone who thought it would be funny to quote his own writing back to him.

It wasn't funny, it was stupid and terrifying, and between this and the Cant double, Oliver was getting tired of it.

He thought he saw someone at the end of the hall: a girl, standing in front of the window. It was just his mind playing games, though, because the only time it looked like she was there was when the light went out. Every time the overhead on that end of the hall kicked in, he could see the corridor was empty. People who only existed when they were in shadows ran contrary to any physics he was familiar with.

That would make a heck of a ghost story, though. Even if he was currently busy scaring the hell out of himself, he made a note to use that detail someday.

Provided I'm not about to be dragged into some spectral hell right now, Oliver thought.

He considered asking the woman who wasn't there if she was not in fact there, and decided he'd rather close the door, lock it as thoroughly as he could, maybe push something heavy against it, and curl up in a corner of his tiny apartment until morning. That was a much better plan.

He bolted and chained the door and hoped nobody decided to bang on it again. It was solid wood and reinforced along the edges with metal, so nothing short of a battering ram could knock it down, so far as Oliver knew. It was probably okay, then, that he didn't really have anything heavy to push in front of the door, and decided that positioning a bunch of lighter things there would only make it harder for him to get out in the morning, when all of this would seem silly and he was late for work.

He got back on the bed. The romance story outline seemed like a distant thing now. He had been thinking about maybe starting to write some things around Athena, but that wasn't going to happen. Maybe tomorrow.

Oliver picked up the phone, which remained harmlessly not-ringing.

"You have their number, stupid," he said.

It was right there in his call history: 2 calls, with the right timestamps and everything. These were real things that actually happened and didn't occur only in his head, and this he found to be an immense relief.

So if it was a prank, whoever was doing it probably owned this phone number.

He took a deep breath, held it for a little while, and hit the callback button on the exhale.

Six rings, and then a static-free pickup.

"Hello?"

It was Minerva.

"Oh, hi," he said, not knowing really how to proceed from here.

"Hi, who's this?"

"Minnie, it's... it's Oliver."

"*Ollie?* Hey, what's up?"

"I, um, I have a funny question for you: did you just call me, like in the last five minutes?"

"No...? I don't even have your number, man. I mean, I guess I do now, right? Cool, now you can't escape me."

In any other context this would be exciting. In this one it was a little scary.

"Yeah, look, are you sure..."

"I wasn't even near my phone five minutes ago. It was on the charger. Hey, how'd you get this number? Did Wilson give it to you? I wish he'd tell me when he did stuff like that, he acts like I'm his secretary sometimes."

"I didn't know it was your number until I called," Ollie said, which sounded crazy, and he knew it did, but it was too late to back this up. "I was calling back whoever called me."

He explained the static on the line, but omitted the part

where the caller was a woman who could easily have been Minerva, who quoted a story only a dozen people knew about, one of those people being Minerva. Because that sounded a good deal further along the path to crazy, in the rough direction of pathologically deranged.

"That's *so* weird. I wonder if the phone company crossed line somehow. Is that still a thing? I remember that being a thing on old TV shows, but not with cell phones. Or maybe someone was ghosting my number, and it's just a coincidence we know each other."

"Yeah that must be it."

"Anyway, nice talking to you, but I gotta go. Pallas, right?"

"Right."

"You're still on? It's next week, no backsies, and now I have your cell."

"Yes, still on."

"Excellent. Oh, how's my romance?"

"Don't know yet. I'm still working on the outline."

"Hey, anything's gonna be better than that thing Wilson made you write, right? Okay, really I gotta go. Talk soon!"

She hung up before he could say anything else.

Chapter Six

WEAPON

Oliver tried to get back to the romance story, but there was just no way. He couldn't get past the possibility that someone was playing tricks on him, and Minerva was going along with the gag.

It would have been easier if was just about anybody else. He was *sure* he saw her talking to the man claiming to be Cant of the Warven tribe, and the ghost story-quoting phone call came from her phone. That was pretty good evidence. Never mind that the charge sounded ridiculous, and would sound no less so if the person he was accusing was someone other than Minerva.

She remained consistently supportive, though, and that really seemed genuine. There were quite a lot of people he could accuse of dissembling, about which he'd be okay. Wilson, for instance. He certainly acted genuinely honest about a lot of things, but there was a "jerk" undercurrent there. If someone wanted to convince Oliver that Wilson was coordinating some kind of involved practical joke, he might believe it.

By morning, Ollie was just about ready to dismiss it as paranoia. He went to work, thought about the story, got home again, sat at the laptop, and started writing that romance for Minerva.

≈

≈

It was four in the morning and Athena was worried.

≈

≈

"Where's the rest of it?" Wilson asked.

"That's the whole thing."

"It was four in the morning and Athena was worried."

"Yes. I couldn't get any further. I don't think outlining is for me."

"I think you may be right."

They were in Wilson's apartment. TAWU was starting in another half an hour. Oliver's latest story was supposed to be workshopped, but he had a feeling Wilson wouldn't bother to share his ten-word sentence, however epic that sentence might be.

"Maybe I should have a look at your outline," Wilson said.

"No! No, that's... I mean, I'm not used to writing stuff that isn't meant to be read, but this isn't meant to be read."

Wilson nodded. "That might be why the outline exercise didn't work too well. Do you take notes? Ordinarily, when you write."

"No, I mostly just write."

"You don't write throwaway scenes or character sketches?"

"No. Am I supposed to be doing that? You never said."

Oliver got the sense that maybe he *was* supposed to be doing that.

The more time he spent talking to Wilson the more Oliver got the idea that he had a problem and Wilson was trying to fix that problem, and the problem had to do with Ollie's inability to finish things. He didn't think he had any such problem; it was only that he never gave himself more than a week.

Although, it was true that for the most part he stopped when he couldn't think of anything else to write, and *that* was going to be a problem. Stories should be finished, and one day he would have to figure out what that was like. It just seemed premature to call it a problem.

"Not necessarily," Wilson said. "Some people do that: full character sketches, backstory scenes that won't be going in the book, that sort of thing. I knew someone in school who had a whole index card system, and another who used to draw maps of her scenes. It's different for everyone. I tried it; it didn't really work for me either. I was just curious if you did it."

From the kitchen, Minerva asked, "What's she worried about?"

"Athena? I don't know," Oliver said.

"Has to be something."

She emerged with a bowl of cheese doodles and something that might have been hummus. She put it out for each TAWU, but Ollie had never tried it. He wasn't sure if he was the kind of person who liked hummus, but felt like this was not the time to find out.

She put the food on the coffee table in the middle of the room and sat on the couch.

"Well, sure, it's *something*," he agreed.

"I mean, you know she's worried. You said so. Was there a noise in the yard? Does she think her husband's cheating on her? Maybe she's late for work. Is there a lump in her breast?"

"Those are all good ideas," Oliver said. "But I don't know if they're right or not. I'm not even sure about the sentence I did write."

That one sentence had gone through several iterations in order to determine if there was a way to get it to initiate a second sentence, and from thence a third, but nothing helped. There was, *Athena was worried* and *It was four in the morning*, and *Athena, at four in the morning, was worried*.

One he nearly went with was *Four in the morning was when the worry got to Athena*, and that led to a partial sentence that he couldn't quite push through. It probed the idea that Athena got worried at four *every* morning, and this was a notable observation, but then Oliver couldn't figure out what was causing her to be worried at the same time of day, what even *could* do that. It would have to be something where the clock turning 4:00 actually triggered concern, and that was just odd. It seemed like something he shouldn't be getting into right off the bat. Like, a deep childhood trauma or something.

So he went back to *It was four in the morning and Athena was worried* and that felt like a really solid sentence.

He just didn't know what happened after that.

"That's crazy," Minerva said. "It's your story, go where you want with it."

"I know, but… she hasn't told me what she's worried about."

"Athena hasn't," Wilson said, for clarification.

"Right."

Wilson nodded. "I understand."

"I don't," Minerva said.

"It's his first female main character, and she's not talking to him right now," Wilson said. "It happens."

"So if you made the male character—"

"Otis," Oliver said.

"Otis! Perfect. If you made Otis the main character you'd have more?"

"Probably, yes. I don't really know."

Minerva got up from the couch, shaking her head as she walked away.

"Writers," she muttered under her breath.

"Well, I get it," Wilson said. "You may not be ready to work the point-of-view of someone who's that different from you. It's okay. It'll come with time. And outlining? That's something you need to figure out for yourself if it's right or not."

"I lost interest in the story before I even started writing."

"That could also be why you don't know what Athena's worried about. You just don't care."

$\sim$

Outlining ended up being the theme of the day. Nobody had a piece to work on for the TAWU meeting, so it became an open discussion that was a lot more interesting than the usual workshop breakdown. Oliver secretly preferred these kinds of meetings, because it meant he didn't have to come up with something nice to say about someone else's stuff. He even preferred it to the weeks when his own stories were getting dissected, because that was more nerve-wracking than anything.

Then Wilson gave a new letter—W—and they were about to break up, when Ivor brought up his piece from the prior week.

"I wanted to know what Oliver thought of it," Ivor said.

At that particular moment, Oliver was working on his thriller idea, which he was coupling with the letter W, because that letter seemed to make all the difference. Someday he would have to figure out why Wilson's prompts worked so well, hopefully before they ran out of letters.

He was thus unaware that he'd been spoken to, at first. W was for Weapon, and the weapon was a dangerous compound developed in a secret lab, and the hero—Orson—was going to have to face off with his arch enemy, a Russian spy-turned-mercenary-for-hire named…

"Ollie," Tandy said, snapping him out of it.

"Sorry," he said, "there was a…" *There was a crash landing, and there was a fight, and a last-minute switch…*

"What was the question?" Oliver asked.

"I wanted to know what you thought of *What's the Matter With Matteo*," Ivor said. "You recall, my story."

"Didn't I give notes? I thought I gave notes."

"You did, yes, but I got the sense that you were holding back."

Oliver looked around at the members of TAWU, not quite sure what was happening. The truth was, they all held back when a "just okay" story came from one of them. It was sort of an unspoken understanding, to be gentle with someone who couldn't do all that much better. They applauded incremental improvement.

Nobody ever really wanted honesty. And if they did, wanting it specifically from Oliver—rather than Wilson, or just about anyone else—didn't make any sense to him.

He looked at Wilson, who shrugged, and gave a little nod. *Go ahead*, he seemed to be saying.

"I thought it was pretty cliché," Ollie said.

There was a pause. People nodded, and waited for him to continue. He thought maybe part of the weirdness came from the fact that these people legitimately valued his opinion.

"Go on," Ivor said.

"I mean, it's obvious from the outset that this isn't... I have a problem with these kinds of stories, because I can't believe anyone would *really* be fooled."

"Do you mean cliché or trope?" Wilson asked.

"I don't even know. This is a certain kind of story, and Ivor is hitting all the plot points. Maybe that's the problem, or... not problem, that's the wrong word. Maybe the *difference* between a trope and a cliché is that a trope is a plot point, a cliché is hitting that plot point exactly when the reader is expecting it."

"Your issue is that you expected it," Ivor said.

"You telegraphed everything. Foreshadowing is great, but it can't be obvious. And when you're foreshadowing something that's not just a trope, but a trope that's going to manifest exactly when the reader expects it to just makes it that much harder to tolerate. Now you have a cliché that's being heralded in advance by *another* cliché, the 'obvious foreshadowing'."

"You make a lot of great points," Wilson said. "How can we tell a story that has been told a hundred times before, give readers who like that story what they want, and at the same time surprise them with something new? Is there a way to do that? What do you think, Oliver?"

"In the context of dream sequence stories?" Ollie asked.

"Just in general. You're becoming our expert on genre writing, and God only knows genre writing is stacked up with this kind of issue."

"Well..." Oliver's voice was drowned out by the WHUP-WHUP-WHUP sound of a helicopter.

It wasn't the kind of sound he expected to hear while sitting in a condo on the seventh floor of a building in the middle of a city.

Everyone in TAWU looked up, first, in the event the ceiling had either vanished or grown a particularly large ceiling fan in the past few seconds. Then Minerva ran from the kitchen.

"Holy crap, you guys, look!"

She pointed to, and then headed for, the windows facing Tenth Avenue.

There were five big bay windows with tastefully chosen curtains and shades, which were mostly closed at the moment to keep the midday sun from overheating the place. There was plenty of space for each of them to get a decent view of what was transpiring outside.

A helicopter was crashing, was the essence of it, but that simple explanation didn't come close to adequately capturing the experience of witnessing this happen. The rotor blades were incredibly loud at this point, because the chopper was essentially at eye level with them. Black smoke was gushing out of the top, and there was evidence of an impact on the side of it.

The tail of the helicopter appeared to be having a disagreement with the pilot, as it kept swinging about left and right, twice coming within feet of the windows, or so it seemed. Oliver thought there probably should have been a moment there when one of them realized their lives were in danger, but nobody said so and nobody moved.

Still, one bad twitch, and that tail would be aggressively joining TAWU's membership roster.

The helicopter continued in a downward direction, at roughly elevator speed, threatening to completely lose control and veer into the side of one of the buildings right up until it hit the ground. There, the rotors had a disagreement with a few of the trees, resulting in a new, different kind of horrible noise.

They didn't see the crash. The angle of their view of the street was such that the only way to get a better perspective was to open a window and look down, and nobody was willing to do that, perhaps out of fear that additional helicopters would be falling from the sky shortly.

"I don't know about you guys," Wilson said, "but I want to go see a helicopter crash up close."

They opted for the stairs. That just seemed like a logical choice given the circumstances, even though there was no problem with the power and the building hadn't been touched by the crash, so far as they knew. *Take the stairs in an emergency*: that was the rule. This certainly looked like an emergency.

The scene on the street was one of stunned silence, at least at first. There was the mangled crash of a helicopter sitting in the middle of the vertical park not far from the statue of a long-dead general and his horse. The stallion was up on hind legs, as if it too was alarmed by what just happened.

Smoke continued to billow from the top of the chopper, which was around where Oliver imagined the engine was probably located. The smoke smelled like motor oil, and also the odor a car gives off when it overheats. Every time the wind blew—which was often on Tenth Avenue—the smoke was forced down and the crash scene disappeared into it.

The damage to the park, immediately around the crash, was pretty bad. Trees had been chopped down, and dirt had been kicked up. Ollie began to wonder if the helicopter landed on anyone. It was, to this point, something that had only occurred in the abstract, despite his proximity to it. The sound of the rotors was real, and the smoke was definitely real, but it still felt like an especially vivid movie special effect.

But the next thing that would happen if this were a film was that the wreckage would explode, and that hadn't transpired. Everyone was expecting it to, though, because nobody was moving. Cars had all stopped in the street. Some hadn't moved since the crash, evidently, since they were covered in dirt. People came out of buildings on both sides, and the already-outside pedestrians were frozen in place. About the only thing all of them had decided to do—aside from not move—was to broadcast as much of this as they could on social media: cell phones were in almost everyone's hands.

Oliver could hear sirens in the distance, which served as an auditory reminder that someone was probably in trouble within the wreck.

It was Minerva, of all people, who decided to do something.

The members of TAWU—there were eight of them on this day —and Minerva had gotten as far as the stoop leading up to the building before spreading out on the sidewalk, where they joined the growing crowd of onlookers and amateur cell phone cine-matographers. Minnie didn't have her phone out. She was polling the bystanders.

"Did anyone see the pilot?" she was asking.

Nobody had, apparently.

"Someone should help him," she said, to Wilson, but loud

enough for everyone to think maybe she was either talking to or about them.

"He's probably... he probably didn't make it," Wilson said. "The fire department's on the way, hear the sirens?"

"That was a controlled landing, Wilson. He made it to the ground. If he's stuck, he'll suffocate before the trucks make it through the traffic."

"I don't know what you expect anyone to do. That thing's going to explode any second now."

"No it isn't."

"Minerva..."

They had a silent glare argument for a few seconds, and then she stepped away.

"Ollie, come with me," she said.

"What?"

"It'll be fine, come with me."

"I agree with Wilson," he said. "You should stay here."

"Fine, I'll go in myself."

Without any further preamble, Minerva took off her T-shirt. She had a bra on underneath, so it wasn't entirely scandalous, but it was still an extremely unexpected gesture. Then, holding the shirt up to her face, she dashed across the street and disappeared into the smoke.

"Dammit," Oliver said, because for whatever reason, her doing that meant he had to do it too. He would have to assess the soundness of this logic later, but all he knew in the moment was that as soon as Minnie ran in, he was going to have to do the same thing.

Wilson didn't, which was another thing Ollie would be reviewing later.

He took off his shirt and held it up to his face. According to the safety videos of his childhood, the shirt was supposed to be a towel and it was supposed to be wet, so he didn't know what good it was really going to do, but it had to be better than nothing.

The smoke burned his eyes, and the motor oil smell cut right through the shirt and stung his nose. His vision was thick with tears well before he reached the impact point in the middle of it all.

"Minerva!" he called out. That close to the crash, he couldn't see much more than a meter in any direction, which was fine for avoiding obstacles but not so good if he's looking for someone who's moving. He discovered a miraculously undamaged park bench, and a lot of bits of helicopter wreckage, but no girl.

"Over here!"

He headed for her voice.

"Be careful," she shouted. "There's debris all over the place."

"I noticed."

She'd found the cockpit. The ground had crushed the helicopter's nose. The pilot was inside, looking mostly undamaged, but not apparently conscious. Minerva was struggling to widen a tear in the hull to get to him. This meant using her shirt against the edge of the torn metal, so as not to cut her hands.

"Help me pull this open."

Using his shirt the same way, Oliver wrapped his fingers around the lip of the tear, and they pulled on a succession of three-counts.

"Thanks for coming," she said, between pulls.

"Sure."

"Hey, this is military, did you notice?"

He hadn't. He didn't know if he would recognize a military helicopter over a non-military one, and didn't really know how she could but that would have to be brought up later.

"It's not budging," he said.

"Keep trying."

"Is he even breathing?"

"He's breathing. Pull!"

They pulled some more. It wasn't working.

"Here," someone behind them said, "let me help."

The voice should have belonged to Wilson, because any reasonable person would expect Wilson to eventually throw in with his girlfriend on something like this, if only to save face. But it wasn't Wilson.

It was the giant bearded man from before.

"Oh, good," Minerva said. "Get over here."

"Stand aside," he growled, to both of them. They did so. Minerva handed him her shirt.

The man crouched down, fixed his hands against the breach in the hull, braced himself properly, and then pulled. The steel screamed, but surrendered.

"That's good!" Minnie said. She jumped through the breach and disappeared. The man pulled some more, and opened up a wider hole, in the meantime, which was useful a few seconds later.

Minvera's head popped out of the opening.

"A little help!" She said, pushing a semiconscious pilot through. She got the head and shoulders out, and then the large man had him by the collar. Ollie jumped in and helped, or tried to.

"I have him, sorcerer," the man who claimed to be Cant said.

"Why are you calling me that?"

He looked bewildered at the question.

"I can carry him out," he said, rather than answering. "You two, get out of this smoke. It isn't safe."

He was large enough to cradle the pilot like a child, and so obviously needed no assistance. Oliver decided to save his many additional questions for a time when he wasn't in the middle of permanently damaging his lungs.

"Minnie, he's clear, let's go," he said, through the hole.

"Find the door," she said. He couldn't see her; it sounded like she'd gone deeper into the helicopter.

"We have to get out of here."

Already, the large man and the pilot were out of view, and the sirens sounded very nearby.

"There might be someone else inside," she said, somewhat more distantly.

Dammit, he thought, before starting in on an uncontrollable coughing fit. He held the shirt up to his face. He'd been right; it didn't help at all. If anything, it made the smell of the burning motor oil something he could also taste.

Oliver felt his way around the side of the aircraft until he found one of the doors. While not fully on its side, the helicopter hadn't landed flat, and it was leaning in the direction of the door.

He worked his way back around to the front, then along the other side until he reached the opposite door. It was pointing toward the sky at a twenty-degree angle, but it could be opened.

He had his hand on the door, when it flew open from the inside.

"There you are," Minerva said.

"Anyone else in there?"

"Nobody breathing," she said, matter-of-factly. Ollie was pretty sure she was saying there were dead bodies inside and she was cool with that, which was alarming on many levels, but since he could barely see or breathe, he just added it to the list of issues requiring unpacking in the near future, and proceeded from there.

"Let's get out of this smoke," he said.

"Yeah. Take this."

She handed over a large backpack.

"What is it?" he asked.

"Help me out."

She took his hand and extricated herself from the craft, which was almost more effort than getting her into it in the first place, as she had the additional weight of a second bag on her back, and the angle of the doorway to the ground made it all that much more awkward.

"What are we doing with these bags?" he asked again.

"Grab yours, let's go find some air."

"Minnie…"

"I'm just saving their gear, I figure it's important. Come on, this thing's gonna blow any minute."

⁓

The helicopter never did blow up, which was equal parts good news and disappointing. In the real world, a large metal craft blowing up would likely create a number of projectiles, and that would be bad for everyone around it. It was good that it didn't do that, then.

Alternatively, it would have been pretty cool. Oliver would have enjoyed seeing it, from a safe distance.

What did happen was that fire trucks arrived and began hosing down the wreckage, the street got buttoned up by the police, and that was about all.

Oliver was told the pilot made it to an ambulance, which drove off before he and Minnie emerged from the smoke. He wanted to know more about the pilot and what could have caused the crash, but he suspected he'd have to wait for the news to uncover that information.

He also wanted to know what happened to the man who got the pilot *to* the ambulance, but nobody seemed to have that answer. Oliver talked to several people before heading back upstairs, and half of them didn't remember the man at all. The other half did, but couldn't say where he went.

"So who was that guy?" he asked Minerva, after they relocated to the condo and got a change of clothes. Ollie didn't have any clothing stored there, but he was essentially the same size as Wilson, so there were options. Wilson certainly had no objections, although that may have stemmed from some form of guilt for not having accompanied his own girlfriend into danger. It was hard to tell, because nobody was talking about it.

Oliver thought that was probably for the best. If there was going to be an argument about it—and how could there not be?—he'd rather not be there when it happened.

"I dunno, some rando," Minerva said with a shrug.

"You didn't know him?"

"No, didn't you?"

"No," Ollie said. He was pretty positive he didn't believe her, but had no idea how to go about challenging her.

"Thought you did. Huh. Well, cool for him, showing up like that. We weren't getting that hull cracked. Maybe he was an angel or something. That'd make a good story, wouldn't it? Big guy going around town, saving people."

Wilson came in with tea. They were in the living room, Ollie in borrowed clothes and still smelling like smoke, and Minerva in a bathrobe and wet hair, having taken a shower as soon as it was convenient to do so.

"Here you go," Wilson said, proffering Ollie a cup. "This should help your throat."

He handed a second cup to Minnie without comment. They shared a look that could have meant anything.

"For the record, I didn't even see the man, so I can't tell you if I knew him or not," Wilson said. "Hell of a day, though, huh? This thing'll probably be national news by morning."

"Probably," Oliver said. "I wonder what a military helicopter was even doing over the city?"

"Was it military?" Wilson asked.

"I think so, yeah."

Ollie looked at Minerva, who shrugged but didn't contribute.

"Hey, what happened to those bags?" he asked her.

"The what?"

"The backpacks. From the wreckage. Did you turn them over?"

Minerva appeared confused. She looked at Wilson, then back at Oliver.

"What bags?"

"The ones…" he laughed. "You know, the ones you went in and got from the middle of the helicopter."

"Sorry, Oliver, I don't know what you're talking about."

Minerva was either an extraordinarily good liar or she legitimately had no clue what he was talking about. He wondered if she hit her head at some point.

Maybe I hit my *head,* he thought. It was a slightly more likely explanation, because the man who might be Cant was beginning to make him question himself in the kind of way people question themselves before seeking psychiatric help. Or so he assumed.

Ollie was pretty positive Minerva knew the large man, and he was very, very positive she emerged from the smoke with two army-issue backpacks containing who-knows-what. That she was now pretending neither of those things were true could really only mean one thing: she was lying for some reason.

Since she was doing it in front of Wilson, he could only conclude she was hiding established facts from *him* specifically. If Oliver wanted to know why, he'd have to get her alone.

But that wasn't going to happen on this day.

"Oh hey," Minerva said, "you haven't forgotten, right?"

"Forgotten what?"

"Pallas! Two days, buddy, you better make it this time."

"Right," he said. "Haven't forgotten."

Although he had.

"Don't worry," he said, "I'll be here. Looking forward to it."

He wasn't, and he was pretty sure when the time came he still had every intention of ultimately bailing. Only now he thought he probably wasn't going to. It could be the only chance he had to get Minerva alone and find out why she was lying.

PART TWO

Palace

Chapter Seven

THE BEST-LAID SCHEMES O' MICE AND MEN

Oliver was never going to be the kind of person who liked going to clubs, but he thought he could probably figure out how to become that kind of person for at least one day. It was the sort of transformation he was just coming to appreciate, as an adult, in general.

When he was younger, he imagined he would grow into who he wanted to be, but that didn't really happen. Writing was a perfect example of this. He wanted to be a writer, but he didn't grow up and just become one, and that was disappointing. But it turned out nobody did. What appeared to work was acting as if he was a writer, until it was true.

This didn't seem like it could possibly be accurate, because the sole obvious defining characteristic of a writer would appear to be the writing itself, but more than one member of TAWU called themselves a writer, but failed to produce writing—until recently, Oliver included. He was pretty sure the only reason he began to actually write was that he managed to convince himself he was already a writer.

He had a suspicion that this was all being an adult was actually about: everyone pretending they were adults until they believed it themselves.

This translated into other aspects of his life as well. He was something akin to a shift supervisor at The Jittery Canary, which only meant that he had a key to the front door and was the person people spoke to when they asked to speak to the manager about something. (This never happened, but it could, and if it did, they would talk to him.) Everyone knew how to do things so he didn't have to tell people what to do, which was good since he had no barista training. Yet, sometimes he had to pretend he did have that training in order for things to go smoothly, and sometimes he had to speak firmly to customers or staff members for one reason or another. And he was able to do that because one day he decided supervisors had straight backs.

There was really no other way to describe it. He lowered his shoulders, which kept the tension from collecting in his neck, and he straightened his back. He made sure his voice stuck to a lower natural register, because he knew it tended to go up when he was nervous. It gave off the illusion of confidence when he was in no way confident, and people reacted to him as if he actually was. Soon, he had convinced himself. He had become the kind of person he thought he needed to be, by pretending he already was that person.

Now he needed to understand how to become a person who goes to a club, through some combination of posture, clothing, and… something else.

"Social engagement," he said to himself, in the bathroom mirror. "This is where you always fail."

The man in the mirror thought he was being a little harsh, but accurate. He was not one of those people, who naturally engaged with other people on an accepted relational level, and he was worried that if he pretended to be, the artifice would be self-evident.

It never worked before, basically. Those early attempts were when he was still in school, and trying to pass as, well, *one of the cool kids*, as cliché as that was. There were times back then when he felt like an alien sociologist attempting to understand human mating rituals, and everyone around him knew it.

The first problem was going to be clothing. He had a dress shirt, decent slacks, and a pair of loafers. Was he supposed to wear a tie? He didn't know. He thought maybe probably not, but he didn't *know*, and that was an early blow to the confidence he was trying to pretend to have. In the end, he chose two ties that went with the shirt—it was a white shirt, so all ties went with it—and shoved both of them in his pocket. He would determine whether or not to wear one based on how everyone else dressed.

Then he left the apartment. It was only two in the afternoon, so he was giving himself two hours to get to Minerva's condo. Since the trip took only forty minutes, he was going to end up being unfashionably early.

But not all that early. The train ride was eventful in the way that the subway could be on occasion, especially when it came to sharing the experience with other humans. Some people were just odd, basically, and there was no way around it.

Oliver ended up on a mostly-empty car. It was a Saturday. The worst commuter traffic for the rail system was always going to be clustered around weekdays, early morning and early evening, but the weekends had moments of high congestion too. It was only that the congestion was a lot harder to predict. The mostly-empty car, then, was a tiny surprise.

He spent half of the ride sitting at one end and examining an M Pallas poster for clues as to how his evening should be expected to go, and which tie would be best. The poster was unhelpful.

Three stops in, a man sat down in the chair opposite, and unlike Oliver elected to stare somewhere other than at a poster. He also didn't bother with a handheld electronic device, as 90% of the train's riders did. He stared at Oliver.

He was an older man, with salt-and-pepper hair and a square face. It looked like that face had experienced its share of scarring over his lifetime.

He looked angry, and that anger seemed to be directed at Oliver, for no good reason.

It was annoying enough that after two stops Ollie decided he'd better speak to the guy.

"I'm supposed to be going there," he said, pointing to the poster. "Never been. I'm pretty excited."

The man glared. Oliver wondered if maybe he didn't speak English.

"You? Ever been?"

"I bet you thought you'd never see me again," the man said. He did have a bit of an accent, but nothing that wouldn't go away if he concentrated on hiding it.

"I'm pretty sure that isn't true. I don't know you at all."

He lurched to his feet and grabbed the handrail nearest Oliver. Ollie was glad the car was only *mostly* empty.

"Next time, old friend, you will remember to make *sure* old Koestler is dead before you walk away, no?"

"I'm... look, I'm sorry, I don't have any idea what you're talking about."

He nodded.

"You do. And you will. We have much to learn, you and I."

Oliver was running the man's face through every memory he had, but didn't think there was a match. Clearly, the guy wasn't all there. The name Koestler sounded familiar, but he couldn't even tell if this man thought that was *his* name or if he was talking about someone else.

The train reached the next stop and the doors opened.

"Until next we meet," the old man said, and he stepped off the train and faded into the crowd on the subway landing.

"Well," Oliver said to himself, "let's not do that any time soon."

"Thank God you're here," Wilson said, on greeting Oliver. "She's beside herself."

"Why?"

"She was sure you weren't going to come. I had to talk her out of calling you five times, and in another half an hour I was going to send someone over to knock on your door."

Oliver laughed, but this was apparently not a joke.

"You don't even know where I live," he said.

"All right, in another forty minutes. I would have needed the ten to find out your address."

"I don't understand the big deal."

"I don't either," Wilson said. "But I've learned not to get in her way when she's like this. She's a killer."

"Ollie!" Minerva said, racing into the living room. She was in sweats, and Wilson was wearing pajama bottoms and a sleeveless tee. Oliver was clearly the only one ready to go, but then he wasn't even supposed to be there yet.

Minnie hugged him, and then stepped back.

"Is this how you're going?" she asked, rather neutrally.

"I have a tie. Two."

He pulled them out and held them up against his shirt for some feedback.

"No, no, no. Pallas isn't a bank. You look like you're going to work at a bank."

"It's a club, this is what I have for clubs."

She laughed.

"It's not a club, not really. I told you, it's something different. It's an experience."

"You know, when you say that, it doesn't mean anything. I don't know how to dress correctly for an experience."

"I would think there's no way to dress incorrectly for one," Wilson said.

"Right, see? What he said."

"You two are going to team up on me all night, aren't you?" Minnie said. "Don't worry, I expected this, and Wilson owns two of everything. You boys go get dressed."

~

"This can't be right," Oliver said, a half an hour later. He was staring at a version of himself in the mirror that didn't correspond to *clubbing* or *dancing* in any way with which he was familiar. It was something closer to *weekend warrior* if that weekend was in the mid-1980's.

"She told you it was themed, didn't she?" Wilson asked. "This is the theme right now. Don't forget the gloves."

The gloves were of the fingerless variety. They were army green, and matched the jacket. Underneath, he had a collarless black shirt that looked like it was raided from the closet of an emo kid. The pants were loose-fitting denim in the same green as the jacket and the gloves. On his feet: black combat boots.

"I don't know what this theme actually *is*," Oliver said. "I look like a military priest."

"Yeah, I don't know. Like I said, I'm just going along with whatever she says. Minerva's the social animal, not me."

Wilson's outfit was similar, in that it also appeared army-issued. The boots were the same, but the rest of him was in camo. He had no gloves, but he did have a canvas hat with a brim. It didn't appear to offer any protection unless they happened upon rain or a particularly harsh sun.

"Don't know how she expected me to know I was supposed to be dressing this way," Oliver said.

"Oh, she completely did not. She was curious to see what you did end up wearing, though."

They stepped back into the living room, and waited for

Minerva to emerge, which took another twenty minutes. It was worth the wait, but not for the expected reasons.

If Oliver were being completely honest, one of the only reasons he decided to actually show for this was because he thought there was a decent chance he'd get to see Minnie in a short dress and heels. That was how women who went to clubs dressed, after all. He's seen it often enough, just going around town on Friday nights.

She wasn't in heels, or in a dress. She also wasn't in anything army-issued, or, not issued by the modern American military version of an army.

"What is *that*?" Wilson asked. He could form words, which was nice. Oliver couldn't seem to.

"Do you like it?" she asked, doing a little turn.

"I do. What are you supposed to be?"

It was a costume dominated by brown leather and cloth, with some elasticity in the joints. It covered her whole body up to the neck, except for a peekaboo spot for cleavage that didn't serve any obvious utilitarian purpose, unless showing off cleavage could be argued to have a utility. It was pretty much form-fitting, with allowances for a tunic-like flap that covered her groin and backside. The material even extended to the wrists, and down two fingers. Only her thumb, ring finger and pinkie were showing.

She also had her hair up in a ponytail, which was a different look altogether.

"I was going for archer," she said. "One from those Japanese films you make me watch."

"Those costumes show more skin."

"I have a boob window, what more do you want?"

"I'm not answering that," Wilson said, wisely.

"I wanted it to be practical. Ollie, what do you think?"

"It's, ah… practical. Very practical."

She laughed.

"I can already tell that wasn't the first word to come to mind."

"It actually is. I hadn't been able to string any words together before that."

"Aww."

Minnie smacked Wilson on the arm.

"See?" she said. "That's how you give a girl a compliment. Thank you, Oliver."

"You're welcome. So, um, before we head off to see the wizard, or whatever, can you tell me why we're dressed like this? Wilson hasn't been helpful. He said it's your plan."

"It's kind of my plan. I had to do some research, follow a few leads, piece some things together. I'm pretty sure once this gets going it'll pick up its own momentum. We just have to start in the right place."

"That didn't at all answer my question."

"The clothing will make sense later, Ollie. I promise."

~

It wasn't even four in the afternoon when they got outside, and Oliver felt wildly out of place. Generally speaking, this part of town had a healthy combination of joggers, people in suits, shoppers and tourists. No army people. Not that he thought he looked anything like an army person, not really. He was too gangly.

Wilson was equally out of place in his full camouflage, but he looked entirely comfortable about it. Likewise, Minerva looked like embarrassment was a concept she'd never been introduced to, much in the same way she saw no issue with taking off her shirt and running around in her bra a couple of days earlier.

Due to some sort of civic miracle, the helicopter was completely gone. The spot where it landed was profoundly messed up—the grass was missing, the trees looked like they were on the verge of an early death, and the whole area still smelled of the fire-retardant foam the emergency crew used—but there was no trace of the wreckage itself.

Oliver ended up staring at the crash site. He did this on the way into the building too, for a lot longer. He was trying to line up his memory of the scene with the current view, but he couldn't get it right. It was as if the helicopter accident was a little less real for existing now only in his memory.

"Hey, let's go," Minnie said. "We got a lot to do."

"How long did it take to clear all that up?"

"Not long." She looked to Wilson for agreement. "Just overnight, pretty much."

"Pretty much," Wilson agreed.

"You guys act like stuff falls out of the sky all the time around here," Oliver said.

Minnie, who was several feet up the sidewalk at this point, circled back around and took Oliver by the elbow.

"Stuff doesn't fall out of the sky all the time," she said, leading him off the stoop as a way to convey, politely, that she would like him to please start walking now. "But that's not as interesting as the fact that we haven't seen *anything* in the sky since."

Oliver looked up and around so as to verify the absence of any flying somethings. Not even the birds on the cornice were around, although he got the impression that wasn't what she meant.

"I didn't notice," he said. "That's weird, huh?"

"It just means we have to get going," she said, cryptically.

"Why does it mean that?"

She didn't answer, but he had started walking so maybe she didn't feel like an answer was necessary.

Oliver looked at Wilson, who shrugged. He was not going to be providing translation services for his girlfriend on this particular outing.

"All right, well are we walking far? The train station's that way."

"Not taking the train," Minnie said. "Not right now. Come on, it's a beautiful day for a walk."

"Just go along with it," Wilson said.

It was hard to tell where they were actually going. Oliver had a decent idea of which direction they should be heading if the plan was to walk all the way to Pallas. He couldn't imagine it made any sense at all to actually *do* this, given the various modes of transportation available to them at more or less every corner, but so far he was just a passenger on this little trip, and not the driver.

The driver was Minerva. That was never really a question, although it probably should have been given the number of times he'd seen her act as a satellite in the orbit of planet Wilson. Maybe they took turns being in charge of things. Ollie never really had a long-term relationship that included cohabitation, so he couldn't say if this was normal or abnormal. He had parents, certainly, but they didn't agree on much of anything, so they were probably not a template he could use.

Minerva was the one, anyway, who took point on this bizarre expedition, with Ollie behind her and Wilson behind him. And so they went, single file, cosplaying soldiers (or something) in broad daylight on a sunny Saturday afternoon.

Interestingly, nobody much cared. The pedestrian foot traffic in the city was dense, and just got worse the closer one was to the hub, which was the direction in which they were heading, so they passed by, through and around a lot of people. Given their *unspecified military cosplay* costumes, then, Ollie expected more staring. But while there were double takes here and there, they mostly involved Minnie's boob window, not the group's fashion sense as a whole.

Another interesting thing was that given the pace Minerva

chose, they were in a hurry. Oliver couldn't imagine why that was.

He decided to take up this point with her at one of the crosswalks.

"Hey, are we late for something?" he asked.

Minnie looked over her shoulder at Wilson, and then to Ollie, as if she wasn't sure she should answer.

"Why do you ask?"

"Well we're practically running, and like you said, it's a nice day and I gotta think nothing's going to be starting at a nightclub before ten or eleven. So what's the rush?"

"It's going to start raining soon," she said. "We have things to do before that happens."

Oliver looked up at a cloudless sky.

"What kind of weather forecast are you working off of?" he asked.

"I told you, I studied a lot."

"And that's still not an answer. What were you studying?"

"Trust me."

"Well all right, so it's going to rain soon. But like I said, it's going to be hours before we can even get into the club and we could always take the subway if it starts raining. Or a bus, or a cab. Maybe a horse, if you have a thing about transportation that comes with a roof."

She shot him an aggravated look.

"We have a lot to do," she said, again, and then the light changed and they were walking again.

Oliver turned to Wilson. "Look," he said, "I know I agreed to go along, but this is getting weird."

I thought this was supposed to be fun, was what he thought but elected not to add.

"A couple of things came up since we invited you," Wilson said. "It's gotten more complicated."

"All right, but I mean, I don't need to go. I don't want to mess up your plans."

"Don't be ridiculous."

~

Oliver's familiarity with the urban sprawl of the city didn't extend much beyond the businesses and high-value residences that existed on the main thoroughfares, which radiated outward from the center of town. He knew that at any given time, on any one of those streets, he was only an extra turn or two away from entire neighborhoods, and those neighborhoods were a complex assortment of row houses, dormitories, fast food joints, liquor stores, and so on. He'd just never been in any of those neighborhoods.

So when Minnie took them past his mental map of the city, it was like he'd entered a new realm entirely; like a two-dimensional Flatland resident discovering 'up', maybe, or an astronaut coming across a parallel dimension.

Oliver wanted to ask where they were, and what they were doing there, but at this point it didn't seem like there was any good to come from such questions. Minerva was acting with the kind of single-mindedness one usually only saw in someone trying to deliver a kidney across town, and Wilson would only tell him to be patient and wait for things to start making sense, as they would soon, surely. Oliver was about ready to excuse himself entirely from the situation and go home, but he couldn't figure out how to do that politely, so he just kept on walking.

"Here we are," Minerva said.

The street they were on was called Mudd Lane, and it was two hard rights and a diagonal left from Dot Ave., the last street Oliver recognized. Each block brought slightly more dilapidated properties. It was as if distance from a central road could be measured in paint flecks and broken windows per square foot.

Minerva came to a stop about halfway down—literally down, as the street was built on a downhill slope. The buildings were three-story apartment houses in various shades of peeling brown and gray. Each one had a tiny yard behind a chain-link fence, with the lawn just large enough to give a dog a place to go and to raise the property values a tiny bit.

The latch on the fence gate she stopped at was a bent metal clothes hanger, crafted into a loop and significantly rusted. She lifted it, and pushed the gate open.

Once through the gate, they went up to the wooden porch. Minnie rang the doorbell for the top floor. The name on the mailbox was B J CODEKS. Oliver had never heard of anyone by that name, but that was not a surprise at this point.

Nobody answered the bell, so she rang again, and looked up and down the street expectantly. Ollie realized how quiet it had gotten, or maybe it was always this quiet on these residential side streets in the middle of the afternoon. They'd gone from high pedestrian traffic to none whatsoever, on a road with no on-street parking and lots of residents who were either all out for the day or were hiding indoors. It didn't feel temporarily unoccupied to him, though; it felt abandoned.

A man answered the second ring.

"Who's there?" he asked, through the intercom.

"It's us, Ben," Minerva said.

"He's here?"

"Buzz us in, Ben."

Ben didn't answer. Minnie looked at Wilson.

"Maybe you should go around back," she said. "Just in case."

"Good idea."

Wilson headed down the three steps from the porch and disappeared around the corner of the row house.

"Why is that a good idea?" Oliver asked. He had a dozen questions, but that was a good one to start with, he thought.

"In case Ben tries to go out that way," Minnie said, in a tone suggesting he should have thought of this himself.

Then the door buzzed, and the front door unlocked. A few seconds later, they were climbing a narrow, creaky wood staircase up to the third floor landing. The door to the apartment was ajar.

Minnie stared at it for a few seconds before pushing it open, slowly. Like everything else in the place, it creaked.

"Ben?" she called out.

"Back here."

The apartment layout was simple enough: a main entryway with a living room/dining room on the left and doors to what were probably bedrooms on the right. The voice came from neither of those places, but straight ahead and slightly left. That was the direction of the kitchen.

Ben was an old man. Oliver had no real expectations about who they were going to see, but even then, *old man* wasn't one of them. He was a square-set, shortish guy with hair going blond-to-white and losing to a receding hairline. He looked like someone who used to be athletic, but that athleticism took place in black-and-white. He did *not* look like someone who went to a nightclub.

Ollie was expecting to run into another person in an exotic costume. What he got was someone who looked like he was late for dialysis.

He was eating a turkey sandwich at his kitchen counter. They had evidently interrupted an early dinner.

"Is this him?" Ben asked, adding, "Where's the other one?"

"Wilson's around back," Minnie said.

"Hah! You thought I was gonna rabbit on you."

"It crossed my mind, yes."

"Well, girlie, it crossed my mind too. I don't like how this story ends."

"I understand."

I don't, Oliver thought.

"Let me get my things," he said. He put down the other half of the turkey sandwich and disappeared into another room.

"Is he coming?" Oliver asked.

"We can't get into Pallas without his help."

"So he's coming."

"I didn't say that."

"I thought you guys had been to this club before?"

"We've been *to* it. We've never made it in."

"So, he's getting us a VIP pass or something?"

"Sort of. He's taking a long time."

She exited the room before Oliver had a chance to get another question in, like why an old man living in a crappy neighborhood in a crappy part of town had VIP passes to the hottest place in the city.

Instead, he stood alone for a few minutes, staring at the turkey sandwich and wondering if he should let Wilson in through the back door, which was in the far corner of the kitchen. He decided not to, because maybe he wasn't supposed to *do* anything at all. That was the consistent message he'd been getting to this point: go along for the ride, don't ask questions, don't do anything else, it will all make sense later.

What he kind of wanted to do was have a bite of the sandwich. He wasn't hungry, and it was the plainest sandwich he'd probably ever seen—white bread, one slice of turkey, perhaps some mayonnaise but it was hard to tell—yet he was filled with the weird urge to find out how it tasted.

"Ollie," Minerva called from the front room.

"Are we ready?" he asked.

He left the kitchen and headed for the front door, where Ben and Minnie were already waiting.

Or, they were doing something other than waiting. It was true that they couldn't proceed without him showing up, but the nature of the dynamic was very different than anticipated.

More specifically, Ben had a gun in his hand, and he was pointing the gun at Minnie's head.

"What's going on?" Oliver asked, his voice coming in a little higher than he wanted it to. He remembered the lesson he'd learned in the coffee shop about speaking in a lower vocal register to sound confident, and wondered if that worked in hostage situations too.

"Is that real?" he asked.

"Sure it's real," Ben said. "Now you two are gonna drive me out of here. And don't do anything funny."

Chapter Eight

'TWAS BRILLIG

"Don't do anything funny?" Minnie repeated. "That's what you're going with?"

"I'm ad-libbing here," Ben said.

"Minnie," Oliver said, "Maybe don't heckle the guy with the gun."

"I know, but it's just so cliché. *You* know that."

Ben pressed the gun against the back of her head. He wasn't exactly holding her by the neck or anything, he just had the gun out, while she stood a foot in front of him with her arms raised.

"I'm doing the best I can," the old man said. "I'm on the clock here."

Oliver laughed.

"Oh, this is, like, part of your cosplay thing, isn't it?" he said to Minnie.

In response, Ben fired the gun into the ceiling. This deafened everyone for a few seconds and showered Minerva and Ben in plaster.

"Jesus, Ben," Minerva said.

Ben looked at Oliver, who was no longer laughing.

"Real gun, real hostage situation, son," he said. "Now let's get moving."

"But we walked here," Oliver said.

"What's your point?"

"You said we had to drive you out of here. I mean, it's not like there's even anyone holding you in this place, you don't need our help, but even if you did we walked. We didn't drive."

Ben used his free hand to dig a set of keys from his pocket. He tossed them to Ollie.

"I got something around back we can use. Let's go."

~

They went around the same side of the building Wilson was last seen negotiating, so Oliver fully expected to run into him, resulting in some manner of comic or tragic turn of events, depending on how he reacted to the gun. But Wilson wasn't there, not even on the back porch where one might expect to find someone who was supposed to be covering the rear exit.

What was there, under a tarp in the only parking space the apartment building had, was a box truck. It looked a little like an old ambulance, one that had been retired a long time ago.

That was exactly what it was. It even had the dome lights. They were covered in a layer of dust, but they were up there.

"I'm gonna go 'round the back with the lady, while you get behind the wheel. You know how to drive?"

"Yes. Never driven anything this big before though."

It had been years since Oliver'd driven anything of any size, and never before in the city, but he had a feeling that wouldn't matter. He'd still end up behind the wheel.

"It handles like a big car, just use the mirrors."

Ben walked Minerva into the back doors and past the two crash carts still taking up space in the rear, then sat her down in the passenger seat. Oliver started the engine. It jumped to life immediately, which was a little surprising. The truck wouldn't have been out of place in a junkyard.

"All right, where am I going?" Oliver asked.

"Don't know for sure," Ben said.

"How can you not know? This was your idea."

"Only sort of. Here."

Ben handed a piece of paper over to Minerva, who examined it carefully. It looked to Oliver like a hand-drawn map, one with no clear orientation.

"Not sure if I recognize this part of the city," she said, holding it up for Oliver. "You?"

There was a long oval-shaped road bisected—the long way—by a straight line, with shorter horizontal streets crossing the left and right parts of the oval.

A large X was marked near the top of the lower left quadrant and a smaller check-mark in the far, upper right, on the outside of the oval's curve.

It was problematic for a great many reasons, one being that the X in the bottom half of the left side of the center line could just as easily be an X in the top half of the right side of the center line, because there was no telling which direction one was supposed to hold the map. It also had no scale to it. It didn't even really look like a street map.

"This looks like instructions for how to dissect a watermelon," Oliver said.

"You gotta go to the X," Ben said, his gun still steady on Minerva.

"Which one? There are two."

"The big one, champ."

"All right," Oliver said. "But I'm going to point out again that we don't know where the X is. And it sounds like you don't either."

"It's all I got."

"What's *at* the X?"

"Won't know 'til we get there."

"Just drive," Minerva said. "Like, around. Just drive around. Maybe we'll spot something he recognizes. Does that work, Ben?"

"Sure, fine. Something I recognize."

Oliver put the ambulance in gear and wondered what he would do if they drove past a cop.

None of this made even a little bit of sense. Minerva's considerable calm while having a gun pointed at the back of her head left Ollie with the impression she was collaborating with Ben in some way, but he couldn't see any angle where this would be to anybody's advantage. The presence of a real, live firearm emphasized the point that if there was some kind of performance going on, it was a scary performance he wanted nothing to do with. It also raised the stakes. It was no longer a situation that was quirky and indie film weird. There were actual consequences. He didn't know what most of those consequences probably were, but at least one of them involved somebody getting shot.

It was simultaneously unreal, and too real. And, it was a lot more serious than pretending two army knapsacks didn't exist, or prank calling his cell phone. Whatever Minerva was involved in, it was definitely not anything he wanted a part of.

Oliver put the ambulance into gear and stepped on the gas. They jerked forward quickly, because he wasn't quite used to the pedal's sensitivity.

"Hey," Minerva said, over her shoulder. "Can you at least put the gun down? I don't like the idea of losing my head because of your bad knees and his bad driving."

"Okay," Ben said. Oliver couldn't see him doing it, but he assumed he had.

"You know I didn't want to do this," he added.

"I know."

"Then why is he doing it?" Ollie asked her, under his breath.

Minnie reached out and put her hand on his shoulder, rubbing it gently. It was about the only safe human contact they could engage in while sitting on opposite sides of the ambulance he happened to be navigating.

"I can't explain," she said. "But thanks, you really came through."

He got the ambulance on the street and turned left, heading downhill and away from the center of town. He was putting fewer pedestrians at risk this way.

"What was I supposed to do?" Ollie asked. "You were in danger, I couldn't just—"

"Leave? Run out the back door? Think maybe you could call the cops and have them rescue me?"

"I couldn't do that. What would that make me?"

"It would make you Wilson, probably. That's something he'd do."

He took his eyes off the road long enough to see if she was being serious.

"Nah, come on, he wouldn't do that," he said.

"Sure he would. Then he'd castigate me for being upset that he did the smart thing. Assuming I survived, I mean."

"Well. I think you're worth the risk of getting shot. I can't believe he wouldn't feel the same way if he were in this situation."

Minerva gave him one of her really special smiles, and he nearly drove off the road.

"You two are cute," Ben said.

"Thank you, scary kidnapper," Oliver said.

Minnie laughed, and blushed a little.

They'd driven about three blocks. Oliver really didn't know where he was or where he was going, and was not having any more luck pairing Ben's odd map with any city designs lodged in his memory now that he was navigating. So far, though, he hadn't committed any acts of vehicular violence, so it was a net positive.

"Hey, maybe it's in one of the parks," Ollie said.

"That's good thinking," Minnie said. The city had a half-dozen open grassy areas, not including the ball field.

"That oval could be a footpath. Where's the nearest field? Am I going the right way?"

Oliver narrowly missed a pedestrian who thought a yellow light was something he could be in the street for. The guy said something unkind as they passed, which he probably wouldn't have done if they looked a little more like an ambulance. But, the white paint on the outside of the vehicle was more of a tan-and-rust color, and the signage had been painted over.

""I think so," Minnie said. "Keep heading this way."

"All right. So, um, how'd you two meet?"

"I volunteer at the elderly center sometimes."

"Do you? I didn't know that."

"Gotta keep busy somehow. It's good stuff. Makes me feel better as a person and all that. But anyway, Ben introduced himself and I realized he was going to be important today."

"I don't understand that at all."

"Like I said, we never made it into Pallas before. When you meet a guy named Ben Kodeks, you figure he's going to have something for you."

"Honestly, Minnie, you aren't making any sense. Is there… is there like some kind of scavenger hunt involved? It's just a club."

"It's not just a club. And look, I was right. He gave us this map."

"To… something. We don't know what."

"We'll figure it out."

Traffic ahead of them was starting to show signs of congestion ahead. The taillights were coming on more frequently, and Oliver had to devote more time to braking. He was wondering about committing to another random turn to see if he could get away from it, but that would have required getting out of the lane he was in, and he had cars on both sides. So, he kept piloting them straight ahead, and hoped it would lead them to a park eventually.

"All right so you think the map is important because it can help us get into Pallas. I'm going to let that go even though it doesn't make any more sense when I say it than it did when you said it. Where'd the map come from?"

He looked in the rear mirror at Ben.

"Did you draw it?" he asked.

"I copied it."

"Where's the original?"

"Lemme restate. I copied it from memory. I looked at the original a long time ago."

"And you don't know what it's for?"

"I kinda do. I know it's for treasure. Not like pirate treasure, like, some other kind of treasure."

Ollie rubbed his face. "None of this makes sense, guys," he said, to both of them.

"It's starting to rain," Minnie said, tilting her head to look up out the windshield. "Told you."

The perfectly blue sky had indeed given way to a heavy cloud bank that appeared to have manifested out of nothing in the past ten minutes.

"Is rain bad?" Ben asked.

"Yeah, rain's bad. Rain's really bad."

"*Why?*" Oliver asked. "Why is rain bad, it's just rain? Are you a witch? Are you going to melt? What's so terrible about rain?"

"In this rain, I might, yeah."

Then the sky opened up.

Water came down in heavy sheets, like a tropical event that belonged in a warmer place closer to the equator. Or a monsoon in India. The wind, though not all that powerful, was enough to push some of the water into ropy waves. The ambulance was filled with the sound of drops pummeling the metal roof.

Oliver kicked the windshield wipers up to the fastest available speed, but the deluge between swipes was so significant he still couldn't see.

"We're going to end up in an accident," he said, with a relative calm that belied the circumstance. Sure, there was a man of questionable health and sanity riding behind him with a loaded handgun, but the real threat at this moment was the rain coupled with the forward motion of the vehicle Ollie was trying to steer.

"Hang on," Minerva said. She was examining the middle of the dashboard, above the radio. "Here, this will help."

She flipped a couple of switches.

"What did you do?" he asked. Nothing appeared to be any different.

"The dome lights should be on now," she said. "And the siren. Assuming they work."

"I can't hear the siren."

"I can," Ben said. "Rain's drowning it, but it's there."

Oliver caught the red flash of the ambulance light in the window of a store.

"Okay, it's working," he said.

Cars ahead of him were making efforts to get out of their way too, which was all good, except they weren't actually an ambulance on their way to an emergency. This was the sort of thing that landed people in jail.

"Great, I have a clear path to get to nowhere in particular."

"Just keep going," Minnie said.

The worst of the deluge only lasted about two minutes, before the storm settled into a heavy, but not blinding, downpour. They were still riding with the lights and sirens, but it was getting a lot harder for the cars ahead of them to get out of the way.

Oliver realized he knew where they were: he'd managed to connect them with Dot Ave. Better, the intersection ahead of them was with another major street. Dot Ave. didn't follow a straight path all the way out of the downtown area. It snaked and curled in several spots. One of those spots linked it up to Common Ave., with which Oliver was extremely familiar.

If he was right, and that was the intersection they were about to get through, he thought he could probably drive them all the way to M Pallas. He knew the way.

It was a nice idea. The problem was that Common Ave. appeared to have been converted into a parking lot. None of the cars on the street were moving, and so none of the cars on Dot were moving either. It made the siren and the dome lights useless.

"Something's going on," he said.

"It's just the rain," Minnie said. "Visibility and all. It'll start moving."

Then there was a godawful sound. Considering Oliver could hardly hear the siren coming from the roof directly over his head, the noise he *could* hear—from apparently a great distance—must have been incredibly loud. It was a metal-on-metal grinding sort of noise. It sounded like someone tried to drive a cement mixer under a steel bridge with insufficient clearance, only this lasted about ten seconds too long to be that.

"Well *that* wasn't the rain," Oliver said.

"Turn us around," Minnie said, with some urgency in her voice.

People on Common Ave. were getting out of their cars and running down the street, all in the same direction: away from the center of the city.

"Yeah, maybe I better."

"No," Ben said, "you have to keep going."

"To where?" Oliver asked. "The road is blocked. Look. People are abandoning their cars."

The running people kept looking over their shoulders, as if they were being chased. Maybe they were. Maybe whatever made that noise was barreling down Common, and Oliver couldn't see it because there were too many buildings in the way. He couldn't imagine anything happening in a modern city that would foster a reaction like that, not unless that modern city was Tokyo and this was a Godzilla movie. A building collapse might do it, except that wasn't typically the sort of thing that chased people.

"You have to keep going," Ben insisted, again. To underline this, he held the gun up to Minerva's head again.

"Ben," she said, "be reasonable, you don't even know where we're meant to go. Maybe it's behind us?"

"No, this is the right direction. You have to go that way."

"How?" Ollie asked. "We can't fly."

"You start driving or I will shoot her! I will…"

He trailed off and lowered the gun, not out of some sudden rediscovery of basic common sense, but because something really wrong was happening in his chest. He grabbed his heart, gasped, dropped the gun, and fell down backwards. As he was already on the edge of one of the crash carts, he had a soft landing.

"*Ben!*" Minerva cried, jumping out of the seat to help.

"Is he all right?" Ollie asked.

"Pull over!"

"There's nowhere to pull over to."

"Then just put it in park and help me!"

He did, and climbed in back. Ben was convulsing, his hand still squeezing his chest. He was turning purple.

"Get him on the floor," she said. "Do you know CPR?"

"No."

"All right, I do, sort of."

Oliver helped her get Ben on the floor, which didn't make a lot of sense—he was on an emergency gurney already—until Minnie straddled him and began chest compressions that would have been harder to do on the cart.

"Can I do anything?" he asked.

"Check the cabinets, see if there's anything we can use," she said.

"Like what? You think they forgot to clear the medical supplies before this thing was junked?"

"Just look."

Minerva was counting out beats and pausing to listen to Ben's breathing, so Oliver figured this wasn't the best time to have an extended conversation. But he had so many more questions.

Meanwhile, outside, more and more people who were nice and dry inside of their cars were electing to hop out and run, from something he couldn't see. Considering how hard it was raining, whatever was coming had to be pretty bad.

"Maybe it's a volcano," Oliver said.

"What?"

"What they're running from. A volcano sprung up downtown and they're running away from the lava."

"Oliver, I really need you to focus on what's in front of you right now, all right? Did you find anything we can use to help Ben?"

"No, the cabinets are empty. No defibrillator or needles full of adrenaline. I can see if the radio works, but I don't think it'll help. Oh, hang on."

There was a foot-locker-like box on the floor behind the passenger seat. He flipped it open, and discovered two black bags that looked very familiar.

"What do you got?" Minerva asked, without looking.

They were the bags she pulled from the helicopter two days earlier, and then pretended didn't exist. He was sure of it.

She glanced over and saw what was in his hands.

"Oh good, we'll need those."

"I know where they came from, but what are they?"

And why did you lie about them? he thought.

Ben gasped, and his eyes popped open.

"Ben?" Minnie said. "Are you okay?"

"You two..." he rasped. It was hard to hear him, between the rain and the siren. Ollie dropped the bags he was holding and edged closer.

"You two make a cute couple," the old man said.

"Aw stop," Minnie said, clutching his hand tightly.

"You find my treasure. Find it or…"

His lips kept moving, but the words weren't coming out, and then the lips stopped and so did his breathing.

"Ben? *Ben?*"

She jumped back into chest compressions, but they both knew it wasn't going to matter.

"I think he's gone," he said.

She tried for another ten seconds anyway, before giving up.

"Dammit."

She wiped the sweat from her forehead and sat back against the wall. Oliver wondered if he was supposed to do something. Ben's eyes were closed already, so he couldn't do that, and that was the extent of the knowledge he had gleaned from televised entertainment.

"Ever seen someone die before?" Minnie asked.

"I don't think I have, no."

"That's the sort of thing you'd remember, if you had."

"Have you?"

"Yeah. Couple of times. Elderly center, they'd lose a few now and then. It's where I learned CPR."

She was lost in a thought for a couple of seconds. It didn't look like something to interrupt.

It was interrupted, nonetheless. The weird metal-against-metal sound returned.

"That was closer, wasn't it?" she asked.

"It was. But maybe it's just quieter. The rain's easing."

"Check out front, is there room to move?"

He did. The entire intersection had gone from a metaphorical parking lot to an actual one. All the cars looked abandoned.

They were also sandwiched on both sides and in back. The

only clear path was the lane on the opposite side of Dot, but he'd have to drive over three cars to get to it, and ambulances weren't built for that sort of thing.

"If we're going anywhere," he said, "it won't be in this."

To underscore the point, he flipped off the dome lights and the siren.

"I guess it's time, then," she said. "Let's open those bags."

"What the hell is this stuff?" Oliver asked.

He was holding what looked like a virtual reality headset, attached to a helmet that was probably bullet-proof. It looked expensive. It also looked like a prop from a sci-fi movie.

"The visor will help with the rain," Minerva said.

She had set aside her helmet and was busy slipping on some kind of light armor based on the design of football shoulder pads. The armor went all the way down her arm, though. She strapped it on and then bent her arms carefully to make sure she could. The armor's joint lined up nicely with her elbow.

"How will it help? How will… Minnie, will you *please* just explain all of this?"

A third roar sounded.

Oliver decided that was what he was hearing: a roar. It made no rational sense at all, because there wasn't anything on Earth that made a vocalization like that outside of a special effects studio, so surely it was a mechanized sound. But until he saw what was making it, he was going to think of it as a roar.

"Put on the gear, we have to get moving."

"No. Explain first."

"All right, Oliver," she said. "This is high tech military gear, we're going to be wearing it when we leave the ambulance, and we're leaving the ambulance very, very soon, so you need to pick up the pace."

"That's not an explanation."

She put on her helmet, and hit a button on the side, near the ear. The front of the goggles turned violet.

"This is how it will help with the rain. Is *that* a good enough explanation?"

"No! How do you know this?"

"Oliver, I swear to God, if you don't start getting dressed right now, I'm going to shoot you."

Ben's gun was on the floor next to his foot, but she wasn't threatening him with that. She had her hand in the bag.

Apparently there was some kind of weapon in there too.

"All right."

Oliver slipped the armor on over his head, as she had. The arms each had a loop for the thumb, and straps around the wrist and up the arm. When he flexed, it felt like a tailored fit.

The chest armor hung loosely, but there were straps under the armpits to fix it in place. He did so, as Minerva—who was already fitted—watched.

He slid on his helmet, and the world got quiet.

"Can you hear me?" Minerva asked, through a microphone. It sounded as if the speaker was buried in his skull somewhere. He nodded.

"You can talk," she said.

"I can hear you."

"Good. Hit the button on the left of your helmet. There's only one."

He did so. It added some clarity to the back of the ambulance, but that was about all.

"It will help with visibility in the rain," she said.

"Fine. What are we even doing? I assume we're not going to Pallas at this point. Should we find Wilson?"

"Of course we're still going. Just follow my lead, okay? Now…"

She reached into the bag and pulled out a smaller backpack with a long rod sticking out of it. The end of the rod was attached to a rubber tube that met up with some kind of aperture under the pack.

"This goes on your back."

"Is that a gun?" he asked.

"It's a kind of gun."

"Minnie, who are we shooting at?"

Another roar. Maybe, he thought, it was a dinosaur made out of used clock parts. Or a sentient iron trebuchet.

"Won't know until we see it."

"Well I'm not shooting anybody, that's for sure."

She sighed, and pulled open the pack surrounding her gun.

"Pay attention. This is a second generation ion cannon. It shoots energized pulses of coherent light. Looks like a big fat bullet. It releases a lot of energy on impact, but you can adjust *how much* energy right here, on the barrel. See the knob? You want to break a window, set it to low. You want to take down the building the window is in, set it to high. It uses a zero-energy recursive self-charge battery system, so it can pretty much keep on going forever, but if you fire close to high more than two or three times, you're gonna lose about ten minutes to the recharge. Try and keep it in the middle-to-low region if you can, and probably don't ever turn it all the way to full. It might rupture the battery, and that would be very bad."

She closed it up, and slipped it on her back. "Goes on like this, see? You should be able to reach over your head and grab the barrel, like this. You're right-handed, right?"

"Minnie, I—"

"Yeah, you are. I remember. It should be fitted and calibrated, so just put it on. The on-switch for the cannon is next to the frequency knob."

She pushed the button on her cannon and a green light traveled from the back to the front, blinked twice, then settled into a gentle yellow.

"And you're good."

"Minnie, what the hell."

"What?"

"This is ridiculous. These aren't real. This isn't something that's been invented. You just made all of that up."

"Well I had to make it up, but that doesn't mean it's not real."

"That makes no sense!"

"Are you going to put it on or not? We have to go. Those things are getting closer."

"What things? What things? What the... NONE OF THIS MAKES SENSE! Who are we shooting? What is making that noise? Where did these cannons come from?"

She held up a hand to calm him a little. It didn't work.

"All right, all right. I can see you're getting upset. The problem is I do not have time for you to *be* upset right now, so..."

"Minnie!"

"Right. Fine. Listen carefully, because I'm only explaining this once. The reason I don't know what's coming is because you never got around to *actually describing it*, so we're gonna have to wait and see what it looks like together. I asked you what the aliens looked like, remember? And you didn't know. Now I know you're confused, and I do not care. I'm going to go out the back of this ambulance into this vinegar-smelling acid rain, which, for whatever reason, you *did* describe in detail, and I'm going to shoot some things. Why? Because that's what happens next, that's why. And you're coming with me, soldier, because we're a team and right now I outrank you. Is that perfectly clear?"

She opened the back door without waiting for a response, and jumped down to the rainy street.

Chapter Nine

THERE GOES THE NEIGHBORHOOD

They were running.

Oliver couldn't remember ever being all that athletic in general, or a good runner in particular, but he wasn't having any trouble keeping up, which either meant that he was better than he thought he was, or that Minerva was equally unathletic.

She was the only person he could measure his progress against, since from the moment he exited the ambulance to the several minutes that had since elapsed, they encountered no other people. On the one hand, this was the expected end-state when everyone on the street elects to evacuate, but on the other hand there was a huge difference between *all the drivers fleeing on foot* and *no other living soul anywhere*. Even with the best civic evacuation plan imaginable, there was bound to be a straggler or two, and yet they'd not seen one. Also, nobody was inside any of the stores they ran past, or at the windows of the office buildings, or the residences.

They weren't all hiding, he decided. And they hadn't all fled. They were missing.

This was just one absurd detail in a series. The rain was,

indeed, faintly vinegary. It made Oliver both question his sanity and crave cabbage. Rain such as this had never—to his knowledge —existed in the real world. Its only appearance was in an unfinished story he wrote. Likewise, the impossible weapon on his back and the impossible tech built into his impossible helmet only existed in that story.

If he were dreaming, fine, great, he could live with that. But this wasn't a dream.

"Hold on," Minerva said. It was effectively an order, so he took it that way and slowed to a stop.

"What's wrong?" he asked, although there was so, so much wrong.

She turned around slowly, scanning the road behind them. The ambulance was still in sight, as they had run straight down the middle of Dot Ave., between the cars. Oliver didn't care where they were running, and Minnie perhaps didn't know. It was all absurd anyway.

"Something's coming. Get down."

She ducked down and put her hand on the butt of her cannon. He was wearing his, but at this moment, preparing to actually use it was a step too far. Oliver could tolerate the emptying of the streets and the impossible rain, but the minute the pulse cannon on his back turned out to be a real weapon was going to be a point of no return.

Unless the aliens turned out to be that point.

"What is it?" he asked.

"I don't know, just get down. Something."

Whatever instinct she was relying on worked pretty well, as something was indeed coming. A yellow light reflected off the glass facades of the buildings at the corner of Dot and Common, an indication that a vehicle of some sort was making its way down Common. The problem was that the traffic on the street was so utterly gridlocked, it was simply not possible for anything to be moving rapidly in that direction. Unless, of course, that thing was flying through the air.

"This is a prank, isn't it?" Oliver said, his voice almost at a whisper. The first time he tried speaking to her through the comms when they were outside, he shouted, which she did not at all appreciate.

"What? Is what a prank?"

"I don't know what else this could be. All I do know is this can't really be happening."

"Well Oliver, I don't know what to tell you. Maybe one of the aliens can explain it. Soon as we see one, we'll ask. Now shut up."

The source of illumination was a ball of light, or what was presumed to be a ball at the core. It was too bright to look at directly, so it could have been a square or a triangle in there. Even the visor with the special filter didn't help.

The technology on display was clearly advanced. As he watched, the light came to a standstill several feet above the intersection, froze there for several seconds, and then headed down Dot.

Oliver held his breath and froze, as the object passed a few yards from their position and down the street, where it disappeared around the bend in the road.

"Did it see us?" he asked.

"No idea. Not sticking around to find out. Let's go."

"Where?"

She looked down at the inside of her wrist. There was apparently some kind of portable computer on a wristband, although from his perspective it just looked like clear black plastic. She pushed a spot on the band, then sort of stared into the middle distance for a second or two.

"Rendezvous point," she said, pointing. "Two klicks that way."

"Who are we even meeting? I thought we were looking for Ben's treasure."

"I don't know who we're meeting; we'll find out when we get there. Can you run or do I have to carry you?"

"I can run."

They ran. He had many, many questions, but it was becoming obvious that Minerva either didn't know or wasn't willing to provide any answers. And once he accustomed himself to the idea that as much as none of this could possibly be happening, it *was*, he started to see the things the way she did.

For one thing, the little ball of light—a probe, clearly—was silent. It wasn't what had been making the metallic grinding noise earlier, and it wasn't what everyone had been running from. They had not yet encountered the thing responsible for the noise, but the longer they stayed near the intersection of Dot and Common, the more likely it was they would. And it didn't sound at all like something they wanted to meet.

Running, then, made a lot of sense.

"The military copter," he said, after they'd gotten a few blocks.

"What?"

"It's what I… it's what was in the story. They took out the aerial defenses first. This is what you meant, that nothing in the sky was a bad sign."

"You're catching up."

"And you knew it was going to rain."

She stopped.

"Get your head in this," she said. "We're losing the sun, switch to night vision and pop your headlight."

"What?"

She hit a button on the side of her helmet, and turned on the light attached to the front of her armor. He mirrored her actions, and discovered that for some reason it all felt familiar, like he knew which buttons to hit and switches to throw.

Oliver looked at the panel on his own wristband. The plain black plastic didn't look like plain black plastic through his visor; it looked like a keypad and a series of command buttons. Without thinking, he started punching buttons, and a second later a 3-D map of the city was overlaid atop the actual city as he saw it through the visor. There was a flashing beacon some distance away, with the path leading to it traced out in red. It was the rendezvous point.

I don't know how I did that, he thought.

"We good?" Minerva asked.

"We're good, let's move."

~

After hitting the same intersection the probe had disappeared around, they cut left and into the neighborhoods again. This time, Ollie felt none of the confusion he experienced when piloting the ambulance down the same streets, because he had a map in front of him and because it felt like he had a much clearer grasp of the city layout now. He was pretty sure he knew where they were going, and what the beacon represented. He still didn't know who they were going to find when they got there, but as Minnie said, that was something they could worry about once they'd arrived.

The neighborhoods were jammed with row houses behind chain-link fences. Nobody was on the streets, and if the people were inside—it really felt like there wasn't—it was behind drawn shades. They encountered more cars, abandoned in the middle of the road only without congestion. That was curious. He could understand if someone got out of a car and ran if there was no place to drive and there was something they needed to escape on its way. This was different. It was like everyone in town had engine trouble at the same time.

"Where are all the people?" he asked.

"Gone."

"Yeah, I see that. The city's abandoned, where did they go? Were they taken? Is this an abduction scenario?"

"You tell me."

"No, I really don't know. They're not hiding."

"I don't think they are, no," she said. "I have a theory, but you won't like it."

"Tell me anyway."

"I think… hang on."

Minvera stopped. They'd been running for about fifteen minutes, which was longer than Oliver could remember ever running at one time in his entire life. He didn't feel winded. It was surreal.

"What is it?" he asked.

"Heard something."

They were standing in the center of the street in the middle of a block of low-rent housing in a neighborhood that sat halfway between Dot Ave. and Newton Street. He was pretty sure the beacon was on Newton.

It was a terrible place to stop. The roofs on both sides were flat and the buildings were forty feet tall, and they had no cover aside from a couple of parked cars. This was an ambush point. The only reason stopping there made some measure of sense was that it hardly mattered where one stopped; the whole place was one big ambush waiting to happen. City planners, he reflected, rarely concerned themselves with the potential for snipers.

"This is a bad place to hear something," he said. "We should keep moving."

Then came an ear-splitting screech. It was something out of the same library of sounds as the earlier roar—a metal-to-metal grinding quality—but more urgent, and much closer.

"Where is it?" he asked. His cannon was already out, an action performed automatically. It gave a little whine as it armed.

Minnie was also armed, and spinning slowly.

"Not sure," she said.

The thing—it was an alien, most assuredly, but Oliver wasn't going to be calling it that until he saw it—let out another cry. It came from behind him, and above the ground.

"It's on the rooftops," he said.

"Yeah, I think you're right. Let's get the hell out of here."

They broke into a sprint down the middle of the street, far more concerned about what was chasing them than with the possibility that a car driven by a human might show up ahead.

The thing on the roof followed. He heard it running.

I count six legs, he thought.

The rooftops weren't contiguous, so there were periodic gaps in the footfalls as it jumped—and perhaps flew—between them. There was something like flapping going on back there.

"It has wings," Minnie said.

"I hear it."

They were about to negotiate the turn at the end of the road. Once around the corner they'd be on a street with fewer buildings and fewer roofs, so there was a sense that if they reached the crossroad, they'd be okay.

The creature on the roof must have agreed, because just a few steps away from that turn, there was a rush of air and rainwater and an audible *whoosh* as something large and capable of flight passed directly over their heads.

Once past, it flew straight up to a height of about twenty feet, and then allowed gravity to take it to the ground directly in front of them.

It was… a giant bug. There was no other way to describe it. It had six legs, bulbous eyes, a mouth with four pincers and something that looked like it could be a beak, almost. It had four wings on its back, segmented somewhat like those on a butterfly.

It stood on four of its legs, while the other two were raised like weapons, with sharp talons.

It shrieked at them. When it did so, its mouth seemed to double in size.

Minerva fired her pulse cannon while the bug was mid-shriek and jumped behind a parked car in anticipation of a return volley. The blast struck the alien in the thorax and knocked it several feet backward.

Ollie was about to fire as well, except that he still thought this was a stupid attack, and this bothered him. The alien could have *landed* on them instead of flying past and presenting itself as a stationary target. They were missing something.

"Shoot!" Minnie shouted, while upping the energy level on her cannon. The alien took a blast that would have killed a human and was still standing; more force was needed.

Ollie could have maybe finished it off with a second shot. Instead, he turned, and checked the sky. Two more aliens were inbound.

"Check your blinds!" he shouted, firing his cannon at the nearest airborne alien.

He'd only touched an ion pulse cannon for the first time in his entire life about a half an hour earlier, but when he took the shot it felt like something he'd done a thousand times before. The recoil—far more gentle than with projectile weaponry—was exactly what he expected, and his aim was true.

The blaster setting wasn't high enough to be lethal, but it didn't have to be; he just needed to stun the thing and knock it off course. The shot caught the side of its face and carried into the wings. It plummeted to the ground ten paces away.

Oliver didn't have time to make sure it would stay down, because the other one was still inbound. It had its legs—with the sharp hooks on the end—spread open in an attack formation coming right down on him. With practiced skill that he never practiced, Oliver cranked up the power level on the cannon and fired right between the legs at the naked underbelly. It was covered in a carapace, but the pulse blast was energetic enough for that not to make a difference, especially since he got off the shot when the thing was barely fifteen feet above.

He dove to the side at the last second, as the creature crashed to the ground right where he'd been standing, and shattered like a piñata, if the piñata was a giant cockroach.

"Good news, they can be killed," he said.

"Yeah, thanks," Minerva said. She was checking other parts of the sky. "We gotta get out of here."

The one in the middle of the intersection had shaken off the initial blast, but was still presenting as a nice easy target, so Minnie shot at him again. This time the force was adequate, because the alien's head exploded.

"There's our opening," she said.

They got moving. The third alien—the one clipped by Oliver's first pulse blast—screeched, but didn't give chase. Ollie thought maybe he'd damaged the wing. He had a bad feeling about that screech, though.

"I think that sound is a request for reinforcements," he said.

"I think you're right. Set perimeter."

He thumbed open the option on the wrist console. The visor display added a grid in the top left corner. It was a quadrant grid, nine squares in which he was always the center square.

"Set altitude to thirty feet," he said, not to Minerva but to the computer embedded in his helmet. A blue light flashed a silent confirmation of the order. He now had eyes in the back of his head, and those eyes would be looking for aerial attacks.

"Done."

"Good, set the cannon to seven and aim for their mouth; that seems to do the trick."

"Already on seven."

"Show-off. Let's move."

She found another gear, and then they were sprinting down the road.

The beacon was only a half-klick away, but to get to it they'd have to negotiate a couple of narrow side streets.

"We need cover," Oliver said.

"I know. An armored helo or two would be great about now. Too bad they shot them all out of the sky."

"I'd settle for a bunch of trees."

"Trees? I can get you trees. Follow me."

When they got to their left turn, Minerva continued straight, which caused the map on his visor to have a tiny seizure for a few seconds, until it rewrote the red line he was supposed to be following. Then they ran past the next street, and the next, and he was expecting the computer to start swearing at him. Instead, the bottom left square of the perimeter grid lit up.

"Seven o'clock," he said. "Twenty-five feet."

"I see it," Minnie said. She stopped in her tracks, turned around, took a knee, and fired once. Oliver ran past her without checking to see if the shot hit its target.

She started running again immediately, and now he was on point, which was fine except he didn't know where they were going.

"Console wants me to take a left here," he said.

"Don't. Three more blocks."

They made it two before his grid lit up again.

"Four o'clock, coming in low," Minerva said.

"I see it."

Oliver planted his feet and spun around. The pavement was smooth, and slick from the rain, so he allowed his momentum to carry him into a skid while he oriented himself toward the alien. It was on a flat trajectory a few feet off the ground, and coming right at him, which made for a pretty easy shot. He took it, as Minerva passed and retook the lead. He watched long enough to see the head burst, then got moving.

The street where they finally turned left—to the immense relief of Oliver's in-helmet computer—was wider than the others, with a thin strip of grass down the middle and trees lining both sides. He followed Minnie past the grass strip to the far sidewalk.

"Better?" she asked.

"Better, but now we're pretty far off the mark."

"Picky."

The treetops played a little havoc with the perimeter alarm in his helmet, but it unquestionably made things worse for the aliens who showed a preference for attacks from above. Twice, they heard a tree behind them suffer from an impact, followed by a tremendous flapping noise as the aliens fell back. They were probing the foliage for weaknesses, which was fine with Oliver. The trees might have had a few complaints about it though.

Their way was clear all the way to the corner, where another left turn would be needed. The rendezvous point was only another couple of blocks from there, but without any more cover.

Minnie came to a stop at the trunk of the last useful tree.

"What do you think?" she asked. They could both hear the consternation from above. Ollie's perimeter grid was busily losing its mind because at least four aliens were in the air overhead, and he imagined hers was doing the same. As soon as they broke in the open they were going to have to be faster than an alien in flight. That was a big ask.

The beacon on his visor map was bouncing up and down over the now-visible rendezvous point: the Candle Square subway terminal, which was a collection of polished steel and glass that stood on an island just before the convergence of three main roads. It was one of those places that looked like an architect's name should be attached to it somewhere. It always made Ollie a little uncomfortable. Some days it looked like a larger building had collapsed into a large hole. Other days he thought of something erupting from deep in the Earth.

"Do you think we're the only ones to make it this far?" he asked.

Minerva looked surprised.

"You mean, other soldiers, running around town?"

"It's a rendezvous point. The clear implication is that we're meeting up with someone there. You're the one who's been calling it that, I'm just taking it to the logical conclusion. So do you think there are others?"

"Maybe," she said.

"And if it's a base, it could be manned. And armed."

The station looked like an asymmetrical pyramid, or one that used to be symmetrical before something tragic happened with the foundation. A series of horizontal gashes scored the top third of the triangle. These were vents for the underground air recycling system, but they could also be gun perches.

"You're thinking we might have cover," she said.

"That's what I'm thinking, yeah."

"Seems risky."

"We can't stay here all day. If we fall, we may as well fall forward."

"Never backward," she said. It was a rallying cry they learned during the training they never had: Always forward, never backward. Oliver thought it was a good lesson to ingrain in a foot soldier you were training to run toward danger, although maybe not the best advice to someone who hoped to survive a battle. Cannon fodder needed that kind of motivation.

"All right," Minnie said, "we do this in steps. Hit the tree at the corner, then across to the store with the awning, the pickup truck, and then straight for the mouth of the station."

"Roger."

They bumped fists, then forearms, then slapped each other on the shoulders, a complex gesture of affection honed by years of training and working together, none of which actually happened. It was their secret handshake.

"On three," she said.

It was a slow three-count, because she was actually waiting until one of the aliens above became engaged in the tree, on the assumption that this would mean there was one-less attacker to worry about for at least one part of this suicide sprint.

When it happened, they went. She took the lead, both because she was faster and because she was still, technically, his commanding officer, if they cared about those things.

They didn't make it all the way to the tree across the street before being noticed. One of the flyers spotted them, and swung in low and fast from the left, parallel with the street they were crossing. Minnie slowed down and gave herself up as bait because Oliver had the better shot. He took it, with a dialed-back pulse blast that shredded the alien's wings. It skidded across the street between them. He jumped over the stunned bug's twitching body and kept rolling.

At the new tree, Oliver took a quick look over his shoulder. Three bugs in the air, two landing, all looking back at him.

We're not going to make it, he thought.

From the tree to the awning wasn't so bad, but another quick glance made it clear the aliens were working on a plan of their own.

"What do they even want?" he asked.

"Right now they want to keep us from getting to the rendezvous point, and that's all we need to know."

They made for the pickup truck at the same time one of the aliens dove through the awning, which wasn't nearly as effective at preventing an attack as the trees had been. It ended up tangled in the canvas, though, which was good. But the bugs near the trees were making their play now, and it was a good one. Three new attackers landed in the street in front of the station, called in from wherever these things originated. Five behind, three in front, and nothing above their heads.

"This would be a great time for someone in the station to provide us with some of that cover you were hoping for, wouldn't you say?" Minerva said.

"Sure would."

Just then, a ninth bug dropped in from the sky, right onto the roof of a truck. It came down so fast the perimeter detectors didn't see it until it was landing. They both fell back, Minnie firing before she even hit the pavement. Her aim was a little off; the cannon shot glanced off the bug's face. It shrieked, and jumped directly overhead.

Ollie blew him apart with a blaster setting at nine, showering both of them in bug guts.

"Yuck," she said, getting to her feet. "Move, Ollie."

The bugs were trying a pincer assault, pinning them between two forces, having learned, perhaps, that they could only fire the blasters so often and at so many targets.

Minnie went with a direct charge at the three between her and the rendezvous point. It was a smart call, if only because the next overhead assault would have more trouble with a rapidly moving target. It closed the gap between her and the bugs awfully fast, though. She needed three or four seconds between cannon shots at that energy level. Even assuming she hit her target the first two times, it would be hand-to-hand before the blaster was ready for a third shot. These things didn't look like pushovers in close combat.

Ollie's helmet had gone wonky, meanwhile. He could see out of the visor pretty well despite the bug gunk all over it, but the computer wasn't dealing well with the stuff. It was flashing and firing off all sorts of invalid alarms and notices, and he was having a lot of trouble figuring out what was a real notification and what was a malfunction.

He flung the helmet off. He lost comms, but they were close enough to shout at each other. Rain soaked his face and clouded his vision, but he didn't mind. Through the helmet, it all felt a little less real. This was immersive.

The five bugs at the end of the street had become ten, and they were charging. All the three in front of the station had to do was hold the line until the main assault arrived, and so far nobody was firing a big gun from inside the station. Maybe they *were* alone.

"We might as well be," he said, to himself.

He spun the dial on the blaster to full. Warning lights flashed all over the place as the pack on his back began to vibrate and the barrel heated up.

"Oliver!" Minnie shouted. "Put your damn helmet back on and get up here!"

She fired a kill shot at one bug, but a second was charging her to close the gap. She needed Ollie beside her to take the second shot and he wasn't there.

"Hold the position," he said. Then he took aim, and fired.

No matter how big a blast shot he took, as long as there were ten targets it wasn't going to do much good. Oliver wasn't aiming at any of the bugs, though; he was aiming at the building twenty feet in front of the bugs.

The kickback from the shot was like nothing he'd experienced before: it knocked him backwards about five feet.

That was probably why the cannon wasn't supposed to get dialed that high.

The pulse lit up the whole intersection as it arced into the glass-and-stone façade of the ground floor bagel shop Oliver sincerely hoped was as unoccupied as it appeared. The aliens up the street hesitated, having not taken into consideration the possibility that the humans had this kind of firepower at their disposal. But when the shot landed and did nothing more than completely destroy the shop, they continued forward.

Then the whole building started coming down. Two support walls had been atomized at the base, which turned the entire five-story structure into a hail of brick and granite and chunks of cement, which fell into the street between Oliver and the oncoming horde.

Minnie still needed his help, though, and now his cannon was useless. He turned to see her firing a second shot at the charging alien—and missing. It anticipated, and maneuvered at the last second. She jumped aside as it crashed into the pavement she'd been occupying.

The battery pack on Oliver's back was still vibrating, which was a bad sign. If he was wearing his helmet he'd probably be getting all kinds of warning feedback, but he knew what was happening all the same. You never dial a cannon to full.

He sprinted right at the alien that was about to engage Minnie. She was in the middle of the street, on her back, waiting for the blaster to re-arm, and basically out of time to do anything else but hope that would be happening shortly. The bug had no such timeline to concern itself with, and was up on its hind legs, about to come down on her with two talons.

"Hey, ugly!" Oliver shouted. He aimed the barrel of the cannon at the alien's head. It was useless, but the bug didn't know that. It reoriented on him, and charged.

By now, he was familiar with the mode of attack. The aliens charged, then roared, then closed in for the kill with either those huge pincers or the talons on the ends of their feet. If he had a functioning blaster, he'd take the shot during the creature's roar. The blaster had fired its last shot, but it wasn't done being useful.

When the bug stopped and opened its mouth, Oliver threw the entire weapon, pack and all, into its maw.

The thing made a quizzical gulping sound and halted its attack for long enough to allow Ollie to get on the other side of it.

"Time to run," he said to Minnie, jerking her to her feet.

"What did you do?"

He threw her over his shoulder—he'd be getting hell for this later if they survived—and sprinted for the nearest piece of cover: a parked sedan.

They nearly made it when the pulse cannon that was caught somewhere in the gullet of an alien erupted.

This had a rather final effect on the bug who swallowed it, as well as to the entire side of the street it was occupying. The explosion manifested as a blinding white light that sucked up all the sound, before releasing it and a tremendous amount of force in all directions. Oliver and Minnie had just negotiated the corner of the sedan when the shock wave carried them both back and through the window of a burrito place.

Ollie didn't have his helmet on any more, and this was a really bad time to not have his helmet, but he survived. It may have helped that he had Minnie and her armored torso in between him and the blast when it happened. Or it could have been that he was just really lucky at a good time to be lucky.

"You all right?" she asked.

Oliver's ears had gotten rung pretty good, so she had to get right up into his face to ask the question. He nodded and pointed to the station: they had to go before the aliens recovered.

He tried standing, but that wasn't so easy. She had to help him up, and then help him to walk.

"I'm really dizzy," he said.

"Your body knows what to do, just keep walking."

They got out of the burrito store to the sidewalk, and headed down the street, with him leaning on her way more than he should have been, but the bugs were gone so it was okay.

Except for the one still between them and the rendezvous point. The explosion didn't kill it, any more than it killed Minnie and Oliver, so it shouldn't have been a surprise to end up still facing him. It was a surprise anyway.

Minnie threw Oliver to the ground and drew her weapon, but this wasn't quite fast enough. She was still raising the barrel, and was a half-second away from having her head removed, when a pulse blast from another angle completely destroyed it.

The shot came from the top of the glass wall of the subway station. A remote-operated cannon barrel extended out of one of the vents.

"Didn't I tell you they were gonna end up being bugs?" someone said over a loudspeaker.

"Wilson?" Minerva said. "You're a little late, we could have used that gun five minutes ago."

"I'm early," he said. "You guys are the ones who are late. Now are you going to get in here, or do you want to blow up more of the city first?"

Chapter Ten

TAKE THE LAST TRAIN

The inside of the Candle Square station was smaller than it looked like it should be from the outside. Most of the triangle structure went to the mechanics of the cooling unit—and, apparently, the large guns—so once Oliver and Minerva made it inside there was little else to do but head down the non-functioning escalators to the first landing.

If they had decided to go all the way down to the subway platform, it would have meant a much longer journey. The first landing had turnstiles, on the other side of which was a much longer escalator system that led to a second landing, and a ramp to the inbound trains. The outbound trains were on an even lower platform requiring additional ramp access.

What struck Ollie as soon as they got down to the landing and he had a chance to catch his breath and get his bearings was that the place looked no different than it had any other time he'd been down there. No bunks with soldiers or high tech military gear, no maps of the city with red X's indicating alien attack points, no provisions, nothing. Just a normal subway terminal in a normal city.

Also: no people. The city's emergency preparedness plan for

this immediate vicinity included the local citizens taking shelter in the station, because the place was deep enough to offer decent protection in the event of a bombing raid in which standard, non-nuclear bombs were being used. Oliver knew this because everyone knew this, because there was a sign posted at the surface that said more or less exactly this. Yet, the place was empty.

Maybe the city had different plans in the event of an extraterrestrial assault. Or maybe everyone was down on the lower platform. But he thought if that were so—if there were ten thousand people down there—he'd hear them.

Minerva helped Oliver—who wasn't entirely ready to stand on his own—to the ground in a corner against the wall, about ten feet from something that looked like a pool of pee, which just reinforced how normal this subway station was.

Wilson emerged from the control room door. He was dressed in the same camo outfit as before.

"Is he all right?" he asked.

"He's a little dizzy is all," Minerva said. "Big blast, no helmet."

"I'm fine," Ollie said.

"Yeah you are. Saved our asses."

She smiled at him and he smiled back. Ollie thought maybe there was something nice there, in her smile, that he wanted to keep for himself. He didn't really care that her boyfriend was standing a few feet away. Not after what they'd just been through.

Then again, he was so dizzy he couldn't stand, so a misinterpretation was possible.

"Hey, where's everyone else?" he asked Wilson.

"Who do you mean?"

"It's a rendezvous point. Please tell me you're not the person we're here to meet."

Wilson looked hurt.

"You mean, not *just* me."

"Sure, if that makes you feel better."

"I'm not the only one here," Wilson said. "There's another guy, but he's down below. Little weird, though, I'm not sure we want to hang out with him."

"You mean down at the trains."

"That's what I mean, yes. He seemed to think the only way to get where we're going is through the tunnels."

"Reasonable assumption," Minerva said. "I wouldn't go back up there without an army behind me."

"Is it really that awful? I didn't have a good deal of trouble getting here," Wilson said. "I just headed on over."

"No aliens?" Oliver asked. "They're all over the place, topside."

"None that I saw."

Oliver looked around the space they were occupying a little more closely from his unfortunate vantage point on the floor. He realized the soot marks he thought he was looking at were blaster marks.

"I think this place was overrun," he said. "Must have happened early. What was the problem with the defenses?"

"The what?" Wilson asked.

"The big guns that go bang-bang. The thing you fired."

"Oh, it was offline. Part of the console was shredded. I had to hotwire a few systems to get it started. Didn't even know I knew how to do that."

"There's a lot of that going around."

Minerva pulled out the map she'd gotten from Ben, seemingly two or three lifetimes ago. "Do you recognize this part of town?" she asked Wilson.

"Nope. Where'd this come from?"

"Ben. So it's important. It's where we should be heading next."

"That's going to be a challenge if we don't know what part of town this is."

"Hey guys?" Oliver said. "I know at this point this is probably too much to ask for, but could you explain, in a non-crazy-sounding way, what you mean when you say stuff like that?"

"Like what?" Minerva asked.

"Like that the map is important, because it came from Ben, a guy who held us at gunpoint and made us drive around town for no obvious reason. He didn't even know what the map was for."

"You want a non-crazy-sounding explanation?" she repeated.

"Preferably."

"No, I really don't think we can do that. Can you walk, though? We should get moving. We'll give you the crazy explanation on the way and you can decide for yourself what to believe."

~

*U*nder normal circumstances, the trip to the inbound platform would have required little effort. One had only to get past the gates using whatever token or pass-card was appropriate, then stand on the escalator and wait for it to make it to the bottom, possibly wondering the entire time why it was still called an escalator when it was taking people down and not up.

That's what tended to go through Oliver's head more or less every time it was appropriate. On a couple of occasions, he shared this observation aloud, but never found someone who thought it as perplexing and/or clever as he did.

The city appeared to be without power, though, because the turnstiles didn't work and the escalator wasn't moving. Ollie wondered if he missed an EMP detonation. That would definitely explain the abandoned cars, but became less likely when he considered that the futuristic soldier gear he and Minerva employed was unaffected. Maybe it was technology that was shielded from electromagnetic pulse attacks.

Or maybe none of this makes sense and I'm losing my mind, he thought. *Let's just put that out there.*

They didn't have to jump the turnstiles, because there was a handicapped entrance that didn't have a gate. But the escalator problem was insoluble. They were going to have to climb down.

While undeniably better than going up without assistance, down was a little frightening for someone still recovering from what he thought was probably a mild concussion. Dizzy spells and the stairs didn't go well together.

"So explain," he said, to whoever felt like answering. It seemed like a great way to fill up the time on what had to be a quarter of a mile downhill.

"I don't think we can," Minerva said. "We can tell you what we know."

"All right, what do you know?"

"We know something's wrong with this city," Wilson said.

"You mean other than the alien attack and the helicopters falling from the sky and the fact that all the people seem to have disappeared?"

"Yes, other than that. We started picking up on these things a while ago."

"Like the dead spaces," Minnie said. "Times when we were suddenly in a place, and we were *supposed* to be there, but we didn't know how we got there. Has that ever happened to you?"

"You almost need to be looking for it," Wilson added.

"I guess a couple of times, sure," Ollie said. "But that's normal."

Minerva laughed. "Okay."

"No, it is. The mind isn't always on, right? We're on autopilot sometimes. It's a thing. Happens to long distance drivers a lot."

"All right, but this is subtly different," Wilson said. "Imagine waking up in the middle of a conversation and the last thing you remember was being home, and two days had passed."

"Like an alien abduction or something?" Ollie asked, deliberately invoking the claims of a few of those long-distance drivers who convinced themselves they hadn't just been half-asleep: time had been stolen from them.

"Well yes, I suppose."

"Except without the abduction," Minnie said.

"I mean, we *have* aliens," Oliver said. This seemed worth pointing out.

"Yeah but nobody saw them until today."

"Then just missing time."

"We think of it as not missing, it just wasn't ever created," Wilson said.

"Well that's cryptic."

"Oliver, we think the reason for these jumps is that the story that connected the two points was never filled in."

"I'm not following."

Minnie, who was leading them down, stopped at the next landing. They were nearly to the bottom.

"Ollie, remember you asked where all the people went?" she said. "And I told you I had a suggestion?"

"But I wasn't going to like it, yes, I remember."

"I think they aren't here because the alien attack was supposed to happen in a nearly abandoned city. Nobody else was written in for this part. Just us."

Ollie laughed, and waited for the other two to join in. They didn't.

"But that's ridiculous," he said.

"I get it," Wilson said. "Crowd scenes are incredibly difficult. You never really know how much detail to provide. I can understand not bothering to provide all that background; it just bogs down the action. It's a good call."

"But we aren't talking about a story, Wilson, this is... I can't believe I even have to say this out loud. This is the real world."

"Yes, but this real world is missing some important parts."

"Ollie, look around!" Minerva said. "You know how many

people are supposed to be in this city? And we just repelled aliens with technology that doesn't even exist, I mean, come on."

"Just because I can't explain it doesn't mean your explanation's correct."

"A logical fallacy!" Wilson declared. "That's true!"

He clapped Oliver on the shoulder and started down the stairs again, smiling at Minerva as he went past.

"I told you he wouldn't believe it," he said. "He's too rational. Come on, let's go find that other guy, I bet he can help."

~

There was no other guy waiting for them at the bottom of the stairs, or anywhere along the landing. There also continued to be no other people, and no trains.

Light they had. It came from battery-powered emergency lights along the walls that were just strong enough to create pools of visibility along the darkened platform. It was precisely effective enough to raise concern about what was in the darkness beyond the edge.

Oliver didn't entirely register how discomfiting the environment was, as he was too busy trying to get a grip on the self-evident nonsense his friends appeared to believe.

The whole thing reminded him, oddly, of Ivor's story. Ollie's biggest problem with it—aside from the fact that it was a plot borrowed from *The Matrix*—was that in order for it to work the characters had to be in a dream and not know they were in a dream.

Oliver had been dreaming his whole life, and not once had he been in one where, at some point, he didn't recognize that he was in one. Dreams could be emotionally real, but not physically real. Pain, physical exertion, and just basic physics weren't there, and that was what always pulled him out of the idea that what he was experiencing was reality.

It wasn't even worth it to question if what he was experiencing was real. The whole *it was all a dream* premise made for a good twist in a story, but it never really rang true for him, because real dreams just weren't that substantial. It was a cute plot twist, sure, but not a workable explanation for what he was actually experiencing.

Unfortunately, there weren't any other good options.

"Did he say where he was going?" Minerva asked, once they'd walked the length of the inbound platform.

"No, just that he was going to push ahead," Wilson said.

"That's all?"

"Essentially. There might have been more, but I was occupied with the defense grid at the time."

"What direction do you suppose *ahead* is?" she asked.

Wilson just shrugged.

They headed down another flight to the outbound platform. It was even more poorly lit. Minerva took the headlight off her vest and held it up like a flashlight. It improved things only a little. Oliver reached for his own, but discovered it was missing.

More to the point, the entire armored vest was missing. He didn't remember taking it off, but he must have slipped out of it at the same time he was hurling his cannon pack into the mouth of a roaring alien. That meant the vest was likely spread out over the same vast radius as the insides of that alien. His light was gone, in other words.

"Anybody down here?" Minnie asked.

"Unless he's playing hide-and-seek, I don't believe he's here," Wilson said.

"I thought I saw something."

Ollie thought so too. The shadows were surprisingly tricky on this level, and one of them looked almost like a person.

"Let me see," he said. She handed him the light. He headed toward the 'person'. It was a cardboard display: one of those human-sized cutouts of a spokeswoman for a monthly wifi package.

"Unless you want to change data plans, this probably isn't who we're looking for," Oliver said.

He redirected the light at the floor in front of her display, because something gleamed in the paving stones when the light caught it. At first he thought it was some kind of moisture, but the ground was dry. There also wasn't any metal that he could see.

"So what do we do now?" Minerva asked. "Wait for him to come back?"

"Don't know if he's coming back," Wilson said. "And I don't think we can go back up at this point: nighttime, with only one of those brilliant cannons left, and giant bugs all over the city. We need another way through."

Ollie knelt down to get a better look. It took some manipulation to get the light pointed exactly right.

"What are you doing?" Wilson asked.

"There's some writing down here," Oliver said. "It's weird."

"What kind of writing?"

"Just writing. In some phosphorescent paint or something."

Minnie leaned down to look. She tilted her head three or four times at several angles.

"I can't see it," she said.

Oliver put his finger right under the lettering. "Here."

She squinted.

"Nope, I don't see it."

"What do these words that don't exist say?" Wilson asked.

"That's a complicated question. Can you see it?"

Wilson peered over Minnie's shoulder.

"If there are words near your fingers, I don't see them," Wilson said.

"So I'm either going nuts—some more—or my eyesight is better than both of yours? Or you're screwing with me."

"We aren't screwing with you," Minnie said.

"Why is it a complicated question?" Wilson asked.

It was complicated because Ollie knew, as soon as the message came into focus, that this wasn't written in any language with which he was familiar. The letters were vaguely Arabic, but that was about the best he could do in terms of identification. But even as the rational side of his brain understood this, there was something in the language center that decided it knew what was being conveyed. It was like watching a movie that was subtitled in another language and close-captioned in English at the same time. He could read the words lying underneath the ones he couldn't translate.

Somehow.

"It just is," Oliver said. "But I think we should go that way."

He gestured with the light beam down the length of the tunnel.

"Is that what the message said to do?" Minnie asked.

"More or less."

The message was an annoying bit of doggerel. It read, *to go back for the first time, go in the out.* Oliver didn't get the first part, but the second was clearly saying to take the outbound tunnel inbound. It was useless advice unless the trains weren't running, which was only one way in which this was absurd—there were many others, including what the message was doing there at all, and why nobody else could see it—but he felt instinctively this was the correct interpretation.

A big arrow would have done the trick just fine, of course. If he ever figured out who put the message there he'd have to tell them this.

"Down the tracks, then?" Minnie asked.

"Assuming the electricity doesn't return subway service to the city any time soon, it's probably safe," Wilson said. "Although I'd stay clear of the third rail. That would be a bad way to learn the electricity's back. Doesn't look like there's much in the way of lighting down there, either."

Oliver took the initiative to drop down from the platform to the tracks. He'd been taking the subway for much of his life, and for most of that time he'd harbored a secret desire to jump down onto the tracks and walk around. He felt this way even when standing at the edge and noticing soot-colored mice and rats scampering around down there. He doubted he was the only one who had these thoughts.

Standing in the middle of the tracks, he held up the light and verified that it did very little to stave off the looming darkness ahead.

"You're right, this could stand to be brighter," he said.

And then it was. The lamp in his hand brightened, until it seemed like he was holding a piece of sunlight.

"Well then," Wilson said, jumping down next to him. "I guess that will do."

Minerva jumped down last. Oliver tried handing her back the lamp, since it was hers.

"No, no, you keep that," she said. "I have a feeling it won't work as well in my hands."

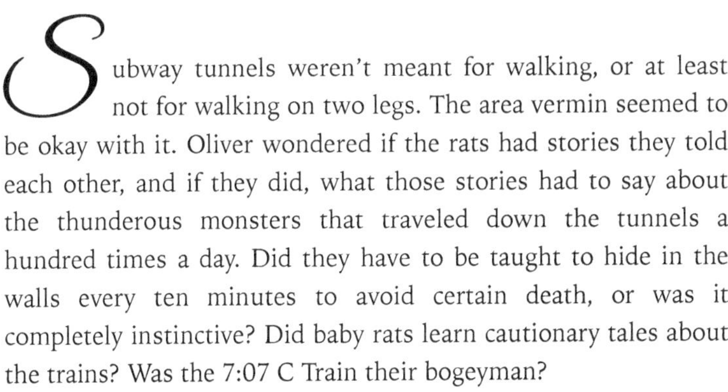

*S*ubway tunnels weren't meant for walking, or at least not for walking on two legs. The area vermin seemed to be okay with it. Oliver wondered if the rats had stories they told each other, and if they did, what those stories had to say about the thunderous monsters that traveled down the tunnels a hundred times a day. Did they have to be taught to hide in the walls every ten minutes to avoid certain death, or was it completely instinctive? Did baby rats learn cautionary tales about the trains? Was the 7:07 C Train their bogeyman?

If the rats had mythologies, surely this day—the day when the trains stopped—would be an important part of the legends.

The larger point was that travel was slow going. The sheer amount of dirt, soot, dust and grease was staggering. They were only halfway to the next stop when Oliver started to consider just turning around, climbing back to the surface, and dealing with the rain and the bugs. It had to be better than the coal lung and the rats.

"How's it going up here?" Wilson asked, stepping up beside Ollie. Oliver had been in the lead because he was the guy with the big shiny light. The others were content to trail behind and follow in his footsteps as much as possible. This was necessary because the ground was uneven, and nobody wanted to deal with tripping. Every direction looked like a tetanus shot waiting to happen.

"Super. I want a shower."

"So do I. It's filthy down here."

"Yeah. Look, I've been thinking about this, and I've decided I don't want to go to Pallas with you guys after all."

Wilson laughed.

"Oh, it's much too late for that now."

"That is where we're headed, though, isn't it?" Ollie asked.

"Ultimately, yes. That's still the plan. But now you understand why we left so early. The commute is challenging."

This made Oliver laugh, which caused the light to bounce around. It seemed as if the entire tunnel trembled when he did that. Footlights along the left and right side of the tunnel were all that passed for emergency lighting in between the stations. They were only there in the event a disabled car needed to be evacuated, or so Ollie assumed.

"So do you want to tell me what's really going on?" Oliver asked.

"I don't have a better explanation, if that's what you're looking for."

"You said you started to notice things a while ago."

"This is true, yes."

"And that somehow these things are connected to me, in ways that make zero sense to anyone with a brain and a basic grip on how reality works. How did you get there?"

"We thought it was Wilson, at first," Minerva said, from behind them.

"That's true," Wilson said. "But once that was proven wrong, we decided to create the writers' underground. Took a while, but here you are."

Ollie shook his head. "I can't go down that rabbit hole with you. I didn't even start writing until a few months ago, how do you imagine I'm… I mean, I existed before then. You did too, didn't you?"

"Well you didn't write *yourself* into existence, Ollie," Minerva said. "We aren't saying that."

"I'm not so sure you didn't," Wilson said. "Just to be contrarian about this. Ollie, what's the name of this city?"

"What? It's… the name is… It's the city. What do you mean?"

"You know exactly what I mean. What is the name of the city we live in? Don't look at me, I don't know."

"But that's crazy."

"I know it is. Where'd you go to college?"

"I went to community college."

"So you said. What was the name of it?"

He couldn't remember. He could picture the buildings, and the classrooms, and a professor he was particularly fond of, but whose name also escaped him.

"This is ridiculous," he said.

"What's your full name, Oliver?" Wilson asked.

"That I know. It's Oliver Naughton."

"Your *full* name."

"Oliver Tennyson Davis Naughton."

Wilson looked impressed.

"Told you," Minnie said.

"Told him what?" Ollie asked.

"We had a bet you wouldn't be able to answer that," Minnie said. "Because other than Ben, nobody else we met could. Wilson has a last name, but that's it. I don't."

"Well that's ridiculous," Oliver said. "Of course you have a last name. It's…"

Then his mind drew a blank again. He was worried if he guessed, and that guess was right, he would somehow be proving them correct in his effort to prove them wrong: would he be retrieving their surnames from his memory, or creating them on the spot? He wouldn't know the difference, and maybe they wouldn't either.

"Okay, but what does any of this prove?" he asked. "I have a name, great."

"It proves you're different," Wilson said.

"It doesn't prove he created himself too," Minerva said. "If that's what you were leaning toward."

"It doesn't disprove it either. Plus, look at the consequences. It would mean someone else is involved. Let's lay out what we're talking about here."

They were coming up on another station, and with that came better lighting, from the platform's emergency lights. Also, it looked like there was another glowing message: something caught in Oliver's light and glittered back at him.

Wilson continued. "We're talking about a situation in which an intelligence is actually scripting us, and we think Oliver might be that intelligence, and that's *completely absurd*. But now if we don't allow for the idea that he's also scripting himself, we've got to go up another layer and find out who's writing for him? Do you see why I don't want to do that?"

Oliver stopped at the wall opposite the platform. There was definitely another message there, just below an advertisement for a department store. He trained the light on the spot, which was covered in the same dust as the rest of the tunnel. The message came through anyway.

"I think that's a much more comforting idea, actually," Minerva said.

"Why?"

"I don't know; it just is."

"Why'd we stop?" Wilson asked Oliver. Clearly, he couldn't see what Oliver could see.

"New message," Oliver said.

"What does it say?"

It said *the good way home is through the home goods* and that was nonsense, but Oliver had already stopped puzzling over that and focused on the advertisement above it.

"I don't know what it means. What stop are we at?"

"Dunston Street, I think," Minerva said. She was looking at the platform. "It looks kind of familiar, but it's hard to tell from this angle."

"Isn't that the stop with the weird underground entrance?"

"Right, yes, through the basement store," Wilson said.

In the somewhat distant past, there was a large department store in what had been the center of the shopping area in the center of the city. This part of the city was no longer considered central, but it was still a major shopping plaza, even as the concept of the department store dwindled in significance over time.

The store had been huge: eight levels of public showrooms, with another eight floors above that containing stock and business offices. It was important enough to the downtown area that when the city decided to create the Dunston Street stop, in the Seventies, they put it right next to the giant department store and added an exit ramp that permitted their customers to enter the store at the basement level. In the winter, shoppers could park at the edge of town, hop on the train, and shop for the entire day without taking another breath of unfiltered air.

The appeal of the all-in-one shopping experience waned over the years, and the store eventually went the way of the dodo and the buggy whip. The spot it occupied had since been replaced by a modest, two-story version of essentially the same kind of department store, which put out its overstock on deep discount in the basement. The entrance-via-subway-tunnel was the most interesting aspect of the store, although most shoppers used it as a pass-through to get to the street and perhaps do some shoplifting along the way.

It was a story everybody who'd ever taken the Dunston Street stop was familiar with, because a nicer version of it was on a plaque affixed to the wall next to the store entrance. Briefly, Oliver entertained the notion that he'd literally just come up with that story, rather than that it was always true, but he discarded the idea because it made his head hurt, and was in every other sense simply not helpful. Minnie and Wilson were messing him up with this craziness.

"We should stop here," Oliver said.

"Is that what the message says?" Minnie asked.

"Not exactly, but we should stop here anyway."

Getting off the tracks was difficult and disgusting. There were ladders embedded in the platform in a couple of places, but needless to say, they were the kind of ladders that cried out for a pair of gloves, and they didn't have those. Once that was accomplished, though, it was nice to be standing in a spot where humans were supposed to be. It felt like rejoining the land of the living. Seeing other people around would have probably helped, but one thing at a time.

"Do you think this is where that other guy went?" Minerva asked.

"Maybe, if he can read the same signs I can," Oliver said. "Or if he's the one leaving them. That's assuming he still exists. I could have forgotten to write about him."

Nobody laughed.

"I'm kidding."

"We know," Minnie said.

The way from the landing to the store was a concourse that had an empty popcorn stand, an empty donut stand, and an entrance that led directly to the street. There weren't any donuts on display, but the popcorn smelled fresh enough.

The door to the store was open. Off-hours, there was a big roll-gate pulled down over the glass doors, and that gate looked like something that could withstand a blast from a bazooka. If it had been closed, Ollie was prepared to ask Minerva to use the pulse cannon on it, because he thought getting inside was important.

He led the way in. The basement shop was a lot of bargain bins full of frequently pawed-over blouses and skirts expertly assembled by children in third-world countries, or so he assumed.

"Why are we here?" Minnie asked.

"Escalator," he said, pointing the way. She shrugged, and followed.

"Where's Wilson?" he asked, noting that she was the only one there, suddenly.

"I dunno, I think he's waiting in the tunnel."

"Why… never mind, we'll go back and get him in a minute. Do you have that map Ben gave you?"

"Yeah, yeah, hang on."

She pulled it out of a side pocket and handed it over. Oliver carried it over to the base of the escalator, which was where the map of the store was located. He put Ben's map up next to it.

"It's not a street map," he said. It matched up to the first floor layout perfectly.

"Look at that," she said. "So X marks…"

"Home goods," he read. "Let's go."

He headed up the escalator to the main shopping floor, which was significantly larger than the basement level. That was obvious almost immediately; he felt as if he'd been deposited into a warehouse.

Curiously, and unlike the basement, the entrance doors on the ground floor were all locked and chained. He wondered if that meant the employees all escaped through the basement, and just forgot to lock it on the way out.

"All right so, if we head that way…"

He stopped when he realized there was nobody next to him to speak to.

"Minerva?"

He'd gone a few steps from the escalator and turned down the first aisle already. He didn't remember doing this, but given where his feet were, there wasn't any other real explanation. But when he backtracked to where he thought the escalator was, he didn't find it.

"What the hell. Minerva?"

There was a support beam near the front door, and on the beam was a map like the one he'd just been looking at. He looked at it again, and was confused by the revelation that it had no spot for an escalator on it. Ben's map, still in his hands, also didn't have a spot for it, but it never did so that wasn't news.

Still, the escalator has vanished somehow, and both Minnie and Wilson had vanished along with it. To make matters worse, now he was trapped in a locked department store.

Then, on the other side of the sales floor, somewhere in an unseen far corner, a cell phone began to ring.

Chapter Eleven

THE GHOST IN THE MACHINE

"Hello? Is someone there?"

The light in Oliver's hand flickered and dimmed, as if the power that compelled it to amplify vanished at the same time the escalator did. It didn't go away completely, though, sticking to something close to the power output of a regular flashlight.

The phone continued to ring. Nobody was around to answer it, but the idea that somebody might be calling gave him hope that an entire city of people hadn't literally ceased to exist.

"Hello?" he repeated. "Wilson? Minerva? Anyone here?"

There was a rustling, to his right. It made him jump, and once he was done jumping, it made him seek out the source of the noise.

The floor layout was racetrack-oval, with paths leading off in both directions. He shoved Ben's treasure map in his pocket and headed around the short bottom part of the oval. Around the corner—there was a wall bisecting the center of the oval—was a mannequin-heavy clothing section with a plastic tarp drooping from the roof. It looked like a tumor that was breathing.

This is ridiculous, he thought.

He'd somehow ended up stuck in the middle of Mad Maggie's Shop-O-Rama, which was insane because he made up Mad Maggie's. He might well have made it up based on a dimly remembered understanding of the very floor layout he was now stuck in the middle of, except that the actual store—it was called Daniel's—wasn't this big.

The possibility existed, then, that the store was now mimicking the story, and not the other way around.

The phone was still ringing. Oliver directed his flashlight down the main drag, past the annoyingly accurate running mannequin display in the sporting good section, to electronics. The same cardboard cutout as the one in the subway greeted him with a cardboard wave and a cardboard smile. He headed her way.

On the route, he got to take in the creepy shadows cast through the joint efforts of the emergency lighting, the display endcaps, and the wide assortment of humanoid dummies in active wear, formal wear, sleepwear, and other miscellaneous wears, ready to jump up and move around. Perhaps they could help him storm the doors, break out, and fight an alien invasion.

Stranger things have happened, he thought, although that was probably untrue.

What he didn't feel was fear or dread, or any kind of anticipatory concern that something in this store was about to jump up and harm him. He thought maybe that was the problem with the actual story: there was no real danger, just the things the main character—*Orrin*—convinced himself of. The fear was all in his head.

It probably would have made a better movie, he decided. He'd never written a screenplay, but maybe that would've been the way to go.

Oliver reached the electronics section, stepped past the friendly, smiling cardboard spokeswoman and found the recycle bin. It wasn't a surprise that the ringing was coming from inside there, because of course it had to be.

There was still a lock on the lid. He reached down to his belt, at his right hip, and was surprised to discover a ring of keys there, which hadn't been there before. The smart thing to do would be to take the keys to the front door, unlock it, and get the hell out of this place. Then he could either go find Minnie and Wilson, or go the hell home and sleep off whatever this was. He didn't think he could treat the entire city losing touch with reality the same way he did a drinking bender, but he was willing to give it a try.

But, he didn't do that, because the phone was still ringing and he was going to have to answer it. And when it was obvious he didn't have the right key—the lock had a tiny keyhole and he didn't have one small enough to fit it—he headed over to gardening supplies, found a mallet, and swung it at the top of the container until it caved in. This took a few minutes, but it was tremendously satisfying, so he was a little disappointed when the lid finally caved. He tipped the container over, scattering outdated handhelds all over the floor.

The ringing came from a flip phone that required an antenna to be extended before functioning properly. Oliver was pretty sure he saw one of these in an old TV show once, but it was the first time he'd held one.

He flipped it open.

"Hello?" he said.

Static. He remembered the night he got a call like this in his apartment, and just the thought of that night made him reconsider how scary or not-scary the moment he was now experiencing was.

"Hello?" he repeated.

"O…You have to…Wilson…"

"Minnie, is that you?"

"You have to come back."

"I can't, the… the stairs vanished, I don't know how to get out of… where are you? Where did you guys go?"

Static. He'd have thought she'd hung up except for the interference.

"Join…"

"What? Minnie, what?"

"Join us."

Then the line went dead.

"Well of course it did," he said, putting down the phone.

All of the phones were supposed to start ringing next, because that was how things went in the story. It was actually where he left off, because once that started happening he didn't know where to go. He figured if he ever picked up the story again, he'd edit out the whole *all the phones were ringing* thing, because that was creepy, but not all that scary.

Also, what's a guy supposed to do with a hundred ringing phones? Answer them one at a time? Orrin would have probably been so freaked out, he turned and headed for the door, and since —unlike Oliver—Orrin could *leave* when he wanted, he'd probably do that.

So for the story to work, Oliver would have to create a situation in which Orrin was trapped inside. Up the stakes, make it so the danger is real, that sort of thing.

How would I keep him inside? he wondered. The key could stop working, or he could lose the key ring, or…

"Or the exit could vanish," he said. "Crap."

For just a half-second, he actually *was* afraid. Not because he appeared to be caught in his own unfinished horror story, but because he was stuck in the middle of a rewrite of that story.

But that didn't make sense. Of course the regular exit was still there, because it had to be. He never introduced anything into the story that would allow for the front doors to just disappear; if he had, it would have blown up the whole thing. The reader would drop out. Any reality-altering event like that had to be telegraphed by something smaller first, and he hadn't done that in any part of the story.

Ergo, the front door was still there. It was just the escalator that was missing, but it was missing because Mad Maggie's had no basement. Weirdly, this made sense to him.

He *was* stuck in a rewrite of some kind, though, because the phones on the floor weren't ringing. As long as that was true, he had no impetus to flee the premises, and yet the story had to head in that direction because there was nowhere else to go.

The scary part was that he didn't know what was supposed to happen next if those phones didn't start ringing.

Then somebody touched his shoulder.

His response was something like the reaction to a live electrical wire: he yelped, jumped away from the contact, and turned all at the same time, which resulted in his feet getting tangled up on themselves and him falling over onto the scattered outdated phones on the floor.

There was nobody behind him, aside from the cardboard spokeswoman, and she didn't look like she'd moved.

"Of course she didn't move," he said, to the nearest mannequin, "she's cardboard."

The mannequin appeared to agree, albeit silently.

He scampered to his feet, clumsily.

"So who did that?" he asked, trying for a confidently loud, low voice but landing on whiny, high-pitched, and scared. "Come on, I just want to know how to solve this."

There wasn't any response, but the tarp at the other end of the room did make a little noise. It wasn't helpful.

"That's the deal, right? You guys are ghosts or whatever, and you need me to do something or fix something or... join you, whatever the hell that means. Is there a curse? What's the issue?"

Nothing. He turned to the mannequin again, the one opposite the electronics. She was a part of the business casual section of the store, and wore a smart pantsuit with a frilly blouse.

"Well, I tried," he said.

The mannequin nodded.

He tried to convince himself that hadn't actually happened, but he was doing that convincing while also fleeing, as this seemed prudent.

The run to the doors was more exhausting than anything he'd done earlier in the evening, and that was crazy because not at all long ago he ran over two kilometers in battle gear, in the rain. Yet he was winded before he even reached sporting goods. He had an awful idea that the reason for it was that the character of Orrin the night watchman was in worse physical shape than the character of Opie, the soldier.

I'm just tired, that's all.

None of the mannequins jumped in his way en route, which was nice. This was probably because the one Oliver saw move didn't move at all, and it was a trick of the lighting, and he was just allowing his own imagination to spook him. Ironically, in this instance, just because it was all in his imagination didn't mean the mannequin hadn't moved. Both of those things could be 100% true.

He got past the tarp and the water-damaged floor and turned the corner. From there it was a straight line to the exit. Already, he had the keys in his hands.

Someone was standing at the door.

He stopped running, of course. That was the proper reaction when confronted with a ghost.

It was a woman. She was barely visible in the shadows that seemed in some ways to partially blur her existence, but he could see enough to conclude that it was a her. She looked a little like Minerva, too. He didn't know what to make of that.

At first he thought she was standing on the other side of the front doors, because she was out of focus. She wasn't; she was on the inside, but she also wasn't anywhere. When he directed the flashlight at her, the light found nothing physical to illuminate. It passed right through.

"I guess this is how the story keeps me from leaving. Cool, cool."

She raised an unfocused arm and pointed at him, which was a little unsettling in a lot of ways.

"What? Look, just tell me what you want so I can fix this or whatever."

Join us.

She didn't say this, precisely. The words appeared in his head, but didn't pass through his ears first.

"No thanks?"

Join us.

"I don't know how you're doing that, but no. I wouldn't even know how."

It was an annoying impasse. He was kind of spooked by the appearance of a ghost, just like he was unnerved by a nodding mannequin, but these things had only temporary shock value. Connecting jump-scares to real-world threats was difficult; no wonder he never finished the story.

Then he thought maybe that was the problem.

"You want me to finish, don't you? Well I don't know the ending. I had a couple of ideas, but I never really decided which one to go with. And look, you're just a light show and a voice in my head. It's spooky, but a couple of hours ago a flying alien tried to eat me. I don't think you're going to top that."

Join us.

"I went with ghosts because ghosts scare the crap out of me, but now that I'm here... I mean, maybe it would be different if I were responsible for your death. That's how these things are supposed to go, right? But I'm not. Or rather, Orrin wasn't. He was just a night watchman."

We will help you.

"What? What does that mean?"

He caught movement out of the corner of his eye, and directed the light that way. It fell on a dais that until a second ago had a male mannequin modeling flannel pajamas. The stand was empty.

He had exactly enough time to register this fact when a white plastic arm slammed down on his wrist and knocked the light out of his grip. It skittered across the floor, while the owner of that plastic arm grabbed Oliver by the collar.

Ollie shouted and elbowed the dummy in the gut. This didn't have the kind of effect one would expect it to have if this were a person and not a facsimile of one, but since the point he struck was a swivel spot—where the torso was attached to the waist—it was still effective. The mannequin managed to register surprise on its featureless face as it lost its balance and fell over backwards.

But then the other ones started to move, and the enormity of the problem Oliver was facing came into focus: he was surrounded by an army. It was a fashionably dressed plastic army, moving slowly and missing a lot of joints, but he had nowhere to run and they had no reason to stop.

He didn't know what they were planning to do to him once they caught him—*join us* was hardly specific—but it didn't seem like a good idea to wait and find out what they improvised.

I need a weapon, he thought.

But Mad Maggie's didn't carry weapons, because he hadn't written them into the inventory. He would have loved to still have the pulse cannon, but that was long gone, and the only other one he knew about was sealed up in the now non-existent basement with Minnie. Unless Minnie was now the ghost near the door, because why not? Either way, her cannon was not going to be of any help. That was too bad; Oliver was pretty sure the mannequins wouldn't fare well against one of those.

He started running down the near side of the oval, far from the clothing half of the store and hopefully near some things that could be used to defend himself from whatever the plastic army had in mind. The mallet he used to crack open the recycling bin might have come in handy if he'd held onto it, but it wasn't like it was the only one in the store. Hardware was just past home goods…

Then he remembered the map in his pocket.

He stepped off the main concourse into an aisle that featured shag rug tops for toilet seats and decorative plungers. The light wasn't great there, but it was out of the way. Given a little time for his eyes to adjust, he was able to work out the details on Ben's hand-drawn map and line them up with where he stood. The smaller X was just about where the cell phone display was. The bigger one was three rows further down from his current position.

He caught the scent of… motor oil. It was a plot detail he'd forgotten about, a clue to an explanation he never entirely developed. Honestly, it was another element of the story he half-expected to edit out of any final version. It smelled like the smoke from a helicopter crash.

The smell was uniquely helpful in the moment, because it made it a lot easier to find the right aisle. This was especially true when it turned out the spot didn't have an X painted on the floor. There was actually nothing special whatsoever about it at all, aside from the odor. It was in a row of coffee makers, food processors and slow cookers, and these were also pretty unremarkable.

He stood in the spot anyway; perhaps he would beam up somewhere or there was a hidden button or a save point or something, but no.

Mad Maggie's, meanwhile, was coming to life around him. He could hear the slow shuffle of feet—shod and unshod, depending on which section they were coming from—along the industrial carpeting. Did they know what they were doing? Or why? Was there any thought process going on at all?

"If I promise to never leave another story unfinished, will you guys leave me alone?" he asked. That was dumb, because now they knew where he was, but it was hard to take that concern seriously when none of them had ears.

The first mannequin appeared at the end of his row. A female one, in a very fetching mauve tennis skirt, a sporty blouse, and a sun visor to shade the eyes she didn't have. Her hand was shaped in a grip to hold a tennis racket that wasn't there. Either she dropped it getting down from her display dais, or someone forgot to give her one.

She was moving so slowly, it was hard to feel terribly concerned about this development. He walked up to her, and stepped past, around the corner and into the face of a second mannequin. Then the ready-for-tennis one had an arm around his neck and he was taking her *very* seriously.

She was strong. Really strong. And the one right in front of Oliver—businessman-on-the-go—was about to show how strong *he* was by swinging an open palm into Ollie's stomach.

Oliver threw himself forward and down, which flipped the tennis pro over his head and into the businessman. That took care of the immediate problem of him being choked, but there were seven more of them around already. If they were all as strong as that, he was in a huge amount of trouble.

I should have gone to hardware, he thought, *instead of stopping.*

Something hard hit him in the back of the head. He fell to his knees, and got kicked, and lost his breath for about five seconds. In that time, both arms got pinned down, and then both legs.

He was spread-eagled in the middle of the concourse, in a store that didn't exist.

Join us, the girl said. She was there, at the edge of his vision, beside an endcap boasting discount pet food.

"I don't want to join you!" he said.

One of the intimidatingly athletic mannequins from the sporting goods section turned the corner then, carrying a sledge-hammer from the hardware section. It was on his shoulder, and the intent was clear.

They were going to kill him.

This was how he would join them—by becoming a ghost himself.

It was one of the plot solutions he had been considering: a not-happy ending for Orrin. He didn't like that ending. Horror stories were generally cautionary tales of some sort. Yes, there were other kinds of horror stories, with bleaker outlooks. He didn't like those as much.

The problem was, Orrin hadn't sinned, so he shouldn't have to die. He was a good guy who hadn't done anything to deserve it. That was why Oliver preferred not to go in that direction.

Perhaps Oliver *had* sinned, though, in which case this was appropriate. He just couldn't imagine how. There had to be an opening for either redemption or acknowledgement.

But, that kind of closure only happened in stories, didn't it? This was the real world. Haunted mannequins notwithstanding.

"Hey, can we talk about this?" he asked.

Join us.

"Aw, come on."

The one holding the sledgehammer got within striking distance, and was about to swing it into Oliver's chest, when some sort of commotion caused the mannequin to turn around.

"HAVE AT IT, YOU UNDEAD FIEND!" someone shouted. There was a whoosh, and the sledgehammer mannequin's head bounced along the concourse.

They jumped up and ran at the new attacker, and Oliver was freed.

All he could see at first was a massive sword swinging around. The man wielding it roared, and plastic parts flew everywhere.

It was Cant.

"Sorcerer," he roared. "What manner of beasts are these?"

Of course, it couldn't be. Cant wasn't real.

It was, undeniably, the large man Ollie had encountered previously, who either claimed to be Cant or starred in a hallucination in which he claimed to be Cant. But where before he'd been dressed somewhat appropriately for a citizen of the modern world, he now wore animal furs with patches of leather armor, a heavy cloak, and enormous metal-tipped boots. In his hands was the largest sword Oliver had ever seen. This wasn't necessarily saying a lot, since he'd had few encounters with swords in his life, but it was still very large. It was the sort of thing that made more sense as a prop for an oversized statue.

"They're mannequins," Oliver said. "I don't know how they're moving around like that, I think they may be haunted."

"Possessed by wraiths? Yes, I have heard of such an enchantment. It is very powerful."

He fought his way to Oliver, littering the floor with plastic body parts but somehow not reducing the overall number of attackers. It was a big store, but not *that* big.

He took a defensive position between Oliver and the army.

"I cannot kill what is not alive," Cant said. "Do what you are here to do so we can be freed of this place, before they challenge my limits."

Oliver realized they were reassembling themselves, outside of the reach of Cant's sword, and then coming back at him. No matter how much power he put in his swings, he could only break them at their connection points. If nothing else, it spoke to the durability of the modern mannequin when facing medieval weaponry.

"I don't know what I'm here to do, though, and I don't really know who you are. How did you even get inside? This place is locked down."

"I entered through the flexible barrier in the roof. That portal remains open, if we must retreat, but better to find your treasure first."

Cant pushed back the attacking force with a quick and furious charge, and then closed off the concourse by toppling a display.

Dozens of fashion-forward serving bowls and stand mixers scattered on the floor.

"And you know well who I am," Cant said. "I am Cant of the Warven tribe, and you are a sorcerer under my employ, in a quest to locate the Kingdom. These are all things you know, Osraic Tal Nar Drang. Atha cautions patience, but we have no more time for you to recover from your addle-brained state. These creatures do not respond to force, only magic. I am here for violence; magic is your domain. Now why are we in this place?"

"I don't know! And my name is Oliver, not Osraic."

"Govern your own name as you'd like, but know that you led us here. You read the signs in the stone that none but a sorcerer could glean, and they brought you to this... merchant storage. Now enchanted guards block our way. We are well past your insistence that you understand nothing of what's happened when your actions have made it so."

"They aren't enchanted."

"Creatures who do not bleed, feel no pain, and can re-form themselves using the component parts of their fallen comrades are not natural beings."

"I know, but... I mean to say it isn't magic. It's the supernatural. There's a difference."

Thinking Cant distracted, one of the mannequins pounced from atop a shelving unit two rows away. Cant saw the attack coming, though; he grabbed the dummy out of the air and knocked off its plastic head with a single blow.

"All right, what is the difference?" he asked.

"Ghosts aren't magic, they're something else. Supernatural and magical are different things."

"Just break the spell. I am quickly running out of patience with your delays."

"Look, I didn't even want to do this."

Oliver was talking about not wanting to go to Pallas in the first place, but for a moment there he felt like what he was really talking about was being drugged and tied to a horse and taken through the mountain pass against his will. In that moment, it felt like a sense memory, rather than a plot point in a story that only existed in his head and on his laptop. He remembered how sore his behind was, and the smell of the horse, and the color of Atha's eyes.

It was just a moment.

"Sorcerer: whether these beings are puppets haunted with the implacable spirits of the dead, or soulless guards propped up by a magical spell, there is no-one here but you. Cut their strings or counter the spell, I care not how. But we are going to lose if you fail to act."

"I'm just not sure what kind of story this is any more," Oliver said.

A proper regroup had taken place among the mannequins on both sides of the aisle. They'd put themselves back together somewhat haphazardly, with two and three different departments represented in the clothing choices of each one. There was a real possibility Oliver was about to be bludgeoned to death with a field hockey stick by a dummy in a suit jacket and bikini. At least they hadn't figured out how to throw projectiles yet. That was probably coming.

They were, anyway, about to charge. Cant may have failed to grasp the layers of absurdity that led to this moment, but he was right about the rest of it.

"There's something under the floor," Oliver said.

"The floor is made of rock," Cant pointed out.

"Cement, yes."

Oliver spied the sledgehammer, still at rest where the beheaded mannequin dropped it. He picked it up and took it to the spot on the map, where the smell of burning oil filled his nostrils.

"Can you cut through the carpet with that sword?" Ollie asked.

Cant pulled a dagger from a sheath on his hip and handed it over.

"Make quick work of it, whatever you plan."

Ollie dropped to his knees and cut an X with the blade. It wasn't quite as sharp as the average carpet knife, so it took multiple passes to get through. He tore open the material, which kicked up a cloud of dust and particulate matter from eons of foot traffic, and all of it smelled like oil.

Why burning oil? he wondered. It wasn't even an odor he was familiar with, although that didn't stop him from the certainty that this was what he was smelling.

Underneath the carpet, only a little off the center he'd defined when he cut the rug open, was a large X, glowing brightly on the concrete surface. Whatever marker that was used to scrawl the messages he'd seen on the walls earlier also made this mark.

Oliver jumped to his feet, grabbed the hammer, and swung down on the X. The heavy end bounced against the surface, and that was all. He lifted it for another swing, and wondered if he was even strong enough to do this.

There was a fire, he thought. That was going to be the big reveal in the story. But he never could decide on the particulars, or how Orrin was going to come across them.

"Where was the fire?" he said aloud, still swinging the hammer. The cement continued to reflect the impact back into the hammer, but there were signs that it was starting to give in.

"What did you say?" Cant shouted. He was trying to defend an attack on two fronts alone, which looked really exhausting.

"There was a fire, but I can't decide where it happened. This building was where fire trucks used to be stored, so the fire could have happened somewhere else but then why would the victims haunt this spot?"

Cant didn't answer right away, because one of the dummies was coming at him with a barbecue fork. Ollie took a couple more swings at the floor. The cement was starting to chip.

"I do not know the ways of magic so I can be of little use to you here, sorcerer."

"I know. I wish I could talk to Wilson about this."

"I know not who this person is."

"Oh he's my, my teacher I guess."

A real crack was showing now, and fragments were flying away with each strike.

"You are the master now," Cant said. "Teach yourself. And in the event I have not stressed this enough as yet, do so quickly."

"He's right, you're really on your own."

It was Wilson's voice, coming from the far end of the row, on the other side of the hole Oliver was attempting to make in the floor.

"Wilson?"

And then he was standing there.

"Yes. Hello. Sorry. It's the camouflage; it really works. I've been here for a while."

"For how long? You couldn't have helped?"

"I don't know, but I'm here now. So what's the issue?"

"Is Minerva here?"

"No, I haven't seen her. I thought she was with you. Things got weird. How can I help?"

"I was trying to explain why ghosts aren't magic. To Cant, who can't possibly really be here. He's fighting animated mannequins who can't possibly exist either."

"Like I said," Wilson said, "things got weird. Ghosts *are* magic."

"This is what I was saying!" Cant shouted. He was free-swinging his massive sword with one hand while beating back the army with their own body parts. This seemed smart, given they couldn't use the parts if they were getting hit by them.

"I mean technically," Wilson added. "In the sense that magic doesn't exist and neither do ghosts. I suppose you could say ghosts are supernatural while magic is unnatural."

Oliver took another swing at the floor. A real crevasse had begun to form, but there was nothing on the other side but more cement. He became concerned that the floor was too thick to get through. This was assuming he wanted to reach dirt in the first place. Maybe he did. If he was dealing with normal physics what he'd hit first was the basement, but that was probably gone.

"You're being too general," Ollie said. "I'm thinking a ghost story can't be a magic story. They serve different functions."

"But you could have a ghost in a fantasy story, and a magic-user in a ghost story."

"I appreciate that, but I need to know what kind of story *this* is."

"I never liked either kind of story. Hey, hang on a second. Looks like it's getting tight out here."

Wilson stepped past Oliver and the hole he was making and onto the concourse.

He had a pulse cannon on his back.

"Where'd that come from?" Oliver asked.

"Minnie handed it to me. I forget when. We should really find her when this is over. Hey, big guy, stand aside."

"Is this a magical device?" Cant asked, looking skeptical.

"Sure."

Wilson fired a high-energy blast at the center of the army of mannequins. Then he turned around and fired another pulse in the opposite direction. The mannequins on both sides scattered— or rather *were* scattered—all over Mad Maggie's.

"That is great magic indeed!" Cant said. "I can see why Osraic called you master, even without a beard."

"Well, forget this," Oliver said, "turn it up, point it at the wall, and let's get out of here."

"I can't, it's damaged. Probably from when yours blew up. I was surprised it worked twice."

"Of course it is."

The component parts of the mannequins remained intact, and

already Oliver could see them begin to pull themselves together. Wilson had bought only a few minutes.

"So you were saying," Wilson said.

"Right, they're fundamentally different kinds of stories. Magic reaffirms man's need to feel in control of the natural world. It's the idea that we can impose order through force of will. Ghosts are reminders that there's disorder and chaos and we aren't in control and we don't know the rules."

"The world is your oyster versus don't go out into the woods at night."

"Exactly."

"So, children's stories is what we're talking about now."

"No, stop, you do that with everything you don't understand: reframe it as childish."

"It *is* childish."

"Stories have value… you know what, I'm not going to get into this with you. The problem, right now, is that I don't know how to make the ghosts animating those mannequins stop. If this is a ghost story, I have to find out why they're so angry. If this is a happy ending kind of story, I'll live, free them, and probably suffer a lot anyway. If it's not a happy ending, I'm gonna die and haunt this place along with them. Either way, I first have to figure out what the big secret is. But, if this is a magic story, I just need to figure out how to break the spell."

"I vote for the second one," Wilson said.

"I do as well," Cant said, "if we are voting."

"The problem is, even with all the fantasy and sci-fi mashup going on here, I think we're all stuck in a horror story."

"So we do *not* get a vote," Cant said. He looked disappointed.

"All right, what's the big secret, then?" Wilson asked.

"I don't know."

"You mean you haven't finished revealing it yet." He gestured to the hole in the floor to make his point.

"Yes. No, that's not really what I mean. I mean that when I

wrote this story I didn't know what the big secret was and I still don't."

"Not a problem. You're here, just make up something."

Wilson dropped the backpack with the pulse cannon on the floor and picked up the sledgehammer. He got going on the floor as if this was what he was supposed to be doing.

"Just make up something?"

"Well, I don't know, Oliver, I'm not the expert on genre fiction in the room. I told you to work on literary fiction, and you didn't, and now here we are."

"Look, it has to be a big secret, okay? It has to be something jaw-dropping, something that makes the reader gasp and think, you know what? If this happened to me I'd be haunting that place too. Someone has to have been wronged."

"And you don't know what that is."

"*I never worked that part out!* And now you want me to come up with it on the fly?"

"All right, all right, I understand. But look, you had some subtext, right? Something about a fire? Burning oil? Something connected to the military, maybe. I assume since they're haunting this warehouse you're leaning toward an Indian burial ground kind of twist. The secret-burial-site or whatever."

"Yes, that was where I was heading. I just didn't like it."

"So we're digging up bodies over here."

His last hammer strike had dislodged the under layer of cement, with the first evidence of the ground underneath it starting to show. With dirt, there could be bodies. There could be a lot of things.

"It's just cliché. I wanted something bigger. And that doesn't even solve the problem. It doesn't explain why the ghosts are turning up *now*, why they picked on m… on Orrin, and it doesn't explain why or how they died."

"So what?"

"So it should be monstrous, or it'll just be like every other ghost story. I mean, who doesn't expect the secret burial ground angle? It's not even worth finishing."

Wilson set aside the hammer.

"Look, if you tell anybody I said this I'll deny it, but maybe it's okay to write the by-the-numbers cliché everybody can see coming from a mile away if it gets us to the end of the story."

"I agree with this one," Cant said. "Whatever you can do that works in stopping these monsters, you should do. Here they come."

Problematically, the ghost-animated mannequin army appeared to be learning. This begged the question; why would such beings behave like a mindless horde in the first place given they were thinking beings at one time—as always, assuming first that ghosts were even real. Perhaps there was something about dying and becoming a ghost that robbed a (former) person of their intellect. More likely it was just easier to have a mindless horde than it was to have a large mob of discerning undead individuals, from a writing standpoint.

Oliver decided it was probably his fault, indirectly, since this story was evidently his. He had no regrets as far as this point went, because the horde was easier to defend against when they were collectively stupid and predictable. At the same time it was probably his fault when they started throwing things, given that was something he predicted would be happening eventually.

The things they were throwing weren't all that lethal—charcoal briquettes—and their aim was terrible, but the fact that they decided to try it at all meant he could count on their learning curve to continue to trend upward. Once that happened, and they located the cutlery a couple of aisles over, things were going to get pretty dicey.

"All right, well, let's find your secret burial ground evidence," Wilson said. He got down on his knees and started digging at the dirt with his hands.

Oliver crouched down next to him to help. The earth was

cold, and a lot easier on the hands than it should have been. Loose topsoil is not what one should expect to discover underneath the floor of a warehouse.

But, they had no shovels. Those were four aisles down, on the wrong side of the mannequin horde. So it was a good thing, even if it didn't make a lot of sense.

"Got something," Wilson said.

He leaned in deeper, to his elbows, then started pulling. Oliver thought that if this was a very different kind of story, the thing he was grabbing would end up pulling Wilson down instead.

Nice twist, he thought. Then he held his breath until Wilson got his arms out of the dirt.

What he'd found was a human skull.

"Yuck," he said. "You know, if you'd taken my advice, we'd be at a cocktail party on the seaside or yachting or going to a family reunion, instead of digging up bodies. You and your genre fiction, I swear. But this should do the trick, right?"

"It might."

Wilson got to his feet and stepped out onto the concourse, the skull aloft.

"We've found the bodies!" he shouted. "Very tragic, I'm so sorry, we'll go tell the world and... I don't know. What else, fellas?"

"We will vindicate you!" Cant added.

"Yes, that's very good. Vindication!"

The response of the dummy army was unspectacular in that they continued to exist, a fact that was particularly acute in Wilson's case after he took a briquette in the forehead.

"Aowww!" he said. "Oliver, it isn't working. Should we find more skulls?"

"Maybe the ghosts think that idea's been played too," Ollie said.

"This is stupid, just make this the ending and, I don't know, fix it in a rewrite."

"Pretty sure we're not allowed a rewrite here. Hang on."

Oliver reached into the dirt. He thought he saw something else in there while Wilson was intent on discovering a bone. Something that wasn't in the shape of human remains.

What he came up with was a small box. It was rectangular, metallic, and looked the right size to hold a set of decorative fountain pens.

"What did you find?" Wilson asked. "It is better than my skull?"

"Could be."

There was some kind of legend stamped in the metal on the lid. Oliver brushed off the dirt to get a better look, which was a challenge in the half-light of the room. He spat on it, and rubbed with his sleeve.

Lot 42.

Someone appeared out of the corner of his eye. He'd been dealing with highly visible animated plastic mannequins for so long he nearly forgot this all began with a decidedly scarier-looking ghost. And there she was again, at the other end of the row. She was speaking words he couldn't hear, and pointing at the box in his hands.

"This is it," Oliver said.

Wilson looked at what he had, not particularly impressed.

"That? What is it?"

"It's a box."

"I see that, what's inside?"

"I don't know, I haven't opened it yet."

Oliver stood up and held it out for all the mannequins to see it with their non-existent eyes.

"LOT FORTY-TWO," Oliver announced.

He was *not* hit in the head with a charcoal briquette, which was nice. Instead, a curious occurrence: the army stood still, as if at attention. Then there was a weird doubling effect that looked like a trick of the eyes, as the specters inhabiting each of the dummies took one step forward, and then melted into the ground.

That left nothing to hold up the mannequins, and while they were designed to stand upright for long periods, that required an exactness of positioning that was absent in this case. Thus, they all fell to the ground in a collection of heaps.

"Okay, why did that work?" Wilson asked.

"Magic," Cant said. "He spoke the words which broke the spell."

"Or found the clue which released them," Oliver said.

"But what *is* it?"

"I don't know what it is and I don't know what it means. That was the key."

"Not knowing was the key? Open the box, maybe it *is* a key."

Oliver checked the front of the box. There was a latch, but no lock. Slowly, he unhooked it and lifted the lid.

"It's not a key," he said. "And I have no idea what I'm looking at."

The box contained a glass vial of blue liquid in a cushioned interior that looked designed specifically to safely transport a glass vial.

Oliver showed it to Wilson, and then to Cant, who shrugged.

"We should find our way from this place," he said, kicking one of the dummy legs on the floor. "I have no interest in your potions."

"What did you mean, this was the key?" Wilson asked.

"The key to the plot. Since there was no back-loaded mystery to solve, it had to be front-loaded instead." He looked at Cant. "Any idea how we get out of here?"

Cant pointed with the tip of his sword down the concourse.

"There is a barred exit ahead. Is it a door you can open?"

Oliver checked his hip.

"I think so. I have the night watchman keys."

They picked their way around the mannequin carcasses, slowly, as if they were all sleeping instead of just being inanimate objects. Oliver kept waiting for one of them to grab his ankle or something.

"So you cheated," Wilson said.

"What do you mean?"

"You couldn't come up with a big reveal in the parameters of your ghost story, so you put the introduction of the mystery at the end of the story instead."

"I guess you could call that cheating, sure."

They got to the door. Oliver began fumbling for the keys, but didn't have to bother. Cant took one look at the chain, gave it a yank, and let it fall away from the handles. On seeing the impressed faces of his companions, he shrugged.

"I am not that strong. It wasn't locked."

He pushed open the door, which led to a vestibule, and an opaque steel panel gate that rolled down from the top of an overhang. Cant leaned down to grab the bottom of it. Assuming it wasn't locked, this would expose them to the night.

"Hang on a second," Wilson said. "Oliver, it's cheating because instead of ending the story, you're starting a new one. So what kind of story is it now?"

"I have no idea," Oliver said. "But I'm pretty sure when he opens that gate we're going to find a city still under attack by aliens. That's how we left it."

Cant ignored the talk of aliens, and opened the gate. Oliver felt like he should be reaching for his cannon, but he didn't have one any more. Old instincts.

There were no aliens waiting for them outside. It looked like the city was just as abandoned as before, but the rain had stopped. No giant bugs were in sight.

Minerva was there. She was standing in the middle of the

street, looking like it was perfectly normal for them to have emerged from this exit at this time.

"Minnie!" Oliver said.

At the same time, Cant was taking vast strides in her direction.

"Gods, Atha, where have you been? Lazy elf."

Oliver had no time to register this, because Minnie was backpedaling from both of them.

"Stay away, both of you," she said. "It's armed."

She had on a jacket Oliver didn't remember her wearing the last time they were together. It was an overcoat that was a little big for her, which made sense as soon as she removed it.

There was a bomb vest strapped to her chest.

"You have to do what he says or he'll set it off."

"Oh," Oliver said. "So it's that kind of story now."

Chapter Twelve

THE WISDOM OF OWLS

W hatever process transformed the interior of the real department store called Daniel's into the thoroughly imaginary department store Mad Maggie's had not impacted the rest of the city. In Oliver's imagining, Mad Maggie's existed as a large warehouse in a parking lot oasis, a standalone building in the exurbs. Conversely, Daniel's was the place you took a subway train to reach, or to come across because it was next to a host of other shops.

The shopping village aspect was still all there. They were downtown, much closer to the hub—and Pallas—than before they took to the underground at Candle Square.

This area of the city was sort of like an outdoor mall. The streets had been surrendered to pedestrian traffic over a decade earlier, and there was a constant rotation of stores through the high-rent storefronts. It lacked the singularity of vision one might see in a real outdoor mall, with several landlords instead just the one, but that just made it less homogenous, and also less artificial.

Ollie liked the area, although he never shopped in it, even though it wasn't at all far from his apartment. These stores catered to a clientele that had money, which he did not have. Wilson and Minerva, perhaps, would be more familiar with it.

Of course, all of that was before there were aliens, a warrior from an imaginary timeline, ghosts, and whatever was going on with Minerva at this moment.

"Who is *he*," Oliver asked.

"There is no other man here," Cant added. He was scanning the area like any good warrior would. "We are alone."

"I don't know who he is. He jumped me in the basement."

"All right, what does he want?" Ollie asked.

"This garment you wear. Is it enchanted?"

She addressed Cant first. Minnie didn't seem to be having any trouble with him being there, and also had no problem flipping from modern woman in a modern city, to Atha the elven archer.

"The vest is cursed," she said.

He gasped.

"We require a blessed token! Sorcerer! With all of those trinkets of yours, do you have a charm?"

"If you recall, I didn't exactly pack for this trip," Oliver said, "so no."

"Then use your magic!"

Oliver decided he'd be better off ignoring Cant for the time being.

"What does he want?" he repeated to Minerva.

"He said there was something he needed inside that store, and he didn't know where it was, but you would find it. He seems to have a strong opinion about what you should do with it next."

She held up a cell phone, high over her head, and walked it over to Oliver.

"Don't do anything crazy," she said under her breath, "I think he may be able to see us, somehow."

Ollie accepted the phone, while Minerva took several steps back, as if the phone was the bomb and not the thing on her chest. The line was already open. He hit the speaker button.

"Hello? Who's this?" Oliver asked.

"You shouldn't have to ask, Orson." The man on the other end of the phone had a Russian accent. He sounded familiar, but Oliver couldn't place him.

"I'm not…"

He was about to say *I'm not Orson*, before Minerva looked him in the eye and shook her head.

Her eyes were green, and they weren't that kind of green before, and it distracted him temporarily, because she was clearly now playing the part of both Minerva and Atha, and Atha had unique and not-quite-human green eyes.

"Hello… old friend," he said on the phone. "I thought you were dead."

Minerva made a silent *what?* to which he shrugged. He was ad-libbing, but with the best generic dialogue that came to mind. It seemed to fit the situation.

His old friend laughed.

"And now you have followed the clues right to where I wanted. Do you have it?"

He realized he *had* spoken to this man.

"Not sure what you're talking about, Koestler."

"We've been playing this game for too long, comrade. Please don't make me blow up your lovely little girlfriend. You know I will. Singapore wasn't all that long ago."

Singapore was where I killed him, Oliver thought. *After he murdered my partner. He was holding her captive to force me to betray my country and I wouldn't do it, and he killed her. I hunted him down and had a chance to bring him in alive, and instead I shot him in cold blood and watched his body fall off one of the tallest buildings in the world. He shouldn't be alive.*

"I remember," Oliver said.

"I am sure you do. Now. Do you have it?"

"I have it."

"Prove this to me."

"Lot forty-two."

There was a pause. Then: "Is it intact?"

"Of course it is. It's a lethal poison, isn't it? If it broke, we would be dead."

"The whole city would be dead. Perhaps the country. And yet since the evacuation, we are very much alone. I could have been convinced the contagion escaped, but for the lack of bodies."

"All right so you have your proof. This is your game, how do you want to play it?"

"Ordinarily, I would meet you in public, where your lady friend's kaboom would destroy many more lives, and where you might be less inclined to employ that irrational heroism of yours. But since you've gone to such great pains to remove all the collateral damage from the city, I have had to make other plans."

"I'm not hearing an answer."

"That place you spoke of. Pallas, yes? You will go there and you will await further instructions. You have thirty minutes."

"Yeah, I'm gonna need more time than that."

"What makes you think you are in any position to negotiate?"

"Koestler, look around. There's no public transportation, the cars are all dead, and this is just a guess, but I think sprinting in a suicide vest is a bad idea. Plus, we've been trying to get to Pallas since the middle of the afternoon, it's just not that easy a commute."

"You are going to run out of time in your effort to talk me to death, as always. You now have twenty minutes."

"All right, how about this? She's gonna be holding the vial you're so keen on, so if you blow her up, you blow up your prize too."

"This would aerosolize the pathogen. You would not be so reckless."

"I admit, it's not ideal, but if that happens I'll be dead too, so maybe I don't care all that much about the consequences."

There was a long silence, as Koestler ran through his options.

Oliver thought he was foolish for having arranged all this

without a secondary consequence, like another hostage, and Koestler wasn't a foolish man. This meant Oliver was missing something.

"All right, you have one hour."

"Might take longer."

"One hour, and then I will set off the bomb and let this entire nation go to hell."

Koestler hung up.

"Did you just use our lives as collateral to buy more time?" Minnie asked. She looked a little nonplussed, but that might have been the bomb she was wearing.

"Not really. Pretty sure he's bluffing."

"Why, because he doesn't want to release a pathogen in the city?"

"He's motivated by money these days. When he was younger, it was the cause, but not any more. The vial is worthless to him if he can't sell it."

"How do you know any of that?"

"No idea. Let's just go with it."

He pulled out the Lot 42 box from his back pocket.

"Now, we have a little less than an hour to figure out what this really is and to disarm that bomb."

"I thought you guys said it was a lethal virus or something."

"Could be. I never wrote any of this down. W is for weapon, but that could mean a lot of things. All I know is, Koestler *wants* me to think that's what it is. Just like he wants me to think he's okay with blowing it up. Wilson? I could use some plot advice."

He turned around to the space Wilson last occupied when they emerged from the entrance of Mad Maggie's/Daniel's. Wilson wasn't there.

"Where'd he go this time?" he asked.

"You saw Wilson?" Minnie asked.

"He was with us. Didn't you see him?"

"Just you two."

"He is a sorcerer," Cant said. "Their trickery is no surprise."

"If you feel that way, maybe you should stop kidnapping them. But you just gave me an idea. I need a modern wizard. I need the Internet."

"Is that one of your gods?" Cant asked.

"It might as well be."

"The city has no power," Minerva said.

"But the cell phone towers are working, babe," he said, holding up Koestler's phone. "So let's get moving."

"All right. But, did you just call me *babe*?"

~

The trip to Ollie's apartment was only ten minutes at a casual pace, which they took. It looked like the local alien invaders were on a break.

Minerva seemed a little on edge on account of the bomb she was stuck inside of, and wanted to move faster, but Oliver wasn't kidding when he said it seemed like a bad idea to sprint when wearing one of those things.

He had the irrational belief that he could disarm the bomb vest when the time came. It was irrational because it stemmed from an understanding of how bombs worked that he was pretty sure he didn't actually have, but that Orson likely did. That was good enough, because the other thing Orson had a lot of was confidence. And hyper-competence was a job requirement, so he had good reason.

"Tell me what this is," Minerva asked, when they were about a block from the apartment building.

"It's a techno-thriller. Or something like it. Something with spies. Maybe a Cold War story."

"Did you write one? I don't remember hearing about it."

"No, but it was going to be next. Also, I think Koestler might have been the pilot of that helicopter that crashed outside of your building."

"The one we saved? He doesn't sound very grateful."

"He doesn't, does he? Well, that's Koestler for you."

Minnie laughed.

"Your old friend, Koestler," she said. "I wasn't sure you were going to follow me into that smoke."

"Well, somebody had to."

"Glad you did. I was worried you were going to stay passive. Sure, now I have a bomb on my chest, but it's mostly worked out."

"I guess. I'm pretty positive I've completely lost my mind, sweetheart, but I figured I'd better get to the end of this first and then pick up the pieces. Might as well embrace the absurd."

"That's the spirit. So what makes you think he was the pilot?"

"I don't think he was the pilot; I think he was the guy sitting in the pilot's seat. But that's splitting hairs. I was thinking of this plot when the chopper went down, and the plot I was thinking of had a crash in it."

"So did your military sci-fi. Inferentially."

"Ben from my romance outline had a map to treasure that was hidden in the floor of the store from my ghost story, which I found with the help of a warrior from my epic fantasy. Everything's running into everything else. I wonder why he was named Ben?"

"He was just a sketch. All you wrote was an outline."

"Yeah, but his name was Nathan in the outline. Yet you said the first time you heard Ben's name you knew he was important. I still don't get why. Was it because he had a last name?"

"That was half the reason, yes," Minerva said. "But only half."

"What was this Ben's family name?" Cant asked.

Minerva smiled.

"It was Codeks, Cant," she said.

Cant laughed.

"Ben Codeks!"

Then Oliver got it. Maybe he needed Cant to say it out loud first.

"Ben, for Benja Codex," Ollie said. "That's cute."

"Indeed! The ur-text for the legend of the Kingdom itself, hidden in human form, in this strange land. That potion so coveted by your foe, the sorcerer Koestler, is the key to the Kingdom itself, for that is the only thing the Benja Codex could be leading us to. Where is this man now?"

"He died," Minnie said. "He had a heart attack. We tried to save him."

"This only means you've lost track of the codex," Cant said. "As before, you cannot kill what is not alive."

They got to the stoop of the apartment building.

"This is where you live?" Minerva asked. "Looks nice."

"It isn't. It's an old building and I live in an expensive coffin. But it's what I could afford."

Cant hesitated at the base of the stairs.

"Coming?" Oliver asked.

"No. These places disturb me."

"You mean… buildings?"

"It's unnatural. You southerners mock us for the way we live north of the Ailings and then build your own mountains and live inside of them. I can see enemies approach better from here."

"His people aren't fond of enclosures," Minerva said. Unless she was Atha when she said it, which was entirely possible.

"And elves prefer trees. They hide their discomfort better is all."

"Especially when they're wearing cursed objects and the only available sorcerer wants to go inside," Minerva said.

"We'll be right out," Oliver said, "don't vanish."

"You think I would know how?"

"I think people have been vanishing a lot lately around here, so don't do that."

The inside looked no different than the last time Oliver was there, which was refreshing. No lights, though, and that was a little annoying, because he'd lost the light he'd been using for the past couple of genres. What they had to navigate by was the soft glow from Koestler's cell phone and the blinking electronics on the bomb. This was enough, but only because he already knew the way.

Six flights up creaky stairs was a little unnerving. He was on edge, and not sure if that was a residue of the ghost story he'd just survived—the building still felt haunted—or a component of his new ultra-competence. He thought it was probably the second thing, and wished he had a gun in his hand.

They were too exposed.

But they got to the door okay. He'd changed outfits two or three times by now, and wasn't entirely in charge of those wardrobe swaps, so it was a nice surprise when the key to the place was still in his pocket where it was supposed to be.

"Prepare to be not impressed," he said, opening the apartment door. They stepped in.

"All right," she said. "I'm not impressed."

"Told you."

"I'm kidding. It's dark and I can't see anything. But what's that smell?"

"I don't really know. Laundry, probably. I don't have any food in here. It always smells like that."

"I'm glad Cant stayed outside. My senses appear to be heightened when I'm around him."

"Well, you *are* an elf."

"Not right now. And when did you start talking about this stuff like it was perfectly normal?"

"It's not normal, darling, it's insane. But I'm gonna keep moving forward. No sin in keeping alive."

"I think you like this version of yourself a little too much,

Oliver. Meanwhile, I went from warrior to damsel in distress. If we survive this, remind me to be mad at you about that."

"You can't hold me accountable for a popular trope."

"Sure I can. You had a problem with every other cliché, but not this one?"

"Clichés and tropes aren't the same thing."

"Take that up with Wilson. I just want this bomb off, thank you. And maybe to not be called *sweetheart* and *babe* quite as often."

The laptop was on the mattress, where he left it. He opened it up, which bathed the room in a healthy glow. He used that to find a proper flashlight.

"This is the whole apartment?" Minerva asked. "There isn't another room on the side somewhere?"

"This is the entire place. Enjoy the spacious accommodations. Especially the palatial mattress on the floor that's also the full extent of the seating possibilities."

"It's body odor."

"What is?"

"The smell. You don't go to the laundry enough."

"That's true. Look, if I knew today was the day I'd be bringing you here, I'd have picked up and fumigated."

"Oh, but you planned on bringing me here?"

"I wouldn't call it a plan. An aspiration."

She laughed.

"I think I probably would have come."

It wasn't easy to tell in the light, but he thought he was getting a good smile from her. Given there was hardly any standing room, she was smiling at a time when they were right on top of one another, which resulted in a brief, electric frisson that Oliver was sure he wasn't imagining.

"Look, I would love to talk about any other plans you had for me, Ollie, but I'm going to need to change into something more comfortable first. Something less explosive."

"Right."

He returned his attention to the laptop, sat down in his usual spot and began typing commands. Minerva stood around awkwardly for a few seconds before deciding to sit as well.

"So how do you have Internet access?" she asked. "Without any power?"

"The laptop has a battery, and I'm magic."

"No, I mean really."

"All right, battery power, and the need for expository information to be obtained at this point in the story."

"Seriously?"

"Yeah, I'm serious. We don't have a story to follow here, but every story has beats it's gotta hit. Right now, I need to know more about Lot Forty-Two, so here we are."

"I don't know how you're going to get anything with only that piece of information."

"Oh, I have more than that."

He was actually just entering commands into a search engine, which was the same thing anyone with basic web access and a little free time could do. He expected to hit a firewall at some point that would require a more robust skillset, but that hadn't happened yet.

"Like what?"

"Koestler wants it, and he said it's related to the government in some way, so now I'm looking for Lot Forty-Two plus U.S. Government. I also know it's related to a program that suffered some kind of accident: a fire. People were killed. I think the accident and the deaths were both classified, and I think the bodies were buried underneath the old department store downtown."

"Daniel's? That's been there forever."

"The building has, but the basement and the subway connection only dates back to... 1972, it looks like."

"So a local top secret government program from the late

1960's that ended with a fire and a mass grave. In the city, somehow."

"It's not that crazy. The first nuclear reactor was built in a sub-basement in Chicago. And part of that land... There."

"What?"

He turned the laptop so she could see his screen. She didn't look as impressed as he expected her to be.

"I don't get it," she said.

It was a city map, circa 1967. One block from the corner on which Daniel's sat was a square building identified as a student center for the university. A subway station existed in that spot now.

"I don't think that was really a student center," Oliver said.

He called up images from the street for the same era, revealing a brick building with a glassed entrance and no windows.

"I agree that that's the most uninviting student center I've ever seen, but this is pretty thin," Minerva said.

"The building burned down a year after that photo."

"Okay, now I'm with you. What happened?"

Oliver scrolled through a couple of pages. There was only so much more he was going to be able to get from public resources, though.

"The papers at the time have almost no details. It happened in the summer, during a renovation, and that's all. Nobody hurt, infrastructure damaged, the school sold the property to the city rather than rebuild. That's it."

There was an icon on his desktop he had never noticed before: the silhouette of an owl. Seeing that made everything fall into place.

"He needs my access," he muttered.

"What's that?"

Oliver ignored her, because time was now very important. He

had to know what Lot 42 was and then get out. He clicked on the icon.

A screen he'd never seen before—and yet was somehow intimately familiar with—popped up. It was a security portal for a firewall, and it needed a user ID and a password. Putting zero thought into it, he let his fingers type whatever they wanted.

The user ID that worked was OrsonDTN. The password was fifteen digits, and he entered it so fast he couldn't have repeated it at gunpoint.

Just keep rolling with it, he told himself.

The portal led to a list of files.

"Ollie."

"Hang on."

There were dozens of file names. He didn't have the time to go through every one of them to figure out where he was supposed to be looking. On top of that, this was the first stage of access, and if what he wanted was hidden here, it was poorly hidden indeed. He scanned the page until he discovered an *Archives* link. From there, he found the right era—they were split into five year chunks—where he was greeted with a collection of random character file titles, half with RESTRICTED flags on them.

"It's just that we're running out of time," Minerva said. "The bomb, and all that."

"Oh, right. Don't worry, it's not a real bomb."

"What? Are you sure?"

"Pretty sure."

"How long have you known?"

"About a minute."

The random character file titles were all four letters long. His first thought was that he was looking at DNA coding, but there was far too great a variety of letters in use for it to be something like that. Then he saw what he wanted. The file was called TAWU.

"Tenth Avenue Writers Underground," he muttered.

"Oliver!"

"What?"

"How do you know it isn't a real bomb? This is kind of important, so I'd like to understand your reasoning, if that's okay."

"Our time was up thirty seconds ago, that's how I know. Now give me a second."

He clicked on the TAWU file, and was greeted with another password portal. This one required a four-digit code. After trying TAWU—which unsurprisingly did not work—he thought about it for a few seconds, and then tried Wilson and Minerva's condo number.

The file opened. He began reading.

Lot 42 was the name of the most successful—and last—trial run in an experiment in remote viewing: Project Wise Eyes. It was similar to the MK Ultra experiments the CIA ran, except the subjects in these tests were chemically induced into a state which allowed them to remotely view things.

These experiments worked, or so the team running it thought. The test subjects were able to report back with accurate information, providing details they couldn't possibly have known. Better, the formula could work on anybody: the government didn't need someone who already had psychic powers. They could *give* psychic powers to anyone, temporarily, under extremely controlled conditions.

Things started to go wrong when one subject—a young woman whose picture happened to be in the file—reported that not only was she able to see remotely, she was able to move things around remotely. It got worse from there. Others soon found they could not just move things, they could alter the nature of things: suspend the laws of physics, transform people into dogs, and so on. It was fantastic, and impossible, and entirely unverifiable. In the real world, nobody ended up being turned into dogs, gravity was never suspended temporarily, or any of that.

Despite this, all of the remote viewers insisted their experiences were real. The conclusion of the head scientist attached to the project (his name was redacted, even at this level) was that the test subjects were indeed remotely viewing *something*, but it wasn't the real world. It was some other place.

It read like bad science fiction, which a part of Oliver's brain decided it probably was. At the same time, he couldn't ignore the fact that he knew the face of the woman in the file. It was the ghost in Mad Maggie's. It was also, somehow, Minerva.

"All right," Minerva said. She'd been hyperventilating for the past minute or so, as Ollie read, and she expected to die. "How did you know it wasn't real?"

"Koestler's too smart. If that's a real bomb, he put the power into my hands, since I'm the one holding the Lot Forty-Two samples, and he doesn't want it blown up. He'd like me to think this is some kind of world-ending virus to appeal to my sense of duty, but really he just wanted me to look it up to find out what it *really* is."

"You mean, what you're doing right now?"

"That's exactly what I mean. I have access to information he doesn't have and he's tricked me into using it. Which means somewhere in that vest you have on is a spybot that just airhopped onto my computer's signal and recorded my keystrokes."

"If you know all this, why did you do it?"

"Because I still had to know what the formula really was. Besides, I had nothing better to do; we're already cornered."

The cell phone rang. Ollie answered, and put it on speaker again.

"How'd I do?"

"Very good," Koestler said.

"He's in the building?" Minerva asked, quietly. Oliver nodded.

"Now, I *would* ask you to kindly deliver the samples to me, and promise to let you live if you did this thing, but we both know this is a waste of breath. I am not letting you exit alive."

"You're nothing if not an honest man."

"I would be hurt if you thought otherwise."

There was a small black steamer trunk sitting under the front window. Oliver had been using it as a table to hold up a houseplant that had perished sometime in the past year. He kept watering it anyway, in part because he thought it would eventually recover, and in part because he didn't feel like throwing it away and finding a new plant to kill.

What was interesting was that he could have sworn the thing holding the plant up was an actual table, not a trunk.

"So now what, Koestler?"

"Now you stay where you are. I'll be along presently."

The line went dead.

Oliver shoved the plant aside, and opened the trunk.

"I hope you're keeping track of this, because I'm lost," Minerva said.

"I am. Let's get that vest off of you. He can still use it to track our movements."

Inside the trunk was a layer of neatly folded clothing, which should have been a giveaway that something was amiss inasmuch as Oliver never folded anything. He lifted the clothes aside to reveal a much more interesting layer. Specifically: a bulletproof vest, a Glock G29, and a toolkit.

He removed the toolkit first.

"Step over here," he said.

The bomb vest was locked to her with a high-tension cable wire usually seen attached to bike locks. It didn't look like something Oliver could cut through quickly without a bolt-cutter, and he didn't have one of those. He did have a lockpick, though, and the padlock holding the whole thing together looked pretty basic. That could mean it was a trick.

With the flashlight, he examined the vest closely, top to bottom, on both sides.

"What are you looking for?" she asked.

"A failsafe."

"I thought you said it isn't a bomb."

"It's not, but that doesn't mean there's nothing lethal about it. He can kill you without blowing us both up."

"I continue to not like this in the slightest."

"Noted."

There wasn't anything else there. He saw everything one would expect from a live bomb, which only meant that the wiring and electronics were real. If the C-4 bricks were fake, it wouldn't matter.

Oliver got to work on the lock, which was in the center of her chest. This was slightly awkward, but only slightly.

"You're sure there aren't any other surprises?" she asked.

"Pretty sure, yeah. You want me to cut the red wire first?"

"Or the blue."

"I could start to cut the red wire, change my mind at the last second, and cut the blue. That always seems to work."

"Funny."

"Then I could exhale when the bomb doesn't go off, and say something clever."

The lock opened.

"There we are," he said, pulling the padlock off. "You can remove that now."

"You're sure."

"Pretty sure. I mean, there's a chance this is a misdirect and I'm not actually the hero, in which case the bomb will go off and the real hero will be whoever turns up to avenge my death, but I don't think this is one of those."

"Jesus, Ollie, what if it's just real life? Bombs actually go off in real life."

"True. Take it off anyway. Put this on instead."

He tossed her the bulletproof vest.

"It may be a little big," he added.

"What about one for you?"

"I'll be fine."

He checked the Glock. It was loaded, as he expected it would be.

Minerva took off the bomb vest. They did not die. She slipped on the bulletproof one.

"Now?" she asked.

Now you get taken hostage, he thought.

"We try and get out of here alive," he said. "Let's move."

~

Ollie cracked open the door. There was good reason to think the hallway was clear, only because the building had eight floors. Whatever tracker happened to be in that bomb vest, it wouldn't be all that helpful when it came to identifying the correct floor. GPS is great with north-south-east-west, and not so good with up-down.

This was assuming Koestler had tech that was functioning during a citywide blackout. Since his cell worked (as did Ollie's laptop) he imagined this was a good assumption.

He considered using a hand mirror to check the hallway more thoroughly, but he had no mirror and the hall had no light, so it would have been a fruitless exercise. He did have a flashlight now, but that was going to end up being more useful when it came to getting shot at than it would if he were the one doing the shooting. Better to acclimate his eyes as well as possible and keep the flashlight for emergencies.

When they came out of the apartment, it was in a crouch. Ollie went first, on his knees, checking both ends of the corridor. He crawled out to the opposite wall and then waved Minerva out.

No guns went off, and the floor was quiet. He got to his feet and helped her to hers.

"We make for the stairs," he whispered, "and get you out of here."

"What about you?"

"I don't leave until Koestler does. That's just how this has to work."

She looked like she was ready to argue, but decided this was not the best time to do that.

They made it to the landing, when the floor erupted. Gunfire, from above. Oliver more or less expected it; he was already pushing Minnie back against the wall of the stairwell before the first bullet landed.

It wasn't the kind of place that lent it self naturally to clean sight lines. He knew it, and so did Koestler.

"That doesn't sound like your Walther PP, buddy," Oliver shouted. "Did you finally retire that thing?"

"I'm afraid I lost it when dying in Singapore," Koestler said. He was one flight up. "A shame. But, sentimentality is not best expressed in small arms, I've decided."

Ollie stepped out and fired twice in roughly the correct direction. He stepped back again, and waited.

"You've held onto the Glock, though," Koestler said. His voice was higher up now. "Perhaps your perspective on sentiment differs."

"I just like the gun."

Ollie moved to the base of the stairs leading up. The way looked clear.

"Go down," he whispered to Minerva. "Get to Cant, I'll be out when I'm done."

"Come with me!"

"I have to finish this."

"No you don't. You can just…"

She gestured rather than finishing the thought, which was

fine. The gesture meant surrender, but what she meant by it was, *you don't have to follow this plot if you don't want to.* He was pretty sure she was wrong.

Koestler fired once, a shot that came nowhere near anybody, but caused both Ollie and Minnie to duck defensively. Then they heard him running.

"He's heading for the roof," Oliver said. "I have to stop him. Go, get out of here!"

He didn't wait around to see her head down; Koestler was getting away.

Not this time, he thought. *Not again.*

He reached the next floor and pushed up against the wall in anticipation of gunshots which never came. Then on to the next flight, and then to the top, and the doorway leading to the roof.

The building had a flat rooftop that was officially off-limits to the tenants, and was unofficially the best spot to get a suntan in the summertime. It was possible to go from this roof to either of the adjacent buildings by jumping a five-foot gap. That made it a viable escape route, and a sensible option for an international mercenary.

Oliver knew the roof well. He knew as soon as he exited the door that he was vulnerable to an attack from the side of the door and from above the exit. Other than that there was no place to hide. So, when he pushed through the door he checked both positions.

He'd miscalculated, in two ways. First, Koestler wasn't there, and neither was anyone else. Second, Koestler didn't mean to use the rooftops to escape. There was a helicopter parked on the top of an adjacent building.

He swept the whole rooftop just to be sure. Cigarette butts and seagull poop, a couple of empty beer bottles and an old tube of suntan lotion. No Russian.

He wondered how it was possible for him to have gotten to

the roof first, then he heard a creak. The door to the stairs was opening.

Ollie spun around, and trained his gun on the opening.

"What, did you stop for the bathroom?" Oliver asked. But Koestler didn't emerge from the doorway: Minerva did.

"I told you…"

"I'm sorry," she said. She looked frightened, which he realized was caused by the Smith & Wesson pointed at the back of her head.

"So eager you were to catch me, you ran right past, old friend," Koestler said. "What a tragedy, your young lady elected to follow you up."

The Russian wrapped an arm around Minerva's neck and pushed the gun barrel against her temple. This was hardly the first time he'd picked up a human shield in his travels, evidently.

Koestler was a hard man. He had thin, grey-white hair atop a square block of a head that looked as if it had been chiseled. Every scar and wrinkle looked earned, and his cobalt eyes looked like they belonged to someone ready to tell you about every one of them. He was dressed in a black turtleneck and a brown jacket, as if he'd only just stepped off of a Russian sub from thirty years past. He looked like the kind of man people had to come up with a plan to deal with. He was bad news.

"Why don't you let her go?" Oliver said. "I have Lot Forty-Two. It's yours."

"Yes, we will get to that. You read the file, did you not? Tell me, do you know how they shut down this Project Wise Eyes?"

"The fire."

"Oh, yes, the fire. But that's such an understatement. I will read the documents later, at my leisure, once you are dead but before I sell the contents of that entire database to some extremely motivated parties with which I am familiar. My information comes from a jocular scientist who had no reason to lie after all the torture. This fire, you see, it came only after the test subjects stopped needing doses of the compound. Now, I admit the man who told me this was in a tremendous amount of pain, but he swears that things began happening around the facility. Little things at first, but then… large things. Entire doorways replaced by walls. Objects levitating. Hamburgers lowing like cattle."

"That's ridiculous."

"I thought so as well! But it was a string I had to pull. Now, I feel it is far less ridiculous. Now I believe it is true. And the fire is the worst part. For when it became clear they could no longer control the test subjects, the military—your government—decided to liquidate them. Twenty men and women, in twenty separate rooms, each dosed with Lot Forty-Two, and sent on some mission, just as they had been every other time. It put them in something like a coma, I'm told. Only, on this occasion the dose was laced with a poison. None of them would awaken, and to make certain of that, they sealed up the building and burned the bodies right where they lay."

"Oh, god," Minerva said quietly.

"Yes indeed," Koestler said. "I wonder, what do you suppose happens to you if someone kills your body while you are not inhabiting it? Perhaps you know, Orson?"

You get angry ghosts, Oliver thought.

"Sounds like a fairy tale, Koestler," he said. "But if you want to test it out yourself, here you go."

He held up the Lot 42 tin.

"Just put it on the ground, and kick it aside. I'll collect it once I'm done with you."

Minnie looked like she was about ready to try something. She was gesturing with her hand, out of sight of Koestler. She was holding up three fingers.

Ollie knew the trick. She'd count down to one and then drop, or head-butt Koestler, or elbow him in the groin, and Oliver was supposed to shoot at the same time, all before the Russian had a chance to retaliate against either of them. It was a cool trick that worked great in the movies, the problem being that it wouldn't work here. Their opponent was too well-trained.

"Now place your gun on the ground as well, if you would please."

Oliver crouched down, and had just let go of his gun when Minerva reached her last finger. She went with the head-butt. It missed, because Koestler saw it coming and moved aside. She fell backwards a little, off-balance, before he caught her.

"Such initiative!" he exclaimed. He spun her around and in a quick, and rather elegant maneuver, flung her right over the side of the building. Ollie had his gun again by the time Koestler righted himself.

Koestler fired, but at the spot Oliver no longer occupied. Ollie dove to his left, came up on one knee, and fired a round into the Russian's right shoulder. Koestler's second shot went wide, and there wasn't a third, because he needed the shoulder in order to fire the gun.

"Now we're done, you son of a bitch," Oliver said.

"I don't think we are."

"Oliver, help me!" Minerva cried. She hadn't gone all the way off the roof; he could see her hand on the edge.

Distracted, he didn't see Koestler drop down and grab a handful of roof gravel until that gravel was being thrown in his face. The Russian charged, and nearly took them both over the side. Ollie landed hard on his back, his gun skittering out of reach.

But Koestler only had one good arm. Oliver rabbit-punched him in the wounded shoulder and shoved him aside, and then scrambled over to Minnie. He reached down and caught her by the vest just a second or two before her grip gave out.

"I have you," he said.

"You're letting him get away!"

He was indeed. Koestler scooped up the Lot 42 tin and ran to the helicopter, electing that over finding one of the guns and possibly giving Ollie another chance to kill him.

The chopper's rotors got going. It took longer to get Minerva back up onto the roof than it did for Koestler to get airborne.

"I can't believe you let him have it," Minerva said. "Isn't that formula dangerous?"

"It is, yes."

"So did you switch them out?"

"No. That would have been a good idea, but I didn't have a chance."

"All right, then why don't you look worried?"

The chopper reached an altitude sufficient to clear all the buildings in the vicinity, and then made a bee-line inbound.

"There's a no-fly zone over this city, remember?"

"Sure but that was…"

Then a set of lights swung into view behind Koestler: one yellow, one a little purplish. They split up and flanked the helicopter. A second later a pair of lightning bolts erupted from the alien devices, and the chopper looked like something caught in a Faraday cage. It dropped out of view.

"Ouch," Minnie said.

A plume of smoke rose up from what had to be a pretty rough crash landing.

"I guess he's going to need us to pull him from the wreckage again," Oliver said. "Good thing we're going that way already."

"Are we?"

"Sure. I know it's hard to see with the power down, but he just crashed that thing right in front of Pallas. Hope you're still up for dancing."

Chapter Thirteen

FOR A HORSE

By the time they got back to the street to an impatient-looking Cant, Minerva had undergone a complete transformation, from hostage to elven warrior. There was even a quiver of arrows waiting for her on the stoop.

Oliver wondered if she was even aware of the change. He was learning to roll with all of the shifts in their shared reality—which he was now actively questioning—but it was a self-aware shift. Deep down, he was still Oliver, whether he was also Orrin, or Opie, Osraic or Orson. Her shifts seemed far more thorough.

Cant looked the woman he called Atha up and down.

"I see you are no longer cursed," he said.

"I'm not. But he had to dangle me off a cliff before it was finished."

"Long story," Oliver said. "I think I know the way to your Kingdom now."

"You've read all the signs?"

"I think so. Do you see the plume of smoke in the distance?"

"A great beast was felled there just moments ago."

"It was. That's our destination."

"Pallas," Minerva said, for clarification.

"All roads lead there."

"Of course," Cant said. "There would be a great palace. A monstrous cathedral, even, but hid with magics. I am glad the augurs have revealed the truth, Osraic. I knew all along you were the correct choice."

Minerva rolled her eyes.

"Yes of course you did."

"Now, where is that fool with the horses?" Cant asked.

"Which fool is that?" Minnie asked. "We know so many."

"Ah, here he comes."

Coming up from behind them, looking entirely ridiculous, was Wilson atop a horse. He was still dressed in full camo gear, which just didn't help. But, he had three other horses with him.

"Look what I found!" he said.

"Where?" Oliver asked.

"Where did I find horses in the middle of the city? Not sure. The big guy asked me to hunt some down, so I did. Four Horse Tavern, of course. They were right out front."

"Of course they were. But I meant where have you been?"

"Getting horses, like I said."

"What about the whole middle part, where you disappeared?"

"Look, I'm just along for the ride, same as the rest of you. Now, we have horses, an empty city, and a place to go. How about if we get going, and figure out the rest later?"

~

Osraic the apprentice sorcerer was evidently no better at horseback riding than Oliver himself was, as neither of them were having a grand time of it once the animal got moving. That the horse seemed to require no instructions certainly helped, but Oliver still felt like he was going to fall off at any moment. He thought Orson the superspy probably knew more about horseback riding than either of them did, but had no idea how to access that skill.

Minerva, meanwhile, looked like she was born on a horse.

"Are you ready for this?" she asked, riding beside him. They were in something between a trot and a full gallop, and every stride caused parts of his body to bounce incorrectly somehow.

"What do you mean? We've been trying to get there all night. Sure I'm ready."

"There are forces that don't want you to reach the Kingdom. You must have realized that by now. Remember the greathawk in the Ailing Mountains? The creature's attack was directed at you."

"How can you do that?"

"Do what?"

"Bounce back and forth like that. The Ailing mountain range is from a story. So was the greathawk. I made it all up. You're talking about it like we actually experienced that."

"Does it matter? I think we're well past the point where parsing any of this makes a difference. It doesn't change what we're about to face."

"And what's that?"

"As I said, there are forces that don't want you to reach the Kingdom. The closer we get, the more robust that resistance will be."

"I'm ready."

"Good. We'll need your magic. Sorcerer." She flashed a great smile, and then urged her horse ahead, to run beside Cant in the lead.

"She's right, you know," Wilson said, from behind. He was doing even worse than Oliver with his horse, apparently not even having a fictional version of himself to draw experience from. "All this craziness has been about you from the start. Something doesn't want you to reach Pallas."

"You've been telling me to just roll with it from the moment we left the apartment. Before that, even. That's my plan."

"That only gets you so far."

The distance from the apartment to the center of town was maybe three miles over land, with a couple of turns. It was two miles by air, just about, and could also be measured in subway stops, which was six. Oliver didn't know how it measured in horse, but after a decent distance traveled he was ready to declare that it was a lot further than he thought it was going to be. The blisters beginning to form on his hindquarters concurred.

The first attack on their party took place sometime after the halfway point. It came from the air, but it wasn't a greathawk, or any other variety of epic fantasy beast: it was an alien.

The thing crashed down atop an SUV in the middle of the street, and not gently. This happened in front of Cant, in the lead. His horse went bonkers, reared up and nearly threw her rider.

Cant was still busy getting his mount under control when the alien opened its mouth and roared, which by Oliver's prior experience with these things meant they would be seeing more aliens shortly.

Minerva—or Atha, in this particular moment—acted as if this attack had been coordinated well in advance. Already, she'd pulled the enchanted bow from her hair and commanded it to full size. Her horse, also undeterred, continued in a full charge straight at the alien, so Atha had little trouble loosing a couple of arrows.

The shots struck true, right into the mouth and at the back of the throat. It wasn't a mortal blow—arrows were poor substitutes for pulse blasts—but it was a serious wound. She reined her horse just out of reach of the creature's attack radius, and circled round. Her eyes weren't on the thing in front any more. She was looking skyward.

Cant was off his horse by then, and ready with his sword.

"We can't afford to be bogged down with the likes of this," Atha told him.

"I'll make it quick."

"Sorcerer!" she shouted. "Keep moving! The skies will only get busier from here!"

The horse's accelerator was apparently located in the hindquarters, a thing Oliver discovered accidentally—or perhaps knew instinctively. He gave a tap back there on both sides, with his heels, and they were suddenly going at a speed with which he was far less comfortable. Wilson, who had been doing very well in not vanishing this time around, was close behind. He was a jangly, uncoordinated mess, clinging to his mount like a drowning man to driftwood. Oliver imagined he looked much the same.

As they passed, he heard Cant shout, "Have at it, monster!" and the alien shriek in reply. It would have been a good battle to witness, but the time to spectate was over.

I think I'd better figure out how to be a sorcerer soon, he thought, as the horse rounded the corner on the other side of the battle scene.

The corner he took led to the part of the city most of the residents called *the hub*. This was due to a faint resemblance it bore, on maps, to the center of a wheel, although in truth this was an exceedingly generous comparison. In order to see the convergence of the roadways, one had to ignore a lot of streets that didn't actually meet in the middle.

The dead-center portion was taken up by a roundabout, which was the only sane solution to the traffic mayhem that would otherwise have been caused by the roadway convergence. By all rights, the grassy circular lawn at the core should have had a statue of someone important. Someone on horseback, maybe, looking determined about one thing or another. It would have been impractical, but nobody expected practicality from a spot like that. Instead, there was something akin to an obelisk there, with street names on it and arrows pointing in all the correct directions.

It should have been useful, because enormous signposts that are readable from multiple angles ought to *be* useful. But people driving around this particular signpost, were far too busy watching the traffic and trying not to ram into someone to look to their left for directional assistance. The signs would have made sense, perhaps, in an era when people drove slowly, in carriages, without in-vehicle GPS at their disposal.

It was a shame nobody did spend time looking at the signs, because some years back—on April Fool's Day—the city added new directions: arrows pointing up at odd angles with the names of planets on them. The directions were only correct a couple of days out of the year, but since no one noticed, no one complained. And, nobody bothered to take the signs back down again.

Ollie was thinking about those incorrect directions when he reached the hub. He wondered if the aliens, at least, thought it was funny.

"Pallas is up there," Wilson said, pulling up beside him.

"I know where it is."

The hub was at the bottom of a hill. Three streets, on the other side of the roundabout, went up that hill at different angles. The middle one was a road called Cub Street. Nobody ever called it that; they called it Club Street. It was a long straight road that ended at a dead-end created by the interstate, and all the way down that road was a succession of night clubs, plus a bowling alley, an upscale billiards hall, and more than one twenty-four hour dining establishment.

Oliver had never been down Club Street at any time of day, but knew of it almost by way of osmosis, as if—like everyone else in the city—he absorbed facts about this place just by breathing the air and drinking the water.

M Pallas was at the end of that strip. This was something he also just sort of knew, somehow, although he didn't need to. There were enough billboards around the hub that provided plenty in the way of detailed directions.

Oliver stopped his horse at the grassy part, and checked back the way they'd come.

"They're on their way," Wilson said.

"Yeah."

"We should keep moving. You heard what she said."

"Yeah. Seems quiet, though, doesn't it?"

"Sure. The city's abandoned and we're in the middle of the loudest part of the city and there isn't anyone here but us. It's very weird, Oliver. Please don't tell me you're about to reach for the *it's quiet: too quiet* cliché, I don't think we have time for that."

"Maybe I am. Maybe I just want to turn around and go back to my apartment. What happens if I don't go to the club? Do you know?"

"I think we'll just wake up tomorrow and talk about going to Pallas all over again. And it'll be like this again. Only even more difficult."

"Why is that?" Ollie asked.

"Why would it be more difficult?"

"Why would we keep trying to get to Pallas? I didn't want to go in the first place. You guys talked me into it."

"Because every story has an ending, Oliver. You have to find yours."

"What if I don't want it to end?"

Wilson sighed, and for a second went from camouflaged soldier-of-fortune on horseback to exasperated creative writing mentor. It was nice to see that version of Wilson, however briefly.

"Depends on what you mean. There's the unfinished manuscript, which is literally a thing the writer failed to come up with an ending for. Then there's the ending that isn't an ending. Either it circles back on the beginning again, or otherwise hints that the hard-earned ending isn't an ending at all: it's a fake-out. Those never work out."

"But it's an ending."

"Sure, but it's a cheat. It's better than the unfinished

manuscript, I'll say that. And it might be better than an anticlimactic ending. Look, endings are tough, no way around it. I understand your hesitation. But we have to get there."

"All right. What if I don't like how it ends?"

"Then come up with a better one," Wilson said with a smile. "It's not that complicated. Now come on, I hear something above us and I'm not interested in seeing what that something is. Are you?"

"Not really."

Ollie nudged his horse, who was grazing on the definitely-not-meant-for-grazing grass in the center.

"Head for the smoke, girl," he said to the horse, who he decided was probably a girl without any way of really knowing. The smoke in question was coming from the other side of the crest of the hill. It was the wreckage of the helicopter, and it was hidden from view, as was the rest of Club Street.

If he were imagining this as Cant did, as the entrance to a separate kingdom that was obscured until now, the crest of the hill would be the gateway. All the sights and sounds of the clubs were protected by the natural rise, ensconced in something akin to a bowl valley.

Oliver was unprepared for what was on the other side.

The final pathway to the Kingdom of Cant's Benja Codex was a neon spectacle of garish, rapid-flash lights, a brazen dare for the seizure-prone. It was about how Oliver imagined Vegas probably looked, only more garish. It was singularly uninviting.

The most interesting thing about it was that Oliver could see it at all.

"They have power here," Wilson said. "How about that."

"Maybe only parts of the city were blacked out," Oliver said.

"Or maybe it's magic."

"Sure, why not?"

The helicopter had come down right onto of Club Street, near the top of the hill, still some distance from the clubs. They headed towards it because there wasn't anywhere else to head: it was in the way.

"What happened there?" Wilson asked.

A shot rang out, and the ground ahead of them kicked up some fragments. They brought the mounts to a halt.

"That's Koestler. He was trying to get away with a formula that came out of secret government experiments, to sell it on the black market for a lot of money."

"Oh. Well, he's shooting at us."

"I noticed."

"Come no closer!" Koestler yelled.

"Do you have a gun?" Wilson asked Oliver.

"I did, but I lost it."

"What was this, one of those cold-war spy things?"

"Yeah." He rode forward a few yards; he was just out of range of the handgun he last saw Koestler with. If the man had a rifle, it was too close, but they were in range of a rifle from a lot further back, and Koestler was a good shot. Oliver figured he didn't have one.

"Koestler!" he shouted. "We just have to get through. You can keep Lot Forty-Two if you want it."

Koestler fired again. Wherever the bullet landed, it wasn't in the ground, Oliver, or Oliver's horse. A warning shot, then.

"You think I would believe this? After you downed my helicopter?"

"I didn't do that."

Wilson rode up next to Oliver.

"What was the endgame of his story, anyway?" he asked.

"I didn't have one."

"That sounds about right."

"If I was not brought down by your hand, then whose?" Koestler asked.

As if cued to do so—and perhaps they were—several balls of

light flew over their heads. They were silent, but bright. Oliver felt certain he'd had just been scanned.

They continued past the wrecked helicopter and along Club Street, coming to a stop midway down.

"Dunno who they are," Oliver said. "Why don't you ask them?"

"What are those things?" Koestler asked.

"Those are alien drones. The actual aliens are big scary-looking bugs. They also fly. I think you'll see one of them in a minute or two, if you want to just hang on."

There was silence from Koestler for a while, and then: "Do you think I am an idiot?"

"No, of course not. You just ended up in the wrong story."

"What is that supposed to mean?"

"Look, Koestler, we don't have a lot of time. In a minute those drones are going to rally some aliens to this location, and I'm going to need to be on the other side of them before that happens or it's gonna be a really long night. I'm not armed, and neither is my friend here. At least let us come closer."

"All right," Koestler said, after a moment. "But know that I fully expect treachery from you and am prepared to answer it."

"Of course."

Oliver started riding forward, then noticed Wilson lagging.

"You're sure he won't shoot?" Wilson asked.

"I'm not a hundred percent, but yeah, I'm pretty sure. You thinking of vanishing again?"

"Wouldn't be a bad idea, but I don't think I can."

"Then come on."

It was thirty yards to reach the crash. The acrid smoke got more intense with each step, leading Oliver to wonder how Koestler even saw well enough to recognize him from any distance.

When they got within a few feet, Oliver dismounted and let the horse wander back out of the smoke. Any travel past this point would have to be on foot, because the mount had no way to get around the crash.

Ollie put his hands up.

"Where are you, Koestler?" he asked.

"I am here," the Russian said, from a spot near the cockpit, on the left.

Koestler was pinned under the wreckage. In one hand was his Smith & Wesson, and in the other the tin containing Lot 42.

Oliver crouched down to get a better look.

"How bad is it?"

"My left leg is bent in ways it should not be. I don't appear to be suffering any internal concerns, but I also cannot free myself. Tell me what they really are."

Oliver gestured Wilson over. Wilson was reluctant to do anything other than watch, but came.

"I told you, they're aliens," Oliver said.

"There's no such thing. Your government is using advanced technologies…"

"It's not us, I'm telling you." To Wilson, he said, "When I lift this, you pull him free."

Lifting the edge of the chassis that was pinning Koestler took some work, and the use of a stick. Oliver found a metal one lying free of the wreckage—it was a piece of a strut or something—which gave him the necessary leverage to move the pile about an inch. This was enough to free Koestler.

It didn't really make the Russian any happier, as extricating his leg hurt a great deal.

"Now tell me," he rasped. "What is really going on?"

"He was supposed to get away, wasn't he?" Wilson asked. "Originally."

"Yeah," Oliver said. "But not with the real compound. I was supposed to have switched it out."

"Did you?"

"No, I forgot. There was this whole government cover-up

thing, where I ended up being a fugitive because of what I found out about Lot Forty-Two. I was thinking maybe in the third act I'd turn to the only person I knew I could trust. The whole enemy-of-my-enemy thing."

"That's a lot of story."

"Well it would have been. I didn't write any of it; I was just running it through my head when his first helicopter crash happened."

"Excuse me," Koestler said. "Why are you talking like this?"

He was pointing the gun at them, but in a way that made it seem less like a threat than like a way to make sure someone spoke back.

"You're in a story," Wilson said.

"You weren't supposed to crash," Oliver added. "Putting you in two helicopter crashes in the same story would have been ridiculous."

"You could have just killed him on the roof instead," Wilson said.

"Yeah I guess, but I needed him for the third act. Probably should have added someone with the... right, so maybe the government still has a secret program, and one person left from the original tests. I would need help facing him and *he* could be the big villain. Or she."

"That's pretty good."

"EXCUSE ME!" Koestler said, somewhat louder this time. "What do you mean, a story?"

"I mean, you're a character," Wilson said. "In his story."

"I am a man with my own agency, and I am holding a gun right now, so I would caution you to temper your words."

"I didn't say you weren't a man, you're just a man in a story."

"Meaning, I am not real."

"If you're real, there's no reason to get violent over someone suggesting otherwise, wouldn't you say? My opinion should have no bearing on your reality."

"I am real, and the pain in my leg is *very* real, and so are the bullets in this gun."

He leveled the barrel at Wilson's head, to underline the point he was making.

"Well all right, but you can be both," Wilson said. "Real, but in a story, I mean. We have been all night, and we're also real. Right, Oliver?"

"Call me Orson," Oliver said. "Around him. Just so he's not confused. But sure, probably."

"I will shoot…" but Koestler didn't finish the threat, as at that moment something loud and awful started taking place in the middle of Club Street.

There were eight probes. They split up into two sets of four and began performing a complicated rotation around one another that was reminiscent of the cup-and-ball movements of a street grifter. There were only four colors in each set: blue, purple, yellow and black, with the latter being the most confounding to the eye. It looked like an emanation of the absence of light, which made no sense and hurt Oliver's eyes.

In conjunction with the rotating colors, they were making a horrible rumbling noise that sounded like something mechanical sliding on a track: a train, almost, but with all the sound coming from the engagement of the wheels to the rails.

"What are they doing?" Wilson asked.

"I cannot see," Koestler said. "Help me."

They helped him up onto his one good leg, and led him around to the front of the wreckage. He ended up propped on his elbows atop the helicopter's tail.

"All right," he said. "Aliens, then. Orson, I have a rifle in that cockpit, would you look for it?"

"Stay put," Wilson said. "I'll find it, if you promise not to use it on me."

"For you I have the handgun. For them, the rifle."

"They're moving too fast to shoot," Oliver said.

"As long as the winds keep the smoke away, I have an opportunity. Perhaps when they slow and present a more amenable target. Can you tell me why the world has stopped making sense?"

Oliver sat down next to him and leaned up against the wrecked fuselage.

"I don't think so. I've just been going from crisis to crisis all afternoon, you know? Acting and reacting. When the whole world goes crazy at the same time sometimes it's just the best idea to deal with what's in front of you and keep moving."

"*Da.* A footsoldier in a ground war. You and I… we see ourselves as special. Make the system work for us, and not the converse. We would rise above the ground war. Be our own generals. But there is always someone to answer to, is there not? We are always cogs. We think the mechanism cannot work without us and this is true. But all cogs look the same and we can be replaced with another cog at any time. Our mistake has always been in thinking the machine runs because *we* turn. You speak of a world gone mad and worrying only about what is before you, and this I understand. This has been my entire life. And yours."

"I'm accustomed to a more metaphorical madness."

"As am I. But, if life gives you something to shoot at, shoot at it."

It was hard to describe exactly what Oliver was seeing happen with the probes. Each set of four was starting to form a… tear in the fabric of the world. The night sky in the space in the center of their aeronautic weaving had become fuzzy, and then fog started pouring out. The sky in the middle of the tear looked like a peek into another place entirely.

Wilson returned, with the rifle, and a box of ammunition.

"Glad you didn't have this when we were on approach," he said, handing it to Koestler.

"My leg was pinned or I would have," he said, calmly checking the gun for damage. "Would you like for me to try and shoot them out of the sky?"

"No," Oliver said. "You'll have better targets soon. I just realized what I'm looking at."

"You break the code?" Wilson asked.

"Sort of. CMYK."

Wilson laughed.

"Of course," he said.

"Is this a coded message?" Koestler asked.

"CMYK," Oliver repeated. "Cyan, Magenta, Yellow, blacK."

"Printer ink," Wilson clarified.

Koestler looked back and forth between them, for a sign that a better explanation would be forthcoming. None was.

"All right, fine," he said. "What is it that is being printed?"

"Aliens, of course," Oliver said.

With that, the gaps in the sky widened suddenly, pushed open by the things passing through.

Those things were aliens, of the previously-encountered flying-bug variety. A dozen had just been 'birthed' into the middle of Club Street.

"It's a transport mechanism," Oliver said. "Probably why half the time these guys are everywhere, and the other half they're nowhere. They go home."

"Where's home?" Wilson asked.

Oliver laughed, and picked up the metal stick he'd used to free Koestler from the wreckage. A sorcerer needed a staff. A wood one would be better, but he would have to make do with what was available.

"Koestler," he said, "cover me as well as you can. It's time to wrap up this story. Wilson, are you coming?"

Chapter Fourteen

HERE THERE BE DRAGONS

The twelve aliens took defensive positions along the street, while another five or six passed through the breach overhead. It was hard to keep a running total, because they all looked alike, and none of them were interested in staying still long enough for a head-count.

"So this is what we're doing," Wilson said, matter-of-factly. His voice was tinged with fear, but it didn't stop him from walking along with Oliver. This was definitely an improvement over his historical behavior.

"We have to get to Pallas, right? This is what you guys have been telling me all day. Let's go clubbing, it'll be fun."

The walk was slightly downhill, but only slightly. The various clubs on both sides turned the street into something akin to a canyon, as if they were walking a particularly risky section of the Silk Road. There was no ambush here, though, not when the enemy wasn't bothering to hide. The bugs took up positions along the rooftops and in the street, with a couple more circling overhead. There was no logical explanation for why they had failed to attack already, which Oliver thought might be a good sign: perhaps they were afraid of him.

"Are they guarding the club?" Wilson asked.

"They're guarding something. Not sure what. Minerva said they're here to keep us from reaching Pallas, but that doesn't make a lot of sense in context."

"Which context?"

"The context of their story."

"All right, Oliver, I'll bite: what *is* the context of their story?"

They'd reached a point on the street where they were parallel with the first set of clubs. Paradise was on their left, and Little Big Country on the right. The clubs had velvet ropes out front for crowd control, but of course there were no crowds. As was true for all the clubs, they had rotating lights flashing in time with music that could only be heard if the doors were open.

The nightclubs had no windows, because there was an active interest in keeping the people inside from being fully aware of the existence of an outside world, and/or possibly for safety reasons.

"They're inside," Oliver realized.

"Who is?"

"The people. The city. All the missing."

Wilson did a slow turn.

"How do you figure?" he asked. "There's no way the entire city can fit into these buildings, you know that, right? On top of which, you can't even see inside."

"Maybe not the whole city, then. Maybe just some of them. But the clubs are full, and I think the aliens put them there."

"*This* is how your story was going to work out? They're keeping the people in a zoo?"

"I didn't know how it was going to work out, remember? That's always been my problem. You said it yourself. I don't know the ending until I get to the ending, and I never seem to get to the ending."

"This is why I told you to outline, Oliver. So we knew about…"

A rifle shot rang out. Koestler was firing at something. Ollie looked up.

One of the overhead aliens had decided it was time to commence with a dive-bomb attack, and it didn't look like the bullet had had any impact on its decision.

"Maybe we should fall back," Wilson said.

"No, we're fine here."

Oliver held up the staff the way one would if one were expecting some sort of attack to erupt from the tip of it. That didn't happen, but what did was that Koestler took a second shot. This appeared to find home, because the alien reacted as if it had been hit in the side of the head by a particularly annoying mosquito. Not a lethal shot, but enough to cause it to veer off and circle skyward again.

"I don't think the rifle is enough," Wilson said. "We could use one of those blasters. Unless you've figured out a weakness, and that weakness is the stick in your hands."

"It's not, but I have," Oliver said. He continued walking. The alien would be dive-bombing again shortly, but he saw no reason to let that keep him.

"Great. What is it?"

"The weakness is that they aren't the aliens in the story. We are."

Wilson laughed.

"On Earth?"

"No, no, on Hockspit."

"We're not on Hockspit," Wilson rightly pointed out.

"Tell them that. Look, remember in the story: we changed the planet to make it hospitable to life, but left the oceans alone because they were highly acidic. What we didn't know was that there was an intelligent species living in that ocean."

The bug was coming back in for another dive-bomb attack, which hadn't escaped Wilson's attention.

"Cute twist. So, you were thinking, what? A colonialism allegory?"

"Maybe, yeah. But this has always been my point, these stories are never *just* about aliens or whatever, sometimes…"

"I would *love* to get into another argument about the relevance of genre stories, Oliver, but we're still about to die. How does knowing this help us?"

"You have to ask yourself: why did they bother to attack at all? We had the land and they had the sea. What's their motivation?"

"Um…"

"We're killing them, that's what. They had to defend themselves."

"Ah, colonialism with an environmental message, very nice."

An arrow arced through the sky from a spot behind them. Atha had arrived. The shot found home in the alien's underbelly. It shrieked and turned skyward again.

She was running to them, with Cant hard behind her. He looked covered in the gore of his last foe.

"There you are," Oliver said. "It took that long to kill one alien?"

"Three," Cant said. "And now you face dozens more with nothing but a tall stick and this useless warrior. Have you gone mad, sorcerer?"

"We were concerned," Minerva said.

"Well, I've got a sniper on my side too."

"Until he betrays you," Wilson added. "I mean, if it's that kind of story."

The aliens seemed to recognize that the stakes had gone up with the arrival of Cant and Minerva, because now they were making a concerted effort to surround them.

"Maybe you should explain how we're going to kill them now," Wilson said.

"We altered the atmosphere into something that's poisoning them," Oliver said. "In their mind they're defending themselves."

"That's still not helping us. Unless you can figure out how to get them to wait around for an hour or two to die."

"Indeed, we could do with a more concrete suggestion," Cant said.

"It's the carbon dioxide in our breath," Oliver said.

Minerva fixed him with an amused look, with those elfish green eyes.

"You mean for us to breathe on them?"

"Well, no, that's not a great offensive attack. But I do think their goal is just to drive us away. That's why they're keeping all the people locked up. If we decided to just leave, they'd be good with that."

"How?" Wilson asked. "They've closed off the sky."

"Maybe they think we can transport people instantly, like they can."

One of the healthy aliens—not the one with an arrow sticking out of him—went into a dive.

Koestler fired, and whether it was luck this time or he'd been working out this solution for a while, he discovered the right spot to fire a bullet into. The creature's head rocked sideways, and it plummeted to a loud death several yards away.

"Did you see?" Cant asked Minerva.

"I saw. Beneath the jaw at the top of the neck. Perhaps their hearts are in their gullets." She looked at Oliver. "Your man Koestler is precise with that weapon."

"He's my arch-enemy. But yes, he is."

"Regardless, he's given us something to hit."

"That will only work for a while, they can keep bringing more through the gap. We have to hit those drones."

Cant drew his sword and stepped in front of Wilson and Oliver.

"There are already too many for us to kill," he said. "A few more will not matter."

"You're not listening. The air is toxic to them. They can only be in it for a short time. Those rifts in space they've opened allow them to go back. If we close it they'll die where they stand. Like holding a diver underwater until the air in his tank runs out."

"Then you figure out how to destroy the drones with your magic while we face them on the ground, sorcerer."

Oliver had already figured that part out too, but didn't really have time to say anything because then the attack was underway. Three bugs landed directly in front of Cant, cutting off their forward progress. Two attacked from above, while three landed behind and two on each side. They were going for an attack that appeared to be calculated to anticipate one of the humans being armed with a pulse cannon they didn't actually have.

He wondered, if he thought hard enough, whether he could transform the metal stick in his hand into a blaster. Perhaps it would happen, via some combination of his supposed magical abilities and the fact that the entire night was being dictated by the whims of his imagination. But no amount of concentration, or wishing, or utterance of 'magic' words seemed to change anything. All that did change was that now, he felt a little foolish.

Meanwhile, the three actual warriors on-hand were doing their best to keep him alive. Minerva was firing arrows skyward, and Cant swung his heavy sword so rapidly it was a blur. It was all he could do to keep the three bugs from landing a mortal blow, but at the same time he couldn't do anything permanent to them. Koestler continued to fire from his sniper's nest. Inevitably, one of the aliens was going to figure out where he was settled and take the attack to him, but that hadn't happened yet.

One of the free aliens from the side pounced, perhaps realizing that the two in the middle—Wilson and Oliver—didn't pose nearly as much of a threat as the others. He knocked Wilson onto his back and screeched into his face.

Wilson exhaled back, which didn't exactly kill the bug, but it did make it wince for a half second, which was long enough for Oliver to club him in the side of the head with his staff. The creature fell backwards, regained its feet, and prepared to launch itself again.

They were probably about to die. Oliver came to this thought calmly, because as much as this all felt real to him, he'd reached a point where ideas like his own death no longer seemed really feasible. This was all very much real: he could feel the pain, and his adrenaline spikes as his body dealt with the fight-or-flight impulses that had been running through him all day. He could hear the horrible noise being made by the drones overhead, and still smell the acrid smoke from the helicopter crash up the road. If the next thing the alien did was to close those sharp teeth around Oliver's arm, he was quite sure he would feel the sensation of having a limb severed. Yet despite all of those things being true, he was confident there was no way this story could end with him dying.

It wasn't a story, he told himself. It was real. But it also wasn't.

There came a terrible cry from the heavens. It was the sort of noise that made everyone—alien and human and elf, sniper and soldier and sorcerer—stop what they were doing and figure out what in the name of all that is holy could possibly make a sound such as this.

High above, a cloud—lit only thanks to the ambient glow of the neon signs crowding Club Street—appeared to move. Then a great beast emerged, wisps of cumulus moisture clinging to its leathery wings. It was beautiful, and terrible, and magnificent.

It was a dragon.

"Sorcerer!" Cant shouted. "Did you call her forth?"

"I only expected her arrival, and hoped it would precede our deaths. But the Codex said we couldn't enter the Kingdom without facing a dragon. You know that."

Cant laughed. "Aye."

The dragon let out a second roar, and dove for the alien army. It was almost an optical illusion: the beast had nothing to compare her to when in the upper atmosphere, so it was easy to convince oneself she wasn't as big as it had to be. But as she dove, she grew, and grew, and then the aliens started to look like actual bugs by comparison.

Being a proper fire-breathing dragon, her first attack was fire-based, and it was directed at the only things flying high enough to make for a decent target: the drones. The flames lit up the sky and engulfed all eight of the drones, and they responded by breaking formation. The portals closed.

This got the full attention of the alien army. If the dragon hadn't represented a larger threat initially, she did the minute she went after the drones and closed off their only way home. Their way was clear.

"Let's move!" Minerva shouted, as she ran past Oliver and in the direction of Pallas.

"Hang on," Oliver said.

She stopped and looked back at him, confused. "We have to reach the Kingdom before that thing is finished with the monsters, sorcerer. I don't know if you realize this, but dragons don't choose sides, and we neglected to invite a dragon-slayer on this excursion."

"Maybe you did. But we can't abandon everyone."

She looked around. The street was empty, save for a couple of bug carcasses.

Well above them, the aliens were buzzing around the dragon's head, while the beast spun and swooped, each flap a mini-hurricane that threatened to knock Oliver off his feet. As he watched, the beast swung a mighty claw and caught a cyan-colored drone. It exploded like a rocket from a fireworks show.

"Who do you mean?" Minerva asked.

"In the clubs," Oliver said. "Cant, I need you to knock down some doors."

Cant looked at Minerva, then shrugged. He ran to the nearest club door, which belonged to Paradise.

"But why?" she asked again.

"They're hostages. Kill the aliens, free the hostages: that's the mission, soldier."

Wilson laughed.

"You're killing the aliens with a dragon," he said. "You planning to put that in the story?"

"Well, I improvised."

Wilson said something about nobody wanting to read a story with both aliens and dragons in it, but Oliver didn't catch his exact words, because by then Cant had taken the first door and the middle of Club Street was awash in people.

They knew without prompting that the best place for them to be was away from the fight going on overhead, so there was a huge rush down the road, toward the crashed helicopter. He hoped Koestler didn't start shooting people, thinking he was perhaps under attack.

"There," Minerva said, grabbing him by the elbow. "He's freeing them. Now let's get moving."

Oliver forgot how much he hated crowds. It didn't seem like something someone who hated crowds would just up and forget, and yet he had. Possibly, it was because he'd spent the entire day in an abandoned city.

He didn't imagine the surge of people would be so omnidirectional, either, but the more doors that were opened, the fewer places the city dwellers had to go. Soon, there were as many people between him and the doors of Pallas as there were in the other direction, and he'd completely lost track of Minerva and Wilson.

But at least Oliver knew which way he was supposed to be headed. It was very much an upstream direction, and he was often at risk of simply being carried by the flow of people, but he was able to push forward.

After a few minutes of this, Minerva appeared at his side. She was still in her Atha form—he couldn't think of a better way to put it—but otherwise seemed like the same girl who was trying to convince him only a few hours ago to go on this ridiculous trip to a club he didn't even want to go to.

"Well this was a grand idea," she said. "I'm tempted to start killing people just to clear a path."

"We'd never make it to the Kingdom if we hadn't done it," he said.

"We won't make it now *because* we've done it. I think even Cant has been waylaid by all of this."

Oliver was trying not to look at faces as they went past, because it felt as if everyone he knew was pushing by. There was a barista he worked with a couple of times just a month ago. Behind her was the family who lived in the apartment on the second floor of Wilson's building, next to a guy Oliver saw on the subway one time. And over there was Tandy from the Tenth Avenue Writers Underground, looking scared and apparently not recognizing Oliver.

The whole city rushed past, a collection of half-remembered names and brief inadvertent encounters, all fleeing in terror.

It was utterly overwhelming.

"Why would we have not made it?" Minerva asked. "I'm not seeing your logic."

"We have to finish all the stories, or the way to the Kingdom isn't going to be open."

"That doesn't sound like it comes from any Codex with which I'm familiar. And I have read all of them."

"One of each kind," he said. "We had to bring one of each kind to the gates of the Kingdom. I don't see each race represented here, so I'm electing to interpret *kind* differently."

She nodded, slowly. "Very well. I suppose you would know better."

Overhead, the battle raged on. The dragon was more than holding her own against the combined might of the aliens and their drones.

Oliver witnessed two drones—magenta and yellow—run parallel to the dragon, in an effort to bring her down the same way they'd brought down Koestler's helicopter. But dragons were larger, faster, and more maneuverable than a helicopter, and also equipped with better offensive weapons. They tried, but their electrical bolts found empty air by the time they fired, and then there was a flaming counter-attack, and the drones were gone.

"Out of my way, out of my way!" Cant was bull-rushing the people who failed to move aside fast enough. He was heading toward them from the upstream direction. His efforts cleared the way a little, and made it easier to proceed.

"These city-dwellers would die in minutes north of the Ailings," he declared, when they reached him. "They act as if they've never picked up a sword in defense in their lives, look at them!"

"They haven't," Oliver said. "Has anyone spotted Wilson? Or did we lose track of him again?"

"Your useless cohort lies ahead, at the door I cannot open."

"Which door was that?" Minerva asked. "Do they make doors in this world that are stronger than the mighty Cant?"

"They do indeed. Come on, sorcerer. You've led us to the gates of the Kingdom itself, but they remain locked yet. Now perhaps you can prove your worth."

~

*M*Pallas was far too ostentatious to be mistaken for an ordinary nightclub. Vast white marble ionic columns ringed the front of a huge circular building with balconies and tresses and gables. Gargoyles hung off the roof and glared at the courtyard, which contained a garden of topiaries that had been pruned to look like Greek statues. The yard was surrounded by a high wall and gated by a wrought-iron fence. But for one detail, it looked like a cathedral, built for the worship of a nameless destroyer-god—or perhaps of all destroyer-gods.

That one detail was the singular expression of product branding: on the face of the building, held up by the ionic columns, was a vast letter M foregrounded by PALLAS. The letters glowed a soothing shade of lilac, as if apologizing for their garishness.

Wilson was standing at the gate.

"I hear they redesign the exterior every year. Can you even imagine the cost?"

"Depends on if those are real marble columns," Oliver said. He scanned the façade, waiting for the part where it became obvious that it wasn't as big as it looked—that this was an unusually effective application of forced perspective—kicked in. It never did. The place was actually as large as it appeared to be.

"This is the gate that defeated the great Cant?" Minerva asked.

Cant checked left and right on the other side of the fence.

"Sorcery!" he muttered.

"The way was blocked a minute ago," Wilson said. "Unless we're going nuts. The two of us."

"I don't understand," Oliver said.

Wilson stepped aside.

"The gate's unlocked. Go ahead and try it."

Oliver put his hand on the cold wrought iron of the fence, expecting to feel something more than just the metal's current temperature. But there was no electrical charge or magical excitation, or any other transmission of pain. It just felt like a fence.

He pulled, and the gate opened. Then there was a deafening WHOOSH as a massive boulder landed just on the inside of the gate. Oliver backpedaled so suddenly he fell over.

"There it is," Wilson said. "It blocks the whole entrance, see?"

"That's one hell of a burglar alarm," Oliver said.

"This is what I encountered when first I came to this point," Cant said. "I would have attempted to overcome this by going through or around, but I feared the magical guardian would just drop another boulder, only on my head."

"It disappears eventually," Wilson added. "But you have to close the gate first. I did that, and turned around. When I looked back again, it was gone."

Oliver got back to his feet and reached through the open gate, slowly, as if the massive rock was an unfriendly dog.

"It feels real enough," he said.

"You thought it was an illusion?" Minerva asked. "Yes, that would track, wouldn't it?"

"If it disappears and reappears, it's the most obvious conclusion. But this doesn't seem like the sort of thing I'd want dropped on me. Those columns up ahead probably aren't really marble, but this sure feels like a real rock."

"Maybe we can find another way around."

"Hang on," Oliver said. He was concentrating on the face of the rock.

Orsak's words fell on the stones of the world, he thought.

He'd seen messages all over the city already, in script that he, evidently, was the only one capable of reading.

"So where are you?" he muttered.

Up above, the battle was coming to an end. The aliens were never meant to face a dragon: they were prepared for an armada, and either an ending that resulted in their genocide, or in a peace accord after the misunderstandings regarding the ownership of Hockspit was worked out. Oliver never did decide which kind of ending he wanted to go with, because one was terrible and the other was improbable. He could only see three aliens still flying around, and no drones. One of the aliens looked like it was succumbing to the atmosphere more than to the dragon, which was what happened when an entire city of carbon dioxide producers manifested beneath you.

"Sorcerer," Cant said. "We need…"

"Shh."

He put his hand on the boulder again, and concentrated. And then the word appeared. It was glowing white, right above where his fingertips rested. It was a word he'd seen before.

"Of course," he said. "*Alavas.*"

From the perspectives of Minerva, Cant and Wilson, the boulder vanished. That wasn't accurate, but it may as well have been. He'd used the same spell as the one placed on Atha's bow.

He picked up the much smaller version of the boulder, half-expecting it to be enormously heavy. It wasn't, but if normal physics were anywhere to be found in this situation, it would have been. But this was magic; normal physics weren't being used here.

"Welcome to the Kingdom," Oliver said grandly, waving them through the gate.

"Not precisely," Cant said. "I believe the door we require is the one up ahead."

"Well let's get moving, before more rocks drop down on us."

What came from above—instead of large stones—was fire. A wall of flame ignited the topiaries and blocked the way, as simulacrums of Greek warriors shriveled on the vine.

The dragon had arrived.

She did a second pass over their heads, to make sure the initial wall of flame, however temporary, had discouraged any further progress. Then she alit on the roof, in a spot that appeared to have been designed specifically for this precise function.

"Great warriors!" The dragon intoned. She had a voice that sounded a lot like her roar, which was to say it was deep and terrifying.

Oliver was hung up on the part where she had a voice at all.

"Dragons speak?" he asked, quietly, hoping she didn't hear the question.

"Of course they speak, sorcerer," Cant said. "Who raised you, that you did not know this?"

"You have done well to reach this far, but now I fear your journey has ended," the dragon continued. "The lands beyond here do not belong to you. The Kingdom is for Orsak the great, and he alone."

"Orsak is long dead, great dragon," Oliver said.

"I have heard this said, small man. Yet this does not change the conditions by which you may enter. Only Orsak. All others must face my wrath."

"But if only Orsak may enter, and Orsak is no more, why do you bother to hold open the possibility of his return?"

The dragon shrugged, which was a remarkable thing to see.

"I'm told Orsak is no more, but I have not seen this proven. If he were to appear before me and state that he is long dead, then I will believe this is so. Since he has not done this, I will hold my sworn position until his return, and fight all others. Even valiant ones such as yourselves. Now turn about and leave this place. You may have come further than all before, but this is where your quest ends. Tell any who would listen that you found the great Kingdom, if it pleases you, but warn them as well. I will not be so kind to the next who come across this doorway."

"What is your name, dragon?" Oliver asked.

"None of your concern."

"I would only know it so that when I, or my companions, leave this place, we would give an accurate account."

"My name is Promachos. You may tell them this."

"Very well. Mighty Promachos, how do you imagine a man many years dead might tell you himself that he is dead? This seems an unreasonable expectation from the deceased."

The dragon bared her teeth, which might have been a smile.

"Indeed, it is. But the mighty Orsak is eternal. He told me so himself 'ere besting me in combat and slaving me to this task. He is a man of many faces but one true self. And so it may be that he could enter my presence and declare he is dead. At that time I would be free, and the doors of the Kingdom unguarded to all with the perseverance you've already shown."

"Very well. Then I am the mighty Orsak himself."

The dragon extended her head forward, as if to get a better look at him. Her smile had only grown.

"*Really,*" she said.

"I think that might have been a mistake," Wilson said.

"Quiet, I might know what I'm doing," Oliver said.

"Well, this is splendid," Promachos declared. "Now, simply defeat me in combat and then I'll let you in."

"In combat?"

"As I said, only Orsak can defeat me, and so if you are Orsak, you should be able to do this. We will work out the rest after."

"That hardly seems fair."

"Do you wish to amend your declaration? It's far too late for that. Now you've declared your true name is Orsak the great himself, I'm afraid my curiosity is such that I must determine it for myself."

"No, no, I mean it hardly seems fair for *you.*"

The dragon gave a great, fiery laugh that was fortunately directed skyward.

"Listen to me, *child,* I can end your journey through this world with a breath. Dare not test my patience further."

"What I mean is, it hardly seems fair because if I best you in combat you may be in no position to *be* freed from the promise to guard this door. Yes, I grant that with a puff of your infernal breath, you would incinerate all of us where we stand. But as a great and powerful sorcerer, I can destroy you before you ever got that chance. And then you would be dead. Do you imagine you are as eternal as Orsak?"

"Very well. I am intrigued. I do not believe you are Orsak returned, but I appreciate your logic. What is it you propose?"

"Come down here. Perhaps we can work out another way for me to prove who I am."

She tilted her head. *You aren't kidding?* seemed to be the expression she was going for. Then with a great flap of her wings, she was airborne.

"Oliver, are you sure you know what you're doing?" Minerva asked. For a half-second she was just Minerva, the girl from Tenth Avenue with the fifteen different ways to smile. It was nice to see her again.

"I am not one hundred percent positive, no," he said. "Let's say sixty percent."

"Hey, we could make for the door now," Wilson suggested.

"I would not try that," Cant said. "You would just encourage her to move on to incinerating us. I expect that will be happening in a moment either way. Sorcerer, you play a foolish game."

"It's the only hand I have, Cant. Besides, isn't this why you hired me?"

"We didn't hire you, we kidnapped you."

Promachos swept across the sky, and then came in low along Club Street. When she landed, her body—from snout to tail—extended nearly the length of the entire roadway. If Koestler was still in his helicopter shooter's nest, he would be looking at a clean shot of her tail. He would be wise not to take that shot, because while she probably wouldn't even notice it, if she did it would be the last shot he ever took.

"Now I am here, great sorcerer. Prove yourself to me."

Oliver stepped past the gates. In the event she chose to incinerate him on the spot, he hoped the walls would protect the others from at least that first blast.

"Do you see this coin?" he asked. He pulled a quarter from his pocket and held it up.

"I do."

"Good. Now watch carefully."

Using a standard bit of sleight-of-hand—which Oliver did not know but Osraic did, so he may as well have—he made it look as if the coin disappeared.

"Is that not a great trick?" he asked.

She didn't look impressed.

"That's a parlor trick, you idiot. Of course I am not impressed."

"What if I told you it was behind your ear?"

"I will burn you where you stand and eat what's left."

"All right, all right. How about this? I can… um… I have it. I can give the coin to you, and then with a word, make it reappear in my hand."

"Enough of this."

"Do you have hands? Maybe they're too big for a coin."

"You could try some *actual* magic. Levitate, or destroy a building. Make it rain pheasants. Do something genuine."

"I'm working my way up to that. Look, do you have anything better to do?"

"All right, but when I remain unimpressed, I'm not going to be providing a third chance for you to act foolish. You should greet your ancestors in the afterworld with some shred of dignity left. Throw the coin into my mouth."

"In your mouth? Will you feel it?"

"I will."

"You're sure?"

"You stall. Throw."

Promachos opened her mouth wide, revealing a huge purple tongue and a strong sulfurous odor. Her gullet was large enough to fit a small car.

Oliver threw a rock in, instead of the coin. It slid along the tongue and to the edge her throat.

She closed her mouth again, and fixed him with a stern look.

"Annnd, one two three, here's the coin!" Oliver said, revealing the quarter that hadn't ever gone anywhere.

"Whatever you threw into my mouth, great Orsak, it was no coin."

"But it was!"

"I think we're finished here. You've bored me. Goodbye."

Promachos drew up, and raised her head to call upon her fire breath.

"Wait, wait, wait!"

"Yes?"

"One last chance, Promachos," he said. "Let us pass."

"You are issuing ultimatums to *me*?"

"All right. I'm sorry; I tried. *Alavas*."

The dragon known as Promachos was large, but she wasn't so large that her throat could accommodate the sudden introduction of a massive boulder. Her neck ruptured from the inside out, blasting dragon flesh all over Club Street. Her shocked final expression, as her head collapsed and rolled over unnaturally, no longer entirely connected to the rest of the body, was the kind that made Oliver want to cry.

"Well, that was… awful," Wilson said, clapping Oliver on the shoulder.

"He slew the dragon," Minerva said. She ran up and gave him a hug.

"I can't believe it," she said. "Are you okay, Oliver?"

"Yeah, I guess. I didn't really want to do that. Aliens are one thing, but she was… She was majestic. I didn't enjoy that at all."

"Killing isn't something we enjoy, it's something we do," Cant said. "And you had to do it, to prove you are Orsak himself."

"But I'm *not* Orsak," Oliver said.

"We all heard what the dragon said. She can only be bested by Orsak, and so Orsak has bested her."

"Look, whatever. I think if I was him I'd know it."

Wilson smiled.

"The résumé sort of fits, actually," he said. "But we can haggle later. Let's find out what this Kingdom is all about. Or, M Pallas, depending on which storyline we're going with today."

Oliver looked past Cant and Wilson and Minerva. The door to Pallas was on the other side of them.

It wasn't the club he thought he was going to when he left in the middle of the day, and it was probably also not the Kingdom of legend. He didn't know *what* it was. But the door was right there, and now he would find out.

"Well let's go then," he said.

"After you," Wilson said.

He and Minerva climbed the steps together.

The doors were massive. He squeezed her hand and smiled.

"This is it, right?" he said. "Are you ready?"

"We're ready," she said, stepping back a little. "And we're right behind you."

"Yes, Orsak the great should enter first," Cant said.

"Please stop calling me that," Oliver said, as he put his hand on the knob.

"Hey, what does the M *really* stand for? Does anyone know?"

"Maybe it stands for mystery," Wilson said with a shrug. "Are you gonna open it?"

"Yeah. Come on. Let's see what the fuss is."

He pulled on the handle. It opened easily. He stepped inside.

Chapter Fifteen

WHAT M IS FOR

The eatery was empty, as it was well past the breakfast rush and the trickle that constituted the lunch crowd, and there was no dinner served in the place. All the patrons had moved on to other important matters such as attending church services, watching sports teams, mowing lawns and tending to laundry. As one does.

The door, a light metal frame holding glass, rattled in time with the bell affixed to the top of the jamb, notifying any and all that a person had entered. Oliver was that person, and he was extremely confused.

He let the door close, and assessed the situation.

It was a diner. There was no way around that. It was a diner on a rural street in a small town, and it was late afternoon on a sunny day. The tables were Formica with plate metal trim, held up by wide, center legs leading to four-pronged feet. There were chairs with nominal padding, sturdy and just comfortable enough to be enjoyable for the length of one meal, and no more. There were booths as well, along one wall, and a counter near the kitchen, with round, backless stools.

Ready as he thought he might have been to explore the vast terrain of possibilities that lay on the other side of the massive door leading to the interior of M Pallas, this diner was not anywhere on that list. For a lot of reasons. Most obviously, he didn't appear to be in the city any longer. It wasn't the middle of the night any more, either. And he was alone. He assumed Minerva and Cant and Wilson would enter right behind him—especially Cant, since this was his quest after all—but that hadn't happened.

Even his clothes were different: his military outfit had been replaced by jeans, and sneakers, and a flannel shirt.

A woman emerged from the kitchen, a cleaning rag in her hand and a weary look in her eyes. She had her auburn hair pulled back in a tight ponytail, which flattered her round face and her pale green eyes.

It was Minerva. It was also not Minerva.

"We're closed," she announced with a practiced tone that was simultaneously welcoming and non-negotiable. "Oh, it's you. Hi, Oscar."

"Cydonia," he said.

She looked ready to say a dozen different things, and those things were all having a quiet and rapid argument amongst themselves. None made it past her lips.

"Have a seat if you want," she said, nodding at the counter. "Still got some coffee on. Unless you want tea."

"Coffee's okay."

This was important. There was no reason for it to be important, except that even the tiniest of things in this place were huge things. Tea was what he had when he first came to town, and what he would be drinking again when he returned to the city, as he just promised Cydonia he would be doing soon.

When had I made that promise?

There was no promise. This was all backstory that existed in his head and not in this rural eatery. It wasn't real. Neither was the diner, but they were sitting in it anyway.

Coffee was what he started drinking when he decided he couldn't put mother into a home. Not right away. Too much of who she was, was tied up in where she was. Taking her from the house would have been an amputation.

He could have had tea. The urn with the hot water was there, next to the coffee pot, and the drawer holding generic black tea bags was right beneath it, and he could have asked, but instead he took the coffee.

This was a small thing, and it was everything. It was important. It meant Oliver was confessing something. Unless it was Oscar confessing.

"Stan's done, but… I can make burnt toast if you've got the need."

He laughed.

"I've had my fill, thanks."

Cydonia set out a white ceramic cup and filled it with stale, bitter black coffee. You could tell the coffee was old from the smell and from the way it coated the sides of the cup, but he wasn't going to turn it down. It was an excuse to be in the building, which he appeared to need. There was unsettled business here. The waitress/customer dynamic was the only way to the other side of that business, and they both appreciated this.

After the cup came a tin holding a rainbow of sweetener packets, and a spoon. He took a seat on the stool in front of the cup and went about the business of preparing his drink.

Cydonia dropped a folded newspaper on the counter, and a blue pen.

"What's this?" he asked.

"Saved it for you," she said. "You know Earl never finishes."

She meant the half-completed crossword puzzle, which Earl—who sold life insurance out of a small storefront across the street

—inexplicably attempted to do in pen. As this was Sunday, Earl hadn't made an appearance, which was just as well since the Sunday paper didn't have a regular crossword puzzle anyway. It still existed, only in a magazine insert, and it was much larger and twice as challenging. Earl didn't visit the diner on Saturdays either, which meant when Cydonia said she saved it for Oscar, she'd been saving it since Friday.

This, too, was important.

She stood with her back up against the wall, the bleach-soaked rag still in her hand looking for a surface to purify. Her expression was emphatically neutral. Oliver was supposed to say something to her here, something important, something they both knew but which had to be uttered before it became real. The words he had to say were magic words; they would conjure the unspoken truth into reality.

He didn't know what those words were. She seemed to realize this.

"Hey, I gotta get some things taken care of out back," she said flatly. "Keep an eye on the front for me?"

"Sure," he said, but she was already through the kitchen door before his response had a chance to reach her.

He watched the door swing back and forth for a while. The way into the kitchen was through a thin plastic partition with a little plastic window and a rubber edge, resting in a couple of socket hinges in the floor and ceiling. It existed only to keep the public out front from seeing the chaos in back, and was otherwise too flimsy to keep out anything stronger than a gentle breeze.

Oliver tried the coffee, and decided that was perhaps a mistake. It was possible to hide a lot of sins underneath a high temperature, but this coffee had crossed that border beyond which no amount of scalding could mask the acrid quality.

The crossword puzzle was a mess. It looked like Earl started strong enough, but two quadrants had wrong answers, and one of those wrong answers wasn't even a long enough word to fill the required space, which called into question the insurance man's entire understanding of how crossword puzzles worked.

Earl had also used up the white space around edges of the puzzle to write letters corresponding to one clue or another: it was impossible to piece together what clue the string of letters belonged to, if at all. Oliver wondered if Earl was also playing some kind of anagram game that only existed in his own head.

Earl was preoccupied with six letters in particular. Oliver really couldn't see what the man was after; the letters didn't even form a word.

The front door clanged and the bell rang.

"They're closed," he said in the automatic response of someone who spent a lot of time in this diner after closing time.

Oscar and Cydonia would sit in the closed diner and talk for hours, Oliver decided. It was safe for them, in the confines of this public space: private, but not entirely private. Maybe that was their problem—they always kept it so safe, when they needed to be taking risks.

When Oliver didn't hear a response, and the door didn't reopen, he turned to see where the disconnect might be.

There was a man standing at the door. He was crippled. His left leg was tied in a heavy splint and he had a crutch under his arm. In his right hand was a Smith & Wesson.

"Koestler?"

"Hello, Orson," the old man said.

He stepped forward and nearly fell over. Oliver hopped off the stool, intending to catch him, but Koestler righted himself, and waved off the assistance.

"What are you doing here?" Oliver asked.

"I… don't know where *here* is. I am where you are, which is this curious place, and I am here because…"

He hesitated, either looking for the correct phrasing, or for an answer he didn't have.

Oliver took note of how tenuous the older man's grip on

everything—his balance, the gun, the crutch—was. Pain was written all over his face. His clothing no longer consisted of the black pajamas he'd last been seen wearing. Instead, he had on hiking boots, baggy dungarees, and a flannel shirt that looked like it was buttoned incorrectly. His hair seemed whiter, and the bags under his eyes more ponderous. He had a brace on his leg—over the dungarees—that looked like it was assembled from the spare parts of a helicopter crash.

"You're here to betray me," Oliver said. "Of course. That's the end of your arc."

"Yes, that's right. I... where *are* we? I don't understand any of this. My leg hurts so much."

"Why don't you put away the gun and have a seat?"

"If you don't mind?"

"Not at all. We should call an ambulance for you."

He put the gun into the pocket of his pants, hobbled over to the nearest table and collapsed into the chair, popped up again in surprise, then reached around and extracted the metal box that had been in his back pocket. He relaxed into the seat once more, with the Lot 42 box under his hand on top of the table.

"Is this a trick, of some kind?" he asked.

Oliver took a seat at the table opposite. He slid the unpleasant-tasting cup of coffee across, and Koestler partook of it greedily, as if his being offered the cup was thoroughly normal in these circumstances.

"How do you mean?" Oliver asked. "What kind of trick?"

"I don't know. Nor do I know how it could be. But the pain from my leg, it's just cascading up my body in hot strikes I feel to my fingertips and the back of my skull. I can barely concentrate. I'm afraid I may pass out. I've never experienced anything like this. I fell from a building once, do you remember?"

"I do."

He didn't, but was confident if he were feeling more like Orson than Oscar, he would.

"I broke ten bones and barely survived, and it hurt less than this. Everything is brighter, and heavier and… I don't like it. And so I ask if it is a trick, because the other consideration is that where we last met, you and I, *that* place was the trick, and this is the real world. I can't bear this notion."

It seemed to Oliver as if the formidable superspy in his presence was shrinking into an old man before his eyes. He *was* an old man, of the grizzled veteran variety, a holdover from the Cold War, which may have been still going on when Koestler and Orson crossed paths but was now long over. His skin was gray and mottled with old scar tissue, and his shoulders were hunched forward. Some of that may have been the outward result of the pain he was experiencing.

"I don't see how that could be," Oliver said. "We're in a small town now. I moved here to care for my mother. I didn't want to, but she had nobody else to care for her."

"That is good, Orson. A man should care for his mother. Commendable."

"Yes, I think probably it might be. But I also think she may have died recently."

"You don't know?"

"I think what comes next is the part where I decide if I'm going to stay or not. There's nothing keeping me here."

"You speak as if your own life is something someone else lived through," Koestler said.

"That's sort of accurate. But sorry, that's the wrong story. The right story is the one where you're here to kill me."

"It is." Koestler tapped his fingers on the Lot 42 tin, lost for a moment in thought. "It *could* be a trick. We know of a way this could be a trick. The formula."

"The Lot Forty-Two experiments were about enhancing remote viewing," Oliver said, feeling a little more Orson and a little less Oscar. "There was no reality-shaping."

"You're mistaken. The victims of the experiment: I told you

what I heard. Doorways disappearing and so on. And there was more."

"That's just a ghost story," Oliver said. What he didn't say was that this part of what should have otherwise been a straight spy thriller was thrown in to connect it to the ghosts of Mad Maggie's, and that was only because the ghost story didn't have an ending otherwise.

"Please listen. One of the theories promulgated during your government's secret laboratory experiments was that the test subjects were not in fact visiting distant locations via travel in an astral plane. They were visiting an alternative reality."

"That's ridiculous, Koestler."

"I know how it sounds."

"I mean it. This is a thriller, not a science fiction story. That would be completely out of bounds."

"You talk already as if *none* of these things are real, Orson."

"It's not that they are or aren't real, it's that there are rules. You can't just introduce something like that at the end and expect it to work."

Koestler nodded, and looked at his ruined leg pensively.

"All right then," he said. "I should leave."

"Where will you go?"

Koestler fell silent for a few beats, lost in thought.

"I may never walk properly again, I've just realized," he said.

"I'm sorry."

"It is probably not your fault, but I thank you. I think I will not shoot you today."

He stood. This took a lot of time, and more moving parts than seemed fully necessary. Koestler wasn't only suffering from a leg he couldn't bend or put any weight on, but from arms that were no longer inexhaustible sources of strength. He looked tired.

"I will thank you not to shoot me either," he added.

"I hadn't planned on it."

"Good."

He took a deep, steadying breath, to help find the strength within himself to move.

"I'm hoping, if I walk out of that door, I will discover myself back in the city from which I pursued you. Or elsewhere. Anywhere else would be preferable. The weight of existence here is too great. I would strongly recommend you follow, but perhaps you cannot."

"I might. I have to finish up a conversation first, but I think my only choice is forward."

"Yes. Well, should we meet again, I hope it is as enemies, and we can go about the business of nearly killing one another."

"Until then."

Koestler pushed open the door. A light springtime breeze drifted in: lilacs, with a hint of manure. Someone up the hill was fertilizing today.

Without further preamble, the international spy hobbled outside, through a door consisting mainly of glass, and vanished. More or less. He was never visible through the glass, so it wasn't so much that he was there and then he wasn't there, it was that the doorway didn't take him outside of the diner, but to someplace else.

Oliver watched the door close, and wondered where he would end up if he walked out after Koestler. Would they all be there, in front of M Pallas, just waiting for him to return? He had a feeling Cant would be disappointed to learn his Kingdom was a greasy spoon in rural America.

He turned from the door, and realized Koestler had left behind his prize: the metal tin holding Lot 42 was still on the table. Did he leave it on purpose, or did he no longer care? Ollie retrieved it and the coffee cup, and sat back down at the counter.

"Did I hear voices?" Cydonia asked. She'd changed from her work blouse, which was blue, to her off duty blouse, which was white.

Oliver tapped the metal box and was about to provide a long

explanation for what had just transpired, but concluded he simply didn't have the energy or the time to offer a full accounting.

"Someone just needed directions," he said. "He was lost."

"Oh. Okay."

She took away the coffee cup, which was empty, and returned the sugar to its position under the counter. They were still stuck in that pregnant pause.

"Look," she said, "I have to lock up."

"I'm not ready to go yet."

She stared at him for a long beat, the dirty cup still in her hands.

"All right."

There were always more things to do in a closed restaurant, so she went about doing some more of those things, while Oliver decided what needed to be said and what needed to be done.

The letters in the margins of the puzzle were bothering him, not so much for the fact that they didn't spell a word as for their familiarity. This went beyond the part where they all belonged in the alphabet together: they belonged together for a different reason.

The letters were: K, P, A, E, U, W.

Then he saw it.

"Kingdom, Phone, Alien, Eatery, Unnamed, Weapon."

"What was that?" Cydonia asked.

"The puzzle."

"Ah."

She was cleaning the same spot on the counter. It wasn't in any way in need of special attention.

"They're stories I wrote."

"Oh. I didn't… You're a writer?"

"Sometimes."

"All right."

She tossed aside the cleaning rag.

"No, no, I'm sorry, I can't do this any more," she said. "If you have something to say to me, please just say it. I have to… you know, I had a life before you came here, Oscar. It may not have been much of a life, but I was happy."

"I told you, I'm not ready to leave."

"The diner?"

"I'm not ready to leave at all."

"But you're going to. That's the implication, isn't it? You're not ready to leave, but you *have* to leave. Like you don't have a choice."

"I don't think I do."

"Do you love me? Because *that's* something you don't get to choose. The only choice you have is what you decide to do about that."

"Yes."

Oscar came back home to care for his mother, a woman from whom he had been deeply estranged for his entire adult life. They fought, reconciled, grew closer, fought some more. Family secrets were uncovered, motivations for his mother's actions revealed: horrible stories Oliver never really fleshed out, but from which Oscar still felt the scars. But as much as this was a story about finding peace with the past, it was also about finding hope for the future. That hope was Cydonia, the smart, funny, interesting, pretty young waitress with her own dark past.

Oliver never fleshed her past out either, but what he did flesh out was the connection these two damaged people made with one another.

If they'd had more time, they could have explored their connection at a properly leisure pace, but of course his mother once again screwed that up with historically poor timing.

Mother's unexpected death—Oscar sort of thought she was going to end up living forever, if only because of how inconvenient that would be—freed him to return to the city. He had no reason not to go back. No reason other than Cydonia. He was here in the diner, on the morning he was supposed to be driving back to his apartment in the city, and the friends he expected to miss more, and the job he didn't like very much, to see if Cydonia was enough.

None of that was really true.

"Yes you love me?"

"Yes. But I can't stay," he said. "I can't go back, and I can't stay. I don't know what would happen if I walked out of that door right now, but I don't think it would lead me in the right place. This story ends here, inside this diner, inside M Pallas. It ends with you, whether you're Cydonia, Minerva, Atha, or Epic, or a ghost, or a hostage. You're the Cydonian Kingdom. You're what I've been trying to get to all this time."

"That's... almost romantic. A little weird."

"Do you know all those names?"

"I think I do. But you're here now. That's good, isn't it?"

"Maybe."

"But you can't stay."

"All the stories end here."

She nodded, and wiped a tear. He didn't want to make her cry. Then he'd start crying, and that would be it: he'd never leave.

"We can make a new story," she said. "Isn't that something we can do? You and I can just... start something new. Something different and original. Maybe it isn't a story at all. That happens, right? People live, and grow older, and die, and there isn't some great story to tell about it."

"Everything's a story."

"But... Minerva, did you call me that?"

"I did, yes. It's one of the people you've been. I guess. I don't know how to describe it better."

"I remember Minerva," she said. "I remember Wilson. I remember the other writers too, and you're Oliver."

"Yes."

"Wilson would have said that a story without a conflict isn't a story, but I don't believe him. We can have a life together."

"It's still…"

"Then a very *boring* story!"

"The story has to continue. We have to *go* somewhere from here, and that's… look, we can't just fade into a happily-ever-after."

"Why not?"

"Because we might actually *fade*. The characters don't continue to have things happen to them when there isn't anyone telling their story."

She sighed, exasperated, and began pacing angrily.

"Tell me how this works, then. You called me Minerva, and I remember being her, but I don't know when or how. When did you last see her? When did I stop being her?"

"I'm not sure. I left you, or a version of you, on the other side of that door, when it was a different door. But you were already in here. If you're asking me whether you continue to exist out there too… I don't think so."

"But that's insane."

It sounded insane, but for the first time in a very long while, it was beginning to make sense to him. He hated that it was.

"What's so special about this place?" she asked.

"This is M Pallas. This is where all the answers are supposed to be."

"Are they?"

Oscar had a memory, of the first time he really noticed Cydonia. That was always the problem with service people, you could see them but not *see* them, not as people. The day he saw her as a person, she was behind this counter, and she'd just made light of something he was getting worked up about. Mother could do that to him, make him utterly irrational about the absolute dumbest things. But they were only dumb if you said them out loud, and the person he said it aloud to was Cydonia. When she called him on it, it was like all the tension in Oscar's shoulders disappeared, and the vice holding his head loosened up for the first time since he'd been forced to move back home. He probably fell in love with her then.

Well, Oscar did. Oliver loved her—Minerva—the minute he met her, probably. He couldn't recall what moment did it, or if there *was* a discrete moment. Wilson introduced them, in the kitchen of his condo, and when Oliver shook her hand and looked into her eyes, it wasn't as if he fell in love right there. It was more like, he was already in love before having met her, like he'd just gone about the whole thing in the wrong order.

"Yes, I think I know the answers now," Oliver said.

"That's good, isn't it?"

"Probably not. Look. Cydonia, I'm here to say I love you, and I can't live without you, and I would rather stay and live out that boring life you were talking about, even if it meant ending up on the wrong side of the last page. I would do that for you. But I don't think you're real."

She stared at him for a few seconds, neither registering surprise nor much of anything else. Expectation, perhaps, that he had something more to add.

"Okay," she said finally. "So what?"

"So I think I might be."

"How can you tell? Is this... have I..."

She was getting really upset. He wanted to step around the counter and hold her, but it was far too late for that sort of thing.

"...Is there something about me that makes you think this?" she asked. "Something I said?"

"No."

"I mean, how do you *act* like a not-real person? I don't understand!"

"It isn't you."

"You said you came here for answers, and you called it... you called *me* the Cydonian Kingdom, so if I'm the answer..."

"It's not you," he said. "You aren't what I'm here for."

"Then what?"

"The puzzle."

"The *crossword* puzzle?"

"Not the puzzle itself. The letters in the margin."

"You said they stood for the names of stories," she said. "Is Eatery… is *this* the Eatery story?"

"It is, but there's another message here. I was trying to make one word out of the letters, but I can see now that it's not one word; it's two. And it's a message for me. K, P, A, E, U, W. Rearrange them."

"O…okay. Two words."

She saw it.

"WAKE UP," she said. "It spells 'wake up'."

"This is what I was here to see," Oliver said.

"You think you're asleep?"

"I don't know. Maybe. I don't think so, but maybe."

"That's ridiculous."

"Well, I'm something. I don't know what, maybe there's a coma involved."

"Do you remember *anything* about a coma? Or a, I don't know, a really long nap?"

"I'm not saying it makes a ton of sense, but like I said, I can't go back and I can't stay. The only way forward is to do this."

"To wake up."

"Yes."

"Want me to slap you?"

"No, I don't think that would do it."

"Are you sure? I'm feeling like I want to slap you right now."

He put the Lot 42 container on the counter.

"What's that?" she asked.

"I think this is the key."

"But what is it?"

He opened the tin and took out the vial. Blue liquid, medical seal.

"I received a treasure map in a romance. Then aliens in a science fiction story chased me underground where I followed directions left in the stones of the world from a fantasy story, to a horror story in a department store. I dug this up there, until it was taken from me by an arch-villain in a techno-thriller. Then it was hand-delivered here by that villain, to this diner, which is the centerpiece of a fragment of literary fiction. All the stories got together to give me this. I think I'm supposed to drink it."

"And then you'll wake up?"

"Or die. I mean, it could be poison. It *was* handed to me by an arch-villain."

"That's a pretty steep risk. What if nothing happens?"

He shrugged.

"I guess we stay. I don't know."

She smiled wanly.

"I'd rather that," she said.

He swished around the liquid a little.

"I don't know what's going to happen to you," he said. "If I drink this and it does what I think it will do."

"I guess that depends on if I'm real or not," she said.

"Do you have an opinion?"

Cydonia smiled gently, and propped herself up on the counter a little. She wasn't quite tall enough to lean over without getting her feet off the ground first. The maneuver was to lean into a kiss, which was quite soft, and far too brief.

"I think I'm pretty real," she said. "But I guess I would. I feel real though, don't I?"

"Yes."

He was about ready to put the vial back in its box and explore the extent of her realness for a lot longer.

"But if you aren't?"

"What is it Cant said? You can't kill what was never alive?"

"I don't think that was meant to be comforting," he said.

"It sort of is. So drink it already. You know you're going to."

Oliver peeled the tape off the side of the lid, which was a rubber stopper. Then he popped it open.

"Cheers," he said, and downed the liquid.

There was hardly any to drink, because the vial held maybe two ounces. Oliver was glad for that.

"Blech," he said. It tasted like burning oil smelled. That was, oddly, a good indication he'd done the right thing.

"Do you feel any different?"

"No. Maybe I was wrong…"

Then the world blinked.

There wasn't a better way to describe it than that. It was more than that the lights went out and then flickered back on, *everything* disappeared and then popped back into existence: the stool he was sitting on, the counter, Cydonia, all of it. For less than a second he was floating in a dark void, and then the world snapped back again.

"Oh."

"You okay?" she asked. "You almost fell over."

"I think it's working."

"Or you're dying from the poison."

She reached over the counter and took his hands.

"Hold on as long as you can," she said.

"I'll try to…" he mumbled. He was going numb. "I'll try to take you. Take you with me."

"Okay."

A shock wave passed through the diner. He felt it, and saw it. It was like looking through a traveling funhouse mirror.

A line of bright light was forming, left-to-right, across his field of vision.

He had a revelation.

"I just figured out what M stands for," he said.

She squeezed his hands.

"What's that?" Cydonia asked. It sounded like she was standing next to him instead of on the other side of the counter, but he could still feel her there.

The line of light widened. A door was opening.

Not a door, an eyelid.

"M stands for memory."

The eyelid opened, and the world disappeared.

Chapter Sixteen

PERSONA NON GRATA

Something in the room was beeping.

That was the first thing Oliver noticed, before he blinked the fuzziness out of his vision and got a decent look at the room he happened to be lying in. *Beep, beep, beep.* It was the kind of sound most people associated with hospital rooms.

And so, when his vision cleared, that was what he expected to find. He didn't. This was a different kind of room.

Underneath him was a soft bed that he wasn't quite lying flat in. It had been adjusted so his back and knees were at angles. His arms were tied to the bed, and he had a needle inserted into his arm, attached to an intravenous drip, and there were sensors attached to his chest that were connected to a machine, possibly even the one that was beeping, and all of this was certainly hospital-like. He was also in a gown. All these things supported the assertion that this was indeed a hospital.

But, again, it probably wasn't. The room was too large, for starters. The floor was dark wood with area rugs, and the walls white plaster with embedded fake Greek columns. He couldn't see a door to a bathroom, or to closets, and there wasn't any window to the world. He'd never seen a hospital room without a view of the outside. Perhaps they existed, but he never saw one.

There was a single door, standing next to what was clearly an observation window with one-way glass. Beneath that window was a complicated assortment of electronics, including what looked an awful lot like server towers. He didn't know a great deal about computing, but he was pretty sure the server space he was looking at was tremendous.

A thick metal circle was bolted to the ceiling, which was there to support a ring of lights pointed at his face from a number of different angles. Only a couple of them were on.

Oliver tried to move. His arms weren't going anywhere, but nothing but gravity was holding down his legs. Unfortunately, gravity seemed to be adequate, as he could barely lift them. The blanket was tucked in tightly, and certainly that was a factor, but it felt like it had been a long time since they'd been used.

Next, he attempted to lift his head from the pillow. This went about as well, but less because of any kind of neck muscle atrophy and more due to the thing he was wearing on his head. He couldn't see what it looked like, but weight-wise, it felt like a helmet. Except most helmets had padding at the contact points with the scalp. This one didn't. It felt raw at those spots. When he moved his head, he was greeted with little stabs of pain.

The very last thing he noticed was the other person in the room. She was sitting on a chair in the corner to his left, which put her out of his direct line of sight entirely, unless he turned his head, which he wasn't all that interested in doing. He picked her out in his peripheral vision, but only when she moved to turn the page of the magazine she was engrossed in.

"Hhhhh…"

The word was supposed to be *hello*, but he didn't get that far. His mouth was horribly dry, and there was this acrid aftertaste in it.

It was enough of a noise to get her attention.

"Oh!" she said. "Hello!"

She got to her feet and moved to where he could see her without too much effort.

"Hi, you're awake!"

He blinked, a silent acknowledgement that yes, he was indeed awake.

She was an older woman, a bit on the hefty side, with black curly hair and thick glasses, wearing a nurse's uniform. He'd never seen her before.

"Water," he whispered.

"Yes, oh, right here."

A second later there was a straw in his mouth. She had a cup of water on the bedside, with a lid, like the kind you'd give a child. The water tasted dusty, but otherwise wonderful.

"Not too much," she said sternly, taking the straw back. "Don't be greedy, you'll make yourself sick."

Oliver wanted to drink all the water that existed in the world, but she was right. His stomach sounded an alarm declaring its intention to start rejecting things if he got out of hand. This didn't mean he felt anything for this unnamed nurse at this moment other than white-hot hatred, for taking the water away.

"Where am I?" he asked.

She looked at him for a measure or two.

"I'll let them know you're awake," she said, and then she bustled out of the room.

~

It was an excruciatingly long wait. It might have been only five or ten minutes in real time—there were no clocks in his range of vision—but felt like something closer to forever.

The problem was that the longer he lay there, the more self-aware he became of his physical body. There were the probes touching his head, which only became more painful the longer he was aware of them. That was the worst part of this experience, but there was also every single voluntary muscle in his body. He didn't know how long he'd been there or where *there* was, but it was long enough that all he could think about doing was stretching and moving and bending limbs that hadn't been bent in a while. It reminded him of how his legs felt on long plane flights, only multiplied by a very large number.

Oliver tried to free himself, but only once, and for just long enough to verify that he shouldn't attempt that again. Heavy nylon straps held his arms to the bed's sidewalls. Those straps were padded on the inside, but when he moved his arms even a little, it was painful. Some kind of rash was on his arms, and the skin around the IV needle was tender. He wondered if this was because whoever was in charge of tending to him didn't know bedsores were a thing, or if he had been moving around a lot while unconscious and rubbing his arms raw.

The door opened, and in walked an older gentleman, in a lab coat. He stopped two steps into the room, muttered something to the nurse, and waited for her leave.

"Hello," he said, closing the door. "It's good to see you again."

He strode across the room, grabbed the metal chair from the corner, and moved it to the side of the bed, but didn't sit in it right off.

"Do you know who I am?" he asked.

"You're Koestler."

"Very good, yes. I'm Doctor Koestler. We have met before."

"Here? Or…" He wanted to say the last time he saw Koestler, the older man had a messed up leg, a gun, and a death wish. But he could already tell *that* Koestler and *this* Koestler were two different Koestlers.

"We *have* met before," the doctor confirmed. "Now, can you tell me who *you* are?"

"Oliver."

Koestler didn't react to this, which seemed like a reaction, in its own way. He sat in the chair, crossed his legs, and began taking notes on a pad of paper.

"Oliver, then. What's your full name, Oliver?"

"Oliver Naughton. Sorry, Oliver Tennyson Davis Naughton. My family was weird about names."

Koestler wrote for a little while.

"Look, I'd really appreciate it if you took this thing off my head," Oliver said.

"Do you have any *other* names?" he asked.

"Me personally? Just Oliver. Well, sometimes Osraic, or Orrin, or Opie. Orson was another one. Oscar. There might have been one or two more, I forget."

"And these were *your* names?"

"They were names people called me and I answered to. I made them up."

"You made them up?"

"Look, really, get this thing off of me."

"Right. Of course."

Koestler put the pad down at the foot of the bed and leaned over to deal with the thing on Oliver's head. Ollie could hear things being turned, metal-on-metal, and lots of squeaking.

"I'm sorry, this is going to be unpleasant," the doctor said. Then he lifted the device off, and it was tremendously unpleasant in the same way having skin torn from one's body can be unpleasant. It hurt like hell.

"Owwwww!" Oliver declared.

Koestler looked at Oliver's forehead with a measure of alarm.

"Don't want that to get infected," he said, and then decided on a course of action, which involved a topical cream.

Oliver got a decent look at the thing that had been attached to his head. It wasn't a helmet, in the sense that wearing it would prevent a person from getting a head injury. It was a hat-shaped lattice of wires connecting pentagonal sensors. It looked lighter than it felt.

Koestler rubbed a white cream on Oliver's forehead, which was the first pleasant thing he'd felt since waking up. Then the doctor sat back down and returned to his pad of paper.

"Do you know where you are, Oliver?" he asked.

"No. I have no idea. Can you tell me?"

"But you know who I am."

"I know your name is Koestler, but I'm betting what I think I know about you is different from anything on your résumé."

"I see. We'll loop back to that."

"Can you untie my arms?"

"We'll get to that shortly. We need to make sure you're stable."

"Stable," Oliver repeated. He felt pretty stable.

"Yes, we have to make sure you're all the way out. I'm not yet."

"All the way out of what?"

Doctor Koestler had an annoying habit of ignoring direct questions. In this instance, instead of responding, he pulled a small hand mirror from his pocket.

"I'm going to show you your reflection, is that all right?" he asked.

"Sure."

Koestler held the mirror a few inches from Oliver's face, and he had a good look. He was pale, as if he hadn't seen sunlight in ages because, perhaps, he hadn't. He looked scruffy, and he wasn't at all fond of the facial hair. He thought probably it had been trimmed a few times, but that didn't mean it wasn't itchy. He suddenly and very desperately wanted to scratch his face.

"Who did you see in the mirror?" Koestler asked.

"I need a shave."

"Please answer. This is important."

"Doctor Koestler, I've been looking at my own face my entire life, and I didn't see anything unexpected just now. It's me. Can you please start answering *my* questions?"

"Soon, yes. Do you know what Project Wise-Eyes is?"

"I... yes, it's a secret government experiment. Or it was. It was supposed to be something to do with remote viewing. But it wasn't real."

"It wasn't real, you say?"

"I made it up. It was part of a story. There was no such thing."

"And do you imagine that, when you make up a story, there might be things you borrow? Street names, people you know... When you say you and I have met before, do you recall that meeting taking place here, or in one of your stories?"

"You were a spy."

"A spy!"

When he wasn't ducking questions, Koestler repeated what Oliver just said as if he didn't quite believe him and that was possibly even more annoying.

"Yes," Oliver said, "but... yes, to answer your question, I think it's possible I borrow from other places when I decide on names of people or places. I think every writer probably does."

Koestler nodded.

"All right. Now, to answer some of your questions, Oliver, Project Wise-Eyes is indeed a secret project, but it's not related to remote viewing and it isn't government-sponsored. We're privately funded."

"*This* is Project Wise-Eyes?"

"Yes, although I have to correct both of us. The project's actual name is L'Oiseaux."

"The bird?"

"Birds, plural. Yes, very good. Wise-Eyes is a nickname. Bastardization, in truth. Some of our volunteers were less than successful with the pronunciation. We heard 'wise-oh', and for some that became wise-eye. And our signage doesn't help. Birds, of course. An owl is especially prominent in our seal. Wise owl with wise eyes. You understand."

"That sounds like you have a real branding problem there."

"Yes. And is this the first time you've heard this story?"

Oliver didn't know what he was supposed to think.

"Yes?" he said. "You just told me for the first time, so yes."

"What do you remember before you woke up in this room?"

"You mean, when I was in the other place?"

"No. We'll talk about the other place in a moment. Before that."

"I don't understand the question."

"I guess you don't," Koestler said. "All right."

"Can you untie me now?"

"Nearly. Let me explain what we do here. Project Wise-Eyes is —was—developing an immersive web experience. The device that was just on your head had been paired with an optical/auditory headset, which we removed when it was obvious… I'm getting ahead. To go along with that technology, we developed a compound to assist the brain in disassociating from the physical. This aided in the immersion."

"Lot Forty-Two."

He looked surprised.

"Yes, that's exactly right. We're still beta-testing the entire thing. Or, we were."

"You're out of beta?"

"We've stopped the tests, sent home the volunteers, buttoned up the research. Because of what happened to you."

"Okay. Then what happened to me?"

Koestler looked incredibly uncomfortable.

"I'm going to tell you a few things," he said, "and they will be shocking, and I apologize for it, but there's really no other way. You were one of our beta testers. You came into the project very early, and actually helped us with some of the conceptualization. We didn't recognize the complete opportunity, you see, not until you came along. We saw only a toy, something for gaming, or perhaps as a therapeutic solution. We focused on escapism. Your innovation was in seeing a tool: a way to expand the mind. You saw these server towers and the terabytes and decided to create something entirely different."

"A memory palace."

"Yes. Yes! How did you know this?"

"I was inside of it."

"And then you escaped."

"I'm here, aren't I?"

"So you are."

Koestler cleared his throat loudly, and made eye contact with the one-way mirror. Oliver realized there was someone on the other side of that glass, and thought that this conversation was probably being recorded. Any minute now this would all start to make sense.

"So you built your palace," Koestler said. "It was a city. You named streets and so on, and began doing what one does in a memory palace: inserting your memories into these places. We could watch all of this, because the lattice was providing feedback to our team. We could see the build-out as it happened. And this was *remarkable*, because it gave us another new idea: an immersive experience in a world designed by a subject instead of a programmer. Imagine the implications!"

"You'd put game designers out of business overnight."

"It was an exciting time. But then something went wrong. We never asked you to start inventing stories, but perhaps you saw the same thing we did, from the inside, because you stopped inserting memories into your city and started to interact with it differently. You—or someone--were writing stories on an imaginary computer inside the program. And then... you decided not to wake up."

"I don't remember any of this."

"Yes, I know, and there's a very important reason for that. A split occurred, inside the program. One day we were able to see your entire memory palace, but then we lost contact with your mind, and the only feedback we were able to receive was the text of the stories. All this equipment became nothing but a word processor for a writer who was trapped on the wrong side of things. And thank goodness we had that, because then we knew you were still in there. Still, we thought we'd never get you back. And... we aren't sure that we have."

"I'm right here."

"Yes. In a way. Our problem right now is that your name is not Oliver Tennyson Davis Naughton. Your name is Wilson Knight. Oliver Naughton doesn't exist."

Chapter Seventeen

FOUR IN THE MORNING

It was a couple of days before he was able to walk around on his own, owing more to his legs not having been used for six months straight than for any other medical problem or security concern. He also got winded easily, so even though bipedal motion was well within the scope of his abilities, even if he wanted to flee the facility he couldn't get far.

It was a campus. He didn't know where it was located for certain, but he could see tall buildings in the distance, and they were near the top of the hill, so he was guessing it was somewhere on the outskirts of Boston. That felt right.

All he had to go on, for a whole lot of things, was feel. If what Doctor Koestler said was to be believed –and that was in *no* way a definite—Oliver had never been to the campus, or to Boston, or anywhere else. Oliver had never left the city of the memory palace, because Oliver hadn't existed six months ago. Oliver wasn't real.

There was a part of him that was indisputably Wilson. The person he knew of as his writing mentor was like a phantom limb, or if that was too cliché, like the password Oliver knew well enough to type but wouldn't have been able to write down if asked. He had all of Wilson's instincts, but none of his active memories. Everything felt like a permanent *déjà vu*.

The campus consisted of four L-shaped buildings, which combined to wall off an inner courtyard. The trees in the yard were turning pleasant shades of orange and red, which also spoke strongly to a New England locale. There was a table in the middle of the grassy center, and a number of scattered Adirondack chairs made out of a material that only looked like wood. When Oliver wasn't getting examined, sleeping, answering a battery of questions, or reintroducing solid food to a body that hadn't had it for a while, he was sitting in one of those chairs.

He was usually alone, in the sense that nobody else was also sitting in the chairs, but not alone in the sense that nobody else was around. Koestler had someone keeping an eye on him: a large man who kept his distance but who didn't make any effort to disguise the fact that he was following Oliver around. It was Cant.

It *wasn't* Cant, because Cant wasn't real, but Oliver didn't know the man's actual name and he looked exactly like Cant—from a distance—and so that was who he was going to be until Oliver decided otherwise.

This was probably unhealthy. He was supposed to be learning how to become Wilson again, or something. There were undoubtedly many weeks of psychiatric examinations to look forward to, as experts tried to find Wilson's memories inside of Oliver's head, or maybe they would just tell him he wasn't who he thought he was until he believed it himself. Or they would have him committed.

He didn't know how it could come to that, but it probably would. Could they declare you insane for not being the person everyone wanted you to be?

"Hello, Wilson."

He turned at the sound of the wrong name, because he knew

he was supposed to. Also, because the woman who'd said it wasn't supposed to be there. It was Minerva.

She was in jeans and a brown Fall-appropriate suede jacket over a white blouse. Her hair was brown with a touch of blonde highlights, pulled back into a ponytail. It looked longer than he remembered it ever getting.

There were wrinkles around the edges of her eyes. It felt like he was seeing her without makeup for the first time, only without knowing she'd had on makeup all those other times.

But it was still her.

"Hi," he said.

"Can I sit?"

"Please."

She took a seat at the nearest Adirondack. They were face-to-face, if he turned his head a little to the left.

"Do you know who I am?" she asked. She sounded scared, and tired.

"You're Minerva."

She smiled, but faintly.

"Athena," she said. "My name's Athena. I'm your… I'm Wilson's friend."

Every word from her sounded wary. It reminded him of the way people spoke to dangerous animals.

"Of course," he said. "That makes a lot of sense."

"Does it?"

"Minerva is what I called you, in that other place. I also called you Epic, and Cydonia, and Atha. Were you and Wilson… I mean, were we…?"

"More than friends? Yes. You can say that."

"I tried to write a romance with the name Athena, but I'm not good at those. I wrote the outline, though."

"Is that why you said my name makes sense?"

"All those names are variants of the goddess Athena. I should have seen that. And Pallas Athena, of course."

She smiled one of those smiles you give to someone who's either a child, or a demented adult.

"Sure," she said.

"There was a version of Wilson, in that other place. He was my writing tutor."

She nodded.

"That sounds like him."

"We used to argue constantly. I'd write these genre stories and he *hated* them. He kept wanting me to 'write something important!'"

They both laughed then, and after that fell into an awkward silence.

"This must be terrible for you, after all this time," he said. "You were waiting for him, weren't you? To wake up."

"It's been a difficult six months, yes."

There were loose hairs, not long enough to stay in the ponytail and dangling over her eyes. She brushed them aside with an automatic gesture, and he nearly fell apart. Minerva was alive in Athena's personal tics, and it made him want to cry.

"I'm sorry," he said. "For so many reasons. I'm sorry I'm not him. We didn't know. When were in there, I mean, we didn't know only one of us was getting out. We didn't even know there was an out to get to. We were just following the story."

She curled up in the chair and hugged her knees. He wondered if she was cold, and if he should offer up something to keep her warm. He could call the not-Cant guy over and have him get her a blanket. That'd be almost chivalrous.

"I'm not so sure you *aren't* him," she said. "I think what happened when Wilson went in there… you know, he was always pushing himself. He wanted to be a better writer, and that's what… that can drive people. Study, read, practice, get feedback, push that envelope, all that. He's a person of singular drive and intent. It made him *really* difficult sometimes. But I think he saw that he needed to become a different person to improve. For most of us, that's not literal."

"You're saying I'm a better version of your boyfriend?"

"I'm saying that's what Wilson Knight thought of Oliver Naughton. Don't get carried away."

"Got it."

"But yes, I think so. At some point in that place, Wilson created you, and somehow handed you the keys to the psyche. I think there's probably going to be a lifetime of doctoral theses written on the subject of exactly how that happened. And I mean except for the problem with your memories… maybe you *are* still him. You look like him. You know that, right?"

The one thing Oliver did to improve his appearance—after a shower that felt simply fantastic—was to shave. When he did, he saw only his own face looking back at him, as it always had.

He didn't remember the Wilson of Tenth Avenue looking identical. They had the same height and the same basic build, and if there was someone out there who didn't know them well, that person could confuse them with one another. But the face was definitely different.

"So I'm told," he said. "I don't see it."

"Maybe it's like hearing your own voice in a recording. So what was she like?"

He smiled.

"Minerva."

"Yeah."

"She looked like you. Not exactly like you, or not always exactly like you. She was smart, and funny, and interesting. And a quick thinker. She was on top of the story changes faster than I was, at first. She seemed to know what was happening before anybody. And she wanted to come with me. But I couldn't take her."

"I'm sorry."

"Thank you."

She thought of something. It was amazing how easy it was to read her face and recognize little telltale signs of what was going on inside her head. Oliver didn't know if he was seeing her with this kind of familiarity because of Wilson's ghostly presence, or because everything that was Athena was reflected in Minerva. Maybe it didn't matter.

"Did Wilson get any better at women?" she asked.

"At women?"

"At writing women. It was one of his biggest things; he could *not* invent a credible woman. It was terrible. I used to have to mark up all his drafts."

"Are you a writer too?"

"No, but I'm a woman and, I mean, it's sad, but that was enough."

He laughed.

"I think he got better. Maybe not at first, but as the plot got going. Should I be saying 'we'?"

"Not if you have to ask. I do think there are a lot of folks here who would be overjoyed if you just started calling yourself Wilson and they could forget about this whole mess, but it's your identity. If you came back feeling more litigious, you'd probably have a good case on your hands."

He assumed Wilson signed some sort of agreement that would have made a lawsuit difficult, and Oliver surely would not help his own cause by declaring that not only did he not recall signing the disclosure, he wasn't *him* when it was signed. Any attorney willing to follow that trail of breadcrumbs to its logical conclusion would find that were it not for this little accident, Oliver wouldn't even exist. Therefore, shouldn't he be thanking them and not suing them?

Taken a little further still, if that were established in court, the L'Oiseaux Institute could be charged with the wrongful death of Wilson Knight.

It made for an entertaining story, anyway.

"You loved her, didn't you?" Athena asked.

"Very much."

His voice caught on the words a little. That was unexpected. He hadn't really mourned Minerva's loss. It was going to catch up to him.

"Even though she wasn't real."

"I don't know how much that matters."

She nodded. "I guess that's true, isn't it?"

"I don't even know who gets to decide these things."

"What do you mean?"

"Who decides who is and isn't real?"

"She was inside of a computer simulated reality. Wilson invented her. Or you did. Based on me, it sounds like."

"Minerva was real when I was in there with her. Isn't that enough?"

"I don't think so, Oliver. I wish it could be. But no."

Something like pity showed up in her eyes. It probably should have been of a comfort, seeing that, but it made him feel worse.

"We all knew," he said. "That was the interesting thing. In the middle of it, we all knew we were fulfilling roles in a story. In stories, plural. A bunch of them. And we knew I'd written those stories. And the part that's really getting to me is I didn't feel any different then, than I do now. Not really. I guess that could be an endorsement of the effectiveness of Koestler's artificial reality, but…"

"But you don't think so."

"I have an interpretation I like better. Nobody else will, but I do. I don't think this reality is any more or less real than the other one."

She took a deep breath. He got the sense that she was told to look out for this kind of declaration. Maybe they gave her a signal, and if she used it, men would run from one of the buildings with a strait jacket and carry him away.

"Do you think you're writing this?" she asked. "Like you were in the memory palace? Is this one of your plots?"

"No. But *someone* is."

"Who?"

"I don't think that matters. Not in the way you're thinking. Like, I'm pretty positive we can't wander around here until we find the writer, because they aren't a character in this story, like we are. Like I was, on the inside. It doesn't mean they don't exist."

"You find that comforting?"

"I do."

"Why is that, Oliver? What difference does it make?"

"It's probably going to sound crazy. I guess everything I have to say sounds crazy anyway. I want a happy ending, Athena. When I look at all I went through to get here, it's obvious I'm at the end of this story. If that's true, I'm holding out for my happy ending, and I could have had it if I stayed in there. But to get one here, this has to be a story first. Otherwise, who knows?"

She smiled a gentle smile that was quite affecting.

"Well," she said. She was uncurling her legs and finding her feet. "Don't say that to anyone else. I think the reaction you get won't be much to your liking."

She extended her hand. He shook it.

"It was a pleasure meeting you, Oliver," she said.

"And you. Will you come back?"

"Yes, I probably will."

"I look forward to it."

She grinned, and started walking away.

"You know," he said, "I told myself not to go."

Athena stopped and turned.

"How's that?"

"The letter prompts Wilson gave me spelled the word 'wake up'."

"And?"

"It was an anagram. There was another anagram, but I never saw it. My name."

"Oliver Naughton?"

"Oliver Tennyson Davis Naughton. O T D N. Every name I gave myself in the stories was a combination of those letters. Move it around: D O N T."

"Don't?"

"Don't Wake Up. That was the full message."

"Well," she said. "Too late now."

"Yes."

"Goodbye, Oliver."

❧

*H*e left the yard soon after, returned to his room and tried to get some sleep. Ironically, since he'd woken up from the memory palace, his sleep cycle had been completely messed up. He knew lying down while the sun was still up wasn't going to make that any better, but he was tired, and he had nothing better to do.

Of course, then he woke up in the middle of the night.

They'd given him a room with a window on the top floor of one of the L-shaped buildings. The window faced away from the inner compound and looked down the hill at the city he couldn't positively identify. This was his third night in the room, and his third night awake at some point past midnight.

The view was nicer than the room, which was quite small. It had a prison-like feel, except for a lack of bars. The campus was a converted monastery, which naturally lent itself to the austerity that was also common in prisons, and college dormitories.

Oliver was staring out the window and wondering what the downtown was like, when the door opened behind him.

"You're awake," his visitor said. "Good. We thought you might be."

It was the big guy who'd been following Oliver around.

"We? You mean Koestler?"

"No, not him. Athena sent me."

"In the middle of the night? What time is it? What's going on?"

The man checked his watch.

"About four A.M. And I don't really know. She said she wanted to get you out of here. She picked the time."

"And… you take orders from her?"

He sort of smiled. It was alarming how familiar that sort-of smile was to Oliver.

"Technically, no, but she and Wilson… sorry, this is real weird. You're kind of Wilson and kind of not. Probably weird for you too."

"In so many ways, yes."

"Well they got me this job. I owe them a lot. I'd follow her—and him, um, you—anywhere."

"What, like a blood oath or something?"

"Something like that. I can explain later, but maybe after we're out of the building."

"I feel pretty safe right here. How do I know I can even trust you?"

"Wilson did."

"But I'm still not him. What's your name?"

"Bobby Canton. My friends call me Cant."

"That's good enough for me. Then let's go."

"So are you some kind of magician or something?" Bobby Canton asked.

"How do you mean?"

They had exited the room, and gone to the end of the hall to a stairwell that was inaccessible without a key card, which Bobby had. From there, they went down two flights and entered an unused wing. Oliver was already completely turned around, so he was glad his guide knew where they were going.

"The way they talk about you," he said. "I don't think they know how you ended up here and Wilson didn't—I mean if that's what happened, I dunno—but I heard more than one guy use the word 'magic' to explain it. And these are scientists."

"There was magic in the world I escaped from," Oliver said, "so maybe they're right."

"Huh. You'll have to show me some. I always wanted to see real magic. It's through here."

Cant opened a door that looked about the same as every other door on the floor. Oliver walked into a dark room.

"Were you followed?"

Athena was in the corner, near an open window. He didn't see her at first, because between visits she'd changed into black clothing.

Oliver started to answer, but the question was directed at Cant.

"No," he said. "They're confident he doesn't want to leave, and that he wouldn't know how if he did."

"Good. This is probably our only chance."

"What's going on?" Oliver asked.

"There's a lot you weren't told," she said. She had a knapsack on her back, which she dropped on the floor between them. "We don't have a lot of time, though. Do you trust me?"

"I do."

"Good. There's clothes in the bag that'll fit you. Change, and let's get out of here."

He took the bag to the opposite corner of the room. This involved negotiating a number of tables and chairs that were apparently just being stored there.

"What wasn't I told?" he asked, as he felt his way through the bag. It was a complete change of clothes, convenient given he'd been walking around in scrubs and a heavy bathrobe. That and a thick pair of socks was fine for the courtyard, but maybe not for a foray into the real world. He began to strip down.

"Koestler needs to keep you here," she said. "Whether that's what's best for you or not."

"Why is that?"

"Because this place is largely funded by money from Wilson's family estate."

"So for that I have to stay?"

"If you're here, he can control you, and if he controls you he controls your money. And I can't challenge him legally because I'm just Wilson Knight's girlfriend. We live together, but that's all. The person with the best claim on the estate is you, up until Koestler figures out how to get a court to say otherwise. And the answer to your next question is, Wilson's parents are both dead and he has no siblings, and it's a *lot* of money."

Oliver finished changing. Dark clothing, like Athena.

"So we run away? Is that your solution?"

"One thing at a time," she said. "We get you out of here, and then to the city. Wilson and I have a condo."

"Tenth Avenue."

She smiled.

"Yes. Tenth Avenue. We'll get you home and then figure out our best options. Is that okay?"

It was four in the morning and Athena was worried, he thought.

He took her hands.

"Like I said, I trust you. Both of you."

"Good. Let's go."

The way out the window required negotiating a ladder, since they weren't on the ground floor. He was halfway down when he took a second to check out the night sky. The air above was awash in the reflected light from the city, so he didn't see much in the way of stars, but there were clouds up there.

One of them was shaped like a dragon, and Oliver's heart skipped.

But it wasn't a real dragon. It was just a cloud.

"You know," he said, "I think maybe I was wrong."

"About what?" Athena asked. She was leading the way down, while Cant held the ladder steady from above.

"Maybe this isn't the end of the story at all. Maybe this is just the beginning."

ACKNOWLEDGMENTS

Thanks to my wife, Deb, for insisting I finish this crazy idea and putting up with me while I did it. And to fellow author Xio Axelrod for hearing about this back when it was only an idea called M Pallas, and not telling me I was crazy.

I'd also like to thank Julie Gray, my editor, whose first and most important responsibility was to convince me I needed an editor, and Kim Killion, the cover artist who has to put up with some ridiculously sketchy design proposals. (Six genres! Here's ten objects to put on the cover! Go!)

Finally, I want to thank the many contributors to the KBoards, for the title of the book, (and the blurb) and for helping me see genre fiction in a way that informed a lot of the things in this novel. You guys are the best.

Gene Doucette is a hybrid author, albeit in a somewhat round-about way. From 2010 through 2014, Gene published four full-length novels (*Immortal, Hellenic Immortal, Fixer,* and *Immortal at the Edge of the World*) with a small indie publisher. Then, in 2014, Gene started self-publishing novellas that were set in the same universe as the *Immortal* series, at which point he was a hybrid.

When the novellas proved more lucrative than the novels, Gene tried self-publishing a full novel, *The Spaceship Next Door,* in 2015. This went well. So well, that in 2016, Gene reacquired the rights to the earlier four novels from the publisher, and re-released them, at which point he wasn't a hybrid any longer.

Additional self-published novels followed: *Immortal and the Island of Impossible Things* (2016); *Unfiction* (2017); and *The Frequency of Aliens* (2017).

In 2018, John Joseph Adams Books (an imprint of Houghton Mifflin Harcourt) acquired the rights to *The Spaceship Next Door*. The reprint was published in September of that year, at which point Gene was once again a hybrid author.

Since then, a number of things have happened. Gene published three more novels—*Immortal From Hell* (2018), *Fixer Redux* (2019), and *Immortal: Last Call* (2020)—and wrote a new novel called *The Apocalypse Seven* that he did not self-publish; it was acquired by JJA/HMH in September of 2019. Publication date is May 25, 2021.

Gene lives in Cambridge, MA.

For the latest on Gene Doucette, follow him online

genedoucette.me
genedoucette@me.com

ALSO BY GENE DOUCETTE

<u>SCI-FI</u>

The Spaceship Next Door

The world changed on a Tuesday.

When a spaceship landed in an open field in the quiet mill town of Sorrow Falls, Massachusetts, everyone realized humankind was not alone in the universe. With that realization, everyone freaked out for a little while.

Or, almost everyone. The residents of Sorrow Falls took the news pretty well. This could have been due to a certain local quality of unflappability, or it could have been that in three years, the ship did exactly nothing other than sit quietly in that field, and nobody understood the full extent of this nothing the ship was doing better than the people who lived right next door.

Sixteen-year old Annie Collins is one of the ship's closest neighbors. Once upon a time she took every last theory about the ship seriously, whether it was advanced by an adult ,or by a peer. Surely one of the theories would be proven true eventually—if not several of them—the very minute the ship decided to do something. Annie is starting to think this will never happen.

One late August morning, a little over three years since the ship landed, Edgar Somerville arrived in town. Ed's a government operative posing as a journalist, which is obvious to Annie—and pretty much everyone else he meets—almost immediately. He has a lot of questions that need answers, because he thinks everyone is wrong: the ship is doing something, and he needs Annie's help to figure out what that is.

Annie is a good choice for tour guide. She already knows everyone in town and when Ed's theory is proven correct—something is apocalyptically wrong in Sorrow Falls—she's a pretty good person to have around.

As a matter of fact, Annie Collins might be the most important person on the planet. She just doesn't know it.

The Frequency of Aliens

Annie Collins is back!

Becoming an overnight celebrity at age sixteen should have been a lot more fun. Yes, there were times when it was extremely cool, but when the newness of it all wore off, Annie Collins was left with a permanent security detail and the kind of constant scrutiny that makes the college experience especially awkward.

Not helping matters: she's the only kid in school with her own pet spaceship.

She would love it if things found some kind of normal, but as long as she has control of the most lethal—and only—interstellar vehicle in existence, that isn't going to happen. Worse, things appear to be going in the other direction. Instead of everyone getting used to the idea of the ship, the complaints are getting louder. Public opinion is turning, and the demands that Annie turn over the ship are becoming more frequent. It doesn't help that everyone seems to think Annie is giving them nightmares.

Nightmares aren't the only weird things going on lately. A government telescope in California has been abandoned, and nobody seems to know why.

The man called on to investigate—Edgar Somerville—has become the go-to guy whenever there's something odd going on, which has been pretty common lately. So far, nothing has panned out: no aliens or zombies or anything else that might be deemed legitimately peculiar… but now may be different, and not just because Ed can't find an easy explanation. This isn't the only telescope where people have gone missing, and the clues left behind lead back to Annie.

It all adds up to a new threat that the world may just need saving from, requiring the help of all the Sorrow Falls survivors. The question is: are they saving the world with Annie Collins, or are they saving it from her?

The Frequency of Aliens is the exciting sequel to *The Spaceship Next Door*.

Unfiction

When Oliver Naughton joins the Tenth Avenue Writers Underground, headed by literary wunderkind Wilson Knight, Oliver figures he'll finally get some of the wild imaginings out of his head and onto paper.

But when Wilson takes an intense interest in Oliver's writing and his genre stories of dragons, aliens, and spies, things get weird. Oliver's stories don't just need to be finished: they insist on it.

With the help of Minerva, Wilson's girlfriend, Oliver has to find the connection between reality, fiction, the mythical Cydonian Kingdom, and the non-mythical nightclub called M Pallas. That is, if he can survive the alien invasion, the ghosts, and the fact that he thinks he might be in love with Minerva.

Unfiction is a wild ride through the collision of science fiction, fantasy, thriller, horror and romance. It's what happens when one writer's fiction interferes with everyone's reality.

Fixer

What would you do if you could see into the future?

As a child, he dreamed of being a superhero. Most people never get to realize their childhood dreams, but Corrigan Bain has come close. He is a fixer. His job is to prevent accidents—to see the future and "fix" things before people get hurt. But the ability to see into the future, however limited, isn't always so simple. Sometimes not everyone can be saved.

"Don't let them know you can see them."

Graduate students from a local university are dying, and former lover and FBI agent Maggie Trent is the only person who believes their deaths aren't as accidental as they appear. But the truth can only be found in something from Corrigan Bain's past, and he's not interested in sharing that past, not even with Maggie.

To stop the deaths, Corrigan will have to face up to some old horrors, confront the possibility that he may be going mad, and find a way to stop a killer no one can see.

Corrigan Bain is going insane ... or is he? 

Because there's something in the future that doesn't want to be seen. It isn't human. It's got a taste for mayhem. And it is very, very angry.

～

Fixer Redux

Someone's altering the future, and it isn't Corrigan Bain

Corrigan Bain was retired.

It wasn't something he ever thought he'd be able to do. The problem was that the *job* he wanted to retire from wasn't actually a job at all: nobody paid him to do it, and nobody else did it. With very few exceptions, nobody even knew he was doing it.

Corrigan called himself a fixer, because he fixed accidents that were about to happen. It was complicated and unrewarding, and even though doing it right meant saving someone, he didn't enjoy it. He couldn't stop—he thought—because there would always be accidents, and he would never find someone to take over as fixer. Anyone trying would have to be capable of seeing the future, like he did, and that kind of person was hard to find.

Still, he did it. He's never been happier.

His girlfriend, Maggie Trent of the FBI, has not retired. Her task force just shut down the most dangerous domestic terrorist cell in the country, and she's up for an award, and a big promotion.

Everything's going their way now, and the future looks even brighter.

Unfortunately, that future is about to blow up in their faces...literally. And somehow, Corrigan Bain, fixer, the man who can see the future, is taken completely by surprise.

Fixer Redux is the long-awaited sequel to *Fixer*. Catch up with Corrigan, as he tries to understand a future that no longer makes sense.

<u>FANTASY</u>

The Immortal Novel Series

Immortal

"I don't know how old I am. My earliest memory is something along the lines of fire good, ice bad, so I think I predate written history, but I don't know by how much. I like to brag that I've been there from the beginning, and while this may very well be true, I generally just say it to pick up girls."

Surviving sixty thousand years takes cunning and more than a little luck. But in the twenty-first century, Adam confronts new dangers—someone has found out what he is, a demon is after him, and he has run out of places to hide. Worst of all, he has had entirely too much to drink.

Immortal is a first person confessional penned by a man who is immortal, but not invincible. In an artful blending of sci-fi, adventure, fantasy, and humor, IMMORTAL introduces us to a world with vampires, demons and other "magical" creatures, yet a world without actual magic.

At the center of the book is Adam.

Adam is a sixty thousand year old man. (Approximately.) He doesn't age or get sick, but is otherwise entirely capable of being killed. His survival has hinged on an innate ability to adapt, his wits, and a fairly large dollop of luck. He makes for an excellent guide through history ... when he's sober.

Immortal is a contemporary fantasy for non-fantasy readers and fantasy enthusiasts alike.

Hellenic Immortal

"Very occasionally, I will pop up in the historical record. Most of the time I'm not at all easy to spot, because most of the time I'm just a guy who does a thing and then disappears again into the background behind someone-or-other who's busy doing something much more important. But there are a couple of rare occasions when I get a starring role."

An oracle has predicted the sojourner's end, which is a problem for Adam insofar as he has never encountered an oracular prediction that didn't come true ... and he is the sojourner. To survive, he's going to have to figure out what a beautiful ex-government analyst, an eco-terrorist, a rogue FBI agent, and the world's oldest religious cult all want with him, and fast.

And all he wanted when he came to Vegas was to forget about a girl. And maybe have a drink or two.

The second book in the Immortal series, Hellenic Immortal follows the continuing adventures of Adam, a sixty-thousand-year-old man with a wry sense of humor, a flair for storytelling, and a knack for staying alive. Hellenic Immortal is a clever blend of history, mythology, sci-fi, fantasy, adventure, mystery and romance. A little something, in other words, for every reader.

Immortal at the Edge of the World

"What I was currently doing with my time and money ... didn't really deserve anyone else's attention. If I was feeling romantic about it, I'd call it a quest, but all I was really doing was trying to answer a question I'd been ignoring for a thousand years."

In his very long life, Adam had encountered only one person who appeared to share his longevity: the mysterious red-haired woman. She appeared throughout history, usually from a distance, nearly always vanishing before he could speak to her.

In his last encounter, she actually did vanish—into thin air, right in front of him. The question was how did she do it? To answer, Adam will have to complete a quest he gave up on a thousand years earlier, for an object that may no longer exist.

If he can find it, he might be able to do what the red-haired woman did, and if he can do that, maybe he can find her again and ask her who she is … and why she seems to hate him.

But Adam isn't the only one who wants the red-haired woman. There are other forces at work, and after a warning from one of the few men he trusts, Adam realizes how much danger everyone is in. To save his friends and finish his quest he may be forced to bankrupt himself, call in every favor he can, and ultimately trade the one thing he'd never been able to give up before: his life.

Immortal and the island of Impossible Things

"I thought I'd miss the world."

Adam is on vacation in an island paradise, with nothing to do and plenty of time to do nothing.

It's exactly what he needed: beautiful weather, beautiful girlfriend, plenty of books to read, and alcohol to drink. Most importantly, either nobody on the island knows who he is, or, nobody cares.

"This probably sounds boring, and maybe it is. It's possible I have no compass to help determine boring, or maybe I have a different threshold than most people. From my perspective, though, the vast majority of human history has been boring, by which I mean nothing happened, and sure, that can be dull. On the other hand, nothing happening includes nobody trying to kill anybody, and specifically, nobody trying to kill me. That's the kind of boring a guy can get behind."

Nothing last forever, though, and that includes the opportunity to *do* nothing. One day, unwelcome visitors arrive in secret, with impossible knowledge of impossible events, and then the impossible things arrive: a new species.

It's *all* impossible, especially to the immortal man who thought he'd seen all there was to see in the world. Now, Adam is going to have to figure out what's happening and make things right before he and everyone he loves ends up dead in the hot sun of this island paradise.

Immortal From Hell

Not all of Adam's stories have happy endings

"Paris is romantic and quests are cool. But the threat of a global pandemic kind of sours the whole thing. The good news was, if all life on Earth were felled by a plague, it looked like this one could take me out too. It'd be pretty lonely otherwise."

--Adam the immortal

When Adam decides to leave the safety of the island, it's for a good reason: Eve, the only other immortal on the planet, appears to be dying, and nobody seems to understand why. But when Adam—with his extremely capable girlfriend Mirella—tries to retrace Eve's steps, he discovers a world that's a whole lot deadlier than he remembered.

Adam is supposed to be dead. He went through a lot of trouble to fake that death, but now that he's back it's clear someone remains unconvinced. That wouldn't be so terrible, except that whoever it is, they have a great deal of influence, and an abiding interest in ensuring that his death sticks this time around.

Adam and Mirella will have to figure out how to travel halfway across the world in secret, with almost no resources or friends. The good news is, Adam solved the travel problem a thousand years earlier. The bad news is, one of his oldest assumptions will turn out to be untrue.

Immortal From Hell is the darkest entry in the Immortal series.

Immortal: Last Call

"I'm something like sixty-thousand years old, and I've probably thought more about my own death than any living being has thought about any subject, ever. I used to be

unduly preoccupied with what might constitute a "good death", although interestingly, this has always been an after-the-fact analysis. What I mean is, following a near-death experience, I'll generally perform a quiet review of the circumstances and judge whether that death would have been objectively good, by whatever metric one uses for that kind of thing. I'm not nearly that self-reflective while in the midst of said near-death experience. Facing death, the predominant thought is always not like this."

A disease threatening the lives of everyone—human and non-human—has been loosed upon the world, by an arch-enemy Adam didn't even know he had.

That's just the first of his problems. Adam's also in jail, facing multiple counts of murder, at least a few of which are accurate. He may never see the inside of a courtroom, because there remains a bounty on his head—put there by the aforementioned arch-enemy—that someone is bound to try to collect while he's stuck behind bars.

Meanwhile, Adam's sitting on some tantalizing evidence that there might be a cure, but to find it, he's going to have to get out of jail, get out of the country, and track down the man responsible. He can't do any of that alone, but he also can't rely on any of his non-human friends for help, not when they're all getting sick.

What he needs is a particularly gifted human, who can do things no other human is capable of. He knows one such person. He calls himself a fixer, and he's Adam's—and possibly the world's—last hope. That's provided he believes any of it.

Immortal: Last Call is the sixth book in the *Immortal Novel Series*, and also the end of a long journey for one immortal man.

Immortal Stories

Eve

"…if your next question is, what could that possibly make me, if I'm not an angel or

a god? The answer is the same as what I said before: many have considered me a god, and probably a few have thought of me as an angel. I'm neither, if those positions are defined by any kind of supernormal magical power. True magic of that kind doesn't exist, but I can do things that may appear magic to someone slightly more tethered to their mortality. I'm a woman, and that's all. What may make me different from the next woman is that it's possible I'm the very first one…"

For most of humankind, the woman calling herself Eve has been nothing more than a shock of red hair glimpsed out of the corner of the eye, in a crowd, or from a great distance. She's been worshipped, feared, and hunted, but perhaps never understood. Now, she's trying to reconnect with the world, and finding that more challenging than anticipated.

Can the oldest human on Earth rediscover her own humanity? Or will she decide the world isn't worth it?

The Immortal Chronicles

Immortal at Sea (volume 1)

Adam's adventures on the high seas have taken him from the Mediterranean to the Barbary Coast, and if there's one thing he learned, it's that maybe the sea is trying to tell him to stay on dry land.

Hard-Boiled Immortal (volume 2)

The year was 1942, there was a war on, and Adam was having a lot of trouble avoiding the attention of some important people. The kind of people with guns, and ways to make a fella disappear. He was caught somewhere between the mob and the government, and the only way out involved a red-haired dame he was pretty sure he couldn't trust.

Immortal and the Madman (volume 3)

On a nice quiet trip to the English countryside to cope with the likelihood that he has gone a little insane, Adam meets a man who definitely has. The madman's name is John Corrigan, and he is convinced he's going to die soon.

He could be right. Because there's trouble coming, and unless Adam can get his own head together in time, they may die together.

Yuletide Immortal (volume 4)

When he's in a funk, Adam the immortal man mostly just wants a place to drink and the occasional drinking buddy. When that buddy turns out to be Santa Claus, Adam is forced to face one of the biggest challenges of extremely long life: Christmas cheer. Will Santa break him out of his bad mood? Or will he be responsible for depressing the most positive man on the planet?

Regency Immortal (volume 5)

Adam has accidentally stumbled upon an important period in history: Vienna in 1814. Mostly, he'd just like to continue to enjoy the local pubs, but that becomes impossible when he meets Anna, an intriguing woman with an unreasonable number of secrets and sharp objects.

Anna is hunting down a man who isn't exactly a man, and if Adam doesn't help her, all of Europe will suffer. If Adam *does* help, the cost may be his own life. It's not a fantastic set of options. Also, he's probably fallen in love with her, which just complicates everything.

9 781953 637109